POPPY DAY

ANNIE MURRAY was born in Berkshire and read English at St John's College, Oxford. Her first 'Birmingham' novel, *Birmingham Rose*, hit *The Times* bestseller list when it was published in 1995. She has subsequently written fourteen other successful novels, including, most recently, *All the Days of Our Lives*. Annie Murray has four children and lives in Reading. You can visit her website at www.anniemurray.co.uk.

Also by <u>Annie Murray</u>

Birmingham Rose
Birmingham Friends
Birmingham Blitz

Orphan of Angel Street
The Narrowboat Girl
Chocolate Girls
Water Gypsies
Miss Purdy's Class
Family of Women
Where Earth Meets Sky
The Bells of Bournville Green
A Hopscotch Summer
Soldier Girl
All the Days of Our Lives

WAR BABIES
POPPY DAY

MY DAUGHTER
MY MOTHER
MEET ME UNDER
THE CLOCK

Annie Murray

Poppy Day

PAN BOOKS

First published 2000 by Pan Books
and simultaneously in hardback by Macmillan

This edition published 2001 by Pan Books
an imprint of Pan Macmillan
20 New Wharf Road, London N1 9RR
Associated companies throughout the world
www.panmacmillan.com

ISBN 978-1-4472-2679-6

3 5 7 9 8 6 4 2

A CIP catalogue record for this book is available from
the British Library.

Typeset by SetSystems Ltd, Saffron Walden, Essex
Printed and bound by
CPI Group (UK) Ltd, Croydon, CR0 4YY

Visit **www.panmacmillan.com** to read more about all our books and to buy
them. You will also find features, author interviews and news of any author
events, and you can sign up for e-newsletters so that you're always first to hear
about our new releases.

For Sam, my son.

Acknowledgements

My thanks to Colin Fox at Reading University who taught me far more about the First World War than could ever be encompassed by this book; to some of the many historians who have written on this period, especially Jay Winter, Denis Winter, Lyn MacDonald and to Terry Carter for his chronicling of the experiences of the Birmingham 'Pals' Battalions, the 14th, 15th and 16th Royal Warwickshire Battalions; as ever to Dr Carl Chinn at Birmingham University; to the Birmingham City Sound Archive and the Imperial War Museum; to my agent Darley Anderson and editor Suzanne Baboneau for their help in every way – I couldn't ask for better; to Marsha Hamilton for just being Marsha and putting up with me turning up now and then.

A special thank you and lots of love to my husband John, technical expert, cell mate and tolerant fellow traveller. xxx

PART I

One

On a freezing evening in March 1914, a young woman was walking through Deritend, the old iron and tin-smiths' district of Birmingham. Jessica Hart was dressed in the serviceable clothes and sturdy boots of a country girl and the bundle she carried, wrapped in a bright patchwork quilt, was hugged close to her as if for comfort. She was looking fearfully about her, longing to see a friendly face, but no one among the drab crowds trudging home from factories and shops even troubled to look at her.

Evening seemed to come too early to these dark streets. At home, dusk would only just be edging across the fields, now green with spring shoots, whereas here, whichever way she looked the light was obscured by buildings, their smoking chimneys pouring out filth which begrimed every roof, every wall and window. A hard lump rose in Jess's throat. The city was a noisy, stinking place.

''Scuse me!' She hurried towards a bobby, strolling his beat along the main road, known as Digbeth. 'Can yer direct me? I want to go to Allison Street.'

The policeman saw a pretty face looking out from under a snug black hat with a white band, wisps of brown hair visible round it. Even in the murky light he could see her rosy complexion which confirmed her as a stranger to the city as much as the desperate look in her eyes. And she was so sweet he'd have liked to kiss her.

'You've passed it already. Tell yer what – where is it yer want exactly? I'll take yer along.'

Soon they turned off the main road and Jess was relieved to be away from the clashing of hooves and loud rattle of the trams, but the sight of this mean-looking side street made her heart sink even further. Is this really where they live? she thought. But what shall I do if they've moved on and no one knows where they've gone? Her mind played with every possibility of disaster. The thought of spending the night wandering these terrifying streets and alleys was more than she could stand.

'Fifty-three, did yer say?' Sensing her agitation he led her along the regiment of blackened dwellings, speaking to her as if she were a child. 'Not far – see – yer was nearly there . . .'

The houses all opened directly on to the pavement. Jess saw someone watching her from behind one of the windows opposite, their breath misting the pane.

'I'll just see yer awright.' The policeman stood back as Jess put her bundle on the step and raised a trembling arm to knock.

In a moment the door opened a little way and the scrawny face and shoulders of a young woman about the same age as herself appeared.

'Yes? What d'yer want?'

'I—' Jess's throat was dry. She could manage barely more than a whisper. 'Are you Polly?'

The girl scowled, pulling the door even closer to her chest as if prepared to slam it shut.

'Why? Who're you then? – Mom!' she called over her shoulder. 'There's some wench 'ere . . .'

'Is your mother Olive?'

This provoked a look of even greater suspicion from the girl, but the door was yanked out of her hand and an older woman pushed herself into view. Her hair was scraped severely back from a tough, worn-looking face and there was a large mole at the top of her right cheek, close to the outer corner of her eye.

'What's going on?'

Jess felt herself recoil. It was as she most feared. They'd gone. This hard-faced woman couldn't be her! And yet that mark on her cheek, the voice . . . 'Olive? Olive Beeston?'

The woman's eyes jerked back and forth between her and the young policeman. 'Who are you?'

'I'm Jess Hart – Louisa's girl.' As she spoke her voice cracked under the pressure of suppressed tears. 'Only, if the Beestons don't live 'ere any more can yer tell me where they went? I must find them 'cause I've nowhere else to go! Olive Beeston's my auntie.'

'Jess! Mom, it's little Jess!' the girl shrieked.

Her mother stared, taking in the dark eyes, the curvaceous shape of the young woman in front of her, then sunk down on the step, leaning limply against the door jamb, her face drained of colour.

For a few moments Olive Beeston could only manage a series of groggy sounds. She sat forward, head down between her knees. Another girl appeared at the door and stood staring.

'She get like this often, does she?' the policeman said.

'No – never!' Polly was biting at the end of her thumb as she stared at her mother.

After a moment Olive began to straighten up again, taking deep breaths.

'She looks better,' Jess said. 'She is my auntie then?'

5

Polly nodded.

Jess thanked the policeman and when he'd gone, Olive Beeston managed to sit up properly and look at her.

'What's going on, Mom?' Polly's voice was gentler now. She looked up at her sister's frightened face. 'I don't know what's come over 'er, Sis. Look – 'er's shaking like a leaf!'

'I'll be awright, stop mithering.' Olive tried to stand up but failed, and sank back on to the step. Glancing across the road she said, 'I'm giving that nosey old bag o'bones over there summat to chew on awright.' She looked up into Jess's face and after a moment the tension in it was replaced by a poignant kind of pleasure.

'So – Louisa's Jessica. God in 'eaven – I never thought you'd grace us with a visit, wench. What're yer doing 'ere?'

'I need somewhere to . . . I've . . .' Jess had held on to her emotions all day, but now she burst into desolate sobs. 'Oh Auntie Olive, please, please say you'll help me!'

Two

Olive poured dark, frothing tea into thick cups and sawed at a loaf of bread. There was silence now that Jess had sobbed out the long and short of her story.

She felt them all staring at her: Polly, Bert and Sis – her cousins, who she wouldn't have recognized if she'd met them on the street, and the babby, Ronny, who couldn't have been more than two or three and could barely see over the table. Jess hadn't known about him.

The room was small and cramped, the table squeezed in close to the range. The mantel was covered by a length of plum-coloured cloth with a pattern of white flowers, a pewter candlestick holding it down at each end and a clock ticking loudly in the middle. On the wall above hung an oval mirror. Olive had lit the gas, trying to control the shaking in her hands, and the room was warm and cosy from the fire.

Jess took a slice of bread and margarine and chewed ravenously on it. She was light-headed from hunger, having had nothing all day but a cup of tea at Leamington station, and her head was aching violently.

Olive didn't join them in sitting down. She took a long, considering slurp of tea and clinked the cup back down hard on its saucer.

'So she wanted yer wed and out from under 'er feet, is that it?'

Jess nodded, tears welling in her eyes again. Her

7

stepmother Sarah had forced her into a loathsome betrothal to a man called Philip Gill, her father's assistant in the forge. Jess's father had raised no objection, however hard she begged him. He took Sarah's side in everything, and it was this lack of care for her, his rejection of her true feelings that hurt most.

She looked across at her aunt, her one hope, and was chilled by the bitterness on Olive's face. She folded her arms tightly and her voice was as grim as her expression.

'And you just took off, without a word or a thought for anyone, is that it?'

'I didn't . . .' More tears escaped down Jess's cheeks and her head throbbed harder. All this way she'd come, terrified and worried sick, and now her aunt was turning against her as well. '. . . didn't know where else to go, what to do!'

Olive leaned towards her with such ferocity that Jess began to tremble. 'And what d'yer think I'm s'posed to do about it, wench, eh? Don't yer think I've got enough on my plate already?' She straightened up again, glaring at her.

'Mom,' Polly protested. 'Our Jess's come a long way – don't go on at 'er.'

Jess was momentarily encouraged by the kindness in Polly's voice. And she saw Bert winking at her across the table, which also restored her courage.

'Jess can stop 'ere for a bit, can't she? She could bunk up with me and Sis.'

'She can 'ave my bed if she wants!' Sis, sixteen and hungry for anything new to happen, was all for it.

'Please,' Jess implored. She could see her aunt eyeing her little bundle and her hat on the chair by the door. 'I've nowhere else to go. I'm not going back there, not for nothing. I'll walk the streets or sleep in a doorway,

8

but I won't go back and marry 'im – I might just as well kill meself!'

'Oh what are yer canting about, yer daft wench.' Olive stood, glowering at her and Polly. Jess waited, face so full of pleading emotion that no one with a heart could have resisted.

'Ah Mom,' Bert said. 'Yer can't turn 'er away, can yer? She's family.'

'Will yer stop carryin' on?' Olive dismissed him. 'I'm trying to think.' She came at Jess again, forefinger wagging.

'Teking off and leaving everyone else to face the music's in the blood in this family . . .' she was shouting.

Jess glanced desperately at Polly. She hadn't a notion of what her aunt was raging about. Polly's expression indicated that neither had she.

Olive brought her face up so close to her that Jess could smell tea and bad teeth on her breath. 'D'you 'ear me?'

'Yes,' Jess whispered. 'Yes, Auntie.'

Olive straightened up abruptly. 'Poll, Bert—' She jerked her head towards the ceiling and the two of them left the table without a word and disappeared upstairs, Olive following them.

Jess put her head in her hands, tears running out between her fingers. 'Where'm I going to go? It's nearly dark, and I'm so scared! What's happened to Auntie? I thought she'd be good to me!'

''Ere—' Sis put a skinny arm round Jess's shoulders. 'What yer carrying on like that for? She said yer could stop 'ere for a bit, daint she?'

Jess looked round, bewildered, her eyelashes wet. 'Did she? When?'

Sis giggled. 'Don't yer speak the King's English?

Course our Mom'd never turn yer away – 'owever 'ard she might be on yer.'

The house, back-to-back with another, had a living room and tiny scullery downstairs with two bedrooms above. Bert slept downstairs on the sofa, Olive had Ronny in with her in one bedroom and the sisters shared the other. In the candlelight Jess saw a tiny room with the girls' iron bedsteads crammed into it, leaving barely enough room to squeeze a straw mattress in between them on the bare floorboards. Olive had no other spare bedding to speak of except an old grey bolster.

'If yer want any more you'll 'ave to put yer coat over yer,' she said.

'I've got the quilt.' Jess showed her.

Olive stared at it. 'Did *she* make that?'

'Yes – it's the only thing of Mom's I've got.'

However poor and spartan the room, Jess felt light-hearted with relief at the sight of her place for the night under a roof with this long-lost part of her family.

Sis, snub-nosed, freckled and cheerful, was full of excitement at having a guest.

'It's gunna be a laugh 'aving you sleeping with us, cousin Jess. I 'ope yer can stop for a long time.'

'Let's just worry about tonight for now, shall we?' Jess smiled. She liked the look of Sis, with her cheeky expression. Polly's face was more severe.

The three of them bedded down together, Polly and Sis's bedsprings screeching noisily as they settled in. Jess lay smelling the fusty smell of the room mixed with camphor and sweat and a faint trace of urine. This last smell was coming from somewhere close by and Jess turned and made out the white shape of a chamber pot near her head.

'Can I move the po' a bit? Could do without it under my nose.'

'Sorry,' Polly chuckled from the bed above her. 'Shove it down the end there.'

Jess's headache had eased a little, and she was exhausted, longing for sleep, but her cousins, agog for details, weren't having that.

'Come on then, Jess,' Polly commanded. 'Tell us all about 'im – this husband-to-be of yours.'

Jess could just make out Polly's angular shape, lying on her side, leaning over her.

'The wedding's s'posed to be Sat'dy.'

'What – *this* Sat'dy!' Polly's tone was awed. 'You really 'ave taken off at the last minute – 'ere, d'you know, you've jilted 'im, 'ain't yer! You know 'ow they say that . . . "She was jilted at the altar!" And now you've gone and done it! Ooh, but they'll be livid with yer!'

'I'm scared stiff they'll come looking for me,' Jess could feel her cousins listening in the dark. She felt ashamed, a failure, not brave and colourful as Polly was making out.

'Who is 'e?' Sis asked shyly.

'Yes – what's so terrible about 'im then?'

'His name's Philip Gill. I've known 'im nearly all my life because 'e worked for my dad at the forge. He's much older than me – thirty already . . .'

'*Thirty*!'

'She – Sarah, my stepmother – decided it. She never said a word to me 'til she'd already asked him, and then 'owever much I argued and begged them it were too late. I was already promised. They 'ad the banns read so

11

quick, people were looking me up and down to see if I was – you know – in trouble.'

She heard Sis give a little snickering laugh in the dark.

'That was after she made me walk out with 'im. 'E just started turning up, Sundays. I was working up the farm and Sunday was the only time I had off. I opened the door and there 'e was, said e'd come to take me out. And I never knew a thing about it before then.'

'And is 'e really ugly and horrible?' Polly was enthralled, as if hearing about the giant in a fairy story.

'Well,' Jess said. ''E's awright really. Kind enough. But 'e makes my flesh creep.'

That Sunday last winter, she'd opened the cottage door to find him on the step, scrubbed up in his Sunday best, hands stiffly clasped in front of him, feet positioned just too far apart to look normal. He'd grown a beard in the last couple of years, which made him appear even older.

'You and I are to go walking,' was all he said.

Jess laid one hand on her chest. 'Me – go walking with you?' she repeated like an idiot.

Philip beamed at her. In the winter sunshine his ears were the dull, thin-skinned red of newborn mice.

Without asking him in, Jess went next door to where Sarah was darning, her two children, Jess's half-sister and -brother, Liza, eleven, and Billy, nine, sitting beside her.

'It's Philip,' Jess whispered, pulling the edges of her cardigan together in agitation. 'Says he wants me to walk out with 'im.'

'Oh—' Sarah looked up with a wide smile. 'Didn't I say he'd asked? That'll be lovely for yer! You run along and 'ave a nice time.'

She spoke loudly, making sure Philip could hear.

'*But I don't want to go*,' Jess hissed urgently. 'Why do I have to?'

Sarah's expression darkened. She stood up, a wool sock in one hand, gripping Jess's arm with the other.

'Now you listen to me, miss. Philip's keen on yer and he's a good lad and 'e wants to make you 'is wife. You take yer chances where you can in this life. Now you'll go, and you'll be nice to him, d'you hear?' Her neck was doing its chicken movement, as it did when she was irritated.

Polly was eager for details. 'So you walked out with 'im?'

'For two months.'

'And – what did 'e do – what's 'e like?'

Jess shuddered. ''E's just – 'orrible. I mean 'e wouldn't hurt a fly. It ain't that. 'E lives with 'is Mom and sister still and the house was damp and it smelt horrible – of dogs . . .'

'I'd've thought there's worse things to stink of!'

'Ooh no, it was horrible, Polly – and 'e was like a dog with fleas 'imself whenever I was about. Couldn't keep still. And we'd not a word to say to each other . . .' Jess looked up into the gloom, the lump coming up in her throat again. There were those horrible walks, Philip all nods and twitches and hissing intakes of breath through his teeth, looking at her sideways all the time. Their silence. Jess rooting round for conversation.

'Bit warmer today,' she said, as the winter shrank back.

'Ar, it is,' Philip nodded enthusiastically. 'Warmer now, oh yes . . .' pressing down on his cap, as he often did, as if afraid it was about to jump off his head. 'Spring coming, that'll be.'

More silence. Jess had rolled her eyes impatiently.

Now it's your turn to say summat, she thought. But not much ever came from him.

He grew bolder, taking her hand in his huge, rough one. One day he stopped her, at the edge of the estate belonging to the Big House. The field beside them was fuzzed with green, like threadbare corduroy. His big, wet lips fastened on hers. Jess felt a disgusted pressure mounting inside her, as if her blood was trying to force its way out of her veins.

'I just couldn't,' she told Polly and Sis. 'Ooh no, never. Not 'im.' She couldn't put into words the revulsion she felt at the idea of marrying Philip. It was just wrong: it seemed to go against nature.

'Dad would've made me. He never 'ad time for me after Mom died. He just went along with anything *she* said. You can't just be *made* to want someone. Your Mom'd never force yer on someone yer didn't want, would she?' Jess looked up at Polly in the dark. She needed reassurance that she was not wrong and wicked like they'd made her feel.

'Yer an ungrateful little madam!' Sarah had shrieked at her. 'You should take what yer offered and feel lucky like other folk!'

'No,' Polly said. 'Course not.'

'She don't need to – our Poll's courting!' Sis said.

'Oi you – shurrup!'

'Are yer?' Jess asked, finding herself surprised at the fact.

'Well . . . sort of . . .' Her voice came coyly through the darkness. ''E's nice, Ernie is.'

'I think you're brave, Jess, I do,' Sis interrupted. Maybe she'd already heard quite enough about Ernie. 'Leaving like that and coming all the way over 'ere.'

'All that woman wanted was to get me out,' Jess said

14

fiercely. 'Ever since she come to live with us. Well she's got what she wanted now all right. But at least she ain't buried me alive with Philip!'

'I couldn't just go off like that,' Polly said. 'I'd be frightened to death.'

'It wasn't brave. I just 'ad to, that's all. And anyway, I cut up my wedding dress.'

Polly gasped, then Jess heard her loud laugh. 'My God, Jess – you're a one, ain't yer!'

Sarah had become almost motherly once the banns were being read. She'd explained to Jess about the physical side of marriage. It wasn't too big a surprise: there were too many animals about for that. But the thought of the bits of Philip she'd seen, let alone those she hadn't, and the smell of him – was enough to make her sick. And Sarah made Jess's dress.

'Was it really pretty?' Sis whispered.

'Nice enough, I s'pose. Cream with pink flowers.'

It had been hanging on the back of the door when she woke early that morning, caught in the light of sunrise through the window, its frill round the neck fashioned from the same material. She'd had to hurry – to act as if it was a normal day and she had to be out early to work. Downstairs she'd crept, scared rigid that she'd wake one of Sarah's two young children, looked round for Sarah's scissors ... When she snipped across the waist the skirt crumpled to the floor like a wind-swept bird.

'If I went back I should think she'd kill me.'

'We'll help yer, Jess,' Sis said. She sounded, finally, as if she was drifting into sleep.

And Polly added, 'Course we will. Don't worry about our mom.'

'I don't want to cause Auntie any trouble. She wasn't

15

all that pleased to see me, was she? Why did she go all funny? I thought she was 'aving a fit.'

'I don't know. It must've give 'er a shock seeing yer.' Polly sighed. 'She's 'ad a lot to put up with one way or another. But she'll come round. Just don't keep on at 'er. She 'ates people keeping on.' Polly reached over, took Jess's hand for a moment. 'I'm glad you're 'ere. I can remember coming out to see yer, when your mom passed on.'

Jess smiled in the darkness, wiping her eyes. 'D'you remember my mom?'

'A bit. She put my flowers in 'er hair.'

'I do that. Makes me feel like her.'

'Yer won't find many flowers round 'ere!'

''Ave to grow some then, won't I?'

When the others had fallen asleep, Jess still lay awake, hearing them breathing each side of her. One of the memories she held on to came to her: long ago, walking into the kitchen to find her father holding her mother close. Louisa's back was to her, a small crimson rose twisted into her skein of hair, her father's eyes were closed and he looked happy in a way she didn't normally see in him. Little as she was she took in that there could be passion tucked under the flat, practical things of every day, like currants inside a bread pudding. And she didn't see why she should settle for less.

Eyes open, she stared into the darkness, longing, feeling it as an ache inside her.

Three

Jess woke early the next morning and went down into the cramped little living room. She found it full of the irritable chaos of a family trying to get out in time for work.

Bert was at the table, peering into a small hand-mirror, scraping a cut-throat razor across his cheeks and attempting to whistle at the same time. Polly was by the window, cursing over a button missing from her blouse, and Sis, busy stuffing paper into one of her shoes to cover a hole, looked up and smiled. The kettle was boiling away unnoticed on the hob so the room was filling up with steam.

'Get a couple of fillets o' coley for tomorrer...' Olive was in the scullery, rattling something in the sink, shouting instructions to Polly.

Jess badly needed to relieve herself but didn't like to interrupt. Surely they didn't pee in a pot in the daytime here as well? She crept across and moved the kettle, then whispered to Polly who was pinning the front of her blouse together.

'Yer 'ave to go down the entry. Come on, I'll show yer.'

She took an old cotton reel with a bit of string on it from which dangled a key and led Jess out into the street and down an entry between two houses, its walls damp and covered in slimy green moss.

To Jess's surprise she found there was a little yard behind with more houses crammed in all round it, dingy, dark and in very poor repair, and the smell of the place was overpowering.

All round her Jess could hear the inhabitants of the houses going about their morning business – a door was open and a broom flicking out dust and bits. There was shouting, the splash of water, clink of plates, children squabbling. A mangle and a tin bath were pushed carelessly close together in one corner of the yard, and at the far end, a stinking heap of refuse, fresh ash steaming on it in the cold air.

'There yer go . . .' Polly opened the door of one of the three privies for her. Jess stepped inside full of dread and locked herself in. Through the badly fitting door she could still hear most of the racket from outside. At home, when she sat in the privy out at the side of the cottage, all she heard was birds in the trees, or the chickens.

She had no more time to wonder whether running away had been a dreadful mistake because someone was rattling at the door.

'Yer going to be all day on there, are yer?'

She pulled her bloomers up and skirt down and hurried out, red with embarrassment. A middle-aged man with a swarthy, unshaven face stood back to let her out, one hand on his fly, giving her a good look up and down. She could feel other eyes on her as she and Polly crossed the yard.

'No peace round 'ere, is there?' Polly grinned at her. 'Take a bit of getting used to.'

The family all downed their porridge at such a rate that Jess was left way behind. Even little Ronny had nearly finished before her. She looked round as she ate.

Bert, dark haired and stocky, ate fastest of all. When he saw her watching he winked at her.

'Awright this morning, Jess?'

'I remember you when yer was a babby – running round like 'im.' She nodded at Ronny.

Bert smiled back, winningly. 'Bet I was beautiful, wasn' I?'

Olive tutted. 'Don't give 'im any encouragement – 'e's full enough of 'isself as it is.'

'You weren't bad,' Jess said. She calculated – she was twenty and Polly nineteen, so Bert must be nigh on eighteen. He was nice looking – not handsome, but full of friendliness and cheek. He told her he worked in a metal rolling mills in Bordesley, and, moments later, was out of the door on his way, with a 'T'ra then,' over his shoulder.

Polly went to the scullery and came out cleaning her teeth with salt from the block Olive kept out there.

'I'll be off in a tick,' she said through the finger stuck in her mouth.

'Ar – and you will be an' all if yer thinking of stopping round 'ere,' Olive said to Jess. Having fed everyone else she'd finally sat down to eat.

'What – today?' Jess was full of alarm at the thought of wandering round trying to find work in this enormous, teeming place. But she felt a tingle of excitement too. She'd do it. By God she would. She'd prove she could find a job, and be allowed to stay!

'Why not today?' Olive said. 'Unless yer want to stand by me up to me elbows in the maiding tub. Though heaven knows, I could do with someone to keep an eye on 'im.' She smacked Ronny's hand as he'd started rubbing it round the inside of his bowl.

'Where d'you work?' Jess asked Polly who was gathering up a little cloth bag and her hat.

'Oh, not far . . .' She opened the front door. 'Off Bissell Street. Clark's Pens. Sis does an' all. You ready? T'ra Jess, Mom – see yer tonight!'

'See yer later—' Sis came and shyly kissed Jess's cheek. Jess was delighted.

And then they were all gone. The room went still, seemed to settle and expand. They could suddenly hear the fire in the range and voices from the house behind. Ronny had picked up his bowl and was licking round it.

Olive looked disparagingly at him then said, 'Oh well – keep 'im quiet for a bit.' She poured them each a cup of tea and sat down in her apron.

'What work was yer doing out there then?' she asked, as if Jess had arrived from the North Pole.

'I worked up at the farm – churning, collecting eggs – the lot really. I used to carry the milk up to the Big 'Ouse when I were younger, so in the end Mrs Hunter at the farm gave me a job. I thought – now I'm 'ere I could look for a job in service.'

'Oh – yer don't want to do that.' Olive sat straighter. 'Yer life's not yer own if yer do that. You can go and look for summat in a shop or a factory. I won't 'ave any of mine skivvying in service – oh no.'

Jess was encouraged by the way she said 'mine'. So her aunt wasn't planning to put her back on the next Leamington train.

There was silence for a time. Jess watched as Olive stared into her cup, trying to make out the face of the younger woman she remembered. In repose, Olive's expression was less harsh, but she looked tired through and through. The years had obviously taken their toll.

Jess was moved, watching her. She knew next to nothing about what had happened to her aunt though, except that she was widowed two years after Louisa died.

'I've not kept up with yer as much as I should – seen what was 'appening to yer.' Olive looked up at her. 'Things've been hard over the years, no two ways about it. She kept yer awright any'ow. Yer look healthy and you've got meat on yer bones.'

'I liked your letters. I've always kept 'em.'

There was a note every Christmas. In 1902, a black-edged card: 'I'm sorry to say that Charlie passed away in November.' They were always short, the barest snippets of news. Sometimes when she was sad Jess had taken out this pile of little notes and hugged them to her chest.

Olive shrugged. 'There should've been more of 'em.'

'Auntie—?'

'Ummm?' She was standing, stacking dishes tacky with porridge. Ronny solemnly passed his over.

'Come 'ere—' Olive wiped his face and hands on her apron and he squealed until she let him get down and he waddled over and sat on the stairs, bumping up and down the bottom two steps.

'Will yer tell me about Mom? And the family, and that?'

Olive looked up at her. After a long pause, she said, 'What's to tell?'

She took the dishes and Jess heard her put them with a clatter into the stone sink. Her voice came through from the scullery.

'I'm not one for canting, in the 'ouse or out of it. And I'm not about to ask yer any more about what 'appened out there. If it's bad enough to make yer come running to me after all these years, that's enough for me to know.' She came back into the room. 'But we're going to 'ave to let 'em know yer safe—'

'Oh no – not yet, Auntie, please!' In her urgency, Jess got to her feet. 'I'm due to be wed to 'im on Sat'dy! They might come and make me go back. At least wait 'til the day's gone by.'

'Ah well – awright then. We'll leave 'em to stew. At least for a week or two. So – now yer can go out and find yerself a job.'

Jess looked anxious. 'I do want to get a job, Auntie. I want to be able to pay my keep, like, since yer've taken me in. Only I don't know where anything is or what to do. I'll get lost straight away!'

'No yer won't. Wherever yer are, ask for Digbeth. Anyone'll direct yer. I'll give yer a piece to take for dinner, and sixpence for a cup of tea or two. All yer've to do is go round – look out for signs up, or ask.' Olive pulled sixpence out of a little cloth purse she kept tucked in her waistband. 'And Jess – you'll not be used to factory work. Why not try the shops round 'ere for a start – up Digbeth and the Bull Ring, see what's going?'

Jess got ready and picked up her hat, all nerves. She was off to take on the big city by herself!

'T'ra then, Auntie.' Her voice wavered. 'See yer later – when I've got a job!'

'Go easy.' Jess was touched that she showed her to the door. 'And mind the 'orse road. There'll be more going back and to than yer used to!'

Olive stood at the window watching her niece as she left. She knew Jess was in a bit of a state, despite her brave smile, head held high, her quick, bouncy walk as if she might break into a trot at any moment. Still, she was going to have to start somewhere if she wanted to make a go of it here.

The sight of her stirred up Olive's emotions again. She was so like Louisa as a young woman – especially from a distance. That dreamy, innocent look she had, while Olive knew that she herself had never looked pretty or innocent. Never felt it either, she thought bitterly.

Course, Jess looked healthy from the country air as Louisa had never done as a girl. But the way she walked, that beautiful hair ... The loss of her sister swept through Olive again. She ached with it, as she'd done so many times over the years. But it wasn't just Louisa. Jess was even more like ... like ... She could not let her mind pursue that. Get on now. Things to do.

She was about to move from the window when she glanced across the road and caught sight of a face, watching.

'Bugger me – just look at 'er!'

The front door of number fifty-seven was also open a bit – just enough for Bertha Hyde, the street's nosey parker, to peer out in the direction Jess had just taken. Olive felt a terrible, dizzying rage surge up in her.

'What're yer gawping at, yer nosey old bitch?' She was out the front door, striding across the street.

'If you're so keen to know my business why don't yer come and ask me, 'stead of poking and prying, eh?'

The door of fifty-seven slammed smartly in her face, leaving her staring at its flaking green paint. Olive felt herself boil over. She raised her hand and thundered on it with her fist.

'Everyone has to know, don't they? Has to meddle and spread lies!' Her voice shrieked high, verging on hysteria. 'Why can't yer leave us alone – all of yer?'

23

She marched back into her house, kicked the door shut and lowered herself unsteadily down at the table. She was panting, half sobbing, her full breasts forcing at the buttons on her dress. She put her face in her hands, overwhelmed with shame and misery, with fear at the unbalanced tone she'd heard in her voice. And last night – when Jess arrived, seeing her like that, unexpected, with that copper next to her . . .

'What's happening to me?' a frightened moan escaped her. How could she have lost her temper like that? As if a trigger had been pulled inside her, out of her control. She pulled the empty cup and saucer towards her on the table and gripped her hands round it until she thought she might crush it.

All these years she'd been all right – hadn't she? Life with Charlie, having the babbies, bringing them up . . . She'd made herself believe she'd forgotten. Past was past.

But now, suddenly – seeing Jess, then feeling the merest hint that she was being watched . . . It brought it all back with heightened, uncontrollable emotion. The persecuted years of her childhood. Tongues wagging, the insults, the horrified stares . . . She'd thought she was free of it.

Her legs felt unsteady as she got up and squeezed the last dregs out of the teapot, stewed dark as dubbing. She was shaking all over.

'Could do with a drop o' hard stuff if there was any . . .' Her hand rattled the cup on the saucer as she picked it up. She became aware of Ronny watching her, staring in the doorway.

'It's awright, son . . . just 'aving a last sup of tea.' To herself she whispered, 'Dear God, help me . . .'

Four

Jess set off in the weak sunshine that chilly morning, walking tall in her dark coat and hat, full of determination to make a success of her day and prove she could earn her keep and meet her aunt's approval. Although she was very nervous she felt strengthened and comforted by the friendliness the Beestons had shown her, especially Polly and Sis. She had been welcomed and taken in by the only people she could now call family, and she knew in her heart that they were kin and that she belonged to them. She had such strong memories of their place in her childhood, even though she had only met them twice before in her life.

The first time she had seen them was long ago in 1898 when she was a tiny girl, four years old. Olive had come out to Budderston to her sister Louisa's house, the old cottage next to the Forge.

They came on one of the trains that Jess could hear each day chugging across the far side of the farmland, stepping on to the platform, skirts catching the breeze, hands going up to hold their hats on. After a moment of looking, bewildered, round the country station, Olive was waving, other arm corkscrewing high in the air, her voice carrying right along the platform.

''Ello, Louisa – ooh, and look at little Jessica – ain't she got your hair!'

'Listen to that, Jess,' her mother had tugged at her

arm. 'Them Brummies are 'ere! That's your auntie, that is. Oh Olive!' Her voice was thick with emotion. It was the first time they had seen each other's children.

Jess felt herself caught up in Olive's sturdy arms, face pressed against the soft cotton of her frock. She smelt of smuts and lavender.

'She's beautiful, Louisa – a proper little pet. Ooh—' holding Jess away from her. 'Yer bonny, you are!' She studied Jess's face, and for a moment her eyes met her sister's.

Louisa was exclaiming over Bert, a stolid toddler with an expression of pure cheekiness, and skinny little Polly, socks a-dangle over the top of her boots.

'Oh Olive – it's lovely to see yer, it truly is!' The sisters linked arms and walked out of the station chattering about their husbands and their children, who trailed behind. Polly dragged Bert along by the hand. Jess was too young to notice, but as well as these two children who came with Olive, her aunt must have been expecting then, because later the child was born – the one before Sis – a boy who died very soon after. They learned this news by post. Jess's mother cried after she read the note in Olive's childish copperplate, and stood for a long time staring out of the back window over the yard.

That first time they came was during summer. In the hayfield over the wall, the seeded tips of grass reached higher than Jess's waist. Jess was several months older than Polly, and taller. The two of them stood apart, giving each other sidelong looks, each fishing for fistfuls of their mothers' skirts: Louisa's a buttercup cotton, Olive's a cream background with mauve swirls which cheap soap and wear had reduced almost to grey.

'Oh go on with yer, Poll,' Olive ordered her wearily.

'Look – 'ere's our Jess to play with. She won't bite yer!' She groaned, a long-suffering smile directed at her sister. 'Proper titty-babbies they can be when they want to, can't they?'

'She'll come round,' Louisa said. ''Ere, Jess – take our Poll 'ere and show 'er the pig.' Jess felt her mother unlock her fingers from the skirt. 'I'll get yer some scraps to give 'er. Off yer go – 'er Mom and I want to have a good natter!'

Jess sized Polly up without saying a word. The girl had pinched cheeks, a pasty face and squinty grey eyes. Her hair was brown rat's tails and she wore a tunic dress in a sludgy brown and sagging button up boots. To Jess she looked foreign and unwholesome. Jess with her plump, tanned arms, pink cheeks and her mop of thick curls, shiny as a newly polished saddle.

'Come with me,' she commanded. Polly followed, a finger in her mouth.

Carrying a paper bag of food scraps, Jess strode off, sturdy legs pushing through the grass at the edge of the cottage garden. Louisa was a townie, but she had taken to growing things as if born to it. Potato plants lay tilted over, arms open, rows of beetroot shoots, their spines river valleys of maroon: cabbages, leaves a silvered green. The air was heavy with risen dew, bees knocking against flower heads, tiny, tight apples on the orchard trees.

'What a stink!' Polly said in a reedy voice. You could smell the pig long before reaching the sty: urine and rancid food trampled to a mush on the brick floor.

''Ere y'are, Sylvia.' Jess ignored Polly and tipped in the bag of apple peelings.

Sylvia lurched to her feet grunting throatily and trotted over, pushing her wet, wiffling nose between the wooden bars of the gate. Polly squealed and stumbled backwards.

'Down there, yer dafty,' Jess addressed the pig. Polly was already well beneath her contempt.

Ecstatic snorting and squelching noises came from the pig. Jess reached through and scratched a bristly shoulder.

'Now—' she turned to Polly. 'What d'yer wanna do then?'

But Polly was kneeling in the orchard picking flowers, already grasping buttercups and a lacy head of cow-parsley in her fist.

Huh! Jess thought.

For most of the day, in rapt silence, the little Brummie girl gathered clumps of blossoms from the orchard, the lane, the hayfield. Buttercups, moon daisies, poppies, bunches which she presented to Olive and Louisa, flecked with blue viper's bugloss, shaggy with tough shreds of ragwort.

'Why don't yer play with Polly?' Louisa said to Jess now and then.

'She don't want to play,' Jess said sulkily.

The sisters agreed that the girls were both 'daft little nibs' and went back to their chatter, sitting out on the grass at the edge of the orchard. Louisa sat with her legs stretched out, arms behind her taking the weight, a gold seam through the orchard green in her buttery frock. Her hair was gathered up at the back, soft tendrils of it round her face. She liked to decorate it with flowers, or bright hips and haws, lustrous jewels, in season. Today she took three of the big field daisies from one of Polly's bunches and threaded them in so they rested over one ear. Olive was so much more sober, her bent knees pulled up to one side, skirt covering her feet, lank hair fastened in a bun with a straight fringe.

For some reason – Jess always connected it with the flowers, although that couldn't really have been it – Olive became suddenly furious, face screwing up with anger.

Their heads had been close together, faces long, talking in secret, grown-up whispers. Earlier on Jess had seen tears on Louisa's face. Olive reached over and clasped Louisa's hand, talking, talking, words a half-whispered jumble to Jess, but Jess thought it must be babbies they were talking about because her mom had lost two and that always made her cry. Then Polly sidled up and presented her aunt with a bunch of flowers from which she dressed her hair, and after, for no reason Jess could see, Olive's face was red and puffed up with anger as if she was going to burst, and they were arguing, straining to keep their voices lowered.

Snatches reached her like torn up notes – 'That's not how it was ... I was the one always kept in the dark ...' and, '... you should've put it behind yer ...' from Louisa.

'Yes – you were always the one who ...' and Olive's voice sank too low for Jess to hear, then rose, finishing, '... to be together. That's what I always wanted.'

But later, again, as if some solemn business was over, they relaxed, joking and giggling. Jess couldn't remember seeing her mother laugh like that before, and never saw her do so again, her head back, having to wipe tears from her eyes.

Nothing else they said stayed with Jess, and she was too young to understand how deeply troubled the two sisters were by their past. What she did keep, though, as a memory from the midst of that green orchard, along with Polly's dumb quest for flowers and Bert having to be retrieved sweaty and truculent from the hayfield, was a sense of rightness. That blood ties counted, no matter what. She had no memory of her father being there that day. He must have greeted Olive, shyly stroking his beard the way he did. Perhaps he ate with them too. But what she remembered was seeing Louisa as enlarged, strung as she had been in Jess's mind until then, between the cottage, forge and village, between her father and herself. There was more to her mom: a past, relatives, Birmingham, which as she grew up she heard spoken of as a huge manufacturing town, way over there, further than she could ever see, beyond the soft curves of Warwickshire.

It was winter the next time, 1900, icicles hanging from the eaves, tongues of ice between the furrows. That morning, which cruelly sliced one part of Jess's life away from the other, had begun full of excitement. The Shires were coming from the farm to be shod!

'If yer can walk without fidgeting about, you can help lead 'em down,' her father said. He was gentle then, although unsure how to talk to her even in those days, as if she was not his business. She was her mother's province and Louisa made sure it stayed that way. Jess was her one, precious child.

The farm boys helped walk the 'big girls', Myrtle and Maisie, the two black and white Shire horses, along from Lea End Farm, their fringed hooves striking on the frost hardened track, breath furling from their nostrils.

Jess tore along to meet them, hair a crazy bird's nest,

holding up her thick winter dress. The arrival of the Shires felt like a dignified royal occasion. Jess's father was ready for them, with Philip Gill. The forge was open on one side, facing the yard. Smoke curled out into the sharp air. The furnace was stoked high and it was dim inside even in the winter sunshine. Rows of tools hung on the main ceiling beam, and alongside the fire.

William Hart, clad in his working apron, tucked the end of his long beard between the buttons of his shirt to keep it out of the way.

'Can I hold Maisie while you shoe her – *please*? Dad, Philip, let me!'

Philip, eighteen then, stood rubbing one of his enormous ears, making hissing noises of amusement through his teeth. 'You know 'ow to keep on, don't yer?'

William Hart said nothing.

He prised the old shoes off, working his way round the horse, clicking at her and leaning against the hard flanks to make her lift her hooves. Jess talked to her, kissing her nose. Maisie tolerated this for a time, then lifted her head with an impatient jerk.

'Eh now,' Jess said, trying to sound grown up. 'There's a good girl.'

When it happened, she was standing with a hand on Maisie's neck, wrapped in the hot smell of horse. A shaft of sunlight cut into the dark forge, shot through with motes of smoke and dust. William, a shadowy silhouette in the firelight, hammered a glowing cresent of iron.

From the doorway of the cottage her scream broke along the yard.

'*William! Help me – for God's sake!*'

There was Louisa, doubled up, gasping on the step,

31

face contorted in agony, hands thickly smeared with blood, and William Hart was running, hammer slammed down, the air abruptly emptied of all other sounds but his boots along the yard. Even the horses stared, rock still.

Jess felt her mother's agony and fear pass into her and her limbs turned weak.

'Mom! Mom!' She was struggling, crying, everything else a fog around her. Strong arms caught her. Philip carried her into the forge, sat her on a stool.

'There now – there,' he said, mopping her cheeks. Jess screwed up her nose at the smell of him.

She was not allowed in the house all day, freezing as it was. The widow Mrs Guerney was sent for from the village, and the doctor. William stayed inside and Philip shod the horses. All day there was a dreadful quiet over the place which frightened her as much as her mother's screams. Left alone, wrapped in her old coat, Jess wandered to the back gate which led to the path, then the hayfield. Atop the wall, on that diamond-hard day, cobwebs had frozen, crystalline and perfect across clusters of blood-red berries. Jess whimpered, hugging herself. Nothing felt right or safe any more. She kept seeing Louisa's red hands, hearing that bloodcurdling cry, the last sound she would ever hear her mother utter.

Late that night she saw Louisa laid out. Her hair was arranged loose on the pillow. She was cold and there was no expression in her face.

Jess looked up accusingly at Mrs Guerney. 'That ain't Mom,' she whispered. Then screamed, 'What've yer done to my mom – that ain't 'er! Where've yer taken 'er?'

Sarah Guerney made clucking sounds with her

tongue, led Jess briskly downstairs again and fed her bread crusts dipped in sweet milk. Her father sat by the range, staring ahead of him. He didn't speak to her, didn't even seem to see her.

'Your mother's gone to Heaven to be with the angels,' Mrs Guerney told her. Jess thought she looked pleased about this, and hated her.

When they took Louisa to be buried, the dead child, a daughter, who had cost her her life, was laid to rest in the same coffin.

And Olive came. The only break between her black garments was her face, raw with grief, the mole on her cheek very dark against her pallor. Louisa was her younger sister by two years.

With her she brought Polly. The girl was still bone thin and pallid from city life, but she had more presence now, and a wry look in her eyes.

William Hart, Philip Gill and a group of neighbours carried the coffin from the curtain shrouded cottage, their feet moving to the toll of the church bell. William was dressed in his Sunday best, his beard brushed flat. He kept his gaze ahead, not looking at anyone. The love of his life was gone, a small daughter no substitute at all. That morning, when Jess tried to go to him, looking for comfort, he had pushed her away.

'Leave 'im be,' Mrs Guerney commanded her. 'He's in no fit state to talk to yer.'

Olive walked holding the girls' hands. Jess was dressed in navy, her thick hair gathered into two plaits. She insisted on picking up a brown, stiff leaf and holding it. She had to hold something or she would float away, lost. Her toes roared with the pain of chilblains. Now and then the stiff black stuff which swathed her aunt's arms brushed against her cheek. Olive squeezed Jess's hand with her own.

Friends and neighbours walked with them. At the church Olive waited with the girls at the end of the path as the coffin withdrew. The backs of the men carrying Louisa moved in a stately sway along the little path, and as they disappeared inside, Jess felt Olive's hand tighten convulsively and a strange shudder seemed to go through her. She drew herself up.

'Come on. That's men's work in there. Time to go 'ome.'

Jess sobbed, distraught as they turned from the church. Looking up she saw tears coursing down her aunt's face. Olive's hand kept clenching and unclenching on hers.

Olive could only stay one more day before going back to Birmingham. She organized for Sarah Guerney to help out in the house. And she tried to take William Hart to task.

'You'll 'ave to take a bit more notice of 'er,' she said, eyeing Jess. ''Er's only six and yer all 'er's got now.'

He was numb with grief, spoke like a winded man.

'I can't be a mother to her, now can I?' Jess heard him say. ''Er needs a mother.'

While Olive was there she seemed like part of Louisa, and was the woman of the house for now. That second day Jess was kept away from school, and played with Polly. Jess took her up the track to meet the farmer's boys, but they were wary, as if death followed you round like a smell. She and Polly went and cracked the ice at the edge of the pond on the green.

''Ave yer got nits?' Polly asked conversationally, shifting a brittle triangle of ice with the toe of her boot.

'No. Don't reckon so.'

'I wish I 'ad hair like yours. It's ever so nice, yours is.'

They were drawn to each other this time.

The night after Olive and Polly left, Jess lay in bed, cuddled in the deep dip of the mattress. The house was quiet and dark. After a time the stair treads creaked as her father came up, a candle stuck on a saucer. The door squeaked as he crept into her room, the flame wavering.

Jess pretended to be asleep. Through her lids she sensed the light thinning, bulbing outwards as he held the candle high over her. He looked down at her for a time, then sighed, a massive expulsion of breath from the depths of him. In a moment he went out again, crossing the landing to his cold, silent room. It was the closest he ever came to trying to comfort her.

Jess lay still, the blackness seeming to pulse round her. She thought about the dark yard below her window: outside it, black fields lit only by an ice-flake moon . . . And beyond them more darkness reaching on forever . . . She began trembling, sobbing, curling into a tiny, tight ball, crying out her distress into her pillow.

'Mom! Oh Mom . . . Mom . . .!'

Five

Sarah Guerney was in her late thirties when Louisa died, a lanky woman with black hair, rather hooded brown eyes and a surprisingly thin neck, giving her head an unbalanced, chicken-like appearance made more pronounced by the pecking little nods she gave when nervous or irritable. Jess had never taken to her, even at the beginning.

Sarah had married first at twenty and been left a widow two years later with a daughter to bring up and a grocer's shop to run. As time passed she took on an assistant in the shop and started to attend births in the village, supported the women until they were Churched, and laid out the dead. As well as gaining a certain status, she earned a small fee for each attendance, or a basket of eggs or fresh vegetables if money was short.

'I see 'em in and I see 'em out,' she would say, full of her own importance.

She set her sights on William Hart almost as his lovely young wife was breathing her last. She did not expect her objective to be achieved quickly, nor did she expect love. What Sarah saw before her was an opportunity for combining assets – she had the shop, he the forge.

So in the year after Louisa's death she left her daughter in charge among the tins, packets of Bird's Custard and motley array of local produce, and set out to make herself indispensable to the Hart household.

She worked for William Hart with the tireless commitment of someone who's after something. She carried water from the pump, cleaned, cooked and tended Louisa's kitchen garden (the spare produce from which she could sell in her shop). She took brisk – not unkind, at the start, but never tender – care of Jess. She scrubbed, washed and darned, her gaunt energy adding a domestic pace and wholesomeness to a house which would otherwise have been bereft. As the months passed, like sand trickling into a hole she began in some measure to fill the space Louisa had left.

Sarah was a practical woman who had always made her decisions on the basis of what she could get out of a thing. She was not prepared for the violence of feelings this situation would lead her to.

She fell devotedly, jealously in love with William Hart, only to inhabit a house haunted by the presence of the woman he had adored – and her daughter. Brooding Jess, whose eyes held only resentment towards her. Sarah was all sharp fingers and elbows, and a sharp tongue to match – no cuddles against a soft body, or feminine prettiness. With all of her being, Jess wanted her mother.

She was almost eight when she had to be Sarah's bridesmaid and followed her new stepmother up the aisle, face gaunt, giving off no joy at all. Once the ceremony was over, the neighbours departed, she went to the end of the garden with the bouquet of carnations she had been made to carry. She stood them in a jar on the wall of the sty and set fire to them. They didn't burn well, being fresh and moist. She lit more matches until the petals were wizened and black, and left them there, an offering of resentment and loathing. Sarah found them the next day.

'What's this?' She held out the jar, quivering with fury and upset.

Jess looked back at her. 'Wedding flowers.'

There was a terrible expression in Sarah's eyes. 'I've tried with you, my girl, by God I have. And this is how you repay me.'

'You're not my mom. You'll never be like her.'

The new Mrs Hart came closer, hand raised to strike the girl. Then she sank down at the table and burst into tears.

Sarah had her two children by William Hart, Liza and Billy, and they always came first. Jess was pushed aside, barely clinging on to the edge of this new family. Her father mostly ignored her. Chose not to see what was happening. Dealing with children, girl children especially, was 'woman's work'. Sarah made sure he was out of the way when she slapped Jess, or screamed at her with poison in her voice. Jess was a sad shadow of the child who had once been the centre of a mother's love, growing up now with only the most basic attention paid to her, and almost no loving care.

As she grew older Jess got a little job. Before and after school every day, she carried cans of milk from the farm to the Big House at the edge of the village, and earned half a crown a week, and Mrs Hunter at the farm was kind to her. There was one afternoon in particular which stuck in her mind. The day was much like any other except for the torrential rain outside, the clouds swirling like thick smoke, and Jess got caught out in it. When she trailed in from school late, clothes saturated with rain, the new Mrs Hart was storming round the kitchen of Forge Cottage in a furious temper.

'Where've yer been? Always in a flaming dream you are – no use to anyone!'

The sight of Jess only increased her fury. Beautiful in a way Sarah could never be, pensive, a sprig of blackthorn blossom twined in her wet hair, her large eyes looking back with a combination of loathing and fear. 'You've not even taken the milk up yet and there's no end to do 'ere! I s'pose yer've been hanging round the cemetery again? Talking to 'er grave ain't going to bring 'er back, yer know, so yer might as well get that into yer head once and for all. And get that muck out of yer hair!'

She went to pull at the flowers hanging on Jess's ponytail but Jess backed away, eyes narrowing.

'No! Why should I take it out? What harm's it doing yer?'

Sarah thought she would boil over. Lord, she had only to set eyes on the girl and she wanted to scream!

'Yer should do what I tell yer. Have a bit of respect.'

Jess's gaze burned into her. She didn't say a word. Didn't need to. Her eyes said it all. Why should I? You're not my mom. I hate you.

Their mutual loathing crackled round the kitchen. Jess moved away and put her cloth bag down wearily. Little Liza, five, was at the table toying with bread crusts on a blue and white plate. Jess looked longingly at them. She was frozen, soaked to the skin and ravenously hungry.

'You'll 'ave to wait,' Sarah said with harsh satisfaction. 'That's what happens to yer if you fiddle about and don't get on – yer go hungry.'

Billy, aged two, was on the floor, banging at the tiles with a child's rolling pin. Sarah suddenly whipped round from by the range and snatched it out of his hand. He started yelling.

39

'You'll drive me to distraction – all of yer. Now go on – clear off up the farm out of my sight, or they'll get someone else to do the job.'

Jess trudged along the muddy track as more clouds were piling up, swollen with unshed rain, and the wind swept across the fallow winter fields. She was a lonely, bedraggled figure, her clothes too small, hugging her wet coat round her, teeth chattering so much she had to clench her jaw to keep them still. Her boots kept slipping and sliding, wet rat's tails of hair lay plastered to her forehead, and under the weight of her cold and misery her heart was so heavy she thought it might fall out of her body. She was so wretched that afternoon that she started to cry, tears mingling with the rain as it began to fall again, sobbing out her longing to be loved by someone, to matter to anyone in the world. She cried with longing for her auntie Olive, for the feel of that sleeve of her black dress as it had brushed against her face. Olive who had been kind. Who felt like her only family in the world apart from Louisa's gravestone, the only place where she could go to pour out her feelings.

Jess remembered that afternoon as she set out from Olive's house along the strange city streets, still able to recall it so sharply that for a moment tears stung her eyes. After so many moments of doubt on her way to get here, after all her soul searching and worry, she knew at that moment with fierce certainty that coming to Birmingham had been the best decision she had ever made.

Six

May 1914

'Jess, what the hell are yer *doing*?'

Polly turned, lifting a pail of ash to take out, and stopped short at the sight of her cousin dreamily rubbing condensed milk all over her face.

Jess's mind was obviously miles away. She stared at her gooey fingers, then back at Polly.

'Yer a case, Jess – yer really are!' Polly burst into her loud laugh, and Sis started giggling too.

'S'good for yer skin, milk is. Mrs Hunter at the farm told me – top of the milk.'

The farmer's wife had dipped a spoon into the thick surface of the cream and rubbed it on Jess's cheeks with her rough index finger.

'Keep yer skin lovely, that will.' And Jess believed her. Mrs Hunter's eyes were sunken with exhaustion and her body sagged like an old mattress, but her cheeks were radiant as rose petals.

Polly was chortling away. 'But that ain't fresh, Jess – it's out of a tin!'

'I weren't thinking. It were just force of habit.' She laughed and laughed, then suddenly found she was in tears.

'We was only teasing, Jess!' Polly dropped the pail and slipped her arm round Jess's shoulders. 'This ain't like you.'

Jess was laughing and crying together.

'I'm awright,' she spluttered. 'Don't know what's come over me. I just feel a bit strung up, that's all – oh ta, Sis.' The girl had poured her a cup of tea. 'Better wash me hands and face first, hadn' I?'

She went into the scullery, bewildered at the odd mix of feelings inside her.

She'd been in Birmingham two months and it had been an emotional time. She'd caused the family a lot of laughs with her strange ways. Used to the freedom of her own room she stripped her clothes off with no hesitation, not mindful of who might be about, looking through windows. Polly and Sis who were more coy and easily embarrassed went into fits at the sight of her.

'Yer want to watch it, Jess – plenty of peeping Toms round 'ere!'

So Jess tried to be more modest. She learned lots of new things. That each family took turns cleaning out the stinking privies in the yard and she'd be no exception. That she'd be taking a bath in the tin tub by the fire once a week if she was lucky and sharing the water with her cousins. That if she wanted to grow flowers and herbs she was going to be hard pushed to find anywhere to do it. She spent a few pennies on seeds: chives, parsley, pansies and Sweet William and planted some pots, but she didn't trust the children in the yard not to knock the tops off. So she stood them out the front and they struggled to grow, poor, sickly looking offerings. Jess decided it was probably more effort than it was worth. She learned that if she suddenly felt like running and jumping in the street as she might have done on the farm track at home, everyone'd look at her as if she was stark staring bonkers and probably tell her so too. And she learned, for the first time in her life, what real family teasing was like, and that she had a sense of humour which had never found a proper outlet before. She loved her cousins and the longer she stayed the more she spoke like them and understood their teasing. She found Bert and Sis easygoing enough. Polly and Olive were more tricky. Polly could be moody and liked everything just so, although Jess found she could often tease her out of being crotchety. Olive was more of a puzzle. She could be warmth and kindness itself, then the next minute distant, angry. And though Jess kept trying to find different ways of asking about her family, all the relatives she'd never seen or known, she got nowhere.

'There's nowt to say. Stop keeping on,' was typical of the abrupt response she got. She found it odd and disappointing.

She had, though, found a job that first day, setting off past small workshops making screws, and copper piping, out into the wide main street which led uphill to the Bull Ring market and St Martin's Church. All the trams and carts and people seemed to be heading there. The street was busy, a bobbing mass of hats in front of her: caps and homburgs, straw hats and bonnets.

Away from the back streets, and the nearer she walked to the Bull Ring, a host of smells mingled together: roasting coffee, freshly baked bread, fresh horse manure and the rough smoke of cigarettes. There was so much to see, and smell and hear, the clatter of carts, the delivery men and market stallholders bustling about hollering at each other.

Jess felt her spirits soar. This is my new home, she thought. It's where Mom came from and I'm going to like it here, even if it is rough and ready. At least it's nice to see a place with a bit of life in it for a change!

The Bull Ring teemed with people moving round the

stalls which seemed to sell everything you could possibly imagine. Jess wove a path between piles of fruit and veg and crocks and rags, looking at everything. There were flowers and birds in cages, live chickens clucking, women with trays of lavender, sweets and cakes, a knife-grinder, sparks showering from his grindstone . . . Tarpaulins over the stalls protected the holders from heat or rain and they stood behind their stalls waving and all trying to see who could yell the loudest.

'Get yer peaches 'ere – luvverly peaches!'

'Best spuds in town . . .'

'Oranges over 'ere – sweet and juicy!'

In the background the shrill voices of lads selling the *Despatch* competed with them. Jess saw a man walking in small circles waving a Bible and shouting and the stout lady selling flowers was in full voice. She found herself grinning affectionately. Flipping noisy lot, these Brummies! And now she was going to be one of them.

The thought of getting a job almost slipped her mind for a time. She wandered on, up New Street, past the Great Western Railway Station at Snow Hill. Dinner-time came and went. She ate her piece of bread in a church yard and ambled on, until gradually it dawned on her she had no idea where she was.

On the corner of a main street she saw a policeman.

'Please – can yer tell me where Digbeth is?' she asked.

He stared stonily ahead and there was such a long silence she thought he wasn't going to answer. Then suddenly he said, 'Well unless you was thinking of going via Wolver'ampton, yer'd be best advised to turn round.'

Eventually, tired now, she found herself back in the Bull Ring again. In a side street the aroma of coffee

44

made her mouth water. Perhaps she could afford a minute or two for a drink . . .

The little shop had a sign outside saying 'A.E. Mather – Coffee and Tea House'. In the window Jess could see plates with a few cakes still left on them. A little girl in filthy, ragged clothes was standing with her face pressed up against the window.

Poor little mite, Jess thought. I wonder when she last had a meal in her belly.

She was about to offer her a penny for a cake when the child scampered away and in the place where she'd stood Jess saw the little sign in the window. 'Help Required.'

It was gloomy inside, sawdust on the floor, a few plain wooden tables squeezed in round the room. At one sat two women with tall, thick glasses of tea in front of them. Jess felt them sizing her up.

'What can I get yer? Coffee or tea?' A thickset man with a moustache spoke to her from behind the narrow counter at the back. On it sat two or three plates draped with white cloths.

Jess went to him shyly. 'I've come about the sign.'

'Sign?' The man's eyes twinkled. 'A sign in the celestial 'eavens, would that be? A portent and wonder?'

'No,' Jess said earnestly. 'The one in the window.'

'Ah, go on with yer, wench – I were pulling yer leg.'

'Oh. I see.' She felt foolish, but the man was smiling at her.

'Why – you offering? Only we're short-'anded, see. The wife's just 'ad another babby and she ain't back on 'er feet yet. It might be only for a week or two, like, but I could use yer.'

Two little children with Mr Mather's slate-coloured

eyes were staring at her from the doorway behind him. She smiled at them and the older one smiled back.

'I'd like the job,' Jess said. 'I need to start some-where.'

'Not yer first job, is it? Yer look more'n fourteen.'

'Oh no – but I've only just come to Birmingham. I don't 'ave any references to give yer.'

Mr Mather snorted. 'We take yer as we find yer, wench. References be damned. If yer don't come up to scratch yer'll be out and that's that. Awright?'

He explained that her job would be to wash up, keep the tables and floor clean and generally keep the place nice while he brewed coffee and tea and looked after the customers.

'Think yer can manage that? It'll be six shilling a week – I can't spare more.'

'That's awright,' Jess was pleased. She'd have that to give to Auntie Olive for her board and food. 'When do I start then?'

Mr Mather's eyes filled with mirth again, looking at the pretty, and somehow unworldly girl in front of him.

''Ow about this minute?'

'That's all very well,' Olive said when Jess proudly presented her with her first week's earnings. 'But yer've got to keep yerself clothed and shod as well.'

Jess's excitement subsided a little. 'Oh – I 'adn't thought of that. Sarah made a lot of our clothes, see . . .'

Olive perked up, hearing this. 'Did she teach yer? You any good at sewing?'

Jess absolutely loathed sewing, but she was anxious to please the hard-faced woman in front of her.

'I can sew a bit.'

'Well that's summat, 'cause we're a right cack-'anded lot 'ere, all of us. Why didn't yer say? You could get yerself a job as a seamstress.'

'I never thought,' Jess said, vowing silently that that was the last thing she'd ever do.

'Not to worry – yer can move on when yer've found yer feet a bit. Factory pay's better, no doubt about it. Tell yer what – you keep this family in darned stockings and yer can keep 'alf your wages every week. 'Ow about that?'

Over the first week as she settled in, they had a mattress stuffed for her and got some bedding from a pawn shop sale. She lay down to sleep between her cousins every night and it was cosy, chatting before they slept. That was, until Bert shouted up to them.

'Shurrup gassing, will yer, and let us get some kip!'

Sometimes they could hear him snoring, and Olive snored like a dormant volcano as well.

'It's a wonder the house can stand it!' Polly giggled sometimes, when they were both at it.

The weeks had passed and Jess hadn't reminded Olive about writing to Budderston. It was only now that Olive remembered.

'I reckon it's about time you let 'em know where yer've taken off to. Yer father wouldn't've kept a note of my address, would 'e?'

'No. It was only on your letters and I've got them.'

Olive painstakingly penned a note saying that Jess had come to live with them, had found work and was in good health. She wrote her address clearly at the top of the paper.

'Right – you go and post it.'

Jess felt churned up as she slipped the letter in the post. She walked back slowly down the road.

I miss 'em, she thought, in a funny way. Even though being ignored and used as the family drudge was what she had been used to. She longed to know whether her father would forgive her for taking off, even though she knew it was his fault she had had to go.

And as much as that she missed the beauty and familiarity of the countryside, the peace of it. Faces she recognized all round the village, when here she saw only strangers.

I wish I could just go for a visit and come away, she thought. See the house again, and my room and the apple trees. She imagined walking along the edge of the hayfield, the rustle of the dry grass which she'd heard every summer of her life, until now. At that moment the city felt such a big, noisy, squalid place. Jess felt suffocated by it, longed to breathe fresh country air, be away from the turmoil and human squalor.

I don't belong here, she thought, in this miserable mood, walking back along Allison Street. I don't really belong anywhere.

As the spring passed, along with the fun and warmth of living with the family, sitting round the table to eat, the jokes, there were other things Jess was starting to notice. Polly was worried about Olive.

'Mom—' she protested when Olive gave her another long list of shopping to fetch in after work. 'I can't carry all that back on me own – and I won't 'ave time! Why can't yer get it this morning?'

'I'll do some,' Jess was always glad to feel useful. 'If you go up Jamaica Row, I'll go in the Market Hall and we can do half each.'

Gradually the girls got into the habit of doing all the

shopping between them. If anything extra was needed Olive sent someone out – Sis, often, on an errand.

'I don't know what's got into our mom,' Polly said one night. 'She don't seem to want to go out the house nowadays. I think she'd get us to go to the lavvy for 'er if we could.'

'Yer'd think she'd want to get out and 'ave a bit of a gossip for a while,' Jess said, remembering that Sarah had usually come home in a marginally better temper from a walk to the village to fetch groceries and chat to anyone she met.

'She don't want to see anyone,' Sis's voice came softly through the darkness. 'It ain't like 'er.'

'She won't say why,' Polly said. 'I've asked 'er.'

Jess thought about the night she'd arrived, her aunt's reaction.

'It's not summat I've done, is it?'

'No – why should it be? I s'pect she'll get over it. P'raps she ain't feeling too good and don't want to make a fuss.'

When they'd lain quiet for a time, Jess asked, 'Poll – this is nosey to ask, but – Ronny. Who's 'is father?'

But there was no reply. Polly was either asleep, or pretending to be.

Jess also started to notice the way Olive quizzed Polly – not herself, just Polly – almost every time she came in from work or shopping.

'Seen anyone?' This was said in a casual way, but Jess could hear an edge of anxiety in her voice.

'No,' Polly would reply, puzzled. 'Who am I s'posed to 'ave seen?'

Jess wanted to say, 'But you must've seen *someone*. It was swarming with people out there!'

Once Olive asked, 'No one following yer, was there?'

'No!' Polly laughed, then looked solemn. 'Mom? Why d'yer keep asking all these funny questions?'

'Oh – no reason,' Olive said. 'Just wondered.'

Polly's worried eyes met Jess's for a second. They were coming to understand that 'anyone' meant 'someone' in particular, and that this 'someone' was someone who was preying on her mind, who she seemed afraid of seeing.

But they couldn't get any more out of her, could all feel the strength of emotion round the subject. And Olive continued to stay in. She was all right in the house with them, but she seemed scared to step outside her own front door.

Seven

'Shift yerselves, you lot, and see what's coming down the 'orse road!'

Everyone else was in a Sunday afternoon stupor: Bert sleeping off a few pints, Olive dozing. Ernie, Polly's beau who was round for the afternoon, was entertaining Ronny, tossing him about on his lap, a game Ronny never tired of. Jess watched them sleepily through half-closed eyes. She'd liked Ernie straight away, his chubby face and gingery beard, the way he was good with Ronny. It was Polly who'd got up to put the kettle on and looked out of the window.

'Come out quick and look!'

Jess, Ernie and Sis followed her. Olive stood in the doorway, craning her head round. Bertha Hyde opposite was at her window having a good nose. Sis took one look and started running down the road, laughing and calling out.

'Don't flap yer arms about and frighten it!' Polly shouted after her.

The grey mare came towards them along the road, hooves slowly clip-clopping. Her ears were swivelling back and forth in a startled sort of way, perhaps because her rider, with no saddle, and no shoes on, was standing up on her back, holding the reins high, his boots slung over the horse's withers with their laces tied together. He balanced, knees bent, concentrating hard, but as they

51

came nearer he looked up, a smile spreading across his face.

'Well I'll be . . .' Olive gasped. 'It's our Ned!'

Jess remembered hearing his name mentioned, Ned Green, the lad Olive had known since he was knee-high. He was now a fireman and Olive obviously thought the world of him.

Bert came out yawning and stretching his arms. 'What's 'e playing at! Awright, Ned, yer silly bleeder!'

Ned loosed a hand for a moment to wave. Jess found herself grinning. The sight cheered her up no end. She'd seen pranks like this back in the village but she certainly hadn't expected anything of the kind in Allison Street. And what a lovely animal! Then she looked at its rider, drawn to him, curious, seeing a strong body, a face with a wide, smiling mouth and fair wavy hair.

'Whoa there now, Bonney – eh, stop, yer daft wench!'

Bonney, who seemed to be enjoying her stroll in the sunshine, stopped with reluctance and Ned slid down to the pavement. Sis pulled his boots from off the horse and handed them to him.

'Ta.' He gave her a wink.

'We thought yer was too good for us these days.'

Jess looked round, hearing the gruffness in Olive's voice. To her astonishment her aunt looked quite dewy-eyed.

''Ow are yer, Auntie?' He came over and kissed Olive's cheek.

'All the better for seeing you. Where've yer bin, yer bad lad?'

'Sorry, Auntie – been busy.'

Everyone was trying to talk to Ned.

''Ow d'yer stay up there without slipping off?' Polly

said. Jess noticed she looked flushed, and saw Ernie watching her. 'Whose 'orse is it?'

'She's from the fire station,' Ned patted her. 'I said I'd give 'er a bit of a walk.'

'Can I 'ave a ride?' Sis cried. 'I've never been on an 'orse!'

Jess went and took Bonney's reins since everyone else seemed to have forgotten that she could just walk off any time.

''Ello, gorgeous,' she stroked Bonney's nose. 'Oh I've missed the likes of you, I 'ave!'

She stood letting the horse fumble in her hand with its lips, but soon her gaze was drawn to Ned. His eyes as he looked round at them all were full of affection and fun. He was wearing a white shirt, the top couple of buttons undone, and a worn-looking pair of trousers. As he stood down to lace up his boots she saw a stripe of his neck, between his hair and collar. The skin looked soft, edged by the thin down of hairs at the margin of his hairline. She felt intensely conscious of his every movement. The hairs on her own skin stood up, making her shiver.

Sis was still clamouring for a ride. Ned stood up and turned, and his eyes met Jess's. To her embarrassment she found she was blushing until she turned hot all over. Her palms were turning clammy.

'Who's this then?'

'This is Jessica, my niece,' Olive said. 'Our Jess. She's come to stop with us.'

Her hand disappeared into his for a moment. His was very warm. 'How long yer staying?'

Jess shrugged, giving a wry smile. 'I don't know!'

'Nice to meet yer, Jess, anyway.'

''Ow d'yer get up 'ere?' Sis was throwing herself

excitedly at the horse's flank, and kept sliding down again.

They all watched, laughing. 'Give us a leg up, Ned!'

''Ere – I'll show yer!' On impulse, Jess, still holding the reins, led the mare alongside the front step, and from there she vaulted up on to Bonney, managing to fling one leg over, her dress riding up to show a length of bare thigh.

'Oh Lor'!' Olive laughed. 'She's a country wench this one, all right. Look at 'er go!'

Jess clicked her tongue, digging her heels into Bonney's sides. She quickly broke into a trot and Jess clung on, even though riding bareback was a slippery business.

'That's a girl!' They trotted off along the street and under the railway arch where the sound of Bonney's hooves echoed until they were out in the sun again, and round the corner. Jess didn't want to stop. She loved the feel and smell of being on a horse again. But she turned Bonney round and trotted back. Her cheeks were pink, hair fastened back haphazardly so some of it hung loose on her shoulders, and she looked the healthy, country girl she was, the joy of it shining out of her. As she drew closer to them all she felt Ned watching her and her smile grew wider.

'I wish I could go on all afternoon!'

'We can see that!' Polly laughed.

'Oh let us 'ave a go!' Sis was jumping up and down with impatience.

Jess swung her leg over, ready to slide off Bonney as if she was a helter-skelter.

'Can yer manage?' Ned came and took her hand.

Jess laughed. 'Been doing it all me life – but ta any'ow. There—' She pulled her skirt down. 'I'm decent now!'

54

As she reached the ground he caught her by the waist for a second to steady her. They held each other's gaze for a moment, then Sis was once more trying to scramble up on to Bonney. Ned let go Jess's hand, but Ernie had already taken pity on Sis and was hoisting her up.

'I'll help 'er!'

Jess was full of energy, as if she was on fire. She ran up and down, leading Sis as she bumped about on Bonney's back, shrieking that she was going to fall, giggling so much by the end that she did slither off the side. Bert had a go, clowning about, then Ronny was allowed to sit up on Bonney's back for a moment.

'Tck 'im off!' Olive protested. ''E looks worried to death! Yer coming in for a cuppa tea now yer 'ere?' She took Ned's arm.

'What'll I do about Bonney?'

'Oh I'll hold her,' Jess hooked the reins round her wrist and sat down on the step. The room was so small that she wasn't left out by sitting down there. Ned sat at the table with his back to the range, the others round him except Polly who was brewing the tea. Jess listened to them talking. She sat quietly, watching him until she felt his eyes on her, watching her curiously for a moment, then glancing away. She couldn't seem to stop looking at him.

But after a few moments she heard Olive say, 'So tell us all about it. Why daint yer bring Mary with yer? 'Ow long's she got to go now? She got over feeling poorly?'

Jess's heartbeat began to pick up speed. She found herself thinking, no – oh please, she can't mean . . .?

'Oh yes, she's got over that, but there's only a few weeks left. She's feeling it now, what with working and

55

that – it's taking it out of 'er. She's gone to bed this afternoon.'

Olive made sympathetic noises. 'She still at Coopers?'

'No – Griffiths. Been there a while she 'as now – over in Vittoria Street, making rings. Ain't I told yer that?'

'Not that I remember. Oh – so yer'll be staying over that side now.' She sounded disappointed. 'I'd 'oped yer'd come back over 'ere so we'd see a bit more of yer.'

'Oh, yer won't catch Mary moving away from 'er mom,' Ned said. ' 'Specially now, with the babby on the way.'

Jess listened with part of her mind, but a shrinking, disappointed feeling crept through her. So Ned was married. How daft could she be, never thinking for a moment that he might be! But he had affected her so strongly – and the way he had looked into her eyes when he helped her off Bonney ... But it must have been all in her silly, inexperienced imagination. She sat closed into her own thoughts, only half hearing now as Ned talked about the Fire Service, about Mary. Her earlier sense of excitement had melted away and suddenly all the joy had gone out of the afternoon. She sat feeling foolish and cross with herself.

She came to as Ned got up to leave and he took Bonney's reins from her.

'So – where did you spring from, Jess?'

'Budderston – Warwickshire.' She answered calmly, glancing at Olive. 'I wanted to come and see my auntie and find work 'ere for a bit.'

'Bit different 'ere in Brum, I'll bet. D'yer like it?'

'Mostly.'

Ned laughed. 'You don't sound all that sure!'

'She gets a bit 'omesick for the country now and then,' Polly said.

'Well, yer can visit, can't yer? The countryside ain't going to run away.'

'She can't.' Bert stated the facts with no malice intended. ''Cause they don't want 'er. Ain't that right, Jess?'

'Bert!' Polly protested. ''Ow could yer?'

Jess felt a blush of fury and mortification burn across her cheeks. This was the truth – of course it was. But it was terrible to hear it blurted out so baldly. Quietly, she said, 'Seems like they don't.'

Ned stopped attending to Bonney and looked round at her.

'How come? Why wouldn't they want yer?'

Jess felt them all staring at her. Olive started to say something, but Jess pulled her shoulders back.

'No, Auntie. There ain't no shame in the truth.' She looked at Ned. 'I ran away from home 'cause they were making me get wed and it weren't what I wanted. So they'd be none too pleased to see me at the moment.'

She felt Ned's interest. 'Why didn't yer want it?'

Jess was startled to be asked such a question. Wasn't it obvious what you should want? Everyone was waiting for her to speak.

'Well,' she said fiercely. 'It ain't no good marrying someone if yer don't love 'em, is it? I mean yer've got to love 'em so that nothing else matters – not just marry 'cause it suits.'

'Think yer might need to lower yer sights a bit,' Olive said. There was amusement in her eyes. 'She's a quaint one awright,' she told Ned. 'All sorts of odd notions 'er comes out with.'

Jess looked down, hands clenched into fists, fury swelling in her right up to the back of her throat. Why had she said what she really thought? Looking up, mutinously she said, 'Otherwise what's the point?'

'The point,' Olive said, 'is sticking together to keep bellies fed so yer don't 'ave the Workhouse hanging over yer. And you'll find that out, Ned my lad, soon as your family starts arriving.'

'Weren't just yer own family you was feeding either, Auntie, when yours were littl'uns. Yer'd even find a piece for me when I turned up like a bad penny.' Jess could tell he was trying to smooth things over. The affectionate cheekiness of his smile disarmed Olive in a second. Jess watched, aching inside. Not only was Ned married, but now she'd made a fool of herself in front of him as well.

As he left, Ned said, 'You are going to come over and see our place, aren't yer?'

Olive didn't promise. She gave him a non-committal nod, from the step. Ned leapt up on to Bonney's back, keeping his boots on this time.

'Bring Mary to see us, and don't leave it 'til I'm walking with a stick.'

Ned gave a salute, smiling round at them. His eyes met Jess's for a second. Then he winked at Sis.

'T'ra then!'

He turned Bonney and they watched him trot off down towards Digbeth, waving a hand.

The others started to go in.

'Come on, Jess,' Polly tried to take her arm.

Jess pulled away, shaking her head, eyes fixed on the horse and rider until they disappeared round the corner.

*

58

'Wasn't it lovely to see Ned?' Sis sat up in bed that night, yanking a comb through her hair. 'Seeing 'im on that 'orse – 'e was like summat out of a fairytale. And 'e's so handsome! Lucky Mary.'

'Why does 'e call yer mom Auntie?' Jess asked.

'Oh – she's known 'im all our lives.' Jess wasn't sure if she imagined a stiff tone in Polly's voice. 'Thinks the world of 'im, Mom does. 'E's like another son to 'er.'

'I can see why.'

Polly sat up. 'I know yer can – it was written all over yer. Yer could've lit a fire off your face this afternoon. But 'e's spoken for. Ned and Mary've known each other for years and now they're wed, so it's no good you coming 'ere getting any ideas in yer 'ead. 'E ain't free, so it's too late for you or anyone else!'

Eight

Ned stepped out of Albion Street fire station the next Sunday afternoon after work. The afternoon was warm and he took off the black uniform jacket and slung it over his shoulder as he automatically set off towards home. After a few yards he stopped and turned back towards town. Mary would be asleep, or round at her mom's so he might just as well go back over to Allison Street again for a bit. There was a warm welcome there all right.

'Making up for lost time, are yer?' Olive said seeing him turn up again. 'Talk about a bad flaming penny!'

'Thought I would. Mary's bad, at the moment.'

'Well yer've missed Bert, and Polly's out with Ernie . . .'

'I came to see *you*, auntie!' Ned said, throwing his jacket over a chair, eyes searching the room. I didn't come to see Polly, he thought, nor Bert, nor even Olive if he was honest with himself. *She* was here, the cousin, the pretty one, prettier even than he remembered. He was intrigued by her, by that smile that seemed to pass right into him. He nodded at her.

'Hello,' Jess said. She had a pink dress on with short sleeves and her arms were tanned, the hairs on them glowing gold. The dress showed off her curves. She's perfect, he thought. He'd never seen anyone like her before, never knew there could be anyone like her.

'Oh Ned,' Sis was saying. 'Daint yer bring Bonney with yer this time?'

He dragged his attention to her. 'Not today. I'll bring 'er again sometime if yer want.'

''Ere—' Olive put a cup of tea on the table. 'Get this down yer.'

He sat and drank his cuppa with them, listening to Sis's chatter, answering Olive's questions about the family. He could only hope he was saying the right things because his mind could only fasten on her, on Jess sitting opposite, close enough to touch, her strong fingers on the handle of her cup, drawing him with her eyes. There was a twist of excitement in his belly like none he'd ever had before, a married man who shouldn't be having thoughts like undoing the buttons down the back of the pink dress, seeing it fall softly from her with her naked under it . . .

'You awright, Ned?' Olive asked him as he sat moving his cup round on the table.

He looked up and smiled. 'Course – sorry. Miles away I was there, for a second.'

'Got a lot on yer mind, I should think, with the babby coming and that. Never mind – soon he'll be 'ere and you'll get used to it all.'

Reality chilled him like a bucket of ice water. I don't want to get used to it. I want another life. I want to start again.

He didn't stay long. Said he'd better be getting back, and stood up to slip the jacket back on. He looked broader, taller in his uniform than in the old clothes he'd been wearing before. As he left he spoke to all of them politely.

61

'Cheerio, Sis . . . Jess.'

'T'ra, Ned,' she said. Her soft voice vibrated through him. He looked away from her quickly.

His visit filled Jess with longing. However much she told herself she was being ridiculous, each brief look or exchange of words she had had with him seemed charged with significance. She relived his visit over and over that week, lying on the prickly mattress after Polly and Sis were asleep, or standing with her hands in tepid water, washing tea and coffee dregs out of thick glasses at the back of Mather's. She kept seeing his eyes turned to her, interested, in some way puzzled, it seemed, when he looked at her.

I've got to stop thinking of him, she thought. We barely know each other and he's married and I bet Mary's really beautiful . . . I'm nothing to him. She was ashamed at the extent of her feelings, her preoccupation with him, hour after hour which she could not seem to overcome by willpower.

Her need to think of Ned blocked out other feelings of longing. Neither her father nor Sarah had written back to answer Olive's letter.

So they don't want me, even enough to drop a line . . . But she no longer felt homesick. For what would life be, if *he* was not there? In two weeks Ned had invaded her thoughts until she could keep her mind on almost nothing else.

The next week he did come with Mary. Jess was in a state of nerves all morning, wondering if they'd come. When they arrived she backed into the scullery, peeping out to get a look at Ned's wife.

She heard Mary's high, slightly nasal voice first.

'Lovely to see yer, Mrs Beeston.' Jess thought she sounded nervous.

'Yer'll want to sit down,' Olive was saying. 'Ooh, yer carrying low awright! Never mind, bab, soon be over now. Come on in and take a pew.'

Trying hard to look casual, Jess stepped out of the scullery. The first thing that struck her was Mary's smallness beside Ned. She was a tiny, pale thing with freckles, auburn hair tied in a high ponytail and arms poking out of her loose stripey frock which were so white and skinny they looked as if they'd snap like kindling. She was carrying the child well out at the front and the burden of it looked enough to topple her over on her face.

Jess was rocked by the violent stab of jealousy that went through her. Savage thoughts ran through her mind. She's barely worth having, scrawny little thing! And look at that thin neck, and those arms! For a second she placed her hands on her own waist, feeling her strong, hourglass shape.

She was ashamed at her thoughts. What right did she have to be so horrible? Mary was bound to be very nice – she was Ned's wife, after all! She knew Polly didn't think much of Mary though. Was there a good reason for this?

She managed a smile at Mary. She had a sweet face, even Jess could see that, with high, arched eyebrows which made her look permanently surprised and interested.

'I'm Jess. Polly's cousin.'

'Oh—' Mary nodded. 'That's nice. Come to stay for a bit, 'ave yer?'

'Sit down and 'ave a cuppa tea – and I might rustle up a bit of cake if yer lucky.' Olive nodded over at

63

Mary. 'Look as if yer could do with feeding up, wench.' It sounded like an accusation.

They stayed a couple of hours, Mary laughing and joking, full of importance as a young wife who was about to have her first baby. Jess did her best to smile and laugh. She wanted to shine in front of Ned, for him at least to notice her. She sat Ronny on her lap and fed him mouthfuls of cake, kissing his cheeks. He'd get down, play about for a bit, run to Ernie for a time, then scramble up on her lap again.

'Come 'ere,' she said as he approached her again. 'Ooh, yer don't make up yer mind, do yer!'

She felt the strength in her arms, lifting him up, and glanced across, longing to see Ned looking at her. For all she attempted to pull herself together and be sensible, she wanted to know he was watching. His being there lit her up. She felt as if she was glowing in the room. But he never seemed to see her. Was looking anywhere but in her direction, it seemed, whenever she looked up and tried to meet his eyes.

'You're settling over there then, are yer?' Olive asked. 'I was hoping yer might move closer over 'ere.'

'Oh, I wouldn't want to leave me mom,' Mary said. 'She still needs me 'elp like – all me brothers and sisters. I'm the eldest of ten,' she explained to Jess.

'She's got 'er 'ands full then,' Jess smiled.

'None too well either, is she?' Ned was sitting back, legs stretched out. Still he didn't look at her.

'No – I don't know what our mom'd do without me close by. And Ned's been ever so good – says 'e'd live anywhere to be with me.' Mary smiled at him adoringly.

Polly got up and refilled the teapot. Jess watched, saw Polly holding her shoulders stiffly. As she came

64

back to the table she looked directly at Jess. See? her expression said. No good you getting any thoughts in *that* direction. But then she noticed that Olive had suddenly closed her eyes and sat back as if overcome by dizziness. Jess saw Polly exchange a worried glance with Sis.

'You awright, Auntie?' Ned leaned towards her.

Olive opened her eyes, dazed for a second, then took a deep breath. 'Oh ar – I'll be awright. You carry on.' She held out her cup for tea, shaking her head to dislodge the flashes of memory which had appeared in there, unbidden.

Jess held Ronny tight with one arm, looking down and stroking his soft little legs. She felt as if she was in a dream, one in which she was in a familiar place but everything in it felt wrong.

You're so stupid! she raged at herself in her head. You can't work up any feelings for the man who was given you on a plate, and now you're all of a flutter over someone who's married to someone else! Just stop acting so daft and get 'im out of your head, for God's sake!

She looked up again, sensing a movement beside her. Ned was leaning forward, playing a game with Ronny.

'I'm gunna 'ave that!' He tweaked at Ronny's nose, then held his thumb trapped between two fingers. Jess saw that he had wide, flat nails. She could smell him, soap, leather, sweat, breathed him in. 'Look – 'ere it is. I've got it – want it back?'

Ronny looked at him open mouthed for a second, put his hand up to his nose, then gurgled with laughter.

'There yer go – back on!'

He pretended to give the little boy his nose back. As

he touched the child's face he looked at Jess for a second, laughing. She smiled back, but Ned turned, abruptly.

'We'd better be going, Auntie. You ready, Mary?'

As they left, Olive stood on the step waving them down the street. She turned to come inside, still smiling.

'Lovely couple, ain't they?' she said. ''E's done really nicely for 'imself there.'

A few days later, when everyone was out, except the babby, Ronny, Olive stood in her house, her thoughts agonized. It was getting worse. Some days she was all right. Normal. But days like today were terrible. Memories rushing back at her like a flock of ravens flying into her mind. Things she had avoided thinking about for years, as if some cavity in her had opened, spilling over.

'It's no good – I can't carry on like this . . .' Hearing her speak, Ronny looked up from his seat on the floor where he was playing with a handful of pegs.

For a moment she stared at him, distracted. So like his father he was! Her face contorted with bitterness. The child couldn't help it, but by God she would rue his existence to the end of her days. A few moments of weakness, of need. Carried away – her, Olive Beeston carried away by sweet talk and a man's fumblings! If she'd known anyone else be so bloody stupid she'd've soon told 'em . . .

With trembling, clammy hands she pulled open the little drawstring bag she kept tucked in her pocket and counted through her change. She turned over the coins, counting and recounting with the sense of wonder that came to her whenever she handled money. It still seemed a miracle when they brought their earnings home. Polly, Bert, Sis – and Jess was bringing in a small amount ... They had enough now with four earning! Not a princely amount, but enough.

Her days of bone freezing poverty never left her. Worrying about every farthing, not even having enough on many a day for a half pail of slack for the fire, Polly and Bert slinking down the canal to pinch it off the barges, begging outside pubs when ice shone like crystals on the cobbles with her babbies clinging round her skirts, so bad with fever she barely knew what she was doing. If it hadn't been for the charity of the church missions they'd have starved. These memories and many others forced themselves into her mind whenever she handled money.

But the things she most wanted to forget, to block right out of her mind, went further back. God knows she'd tried to force the memories away, but suddenly it wasn't working any more. It all seemed to be bearing down on her like a goods train, with her tied to the track, like those pretty wenches in the films, the hot breath of the train on her face.

'Today's the day,' she said to Ronny. 'I gotta do summat about meself. 'Ow can I go on like this? I can't even get to the shops!'

Polly or Jess were doing all the shopping. She could tell Jess was puzzled by this. After all, Olive was the one who was at home all day. She had the time. That morning as they set off to work Polly had said,

'What d'yer need bringing in tonight, Mom?'

'Don't bother. We'll get by on what we've got,' she said. Polly looked surprised but was in too much of a rush to argue.

It was no good – she'd have to go. They were out of

milk and tea, and there wasn't a heel of bread in the house.

She pulled her coat on like a suit of armour, although it was June now and warm, took her hessian bag from the hook where the coat had hung and picked Ronny up.

'Come on, son—' She was aflutter with nerves. 'You're going to Agatha's for a bit.' She forced herself to the front door and carried Ronny round into the yard and went to her neighbour's house.

Agatha's pinched face appeared at the door. She looked taken aback at the sight of Olive Beeston in her hat and coat. Word had got round that she'd 'turned a bit funny' and wouldn't go out of the house.

'Could yer take Ronny for me for an hour?' Olive said brusquely, trying not to turn her nose up at the dank, sweaty air that gusted out through the open door.

'You going out?' A nosey smile had begun at the corners of her mouth.

'Ar – I'm going out. That awright with you?'

'No trouble,' Agatha said, holding her arms out. Ronny's face screwed up and he started roaring. 'Oh come on, bab, don't start that. You go – 'e'll be awright wi' me.'

Olive left a beetroot-faced Ronny trying to hurl himself out of Agatha's arms. She made it out of the yard, but down the entry stopped and leaned against the wall, all the old fear flooding through her. She bowed her head, closing her eyes, sweating inside her thick coat. Her hands felt clammy, and for a few moments she was panting in panic.

Oh pull yerself together! she gasped to herself, scared stiff someone'd see her. She straightened herself up and walked on weak legs towards the street.

68

It had only got this bad since Jess arrived. She knew that was what it was. Seeing her that evening, that copper beside her. Gave her the shock of her life. All these years she'd kept it at bay. And borne so much alone. No old man to tek care of 'em. No Charlie. He kept her steady when he was alive, those years they had together.

Taking deep breaths she turned down Allison Street. Immediately she spotted Bertha Hyde at her window across the street, like a ghost between her twitching net curtains. Olive's fury at her restored her a little and she gave a mocking wave.

There's nowt to be afraid of. Nowt. Just keep walking. Down to the main road – morning, Mrs Eldon, awright? A smile, that's it. No, I don't see you out often either . . . that's it, round the corner.

Digbeth and the Bull Ring were packed with shoppers. Her fear began to subside a little in the anonymous bustle. She enjoyed the smells of the market, music from someone playing a French horn, felt the early summer sun on her face.

Ain't good to be cooped up inside all day long, she thought. I ought to do this all the time, silly old woman I am.

Stepping into the first shop was a relief though. As if she'd been washed up on a rock. She felt her body relax, and only realized then that she'd been clenching her teeth hard.

But then she saw one of her neighbours from down the road was just turning from buying her bread as Olive's turn came.

'Mrs Beeston, ain't it?' the woman said, not troubling to keep her voice down. 'Don't see yer about much – yer been bad or summat?'

Olive's jaw tightened again. Mind your own cowing business! a madwoman's voice shrieked in her head. Don't go nosing into my business, yer upstart busybody you!

She forced a tight smile. 'My daughter likes to do the shopping as a rule.' She turned away. 'I'll 'ave a large cottage and a bag o' cobs, ta.'

She moved carefully from shop to shop for what she wanted: tins of Handy Brand milk, a quarter of Typhoo Tipps, a pound of cheap mince, onions, spuds and carrots off the Bull Ring. They slung them straight into her carrier for her. Triumphant, she gathered up her purchases and headed across towards Digbeth. Straight home and get the kettle on. She could leave Ronny with Agatha a bit longer and have a morning's peace. She'd done it! It had only taken breaking the habit . . .

A tram was lumbering down the road and she glanced to one side, half looking at it. There was an advertisement for Hudson's Soap plastered along the side of it. She was none too keen on trams passing too close to her. All those faces behind the glass staring down at her. Made her prickle all over. She avoided looking at the windows, and the tram rattled past.

And then she saw it, across the street. Her insides gave a violent lurch of shock so that for a moment she thought she was going to be sick right there in the gutter. Among all those people milling along there, that face turned towards her. The face she lived her life in dread of seeing, eyes staring straight at her from under the brim of a black hat . . . It happened in a second and Olive spun round, pressing herself against the sooty wall of St Martin's. After a moment she turned back, searching the crowd, but there were so many hats, so many people in drab clothes, and her eyesight was not all it might be. She dropped her bag and onions rolled out across the pavement. A woman stooped and helped her pick them up.

She almost fell through her front door, her face wet with perspiration, hands trembling so that she could barely unbutton her coat. She put the kettle on the hob and sank down at the table, panting as if she'd run all the way home.

Everything led back to that house. That room where she'd been found. They'd come towards her, approaching her slowly as if she was diseased or dangerous, leading her away by the hand ... away ...

'Oh God in heaven,' she whimpered. 'Oh Louisa ...'

She sat for a long time, staring across the room. Steam gushed unheeded from the kettle's spout.

'We've got to move on.'

Polly was greeted by these words as she got in from work that night. Olive was huddled up in the little room which seemed very dark after the light evening.

Polly put her bag down, looking round for Jess or Sis. 'Where are the others?'

'Jess ain't back. Sis's round at Enid's.'

Carefully, Polly said, 'What's 'appened, Mom?'

'I saw 'er.'

'Saw who?' Polly sat down at the table, rubbing her hands over her pale face. 'What're yer talking about?'

'I went up the Bull Ring. I 'ad to get ...'

'You went up the shops?' Polly sat up, smiling. 'Did yer manage by yerself? That's really good, Mom, ain't it. Yer could get out more now ...'

'But I saw – this woman. Lived round Saltley when Louisa and me lived with yer Dad ...' Polly could hear

71

the tightly strung emotion in her mother's voice. Olive couldn't seem to stop talking, thoughts which had been pressing in on her all day, rushing out, even though Polly didn't know, wouldn't understand. 'She's aged a bit of course, but it was 'er awright. Oh Poll, I thought my 'eart was going to stop she gave me such a shock. She's after me again, coming to find me . . .'

'Mom, stop it!' Polly shouted. She grabbed Olive by the shoulders, starting to shake her. 'I don't know what yer going on about. What woman? Why's anyone going to be after yer? Yer ain't done nothing, 'ave yer?'

Olive's face was crumpling like that of a terrified child.

'Don't!' Polly cried harshly. She released her mother, frightened by the look in her eyes. 'This's got to stop, Mom. I can't stand any more of it. Yer making a nervous wreck of me an' all. Yer not making any sense.'

'I'm sorry, Poll—' Olive started crying, sobs breaking out from her throat. 'I just can't go on living round 'ere if she knows we're 'ere. She's wicked – evil . . .'

Polly was close to tears herself. 'Mom, I don't know what all this is about. I'm worried about yer – yer don't seem yerself at all lately. Please don't talk like this. You're frightening the life out of me. There's no one after yer, is there? Why would there be?'

As she spoke, Ronny came bumping down on his bottom from upstairs, took one look at his mom and started wailing in alarm.

'Come up 'ere, bab.' With a huge effort Olive rallied herself, sat Ronny on a chair and wiped her eyes and nose on her apron. 'Don't cry, son. I was just telling Poll 'ere that we're going to move to a bigger 'ouse soon. Yer'd like that, eh?'

Polly was protesting that they didn't need to move

anywhere when the door opened, setting the coats on the back of it swinging. The two of them froze. Jess walked in, preoccupied until she saw her aunt's tearful face.

'What's going on?' she spoke cautiously.

Polly and Olive looked at one another. Olive stood up. 'Nothing for you to worry about.'

Jess felt about as welcome as a fox in a chicken run. She couldn't get another word out of them, so she asked Polly later, upstairs.

'She's been acting real funny lately.' Polly sat on her bed, twisting the sleeve of her cardigan round and round. 'I'm bothered about 'er, Jess. The last couple of months – not going out, and now she's on about seeing some woman who's scared 'er half to death and she wants to move 'ouse. She won't say why. I'm worried she's going a bit, well, you know . . .'

Jess sat beside her in the half-light. 'She seems awright in 'erself – you know, not sick or anything. But you're right – she does seem to be acting funny. I saw 'er the other morning looking out the window – up and down the road, worried like, as if she thought someone was coming. Who does she say this woman is?'

'She don't—' Polly looked round at her, wide-eyed. 'I've never heard 'er talk about this woman before. And the worst of it is, Jess – I'm not at all sure there is any woman!'

73

Nine

'Oh sod it!'

Jess caught the hem of her dress on her heel as she stood up from bending to wipe Ronny's face. She heard the waistline rip.

'Well it'll have to stay like that – I ain't got time to mend it now.' More sewing, she thought grumpily. On top of all the mending she was doing for the family.

No one took any notice. They were all rushing to get to work. Jess was in a bad mood because yesterday Mr Mather had announced Mrs Mather would be taking over again in the Coffee House and that she was no longer needed. Having seen Mrs Mather, a terribly thin, sallow woman, with a robust infant who looked as if he'd sucked the very life out of her, Jess had thought she'd be there for some time to come. But no. She'd have to look for a new job.

'Yer've been a good worker,' Mr Mather said. 'If yer do want any of them references anywhere like . . . only yer'll 'ave to write 'em. I've never writ well meself.'

'I know where I'm going to look for a job,' Jess told them at home. 'The Jewellery Quarter.' If that Mary could get a job there, she thought, I don't see why I shouldn't. 'I like the sound of it.'

'Well there's always girls wanted,' Olive said. 'But you'll 'ave a walk – that's the other side of town.'

'It's not that far – I could walk it in a half hour if I hurry . . . I'm going early.'

She downed a cup of tea and a quick bite of breakfast. 'T'ra then!'

'Tara-abit,' Sis called to her.

Jess walked briskly but despondently through town, joining the early morning hurly-burly of people scurrying to work. It was an overcast morning, the ground wet. Soon she felt water seeping in through the sole of one of her shoes.

Darn it, she thought. I've not enough for another pair. I'll have to stick some paper in the bottom. The morning suited her mood. Here she was in this smoky grey place, away from home, no job and now to cap it all, she had holes in her shoes! She felt very glum, as if all the world was against her.

She didn't even see the horse bus coming until someone shouted. It was almost on top of her and she dashed to avoid it, tripping over a tram track and falling on her face in the road. She felt the cobbles scrape along her cheek, heard a horse screaming above her as the driver reined it in to avoid her, prone on the ground. Jess curled up, covering her head as the hooves clashed and scraped round her. All was confusion and the first thing she was properly aware of was a man's voice shouting,

'What in God's name d'yer think yer was doing! I could've bloody killed yer!'

Things gradually stilled. Slowly, dazed, Jess raised her head. Her hat was lying crushed in the road in front of her. She sat up and looked round. There was a crowd of murmuring faces round her, the bus stationary on her left, its horse still jumpy, the harness frothed up round its mouth.

'So – are yer awright or what?' The driver squatted in front of her. Jess stared at the buttons on his uniform.

'Yes. Think so.' She felt giddy, knocked out of shape. Her head was throbbing. 'Sorry. I never saw yer.'

'That's 'cause yer weren't even flaming looking!' He seemed to be calming down now, having seen there was little damage. 'If yer can get yerself up, all these good people and myself can get on.'

'It's all right. I'll take care of 'er.'

Blearily, Jess found herself looking at a pair of heavy black boots. She followed the line of them up, black uniform, brass buttons. He knelt beside her.

'Jess? You awright?'

'Ned?' For a crazed second she wondered if the tram had hit her and she'd died, and was this what heaven would be like.

'Let's get you off the road . . .' He helped her stand, taking her hand with a firm gentleness she noted, even in her stunned state, and led her through the staring people to the pavement and a little way up the sloping street opposite. Her left shoulder and her knees were hurting, and her right cheek stung, bringing tears to her eyes.

'Can yer make it up 'ere? There's a churchyard where yer can sit down.'

Jess nodded, and without a word he offered her his arm and they walked together until they reached the graveyard of a blackened church. Ned held on to her until they reached a bench and sat down. Jess rubbed her shoulder, trying to ease it.

'Is my face a mess?'

''Tis a bit, yes. Sorry – I've got no hanky, nothing like that.'

'Nor me.'

'Yer going to be awright?'

'There's not much wrong. I just feel all shaken up, that's all.'

'Couldn't believe my eyes when I saw yer. What're yer doing over this way? I thought you worked in town?'

She was touched that he remembered. 'I did. Lost me job yesterday. So I come over 'ere to find another one. Only I seem to be making a hash of it so far.' She started laughing until he laughed as well. 'Sometimes I don't think I'm cut out for living 'ere.'

'You'll get used to it. We're awright really, yer know, us Brummies.'

Jess smiled. 'I know. Didn't mean it like that. Shouldn't you be going to work?'

'Just finished. I was sent to run an errand to Newhall Street before going home. I work over in Albion Street.'

'Yer must be tired.'

'Not yet. Takes a while after a night like last night to unwind, like. There was a blaze over in Hockley – not far away.' Close to him now, she saw streaks of grime on his face. 'Listen – if yer want to find a job I'll 'elp yer. I know these streets like the back of my hand.'

'Would yer? I don't know where to go to start. Only – aren't I too much of a mess?'

'No, that don't matter. There's loads of jobs round 'ere. We'll find yer summat.'

He led her through the narrow streets of the Jewellery Quarter, lined with narrow old buildings which had once all been houses, but had gradually been taken over by many different little businesses. Graham Sreet, Vyse Street, Vittoria Street. They walked along, reading the signs over factory doorways. Ned pointed to one: 'Griffiths . . .'

'That's where Mary works.' Jess noticed he didn't suggest she work there, although there was a sign outside saying, 'Girls wanted'. 'Shall we walk on a bit, show yer the lay of the land?'

There was silence for a while as they walked along.

'Did yer really do what yer said?' he asked suddenly.

Jess frowned up at him. 'What?'

'Run away from 'ome – cut up yer wedding dress . . . Only it's not every day someone tells yer summat like that.'

'Who told yer that – about the dress?'

'Sis.'

Jess was silent.

''Ave I put my foot in it?'

'No – I don't mind yer asking.'

'So, why?'

'I told yer why. They wanted to marry me off to someone I couldn't stand for more than five minutes, let alone a lifetime.'

'Oh. I wasn't sure if you was 'aving me on, that's all.'

'Why would I be 'aving you on? 'S'not the sort of thing yer just make up off the top of yer head, is it?'

'I s'pose not. Sorry for asking.'

'S'awright.'

'Look—' He stopped. 'What about this? "Blake's Brooches and Badges."'

Jess looked at him, eyebrows raised.

'They might 'ave summat. Enamelling job. Let's go and ask.'

To get to the entrance they had to go down a narrow alley at the side. Jess followed Ned, feeling as if she was in a dream. With him, she thought, everything felt right. As if she'd come home. The realization was followed by

78

the pain of reality. No! Of course not. She could not think like that. He could never be hers.

'What d'yer want?' a woman's voice said.

'You got any vacancies?'

'Depends what for.'

'My er . . . Miss Hart wants to learn a trade.'

'Miss Hart does, does she?'

'Jess,' Jess said.

The woman's shrewd eyes looked her up and down. 'Where've yow worked before?'

'On a farm and in Mather's Coffee Shop, in the Bull Ring,' Jess told her.

The woman rolled her eyes. 'Well that's gunna be a lot of use to us, ain't it? Yow can only come and start laying on if yer want. That's all I've got if yow've got nothing previous. What's amiss with yower face?'

'I fell over.' Jess looked at Ned. He gave a tiny nod. 'Yes – I'll come and do . . . laying on.' She hadn't the remotest idea what this meant, but if Ned thought it was right she'd do it.

'Yow can start tomorra. Can't be doing with it today. Get a note from yower doctor to say yer fit for work. Yow'll be on ten shilling a week minus stoppages.'

The door slammed shut.

Outside, Jess laughed with relief. 'Well – thanks a lot! I thought that was going to take me all day.'

'Oh you'll get on awright. Just need to learn yer way around a bit.' He smiled at her. Jess thought he looked exhausted.

'Yer can go and get some kip now, can't yer?'

Ned hesitated. 'D'yer fancy a walk?'

'A *walk*?'

'You know – yer keep sticking one foot in front of the other.'

Jess tutted, though her heart was going like a drum. Nothing could be nicer than the thought of spending some more time with Ned. 'What d'yer take me for? I just thought you'd want to get home.'

'Well – you've not got to be at work 'til tomorra and I've done for today. And yer look as if yer could do with cheering up. 'Ow about it?'

'Wouldn't Mary think it were a bit funny – you taking me out for a walk?'

'No – course not,' he said hastily. 'I'll show yer Handsworth Park. It's nice, this time of year. It's a couple of miles. D'yer want to catch a tram?'

'No! Oh no – I'll walk.' All her aches and pains were nothing compared to the thought of Ned asking her to go with him. No man had ever shown such kindness to her before.

'I'll stop yer throwing yerself under any more buses,' he smiled round at her as they started walking. Seeing his dark, mischievous eyes looking into hers, Jess panicked for a moment and she wished she'd said no. How could she enjoy this time with Ned without it being more agonizing knowing he felt nothing for her but sympathy?

They walked north, out of the city, to Soho Hill and the gracious suburb of Handsworth with its fine villas and wide roads. Ned led her to the gates of the park, where a nanny and two small children were climbing into a trap pulled by a skewbald pony.

'Oh – look at 'im!' Jess went up closer. 'Lovely, ain't 'e?'

Ned watched Jess as she shyly went up and asked if she could pet the pony. The nanny nodded, reluctantly, and Jess stroked his smooth neck and tickled his nose before saying goodbye. The woman in the trap stared

Ned up and down, surprised to see a fireman out strolling the park, helmet under one arm, but saw he was oblivious of her scrutiny. All his attention was taken by the sweet-faced young woman with him. He was so obviously captivated by the sight of her as she petted the pony.

'I'll 'ave to bring Bonney out to see yer again, if you like horses that much,' he said as they walked through the gates together.

'Oh would yer? I'd love another ride. I've always loved horses.'

She told him about the shire horses at the farm. The days they came for shoeing, and how that was what they were doing when her mom died.

'I can still remember that day – everything was covered in ice, like sugar. Beautiful. But it was the worst day of my life.'

They were walking round the big pond, brown water to their right, grass on the left. A watery sun forced a bright patch through the cloud.

'What 'appened to her?'

'She died in childbirth. I'd've had a sister. My step-mother – well, later she was my stepmother – told me after.'

'And you didn't like 'er – your stepmother?'

'No.'

'You don't look anything like yer auntie – or Polly.'

'I look like my Mom – Olive says any'ow. I do remember her, a bit, but I wish auntie'd talk to me more about 'er. I can't get a word out of 'er.' Jess looked up at him. 'She thinks the world of you though.'

'I know – she always has. She and Charlie ran their hucksters shop in Sparkbrook and our mom and dad lived just round the corner, off the Stratford Road. I

81

was in and out of the shop for a penn'orth of rocks and she took a shine to me. Gave me 'em for nothing some of the time. She weren't so poor then as she was later. Course, I never knew 'ow bad things were for 'er after Charlie died. You don't see things as a kid, do yer? But she was still pleased when I used to go and see 'er when she lived up by St Alban's Church. Mom and Dad would've helped 'er out if they'd known, but I just said she was all right.'

They strolled slowly round the park talking. Ned told her his mom and dad lived in Selly Oak now: his dad worked for a small firm producing yeast and his elder brother Fred was married with two boys. Jess said she had no one. Told him about her father, and Sarah.

The morning went very fast. After a time they found they had stopped talking, as if something had stalled and they couldn't get it started again. Jess stopped by the boundary with a church yard and looked across the gravestones. A bird was singing.

'Peaceful in there,' she said, but felt desolate, couldn't bear another second in his company suddenly, because with every fibre of her being she wanted to reach out and touch him and knew she must not. As he stood close to her, the hairs rose on her neck and arms. 'We ought to go back,' she managed to say. 'We shouldn't be 'ere. Neither of us.'

He looked into her face and saw her eyes were full of tears.

'What's the matter?'

'Nothing. I just want to go home.' A tear rolled down her cheek. 'I want . . .' She turned away. 'I don't know what I want. Just leave me, Ned. I know the way 'ome. Please.' She put her hands over her face, wanting to pull them away again and find him gone, yet feeling she'd fall apart if he wasn't there. She was afraid of what he would think of her.

'It'll be the shock,' he started to say, but had to stop and swallow to clear the sudden tightness in his throat. 'From this morning. Look – I'll take yer back and make sure you're safe. You might faint or summat. We've had not a crust to eat.'

She'd given no thought to food, but knew it was nothing to do with that. I mustn't say a word, she thought. If I say anything, it'll be all wrong. Silently she wiped her cheeks.

'Jess—' There was a tone in his voice which made her raise her eyes to him, but he'd turned away abruptly, was staring across the park, his broad shoulders black against the green beyond.

After a moment he turned back to her, finding his resolve. 'We'd best catch a tram.'

All the way back, they were silent, sitting on the tram's hard seats, pressed together at the hip. Jess felt cold and desolate inside. Ned stared out of the window. He seemed hundreds of miles away to her. Of course he was, because that was right, he felt nothing for her and she was a fool.

'Will yer be all right walking from the Bull Ring?' he asked as they got off. The afternoon had darkened again.

'Yes, course,' she said flatly. 'And thanks, Ned. For 'elping me, and the walk and that. We'll be seeing yer sometime I s'pose, with Mary.' As Jess spoke her good-byes she was scarcely able to look at him. She crossed the road, not turning to glance back, so she was unaware of how long he stood watching her as she walked away.

He picked her out among the crowds, straight-backed, with a solitariness and proud dignity which made him clench his fists as he fought the desire to run after her. He walked exhaustedly back towards Hockley to meet Mary out of work. His mind was in a tired, feverish turmoil, a confused array of feelings strung between his fragile, trusting wife, and the lonely, bewitching girl with whom he was falling passionately in love.

Ten

'Oi – are yow listening to me or am I wasting me breath?'

Even as the grim-faced woman in charge of the workshop showed her how to lay the coloured enamel powders on small round sheets of metal ready for firing, it was Ned's face Jess could see before her. The way he'd said her name that day – what was he going to say that he never finished, didn't dare to say?

She shook her head to dislodge him from her mind.

'Yow awright?'

'Yes – course.' She tried to concentrate on what the woman was saying to her.

'After they've been fired, they're ready for filing and polishing – so they go to them lot over there . . .'

Once she was left to do the job, arranging the blue and white powders on to make the badges, she quite enjoyed it. Care was needed and she became absorbed, hearing the chatter of the other workers. Eavesdropping was no problem as they worked in such a small, dark room. It might once have been someone's bedroom over the street. But at least there was the work to distract her. The ache in her heart let up a bit. She ate her dinner with a freckle-faced girl called Evie, who was chatty and cheerful. Afterwards she went back to work much less weighed down.

Put him out of your mind, she told herself. He's

someone else's. There's not a thing you can do about it now.

But the next week, one morning she started crying. She wet the enamel powder with her tears and had to start again.

''Ere – what yow playing at – it costs, that does!' the gaffer was on to her straight off, seeing her scraping the powder off the badge again. 'What's the matter with yow today?' She scowled at Jess's tearstained face. 'Look – go outside and pull yowerself together, and then get back in 'ere and make a proper job of it.'

Mortified, Jess went out of the workshop with everyone having a good nose round at her from their benches.

There was nowhere much to go. She sank down on the stairs, put her head in her hands and burst into tears again, sobs rising from somewhere deep within her.

'Oh Ned . . .' she cried. 'Oh God, Ned, please . . . please . . .'

Tears dripped through her fingers on to her work overall as the words poured out. In her state of turmoil she only knew that everything felt wrong. She would have to live with Ned calling on them in Allison Street with Mary and the baby when she had such overwhelming feelings for him as she'd had for no one else and she could not tell him or show him.

He was being kind to me, that's all, she told herself. He doesn't *need* anyone else. Of course he don't feel the same. Even if he did like me he couldn't say, could he?

She pressed the heels of her hands against her eyes.

I've got to stop this. To pull myself together, or I'll lose this job as well.

'Hope yer feel better tomorrer,' Evie said to her as they packed up work. Evie always tried to look on the bright side of everything. 'I feel a bit any'ow meself today. Let's 'ope the wind changes, eh? See yer then – I'm in a rush!'

Jess stepped out along Frederick Street. The evening was warm, the air seeming to stroke her skin. She always walked home instead of using up money on tram fares, and this evening she set off head down, not looking about her. Other people were coming out from the factories and workshops in the surrounding streets. She stopped for a moment as a crowd came out of the Griffiths Works, afraid that Mary might be among them.

Maybe I should move on somewhere bigger when I've done a bit of time at Blake's, she was thinking, when she felt herself gripped forcefully by the arm and pulled to one side against the railings. She let out a cry of alarm before she saw him.

'Ned! What . . .?'

'Can yer come with me – just for a minute?'

He led her quickly away from the factories, back down to St Paul's church yard where she had sat to recover from her run-in with the horse. There were other people about, but all of them on the move, in a hurry to get home and get their tea inside them.

They sat down on the same bench, gravestones behind them. A group of boys were throwing stones at a row of empty bottles. Jess didn't dare speak. She had to know what he wanted to say. She could feel an enormous tension coming from him. For a few moments he sat leaning forward, arms resting on his knees, looking at the ground.

He feels something for me, he does, she thought. But in her mind she was also prepared for the opposite, for this to be about something else completely. Eventually, the silence had gone on so long that she said,

'What d'yer want, Ned?'

He put his hands over his face. 'Don't yer know?'

'No. I can't say I do.'

There was another silence, then he said, 'This is terrible. I shouldn't be here. Neither of us . . . I've got to go and meet Mary in a minute.' He sat up and turned to her.

She looked ahead of her.

'Jess—'

Slowly, frightened, she turned her head.

'Help me . . .' He managed the words at last. 'What yer said about it not being worth it if yer don't feel more than just a bit of fondness . . . I'd never, I mean I didn't know what it was, how I could feel . . .' He looked fearfully at her, then plunged in. 'Ever since you've been 'ere I've thought about yer all the time. You've taken me over – I keep seeing you everywhere. I didn't know it could be like this. I mean me and Mary, we've always been good pals. She's a nice girl, a good girl, and I'm fond of 'er, but . . .'

He waited for her reaction. Her face was solemn, not angry or laughing at him as he'd feared. The emotion in her eyes affected him so he could barely speak.

'Say summat to me. I don't know what yer thinking of me.'

Her voice came out barely more than a whisper. 'You're in my mind all the time as well, whether it's right or not, Ned. I can't seem to help it. I feel as if I belong with yer and I can't make any sense of it.'

He opened his arms and after a second's hesitation she leaned into them, clasping him very tightly, raising her head to search for his lips. She felt them urgent, on hers. Then they sat holding each other, his chin resting on her head, both of them rocking together slightly, as if for comfort.

'You're so beautiful,' he said. 'I've never met anyone at all like you before. When I was at yer auntie's I 'ad to keep looking somewhere else, keep my eyes away, so I didn't just sit and stare at you all afternoon. It was like an ache in me—'

'You're married to someone else.'

Ned pulled away.

Jess was wide-eyed, stricken. 'That's the truth of it. You made vows in church. I'm frightened, Ned, by all I feel. I've been lonely all my life, wanting someone to love, and now I love you it's not right. I can't stop thinking about yer and wanting yer but I don't see how it can be anything but wrong . . .'

He gave a great anguished groan. 'Jess – I 'ad to tell yer – to see yer. It was wrong of me. She's going to 'ave my child any day now . . .'

Jess watched his face as he spoke, her eyes full of tears.

'I'm stuck with it – all those things Auntie Olive said, about sticking together and keeping bellies fed. That's what yer marry for, Jess . . . And there's my mom and dad to think of . . .'

'I know – I know, I know . . .' She was weeping. What she wanted, longed for, was an enormous, inconceivable thing.

'But I can't do it to Mary – and her mom. Yer should see 'em Jess. Her Mom's so thin and ill, and all them children she's got. It'd kill 'er if I broke it off. And Mary ... I've 'ardly slept thinking of it. Not knowing what to do for the best. I 'ad to see yer, to know 'ow yer felt, but I can't just throw it all away ... I'm sorry, Jess.'

She pulled herself to her feet, hugging herself as if to nurse her aching heart, her face wet with tears.

'I don't know if I wish you hadn't come to me and told me. I couldn't stand loving you and thinking you had no feeling for me. But now I know ... what you've said ... us having to go on as we are ...'

Unable to bear seeing her in such distress he went to comfort her.

'Don't touch me!' She slapped his hands off her shoulders. She saw his look of pain and made as if to reach out and stroke his face, but she drew back, wiping her eyes. 'I want you to hold me in your arms forever, Ned, but I don't think I can stand it if you touch me now.'

'Please—' Again he tried to move close to her. 'I love you, Jess. Come 'ere, just for a minute, while we've got the chance.'

She backed away. 'No. No. I'm going now. You go and catch up with Mary. And don't come round to ours when I'm in. I don't want to see yer.'

She walked away, her arms still folded tightly.

'Jess!'

But she didn't turn. Ned stood watching helplessly. Her shoulders were hunched, head held at a dejected angle, her thick hair escaping in wisps from its pins. He felt as if she was taking a part of him with her as she left. His whole being ached for her.

He sank down again on the bench and stared desolately ahead of him. He couldn't stand the thought of going home.

PART II

Eleven

June 1914

Mary laboured long and hard to produce her child. When Ned got in from work that evening the next week, she was well underway. Her mom, Mrs Smith, was up there with her, and Mrs Martin, a local woman who came in to help with birthing. The fire was lit and they were up and down the stairs for water and cups of tea, stoking the range, looking knowingly at him.

'She's doing her best, poor lamb,' Mary's mom said. She was a thin and wrung-out looking woman, forty-five years of age but appearing sixty if a day, though with a genteel dignity about her. 'There's a stew on the fire, Ned. Will yer have 'taters with it?'

He nodded, accepting as graciously as he could. He'd known when he married Mary that they'd live close to her mother in her little terrace in Handsworth. He just hadn't bargained on it being next door. They were in and out of each other's houses, Mary's brothers and sisters too, as if they all lived together and there never seemed to be a moment's peace. He knew he should be grateful. It saved Mary worrying, and Mrs Smith was close by to see her through with the babby.

It was just that sometimes he felt he was married almost as much to Mrs Smith as to Mary.

'That all right for you now?' his mother-in-law laid a plate of scrag-end in front of him, edged with potato. The whole meal was the grey of an old floor cloth.

'Yes, ta.' He tried to tuck in, glad once she'd shuffled off upstairs again in her badly fitting shoes. From the room above his head, he could hear the leg of the bed banging on the uneven floorboards and the women walking about, exchanging a word or two in low voices. Now and then came a low, muffled moan.

Ned ate up his tea in large, hungry mouthfuls, then took his cap and went down to the corner for cigarettes. God knows, he was going to need summat to get him through the evening. He didn't want to think about what Mary was going through. It only stirred up the turmoil of emotion within him even further.

Once he'd bought ten Woodbines he still wanted to stay out. It was a still, summer evening and his pace slowed. The thought of going back to the cramped house full of all the disturbing, female things going on in it filled him with revulsion and guilt.

He passed a church and thought about going in to sit in the musty gloom to try and set his thoughts straight, but he could hear the chat and laughter coming from the pub so he went there instead, settled with his pint at a table awash with spilt drink, amid the smells of beer-soaked sawdust and smoke. He lit up a Woodbine, not wanting company. If he sat here for a bit, he might get home when it was all over. It was fuggy and comforting in there and his mind drifted. He couldn't bear to think about the future or what he was going to do.

It was getting on for ten when he walked in. Nothing seemed to have changed in the hour and a half he'd been out. The kettle was boiling. Mary's mom came down and brewed tea.

'Getting a bit closer,' she told him. 'It's not often very quick the first time you know, Ned. Nothing to worry yerself about.'

It only then occurred to Ned that he might worry. He thought of Mary upstairs, her scrawny body writhing on the bed. That was as far as his imagination went. He didn't know what was involved, not really. He sat by the fire drinking tea, a saucer between his feet on the peg rug Mary had made. Over the mantel, a picture of a puppy with bright eyes and a shiny nose stared down at him. Stew and beer formed an uneasy partnership in his belly. The noises from upstairs were growing louder, coming more often, although he could tell Mary was trying to stop herself crying out. Occasionally the cries crescendoed out of her control, like a lid lifted off something.

The clock ticked. The saucer at Ned's feet filled up with stubs. He sat in the murky light feeling like an old man. The path of his life seemed laid out straight in front of him. Get up, go to work, come home. Mary, babbies, young'uns tearing in and out, struggling to feed them, clothe them, until he dropped dead.

Mary was a good girl, a sweet wife. Cheerful, dutiful, bound up in family, as he'd known she would be. As he'd imagined he would be too, thought that was what he wanted. He'd chosen. But he'd chosen because she was always there, because his family liked her – because he'd barely thought of it as a choice. That was what you did.

He hadn't seen Jess since the day she'd run from him, crying. Memories, her shape, the way she moved, her eyes, came back to him with such force that he closed his eyes, letting her take him over. She moved before him like a cinematic show, her smile, her dark-eyed gaze burning into him, her lithe figure bounding on to Bonney and trotting off along the road. The feel of her lips on his, that once ... The thought made him long for her like a hunger. An agonized scream came from upstairs. He got up and paced the room. Lit another cigarette from the fire.

Upstairs, Mary lay limp as a rag between the bouts of pain, her hair soaked with sweat.

Mrs Smith sat on a chair beside the bed, holding her daughter's hand. Mary almost crushed the bones of it during each contraction, so that her mother barely managed not to cry out too. She was suffering through every pain with her daughter and her face was dragged down with exhaustion.

'Terrible, watching your own go through it,' she said to Mrs Martin.

Mary's teeth were clenching again. She cried out at the height of it, then sank down again, exhausted.

'Mom?' she murmured as Mrs Smith wiped her face.

'Yes, darlin'?'

'Is Ned here?'

'Oh yes – 'e's downstairs, waiting.' The corners of Mary's mouth turned up in a faint smile.

Finally, at three in the morning, when everyone concerned felt tested past endurance, Mary pushed out her baby, a girl, and a 'tiny snippet of a thing' as Mrs Martin called her. She coughed and squeaked and finally cried, gratingly, waking her father from his uneasy sleep in the chair downstairs.

Ned sat listening to the unfamiliar sounds round him. He heard the child and felt it was a dream. But he was excited. Was that sound part of him?

After a long time he heard the slow tread of his mother-in-law on the stairs.

'You've a lovely little daughter.' She smiled, revived by joy. 'Go up and see.'

The tiny face was just visible, a triangle of dark pink flesh between the tight swaddlings. She was lying in the crook of Mary's arm in the candlelit room.

'You'll all be right now,' Mrs Martin yawned. She stood by the door, waiting.

'Oh – 'ere,' Ned slipped coins into her hand. He was shy of her, of what had gone on in this room.

'Thank you,' Mary murmured. All her attention was on the baby.

But when they were alone, Ned knelt beside the bed, looking at the pair of them, awed, but distant from what had gone on.

'Ned?' Mary's eyes fluttered open.

'What, love?' He leaned closer to hear her.

'Can we call 'er Ruth?'

'Awright.' He would have agreed to anything at that moment. 'Ruth's a good name. In the Bible, Ruth is.' He took Mary's hand and kissed it.

'She's pretty, ain't she?' Her voice was fading.

'She's the prettiest girl in the world,' he whispered, gently stroking the infant's cheek with the side of his finger. ''Cept for you.' At that moment he meant it, was humbled and full of gratitude.

Mary barely managed to smile. She was falling asleep.

He stayed there in the deep quiet of the night, the creaks of the old house and their breathing the only sounds. He watched the child, her face twitching in sleep. He had not yet seen her with her eyes open. He felt his sense of himself expanding, taking in this new responsibility. New life. Family. This was where his duty lay. Eventually he climbed gently on to the bed beside them, and they all slept.

'We must take her and show her to Mrs Beeston,' Mary said.

It was Sunday morning. Little Ruth was ten days old, and though tired, Mary was well recovered from the birth. She sat holding the baby, suckling her, smiling down into her face. 'She'll be ever so annoyed with us if we don't pay a visit. We promised, daint we?'

Ned was in the scullery, bent over in his shirtsleeves, trying to unblock the sink. For a moment he froze. Mary didn't see him.

'No hurry. Why don't we leave it for a bit? You'll get tired traipsing all the way over there. It's even further now they moved.'

'Ned!' Mary laughed. 'I want to take 'er out and show 'er off a bit! She's starting to look quite bonny. And Mrs Beeston said she wanted to see the babby, soon as it arrived.'

Ned hesitated. 'We ought to give 'em a bit of warning – take a note to say we're coming . . .'

'Why? What the 'ell's got into yer? You always said she'd be pleased if you turned up anytime. She sent 'er new address, din't she? So she wants to see yer. We'll go after we've 'ad some dinner. 'Ow about that?'

'What's the matter with yer, Jess – yer poorly or summat?'

Jess was lying on her bed in their room in the new house in Oughton Place. Olive had insisted they move. Apart from the fact that the neighbours on one side, the

98

Bullivants, who had nine children, were a raucous and sometimes quarrelsome lot, they'd had a lucky find. The new house was on a terrace which backed on to the railway, close to Camp Hill Goods Yard. It was much more roomy than the back-to-back they'd been in before, with an extra bedroom, and although there were the usual problems of damp and bugs, the previous occupants had done their best to keep it nice. All the rooms were papered and the roof was sound. Olive kept saying they should have done it years ago.

'I'm awright.' Jess lay on her side. Bert had the smallest room, and there was just enough space to squeeze three proper beds into theirs. The wall in front of her eyes was covered with a cream paper patterned with trailing blue roses.

The house was quiet. Olive, feeling more herself since the move, was bolder about going out, and had gone with Sis up the road to the Baptist Church. She wasn't fussy about the denomination, but liked to go to church somewhere. She said she'd had help from all sorts and she'd pray with all sorts, and Sis liked a sing-song when it was on offer. Bert was outside, below their window, slopping whitewash on to the little wall of the yard.

Polly was, as usual, tidying up. They had a small chest of drawers between the three of them, and she was kneeling in front of it taking everything out, folding and refolding their few garments, even the stockings, which Jess had patched and darned until they were almost unrecognizable.

Jess wished she'd go down and leave her alone.

'What yer doing that for?' she snapped. 'Yer always fussing and fidgeting – yer've done that I don't know 'ow many times before and no one's touched it since.'

Polly sat back on her heels. Her mousy hair was scraped back and tied with a piece of string, her face pale and strained. She also looked annoyed at Jess's attack.

'It makes me feel better, that's all. Keeping the place a bit nice. What's wrong with that? If it was left to you we'd live in a right heap. When Ernie and I ... when we 'ave our own 'ouse I'll keep it nice I can tell yer.' She got up and went to sit beside Jess on the bed. 'Look – you're not yerself. What's ailing yer, Jess? It can't be that bad yer can't tell me?'

This wasn't the first time they'd had a conversation like this. Jess's moods had been up and down for weeks, sometimes calm, sometimes silent and withdrawn, and at others viciously irritable.

How could she tell them about Ned? There was no one she could confide in. And all the time she was eaten up with sorrow, with longing.

If I can't have him, there'll be no one else, she vowed to herself. I won't be with anyone just for the look of it, or because that's what everyone else does. I won't have second best. Not like Sarah. My dad never loved her. He was scared stiff of the woman. It wasn't like that with Louisa, not with Mom. If I can't be with Ned, what's the point – of anything?

There were a couple of lads at the works who'd taken a shine to her and asked her out. They were all right, except she found nothing to interest her in their company. She wouldn't go again and they told everyone she was a bit hoity-toity.

'Cor – daint yer like Billy?' Evie goggled in amazement. 'I'll 'ave 'im off of yer!'

'Yer welcome to 'im.' Jess smiled at her eagerness. If only she could feel the same.

People were noticing she'd lost her vitality, Polly especially. She was always on at her, like now, trying to worm out of her what was wrong.

'Jess—' Polly touched her cousin's back which was turned away from her. 'Is it yer family – them not writing or nothing?'

Jess shook her head. 'No – I never really thought they would. I mean if they'd left it that long . . .'

'Is it – well, summat we've done to upset yer?'

Another shake of Jess's head.

'Yer can't go on like this – yer getting scrawny like me – 'ere, I can feel all yer bones! When yer came yer were all bonny and strong. I wish there was summat I could do to help yer. Yer acting as if yer pining for summat . . .'

There was a long silence, then Jess's broken voice suddenly burst out, 'Oh Polly!' She buried her face in the bed.

'What's up, eh?' Polly patted her agitatedly. 'You can tell Poll. Just get it out – you'll feel better.'

Eventually Jess spluttered out, 'It's Ned!'

'*Ned*?' Polly actually started laughing. 'Jess, yer not still hankering after 'im, surely to goodness? I knew yer 'ad a flame lit for 'im when yer first came. I mean everybody goes for our Ned – me included, once upon a time. I know Mary's the last sort of person yer'd think 'e'd go for, but 'e's married 'er and that's that! Yer can't go on like this over 'im. I mean you hardly know 'im, do yer?'

Jess rolled over and sat up, hair in a mess and her face wet.

'I do – more than you know. I've seen 'im – a few times. He said he couldn't stop thinking about me and he – kissed me.' She saw Polly's face sober up in shock.

101

'I love him, Poll, and I know he loves me! Babby or no babby, it's me 'e should be with. If you feel that way about someone, that's where yer belong, ain't it? I can't stand the thought 'e'll be with *her* for ever more. In the wrong place with the wrong wife!' She put her head down on her knees and started crying all over again. 'I feel as if I'm losing my mind over him!'

'Oh for pity's sake—' Polly took hold of her shoulders and shook her furiously. 'What the flaming 'ell're yer going on about? This ain't some threepenny romance – this is life going on 'ere, Jess – they're married with a babby . . .'

'Don't—' Jess shook her off. 'I know it's bad of me – that's the worst of it, but I can't get over it! I can't stop wanting 'im . . .'

Polly got up and stumped over to the pile of clothes on the floor. 'I've no sympathy with yer, that I ain't. Never 'eard such a load of clap-trap. Yer just want to pull yerself together. There'll be someone else. Plenty of men about. Too many if yer ask me. Yer can't go after someone else's, that yer can't. Yer've no right.'

They heard the door rattle open downstairs. Olive and Sis were back. Sis was singing a bit of a hymn with her sweet young voice.

'Don't let on to our mom about this,' Polly hissed. 'That's the last department you'll get any sympathy from!'

'Can't say I've 'ad a lot from you neither,' Jess sniffed.

'Well—' Polly turned, angrily. 'What the hell d'yer expect?

*

102

'Ooh – Mom, look who's paying us a visit. Oh, and the babby – 'ark at 'er blarting!'

The tiny hall was crammed full of people all of a sudden, vying for a space on the lino as Sis opened the door. Dinner was over and the house still smelt of tasty stew. They were all sitting having a cuppa to finish off the meal. Ernie was there, as usual now, on a Sunday.

Polly's eyes whipped round to meet Jess's, full of warning. Jess looked away. She could hear Ned's voice in the hall and she was paralysed. Her hands turned clammy, heart feeling as if it was hammering a path out the front of her. She put her cup down, clattering it on the saucer.

Somehow she managed to stand up and do the expected things that the others were doing.

''Ere she is then, after all the waiting!' Mary held her out to be admired as if everyone's lives had been spent in anticipation of this moment. She beamed round at them.

'You sit down, wench,' Olive said, guiding her to a chair.

Jess took in the sight of Ned as he came round the door. Had he changed? Thinner, a bit. Tired. But still the person she loved, and longed for.

'Poll. Jess.' He nodded at them. He didn't hold Jess's gaze. He looked quickly away, but so did she.

Everyone stood round Mary, cooing over Ruth, even Bert.

'She's a bonny one, Ned. Ain't yer?' He held Ruth up, making playful faces at her. ''Ere y'are, Poll – I can see you're dying for a hold.'

Polly was drawn to the child in spite of herself. She

103

smiled stiffly at Mary and said, 'She's a lovely babby,' and Mary beamed like a cat with the cream and said,

'She's the prettiest babby *I've* ever seen and I don't think it's just me being partial.'

Jess's thoughts raced elsewhere. She could read nothing in Ned's face. He was like a stranger, his expression closed. Had her lips touched this man's? Had he aroused such feelings in her? But her body remembered, making her flushed and unsteady, even if her mind had doubts. She prayed no one would notice, especially not him. Oh, but the effect he had on her. Even a look from him!

She had to go and admire the baby. In any case, she was curious to see what Ned's child would be like. Mary was chatting on, cheerful.

'She's a right greedy little thing,' she told Olive. 'On and off of me all day long. I never knew it'd be like that. Ooh, I was sore to start with . . .'

'It'll settle down.' Olive couldn't take her eyes off the infant. She lifted Ronny up to look. 'See what our Mary's brought to show us – she's called Ruth, look, Ronny.'

'Babby!' Ronny shouted reaching out to her, hands smeary with gravy. 'Babby, babby!'

Jess watched quietly. She found she was standing next to Ned, although she was sure he hadn't intended to come close to her. She felt she must say something. 'She's a lovely babby, Ned. Congratulations to yer both.'

'She is.' He smiled faintly. 'Ta, Jess.' He looked round at her. Jess didn't know if her eyes held any of the hurt she felt. In his she saw . . . something. Longing? Sorrow? Or did she imagine that? Then Olive was saying,

'We can't just stand about all afternoon – park yer-selves on a chair if yer can find one. There, Ned – pull up one of these from the table.'

'I like yer new house,' Mary said, eyes roving the room. This was one of the things that aggravated Polly about Mary, always poking round to see what you've got. Always after more. She had an eye for the main chance marrying Ned, Polly always said. Her family wasn't much, after all.

'It was time we 'ad a bigger place,' Olive said quickly. 'Now Jess's stopping with us, and Ronny getting bigger.'

'That Regency stripe in the front's lovely, ain't it, Ned? We could do with some of that in ours. This is pretty in 'ere, an' all . . . I like a pretty paper on the wall I do. Gives the whole place a clean look . . .'

She chattered on, Jess barely listening, until she realized Mary was talking to her.

'D'yer want to 'ave a hold?'

'Oh – yes. Awright then.'

Blushing, she took the little scrap on her lap, supporting her head. Ruth peered up at her with pebbly blue, still slightly crossed eyes. Her face was covered in pink blotches. A moment after Jess took her she screwed up her face and started crying.

''Ere—' Thankful, Jess held her out to Mary. 'It's you she wants, not me. I ain't no good to her.'

She's going to look like her mom, Jess thought. It was as if there was nothing of Ned in her. She glanced up at him, and he smiled for a moment, rather absently, then turned his eyes towards his wife. Jess saw him quickly look away again as Mary began to suckle the baby.

Jess found those two hours an agony. His being

there, so close to her, yet they couldn't talk and were afraid to look at each other. She wondered if his feelings for her had died, now he had a child.

She barely took any notice as talk turned to the assassination of Archduke Ferdinand in Sarajevo, to the threat of war. Outside was so warm, so breathlessly still that it seemed an impossibility on this summer day, a distant dream, despite all the sabre rattling.

'We must be going,' Mary said eventually. 'It's quite a walk and our mom's expecting us back. Said she'd cook us tea tonight.'

'That's very nice of 'er,' Olive said, a bit sarkily Jess thought, as if to say, it's all right for some. 'Sis – you get the pram outside for Mary, will yer? None of us'll get out the door else.'

Mary got Ruth bundled up in her blanket and they heard Sis struggling down the step with the pram.

They were going through the 'lovely to see yer's and 'come again soon's, Ned nodding round at Polly, and Jess – 'T'ra then' – when Olive shrieked,

'Ronny? Where is 'e? 'E's gone – oh my God 'e'll be in the 'orse road by now!'

'Oh Lor'!' Polly cried. ''E must've got past Sis when 'er opened the door!'

There was a rush to the front, Polly and Ernie, Mary holding Ruth, Olive yelling at Sis – 'Where's yer brother, yer idle wench?'

Jess was on the point of following, when she saw that she and Ned were the only ones left standing in the back room. She turned at the door. All the desperate emotion she had been holding back all afternoon flooded into her face.

'Ned —'

'Jess—' He quickly moved closer. 'I didn't want to come today. It was Mary – you know, the babby ... I ...'

'D'yer love me? Do yer? Say it, Ned. Or say yer don't and yer never did.' Her gaze burned into him. He could feel her trembling, but there were voices outside. He gripped her hand tightly for a moment.

'Meet me – Tuesday night. Snow Hill. Under the clock. Can yer do it?'

There were voices coming to the front door, Ronny's loud, indignant yells.

Jess nodded. 'Course I can do it.' How would she let anything stand in her way?

They loosed hands as the others came in, Olive with Ronny grasped under one arm.

'Oh stop yer blarting – yer lucky not to be under a tram, yer little bugger. Found 'im outside the Friends Meeting 'Ouse! Moves like a clockwork engine, when 'e gets going.'

'You awright, Ronny?' Jess turned and picked him up, kissing him. In a moment when Olive's eyes were turned away she looked at Ned and mouthed, 'Half past seven?' He acknowledged it with a tiny movement of his head.

'Lovely to see yer, Auntie.' He kissed Olive. Jess watched, full up with feeling. He was so handsome, so lovely, and above all, he loved her ... For the first time in ages, she found herself smiling, joy swelling in her.

'You look after 'em both, my lad.' Olive clapped him affectionately on the back. 'That's your job now.'

'I will – don't yer worry on that score.'

They all stood waving them down the road, Mary pushing the pram.

Polly turned to go inside.

'Never seen such a scrawny little scrap of a thing,' she said. 'I'd've fed that one to the cat.'

'Poll!' Ernie sounded disappointed in her. 'That ain't very nice.'

'Huh,' Polly said.

Twelve

'Evie's invited me back to meet 'er family,' Jess said on Tuesday morning. 'So I'll not be back for tea.'

'Where's she live then?' Olive grunted, bending to pick up a cloth from the floor.

'Off Constitution Hill somewhere.'

'She got any brothers?' Sis asked with a cheeky grin. 'Maybe she'll get yer set up, like.'

'As a matter of fact she has – she's got two. One's fifteen –'

Sis groaned.

'– and the other's twenty-one.'

''S'e married?'

'Not as I know of.'

'Oooh!'

'What's 'e do for a living?' Polly asked.

'I don't know, fer 'eaven's sake!' Jess laughed. 'I ain't set Evie up as an official matchmaker – for all I know 'e might look like Frankenstein's monster!'

'Good match for you then,' Bert said.

'Oi – watch it . . .' Jess grinned. She was aquiver with excitement, but was trying to act normally.

'It's put you in a better mood, any'ow,' Polly observed.

It felt terrible, lying to them the way she was. But what choice was there? All day long she was full of pent up nerves. She had difficulty keeping her mind on her work. Each hour seemed longer than the last. Every few minutes she looked up at the clock on the wall. Maybe it had stopped? It scarcely seemed to move.

When work was finally over she clocked off and stepped out into the hazy summer evening. Smells of cooking drifted from the back yards.

She got there five minutes early. Standing under the enormous clock in Snow Hill Station getting her breath back, she looked round at the other figures moving back and forth to the platforms. Every so often one of the trains gave a shrill whistle, and there came the powerful chuffing noise of it getting up a head of steam.

Two men were standing near her. She saw them greet the people they were waiting for one by one and she was left alone, pacing up and down, looking up every few seconds to see the big spider's leg of a clock hand edge past the six and up, up the other side. Twenty-five to eight, twenty to eight. The light outside began to dim as the sun went down. Jess looked round, straining her eyes to see who was coming into the station. Twice, unable to keep still, she went to the entrance and looked out, each way.

By a quarter to, her throat was aching with unshed tears. Stupid fool she was, rushing here to meet a married man who wasn't going to come. MARRIED. The word thundered in her head. She leaned back against a poster advertising Fry's Chocolate and closed her eyes, aware of her heart's painful hammering. All the tension she had felt these months, the waiting, this long, difficult day she had had, and now this. Tears began to well up under her eyelids.

'Everything awright, miss?' Jess jumped, heart pounding. A young man dressed in the Great Western uniform stood in front of her.

Jess stood up straight, tried to make her voice normal. 'Yes ta – er, thanks. I'm just waiting for someone.'

'Right. Only I kept seeing you there – thought you was looking poorly.'

Over his shoulder, in that moment, she saw Ned's face.

'Oh—' She burst into tears, unable to hold back her emotion. 'Oh my God – I thought you weren't coming!'

'Jess ... love.' He wrapped his arms round her. 'I was worried yer'd have left. Only Ruth wouldn't settle and Mary'd got behind – there was no tea ready. I couldn't just go 'cause I said I was going to the pub and I never do that without 'aving tea first ...'

Jess sobbed even harder. Ned's words about what he did or didn't do at home, habits, that married routine, made her feel even more wretched. Mary had so much of him, and what did she have?

She nestled into his arms, as he held her tightly, his coat rough against her wet face. She drank in the sensation of being held in his arms.

'Come on,' he said. 'Look – let's get out of 'ere. It feels as if everyone's watching. No one'll take any notice outside.'

Once out in the street, along the side of the Grand Hotel, they dared to hold hands in the dusk. A horse and carriage clattered past them on Livery Street, hooves sparking on the cobbles. Jess could smell smoke from the trains. Opposite the end of the station they crossed into Bread Street.

'No one'll bother us 'ere,' Ned said.

He turned, holding her again.

'Tell me you love me,' she said. 'Everything'll be all right just so long as I know you feel like I do.'

'Jess ... Jess—' Ned gave a deep sigh, eyes fixed on

111

hers in the gloom. 'I wish I'd met you months before I did. As soon as I saw you it was summat else. Summat much – I don't know 'ow to say – bigger than what I feel for Mary. Beyond everything. It's made me feel, and do things I never thought I'd do in a thousand years. You're 'ere in my head and I can't get you out. I've tried.'

Jess was laughing and crying at once. She stood on tip-toe and they kissed. She felt the urgent force of his lips. When he released her she had to remind herself to breathe.

'What are we going to do?'

He leaned towards her again, not wanting to talk, only to fill himself with the sensation of her. He kissed her until he was drunk with it, his strong hands pressing her close, longing to touch every part of her lovely, curving body, knowing bitterly how wrong it would be, that it was forbidden him.

They stood for a moment, foreheads pressed together, both breathing fast. Then as if knowing a limit had been reached, they moved apart and walked on.

'I can't just leave 'er. Not with the babby. I owe 'er, Jess. And how would yer feel about me if you knew I'd just walk out on a woman and my own child?'

I don't know! she wanted to say. I just want you to be mine. To come with me and start again. But she knew he was right.

'So why're you here, Ned?'

'Because I can't keep away from yer.' He stopped again, taking her by the shoulders. 'She's the mother of my child, and you're the woman I love. I feel knocked to one side. As if I can't recognize myself. When I think of you it's as if nothing else matters. But I know it's wrong, like – to both of yer. We'll have to stop this, to keep apart. I can't expect to 'ave it both ways.'

For a moment neither of them spoke. A train came rumbling out of the station, making the ground shudder, smoke woomp-woomping out in hard-working bursts. The sound of it built, then died away.

'Yes, you can.' Her voice came out very strong, determined. 'If we can't do what's right to be together, we'll just have to live in the wrong. If it is wrong. I don't seem to know what's right and wrong any more.'

'God, Jess – what're yer saying to me?'

'Where did you say to Mary that you was going tonight?'

'Down the pub.'

'So you told 'er a fib. And I said to Auntie and the others I was going to Evie's – she's a girl at work. That makes both of us liars. But if I have to lie to see you, I will. Even though I know it's wrong . . .'

She felt his hand in the hair at the back of her neck, stroking her, saw him smile at her. 'How can this be wrong . . . Feeling like this?' But then he loosed her and turned away, towards the wall. 'How can we? We can't go on telling fibs, sneaking about, pretending to people . . .'

Jess put her hand out and touched his back, felt the tense hardness of it.

'So you'll not see me again? Is that it?'

He turned slowly, looking at her, helpless. Both of them tried to imagine going on now, without the other.

'No – that's not it. Come 'ere.'

His arms wrapped so tight around her he almost knocked the breath out of her. 'You're my woman. Deep down that's the truth of it, no matter what else. I can't change that even if I wanted to.'

'Do yer?'

'No, I don't. If doing the right thing means doing without you, Jess, I'm damned, that I am.'

'And me,' she nuzzled his neck. 'We'll both be damned together.'

Later, he walked her into town and they parted in New Street. On the corner of Corporation Street they stood in each other's arms for a long time.

'I can't let you go back to 'er,' Jess said. 'I can't stand it.'

'I've got to go – she'll wonder what's 'appened to me.'

After a last, long kiss, they parted. She began walking slowly along New Street, in a daze, still with the feel of his arms round her. Her lover, her man. And she his . . . his . . . She stopped abruptly.

'Oh!' she said, out loud. His mistress! That's what she was, however you dressed it up. It sounded bad that did. Terrible. But that was what she was. What she wanted. Because above everything else, she wanted Ned, whatever it involved, because nothing else mattered. She had never felt so loved or needed before, so safe and sure. She stood by the kerb, taking in deep breaths. What in heaven's name would Polly say if she knew?

''Ere – clear off out. Go on – shove it.'

Jess looked round, bewildered to hear a woman's voice, husky and low, directed menacingly close to her.

She was a tiny person, in a wide-brimmed hat with a strip of gold stuff tied round it making a huge bow. In the gloom, Jess could just make out a beauty spot on her cheek, and she smelt pungently of perfume.

'What?'

'I said clear out. Bugger off. This is my patch – yer can eff off and find yer own. Shouldn't try anything down this stretch if I was you – it's all spoke for.'

'What d'yer mean?' Jess protested. 'I was only . . .'

The woman laughed nastily. 'Just get 'ome – go on – get out of my sight before I decide to forget me manners.'

Jess raced the last mile home as fast as she could in the dark, unnerved by this strange woman. What the hell'd she been going on about? She slowed a little as she came closer to the house, panting hard. The ecstatic happiness she'd felt when she was with Ned seeped away and her mood became more sober. His loving her, knowing he felt as she did was the most wonderful thing that had ever happened. But the chill reality which had begun to impinge on her before she met the strange woman flooded through her again. Ned was going to stay with Mary, with his child. So when would there ever be a time, a place for her? When could the two of them ever belong together? By the time she got home she felt near to tears. But outside the house she met John, the eldest of the Bullivant sons from next door, a strong, handsome-looking man.

'Evening – awright, are yer?' he called out. Jess managed a reasonably cheerful reply and it helped her compose herself a bit by the time she walked into the house.

'Nice evening, was it?' Polly called to her.

Jess knew her face was flushed. She was too restless, too emotional. Would her guilt show in her face? She unbuttoned her coat and hung it in the hall with her hat, then forced a grin on to her face.

'It was awright,' she said, going through to the back. 'We had a bit of a laugh and they got some ale in from the Outdoor. Evie's mom's nice, and 'er brothers.'

Everyone was all ears.

'So – what's 'e like?' Sis was tilting her chair next to the table. Olive glowered at her and she lowered all four legs to the floor.

Jess frowned. 'Who?'

''Er brother of course – the one you thought she might set you up with!'

'Oh – well . . .' Jess made a face calculated to keep them all guessing. 'Not bad – not bad at all . . .'

'Better looking than me?' Bert asked.

'Miles better. Anyroad, it were a good evening. Only, on the way back I met this queer woman.'

She told them what had happened in New Street.

'She was ever so sharp with me,' she finished indignantly. 'And I was only getting my breath back! What's so funny, eh? Yer look like a barrowload of Cheshire cats.'

Olive's lips twitched and Polly and Bert were grinning from ear to ear.

'I told yer, didn' I – not to hang about in town of a night!' Olive chuckled, pressing a hand to her chest. 'That'll teach yer!'

'Well, who was she?'

'Yer lucky she daint scratch yer face off of yer,' Polly laughed. 'Ain't you ever heard of Ladies of the Night?'

The penny began to drop. Jess pressed her hands to her hot cheeks. 'Oh my . . . she was a . . .?'

Olive nodded, looking meaningfully at Sis.

'A what?' Sis said. 'Oh go on – a what? Why won't yer tell me?'

'What yer don't know won't hurt yer. And yer should be getting to bed this time of night. Go on – up yer go.'

116

Sis groaned and moaned her way to the stairs, but knew she could ask Polly later.

Jess looked round at them all. They hadn't guessed. And next week she could go again, pretend she was interested in Evie's brother. At least she could see him. Feel his love. That was all that mattered. She smiled.

'Anyone want a last cuppa tea?'

Thirteen

She met Ned the next week, but the third Tuesday he didn't turn up and Jess went home miserable. He managed to find her the next day, outside Blake's when she came off work.

'Sorry about last night.' He sounded very fed up. 'It's our Ruth – 'er's been bad with a fever. Up and down all night. I couldn't just leave Mary to cope all evening as well.'

'What a good father.' She'd felt horribly jealous and tense all day. But soon, out of relief at seeing him, she relented and smiled. She knew he was trying to do right by both of them. 'It's awright. Is she any better?'

'Not much. Look, I'm going to 'ave to go – I just wanted to see yer in case you was thinking – well, you know.'

Before he went he kissed her quickly on the cheek, looking round anxiously in case anyone he knew was about.

'Eh – who was that then? He's a looker!' Evie followed Jess's gaze as she watched Ned disappear.

Still straining to see him along the crowded street, Jess said, 'Evie – I need a favour off of yer.'

'What's that then?'

'Look – come with me. I'll treat yer to a cuppa and tell yer.'

They went to a coffee house nearby which reminded

Jess of Mather's, only it wasn't nearly as well kept. The sawdust looked as if it hadn't been swept up for days.

'Bit of an 'ole this,' she said, looking round.

When their tea arrived the glass felt grimy, a silt of sugar still stuck to the outside, but Jess was too preoccupied to complain.

'I've got to come clean with yer, Evie. I've been using you as an excuse to get out of an evening.'

Evie leaned closer, all agog. 'What – you seeing that good-looking fella?'

'That's it. I told my auntie I come over to see you and yer mom and brothers, Tuesd'y nights . . .'

Evie laughed. 'Jess, I ain't got no brothers! There's just me and Edith and Sal.'

'I know – any'ow, might as well be hanged for a sheep as a lamb. But they've sort of got the idea I'm keen on this brother o' yours. I'm just telling yer, 'cause I feel bad using yer like that and you not knowing.'

'Well I s'pose that's awright,' Evie didn't sound too sure.

'I won't get yer into any trouble.'

'I'm glad you told me any'ow, Jess. What about this feller of yours then . . . ain't they too keen on 'im?'

Jess didn't feel she could tell Evie quite all the truth. After all, she had to protect Ned as well. She looked down at the greyish tea in her glass. 'No. They ain't. My auntie's very strict – looks out for me like. But they've got 'im all wrong.'

Evie was full of curiosity. 'D'yer love 'im then?'

'Like mad. But I don't see 'ow we can ever be together. Not properly.'

''Cause of yer family?'

Jess nodded solemnly, appalled at the way she could lie so easily.

Evie reached across and touched her hand. 'If yer really love each other, you'll find a way. They can't stop yer forever, can they? You could go to Gretna Green. Ooh, it's just like in a story!'

''Cept in stories you know there'll be a happy ending,' Jess said tragically.

'Eh – cheer up. Tell yer what. As you're telling them yer coming over to see us, why don't you come for a visit. Our mom'd be ever so pleased to meet yer!'

'Awright,' Jess smiled. 'I'd like to. Just not on a Tuesd'y night, that's all!'

When Ned met her the next week he looked tired. They walked south, away from the Jewellery Quarter, through St Paul's churchyard. It felt safer, more anonymous to head for the middle of town.

'You awright?' she asked anxiously. 'You look all in. Been out on a blaze?'

'No – I just ain't getting much sleep. One minute Ruth's up wanting feeding and then I'm – well, I don't get to sleep easy. Listen, I've been thinking – whether there's a way we could spend longer together. Away somewhere. It's hopeless here – there's no privacy anywhere.'

Jess's eyes widened in hope. 'What – yer mean . . .?'

'I've been thinking how I could get a day out.'

'A whole day! Oh, that'd be – Oh Ned!' Her face fell. 'But how? I mean we're either at work, or there's no reason we can give for going out. Oh, but I'd do anything to spend a bit more time with yer, yer know that!'

'Could yer get away on Sunday?'

She didn't hesitate. 'Yes. I'll just go and answer questions later.'

'Mary's mom's often round ours of a Sunday. Can't get away from the woman. But if I say there's a reason I 'ave to be at the Fire Station, or summat like that ... Giving it a special going over ... I'll sort summat out. Oh God, more lies, Jess ...'

'Where shall we go?' Jess asked. She was all but jumping up and down in his arms. 'Oh I can't believe it – just you and me!'

'Let's go as far away as we can get. On a train – eh?'

'Oh, I know!' Her face lit with excitement. 'I know exactly where we can go!'

It was a perfect, still, July dawn.

This can't be wrong, doing this, Jess thought as she crept out of bed, cringing as the bed creaked. Otherwise God would've made it rain and be miserable.

She dressed silently in the prettiest of her two summer frocks, white with blue checks. Over the top she wore a cardigan the colour of mulberries, and her old summer shoes with a strap and a button. All the time she watched Polly and Sis, on tenterhooks, but both of them stayed fast asleep. Jess felt even the sound of her heart thumping might wake them, she was so highly charged. She'd barely slept all night. She could hear muted snores coming from Bert's room.

She was too impatient and nervous to brew tea. Taking a slice of bread with a scraping of butter she let herself out, eating it as she hurried along the Moseley Road. It was too early, but she could not have kept still in the house any longer. A clanging sound came from the goods yard behind, but otherwise the road was quiet. The sky was clear, but hazy, and although it was still cool, it was obviously set to be a beautiful summer's day.

She tried to slow her pace and look around her. The Bull Ring was shut up and almost deserted as she walked through, and she was soon in New Street station waiting for Ned.

The station was anything but deserted. Over to one side of the area near the ticket office, a group was gathering. Jess stood, half her attention on them, the other on watching the entrance with impatient excitement. A few more joined the group. They were all women, most smartly dressed in calf length skirts, jackets and elegant hats. She saw that one of them was holding a placard with the initials 'WSPU' on it. Another was handing out sashes which they were all shouldering on over their clothes. Jess squinted to read them. '. . . s for Women' was all she could make out. She turned away as one of them glanced at her, and saw Ned coming. He kissed her briefly and took her arm, steering her to the ticket office.

'Come on – let's get right away from 'ere.' Excited, she clutched his arm.

The train ride was bliss. Away from the danger of meeting anyone they knew, they settled down together, Jess by the window, Ned's arm close round her. She laid her straw hat in her lap and leaned against him, resting her head on his shoulder, smelling the smoky upholstery. They had the carriage to themselves. The train rumbled out through Adderley Park, then Stechford. Jess let out a great sigh of contentment.

'The air feels clearer already.' She twisted her head, smiling up at him.

'Not in 'ere it don't.' He leaned down and kissed the tip of her nose. 'My country wench.'

'I miss it. I want to take you and show you.'

'You going to call on yer dad?'

She was silent for a moment, fear and uncertainty mixed with her excitement. 'I don't know. In a way I want to. But 'e's never writ me even so much as a word. I could be dead for all 'e knows. Or cares.'

'Maybe yer should. Yer might run into someone else who'll let on they've seen yer. And it might make yer feel better.'

'Yes, and it might not,' she retorted. 'I'll see 'ow I am when I get there. I just want to see the place – the fields and everything. That's what I've missed. And how'm I going to explain you away, sunshine?'

'I'll hide behind a wall 'til yer done! Anyroad – they don't know me, do they? We could be married.'

Jess twisted round in his arms. 'We should be married, Ned. We're married in our hearts, whatever else.'

Ned watched her face, the force of her feelings plain in it. Desire rose in him. What would she be like as a lover, this fierce, passionate girl? Mary was sweet and obliging. Didn't refuse him. But her response was nothing more than dutiful, friendly. Obedient even. But Jess – he could feel the taut arousal in her even when they kissed. The instinctive way she moved against him. She made the same sounds of need, of frustration as he did. Yet she was scared. And he knew how wrong it was even to be thinking of making love to another woman. But he hardly seemed to be able to think of anything else these days. His need of her was total, consuming him.

She was intent on the view from the window, hungry

123

for old, familiar sights. The city had faded away behind them.

'Oh look, Ned!' she cried. 'Look at the fields, the colours of everything. It's so beautiful. I want to get out – now!'

'I think yer'd better wait 'til the train stops in a station!' He laughed, ran his hand slowly down her back, feeling the warmth of her.

At last they stepped out on to the platform at Budderston. Jess immediately thought of her aunt, waving in this spot all those years ago, and told Ned.

'She looked like a fish out of water in the country. And as for Polly!'

'Well . . .' Ned was looking round. 'It's a bit quiet, ain't it?'

'It's Sunday – what d'yer expect!'

It was already well on in the morning and the sun was hot. Jess took off her cardigan and carried it over her arm. To her relief, no one was about. Only the station master's black dog snoozed in the shade at the front of the station.

'So – where're we off to then?' Ned asked, suddenly gruff. He was thrown a bit by the unfamiliar surroundings.

'I thought,' Jess turned, uncertain. 'Maybe we should go up to the Forge and get it over – see my dad.'

He saw how vulnerable she was, coming back, not knowing if she'd be wanted.

'It'll be awright,' he said, taking her arm.

'We'll go the back way. I don't want people staring and gossiping.'

Arm in arm, they walked along the back lane, across

the brook. Jess saw that the wood which made a bridge over it had been replaced. The pale, unfamiliar planks now laid there enforced her sense of separation. She'd known almost every grain in the old ones: they formed part of her memories.

'This is my favourite place,' she said, stopping, breathing in deeply. She could smell the long grass, the wheat ripening in the field behind, shifting in the breeze, flecked with red.

Ned put his arm round her shoulders. Gnawing at him constantly was the need to touch her. 'It's very nice. Lovely place to grow up. And you look right 'ere, Jess.'

'I used to play out 'ere for hours on end – and help with the haymaking and that. Our 'ouse is just down there.'

She stopped at the back gate. They looked over, seeing the orchard trees, the path to the house, startlingly familiar when she felt so changed. There was no one about, but a loud snuffling came from their right.

'That'll be Sylvia – the pig!' Jess found she was whispering. 'Oh Ned – d'yer think I should just stay away? Would that be the best thing? I feel sick at the thought of going in.' She laid her hand on her chest as if to slow her heart.

'Yer might as well – now yer 'ere. Yer might not get the chance again in a long while.'

She took several deep breaths, then nodded. 'Awright. With you.'

The first person she saw was little Liza, sitting on the cottage step shelling peas into a basin. The girl looked up. Without smiling, she stared for a moment, then called out,

'Mom. Jess's 'ere.'

In a second, Sarah appeared disbelievingly in the doorway. Jess saw she'd grown a little stouter. She stepped out, stared, seeming neither pleased nor hostile, only wary.

'I'm sorry I cut the dress,' Jess said, eventually. 'I couldn't marry Philip.'

Sarah swallowed. Nodded. She seemed unable to think of a word to say. Eventually she asked, 'Who's yer friend?'

'This is my . . .' she wanted to say 'husband'. Wanted to show she could choose for herself. But it was such a big lie. Bigger than all the others and she couldn't bring out the words. 'This is Ned.'

Sarah nodded at him, then looked back at Jess. 'Yer father's in the forge if yer want to see 'im.'

'Is Philip there?'

'No. Not today.'

As they went closer she could hear William pumping up the fire with the huge bellows, the crackle and spit of the flames. They stepped in, just able to feel the heat on their faces, eyes adjusting to the smoky gloom. She didn't say anything, just waited for him to see her.

When he did turn, he jumped, startled. He peered at her, eyes watering from the smoke.

'Louisa?' It was a whisper of hope, defying time.

'It's Jess. I've come back to see yer.'

'Jess.' The moment of wonder passed and his expression became more guarded. He came towards her, wiping his hands on his apron, beard tucked between the buttons of his shirt. His eyes, always childlike, seemed paler, his skin a little slacker. Jess was moved. Could it have been the shock of her going which had aged him in just a few months?

126

But then, with obvious disquiet, he said, 'Not come back for good, 'ave yer?'

'No!' Hurt and anger burned in her again. Why had she let herself think he might have missed her? 'Not likely. I just thought you might be pleased to see yer daughter once every blue moon, that's all. But I can see I got it wrong!'

'I am pleased to see yer. I just didn't expect yer.'

'Why didn't you answer Olive back when she writ yer? That wouldn't 've cost yer much, would it?' Ned could sense the anguish behind the aggression in her voice.

William shrugged. 'She said you was awright. Come to no harm. You wanted to go, and yer went.'

Jess turned away. What was the point? Nothing had changed. She'd got out of their way and that suited both of them.

She looked back at her father. 'To think I came back wanting forgiveness from you! It's you who should be on yer knees begging me for it. Come on, Ned – I'm not wanted 'ere. Never was.'

Sarah met them on their way back across the garden.

'We won't stop to get in yer way,' Jess said. 'I've done quite enough of that in my time already.'

'Yer upset 'im, going like that, yer know. Took 'im an age to get over it.'

'Well 'e seems to be over it now.'

Jess stood by the vegetable patch, arms tightly crossed. She was infuriated to find herself fighting back tears.

'Yer can come in and have a bite to eat if yer want,' Sarah said. 'I don't mind.'

'No,' Jess retorted. 'Maybe yer don't. But I do. I'm never sitting at a table again where I'm not welcome.'

Sarah took a step away, as if there was work she needed to get back to. 'Give us a bit of warning next time yer decide to come.'

'Oh – there won't be a next time. Goodbye, Sarah.'

They went down to the lane and shut the gate. Jess stopped, leaned against the back wall and put her hands over her face.

'Oh I wish my mom'd never died! God knows, all I wanted was to feel 'e might be pleased to see me.'

Ned's arms came round her, warm and comforting as the sobs broke from her. She had had no idea that coming back here would make her feel quite so desolate. She had done wrong running away, she knew, but could they not see the wrong they'd done her by trying to marry her off to Philip? She had still hoped deep down, that beneath her father's reserved ways he really loved her, that one day he'd be able to show her. But now she felt utterly cut off: more alone than ever. She clung with all her strength to Ned as he held her. He was her life now, her anchor.

'Never leave me, Ned. You won't, will yer, promise me?'

He held her while she cried like a little child.

In a while she wiped her face.

'Let's go over there.' She pointed beyond to where the hayfield met the wheat, the hedgerow a dark line between. 'No one ever goes there, not except at harvest or sowing time. We can just pretend there's no one else in the world but us.'

'That sounds my sort of place,' Ned said. Her tears had roused in him a powerful combination of tenderness and desire.

Jess looked anxiously at him. 'Are yer hungry? We could get summat in the village.'

'No—' He reached for her hand. 'That can wait.'

They walked hand in hand across the hayfield, swishing through the grass, hearing the wind moving through it. The feel and sound of it filled Jess with a wistful longing. It was the sound of her childhood, once happy, then so cruelly spoilt. She looked up at Ned beside her, white shirtsleeves rolled halfway up his arms, jacket slung over one shoulder. Just the sight of him made her want to hold him close: his wavy hair, shaped rather squarely round his forehead, darker eyebrows. She pressed his hand to her lips.

'You suit the country an' all,' she said. 'D'yer fancy being a farmer?'

He laughed. 'Not sure I'd know one end of a cow from another! I'd 'ave to leave that to you!'

Jess thought of Mrs Hunter, the farmer's wife, and her exhausted face. 'It's one of the hardest jobs there is, I reckon.'

There was a strip of unsown land where shorter, scrubbier grass was growing, but it was in the shade, so they walked to the gate and climbed through to the wheatfield.

'That's better,' Ned said. 'It feels even further away from everything.'

'Let's sit down.' Jess took Ned's coat and her cardigan and laid them together. She looked shyly at him. 'Half the day's gone already. I wish we could stop it going so fast.'

They lay resting back on their elbows, looking out across the corn, hearing the breeze, the occasional grating cry of a crow, and smaller birds darting between the heads of wheat. Between its tough stalks, the glowing petals of poppies blew on their curved stems, their blooms wide open to the sun. Jess rolled over and snuggled closer to Ned.

'It don't matter about them any more. I've got you. I mean I know I ain't really got yer – but I have for today, so I can pretend.'

'I wish you could meet my mom and dad. They'd like you.'

'They like Mary though. So they wouldn't, would they? Not as things are. If they knew they'd hate me!'

Ned was silent. He picked a stalk of grass with his free hand and nibbled the end. Suddenly he rolled on to his side and looked into her eyes. They seemed to hold a question, whether directed at him or within herself, he couldn't tell. For a moment she looked deeply serious, then a smile broke over her face.

'My Jess,' he said. 'My wench. Yer lovely, you are.' If only he could tell her properly what he felt! But words were no use. He kissed her mouth, slowly moving his hands over her body. Her dress was light cotton, only her bare flesh beneath. He worked his way, stroking until he reached her breasts and reached inside until he could move his hands over them and they were so firm and beautiful to touch. She didn't object, as she had sometimes in the park, thinking people could see. She arched her back, responding to his kisses, pressing against him until he was aroused past reason.

Jess's mind was awhirl. Here they were, for the first time ever in a place where they were truly alone. The one time where she could have with him what Mary had. She could have his whole body. She felt a throbbing between her legs at the thought. No one would know. No one except the two of them. The idea of this act with Philip had so repulsed her, but now, as

130

Ned touched her, it felt right, the only thing to do, inevitable.

Ned tried to hold on to his self-control. He mustn't go too far, it was wrong. For some time they lay together, wrapped in each other's arms, until he pulled away and knelt above her.

'Oh God, Jess—' he sounded desperate. 'I want you – let me have you . . .'

She gave a small, uncertain nod, then whispered, 'Yes.' She reached out and began to unbutton him, hearing him panting in surprise.

He unfastened her dress, looking around, afraid that despite what she'd said, someone was coming. But there was no one. She raised her arms and he pulled the dress over her head, then took off his own shirt.

They made love beside the rustling wall of wheat, her strong fingers pressing on his bare back, her legs locked round him, urging him closer and deeper to her.

Everything was quiet, then, except for the sound of their breathing, pressed close to one another, and the swish of the corn. She moved her hands over him, in wonder at what had just happened.

'What a woman you are, Jess,' Ned murmured. 'There's no one like you.'

She kissed his neck, holding him close looking up at the tiny puffs of cloud against the blue sky, and the brilliant red smile of the poppies.

Now he's mine, she thought, without shame. Really and truly mine.

Fourteen

Jess bought the *Gazette* that Bank Holiday Monday, a week after her day with Ned. She read it in Aston Reservoir Grounds, lolling on the grass with Olive, Polly and Sis, buying Scattoli's ice-creams as a treat, the tinkling music and roar of engines drifting to them from the Fun Park where they'd come for a day out. It was a hot, festive day, smelling of fried onions and engine oil. The idea of war seemed abstract and far away, despite the talk in the factory all week.

'D'yer think it'll 'appen, Mom?' Polly looked round at Olive who was sitting behind them, legs splayed, shoes off to air her bunions.

'Looks as if it might. They want to get it over with, that they do.'

The next day, 4 August, England declared war on Germany, and three days later, Bert came home jubilant.

'I've joined up!'

Jess had never seen him look so excited. He seemed taller suddenly, shoulders back, proud of himself. The women stood in a ring, giving him their absolute attention.

'Well,' Olive said. 'Yer father was an army man – in the early days.'

'I asked about joining his regiment, but they said I might as well be in the Warwicks – with Sid and Jem. They'll let us know, soon's they want us.' He pulled his boots off, looking up at them from his seat by the cold hearth. 'Can't be worse than all the bloody noise and filth in the Mills, can it? I've always had a hankering to give the army a go, so now's me chance.'

Jess immediately thought about Ned. He wouldn't go, would he? Not a married man with a family? And with her . . . He couldn't leave – how could she bear it?

Bert left a few days later, the family hero, for training at Tidworth, on the edge of Salisbury Plain.

Ernie was next. By the middle of August posters were appearing all over town, Kitchener's handlebar moustache, 'Your Country Needs You'. When Ernie came round that Saturday night, Polly knew immediately.

'Oh Ernie – yer haven't!'

Ernie smiled shyly, stroking his beard. Ronny was throwing himself at his legs and Ernie laughed, picking the little boy up and making faces at him so he chuckled. 'Ooh yer getting too heavy for me!' He swung him to the floor. 'Look, Poll – d'yer fancy coming out, for a walk like?' Jess saw a blush seep into his chubby cheeks.

Olive's eyes followed them as they left. When they came back, Polly was pink-faced and smiling, and both of them looked as if they might burst if they didn't get the words out.

'You two look mightily pleased with yerselves,' Olive said. 'Let's 'ear it then, whatever it is.'

'The thing is, Mrs B,' Ernie said, all blushes. 'What with me going away soon like, I've asked – I mean, Poll and I would like to get wed.'

'Oh, Poll!' Jess cried, delighted for her.

'Oooh!' came from Sis.

Olive was silent.

133

'Is that awright, Mom?' Polly looked uncertain. 'I mean, since I've no dad to ask for permission like . . .'

'When was yer thinking of? Yer getting married in church, proper like?'

'Whatever you say, Mrs B,' Ernie said fervently. 'I want to do right by Polly, and if that's what she wants.'

'Ar, it is what she wants,' Olive said. 'Well – yer'd best get weaving then, ain't yer? We'll sort yer a frock out, Poll.'

Jess went to them, 'I'm very happy for yer. That's lovely news that is.' She kissed them both, making Ernie go red again.

She was indeed very pleased. Polly deserved to be happy and she liked Ernie. Would have trusted him with her life. But that night there was an ache in her heart for the thought of a wedding of her own. A wedding that she doubted could ever happen with the man she loved.

They still met every week, hungry for each other's company. Their lovemaking had brought them even closer, and they spent their one evening a week locked together, walking, talking. The next Tuesday, they went to Handsworth Park.

'It's daft me bringing you 'ere again,' Ned said. 'Too near home for comfort.'

'But it's so pretty – everyone else's in getting on with their tea this time o' day.'

'That first time I came 'ere with yer – you know – after you nearly threw yerself under that bus . . .' He shook his head in teasing despair at her antics. 'I've never felt more wound up in me life.'

Jess smiled. 'Nor me.' After a moment she said abruptly, 'Ned – you're not going to join up, are yer?'

He was silent, then sighed. 'Not for now, anyroad.' Seeing her dismayed face he touched her cheek, smiling. 'Eh, cheer up! They don't want an old married man of twenty-one – we'll let the young'uns with no family go first and see what 'appens! They say it'll all be over in a few weeks anyroad.'

'I can't stand the thought of you going away. I mean, I'm no one – nothing to yer, am I? Not as far as anyone else knows. If anything was to 'appen to yer, it's the widow they'd tell, not me . . .'

She sounded so wretched, Ned turned and held her in his arms. She breathed in the smell of him, salty, sweaty in the heat.

'That's enough of that. I'm not going anywhere, Jess. I'm 'ere.'

They made love again that evening, in a corner of the churchyard beyond the park, hidden behind long grass and a tree. It wasn't planned, but they sat together in the dusk, under the wide branches of the tree, and were overcome with desire for one another. Jess felt her whole body yearning to be touched and loved. She pulled him close into her, knowing as she did she should be ashamed at being so eager, so helpless with need of him. But she was not ashamed. She was moved that he made love to her so urgently. She didn't care about tomorrow or next week, only now. And now, if this was how they spent it, was enough.

When they had become calmer he lay stroking her, kissing her cheeks, her lips, his hand under her blouse.

'Oh Jess, we need to be so careful.'

135

'I know. But sometimes I just don't care. It feels as if there is nothing else. Because there ain't—' she turned and looked him in the eyes. 'Not for me.'

She saw Ned close his eyes for a moment. When he opened them again, he said, 'I'm a coward, I should leave her. Go against everyone and go with you, where I really want to be.'

Jess held her breath, waiting, but he did not speak again, not about that. There was a long silence.

Polly and Ernie managed to organize a whirlwind wedding the next weekend, before Ernie had to report to his regiment, the 10th Warwickshires. They were married at St Agnes Church in Sparkbrook, where Ernie's family were regular members and where Olive had attended as a young woman. Polly looked very sweet in a lilac dress trimmed with lace. Ernie's cheeks popped up over the rim of a tight collar. He sweated both with the heat and with nerves and seemed to find the whole occasion an ordeal, but kept smiling valiantly, clearly happy and in love, as Polly was too.

It was also an ordeal for Jess. Ned and Mary were invited, and sat behind her, Mary holding Ruth on her lap. Jess could hear the baby's little sounds as Mary fed her discreetly to keep her quiet. She felt Ned's presence behind her as if a current was running between them. Her chest was tight with repressed emotions.

They were the only guests who came back to the house. Jess tried to stay away from him, keeping busy making tea and cutting cake. Then she sat with Polly and Ernie, who as usual had Ronny on his lap, and they made jokes about the two of them soon having their own children, which made Polly blush and look happier than ever. The couple left in the evening for three days' holiday, staying in a pub in the country.

Polly came back looking very healthy and said bashfully, that they had had a lovely time.

Work changed abruptly. Now they were making battalion badges with a crest at the top: underneath, the lettering, 'Volunteered for Birmingham Battalion'. Evie was full of pride because her new boyfriend had just volunteered. Polly was also proud, but bereft now Ernie was gone, first to Budbrooke Barracks, then on to Tidworth, like Bert.

Summer waned into autumn, but the impetus for war did not fade with it. The papers showed pictures of Belgian refugees arriving in Britain. Ned told Jess that Bonney the fire station horse had been taken to be shipped to France. They started to hear about battles: Mons, Le Cateau, the Marne. Across the Town Hall, a huge banner read: 'RECRUITING OFFICE: WANTED, 500,000 MEN. GOD SAVE THE KING.'

The pressure on young men to join the fighting was becoming irresistible. Jess knew in her heart that it had to happen eventually.

One evening when she met Ned, he pulled out a white card from his pocket and showed it to her reluctantly. It was his enlistment appointment from the Deputy Mayor.

'It won't be for long. They're saying it'll only last a few months, if that. But I can't stand by and let everyone else go and not be part of it, can I? I feel like a shirker, a coward, if I don't do my bit.'

Ned watched her face. Saw her summon strength inside herself.

'I don't want yer to go, course I don't,' she said. 'But I s'pose I'd feel the same.' She smiled tenderly. 'I'm proud of yer.'

As they parted that evening, Ned walked home with a sense of relief, freedom even. All these months he had been torn between Jess and Mary, so that he was worn down with it. He felt unsettled and deceitful, when he had been accustomed all his life to people thinking well of him. Going away from it all was a way out. Just men round him. It would give him time to think, to see if he could forget Jess, and pull himself round to doing what was right. Stick with Mary. Or find the courage to leave her and face the consequences. At the moment that felt the hardest, most heart-breaking decision he had ever faced in his life.

Fifteen

October 1914

Jess slammed the door of the privy shut and bent over the wooden seat, retching. Nothing came up except a thin trickle of yellow bile. Holding her hair back she coughed and gasped until it was over. The stench of the dry privy was awful and she stepped out into the yard, taking in gulps of bitter smelling air. For a moment she leaned against the wall, hearing the chunk-chunk of a goods train coming out from the yard behind. A dark plume of smoke thinned out in the air. The sun was trying to struggle through cloud.

Two months, she'd missed. And sick – for several days now – always aware of her stomach, as if someone had drawn round it in black. At first she'd thought she was ill. But she knew the signs – Sarah's education again. Knew, in a part of her mind that could barely admit it, that she was carrying a child. The sickness. Everything smelt stronger but nothing tasted nice. Her breasts felt heavy and bruised.

She heard someone else come out the back door. Polly, in her slip, younger looking in her nightclothes, legs mottled as brawn, shivering now there was a nip in the air. When she came out of the privy she gave a little shriek.

'Flipping 'eck, Jess, I daint see yer there!'

'Poll – come 'ere.'

'What?' Polly moaned. 'S'cold out 'ere.'

'Poll – I think I'm 'aving a babby.'

'Oh yes – and I'm flying to the moon!'

Jess hadn't said the words even to herself before. Had hardly meant to speak now. Hearing it said frightened her.

Polly peered at her. 'What yer talking about? You're 'aving me on, ain't yer? By Christ, Jess – yer'd better be!'

Jess was shaking her head, eyes filling with tears. Saying it made it sound real.

'But yer can't be! I mean, whose . . .?'

'Ned's.' She only whispered the name, but Polly leaped towards her, clamping a hand over Jess's mouth. She looked anxiously round at the windows of the house.

'What yer telling me this bloody clap-trap for? Eh?' She put her hands on Jess's shoulders, thin fingers digging in. 'Don't ever come out with any of this in front of our mom or she'll knock yer block off, that she will!'

'Poll – I ain't come on for two months.'

For a moment Polly was speechless. She glared into Jess's tearful eyes, then pushed her with all her force round the side of the privy and began shaking her, slapping her face, sobbing, finally clutching her hands over her own face.

'Yer stupid, dirty little bitch!'

'Poll!' Jess hadn't intended to tell her. It had just swollen up in her mouth and popped out before she knew.

''Ow could yer be so disgusting? So bloody *stupid*?'

Polly was beside herself. 'Mom'll . . . she'll . . .' She grasped Jess's wrist. 'She mustn't know. Yer not to say a word to 'er. It'll finish 'er this will.' She turned, her gaunt face looking round the yard as if there might be a solution there somewhere, then turned again on Jess. 'It's not really Ned's, is it? 'E's a married man – 'e's got Mary, the babby ...' Her nails were digging so hard into Jess's wrist that she pulled away, wincing.

'Sorry, Poll.' She did feel ashamed, then, hearing it spelled out. 'But Ned and me love each other. I know 'e's married to Mary, but really 'e's mine.'

'For Christ's sake, Jess, yer a bloody dupe, ain't yer?' Polly's voice suddenly quietened, as if with despair. 'Now don't you go saying a word to anyone else. Not a word – got it? I need time to think about this bloody lot!'

Seething with anger and upset, Polly strode ahead of Sis down Bradford Street on their way to the pen factory. How they'd got through breakfast she'd never know, with Jess filling up every few minutes and wiping her eyes on her sleeve.

'What's up with you?' Olive asked eventually. She said it so meaningfully, to Polly's ears, that she thought her own heart was going to stop.

'I think I'm going down with a cold,' Jess said in an almost normal voice. 'I'm awright though – honest. Just me eyes keep watering.'

Polly was so brim-full of emotion she wanted to howl. She was very short with Sis on the way to work.

'Wait for me,' Sis complained.

'Keep yer trap shut, will yer. I'm trying to think.'

'But what's the flaming rush?'

'Oh *shurrup*, will yer!'

Sis looked hurt and decided to keep quiet for the rest of the way.

Polly felt her eyes fill with tears and brushed them away. She'd already been anxious and pent up about Ernie being away. They should be finding a house of their own to rent, moving in together, not parted, not knowing when they'd see each other again. She missed him terribly. His quiet, stable nature steadied Polly. She trusted him absolutely, felt safe with him. Now he was gone she felt alone, and frightened.

And it was only now she was facing up to how worried she'd been about her mom. Those funny turns she'd had. They'd always been fighters, the two of them. Mother and daughter standing together against cold and hunger, getting by with no man in the house. Life so difficult – her begging round the factories for food after school. Just as she'd thought everything was getting better, her Mom had turned strange on her – thank God she seemed better now, at least for the moment.

But Jess – the pressure of emotion welled up in her again at the thought of her cousin. She had great affection for her, but this morning she had felt like killing her. Jess just breezes in, takes everything she wants, makes a disgrace of herself with no regard, no idea . . . She felt faint herself suddenly, was afraid she'd fold up, right there in the street, and she leaned against the wall of Clark's, everything fading round her for a second as black panic spread through her. Things were going wrong, getting out of control, when what she needed was to keep order, keep life in check . . . Jess was like a whirlwind, stirring everything to chaos. What in hell's name were they going to do?

'Poll?' Sis's voice was frightened. 'Yer face's gone a funny colour.'

'I'll be awright. Just 'ang on a tick.'

She straightened up groggily and took Sis's arm. Sis smiled at her uncertainly.

Later, at work, Polly kept an eye on a woman called Sally. She was a bit simple, Sally was, had been taken advantage of by some factory lad a year or so back. But her mom'd got hold of her, made sure the babby never came to anything. Polly waited until the break when Sally went to relieve herself. There was only one toilet downstairs, out the back; in a filthy state. Polly caught her coming out. Her misshapen face looked first terrified, then perplexed, as if trying to remember something deeply buried.

'If yer breathe a word about this yer gunna get a beating—' Polly had her face pressed up close.

'I'll not, I'll not!' Sally squeaked. From her mouth, the stench of rotten teeth. In a hoarse whisper she told Polly what she wanted to know.

'I ain't doing that! How can yer even think of it?'

'Yer've not got a choice, yer silly little bitch! Yer don't think 'e's going to stand by yer, do yer? With a wife and babby to fend for already! You don't seem to see what a mess yer in! Face it, Jess – yer carrying his bastard child. You're a fallen woman! You don't think our mom'll let yer carry on stopping with us in that state, do yer? She'll 'ave yer out on the street even quicker than 'e put it in there!'

Jess felt the words rain down on her like bullets. 'I've got to tell 'im,' she said stubbornly. Ned would make everything all right. He loved her more than anyone in

143

the world. If she was carrying his child it made her equal to Mary, didn't it? But in that moment all her certainty deserted her and she was filled with a chill sense of despair. He was married to Mary, so where did that leave her? And when would she see him again? For the moment she was alone. Except for Polly.

'Yer can tell 'im all yer like . . .' Polly put her face up close, teeth clenched. ''E'll be as keen to see the back of you, and *that*—' she pointed at Jess's belly, 'as bum boil, that 'e will. Put 'im out of yer mind – where 'e should never've been in the first place. Face it – it's you and that child inside yer. And yer'll not be able to hide it from our mom for long . . .'

The two of them stood staring at each other in silence. Jess's mind raced round and round. What was she going to do?

'Sat'dy night we'll go,' Polly said. Jess thought for a second her cousin was going to spit in her face she looked so angry. 'Then it'll be over and enough said. What in God's name were yer thinking of?'

''E wanted me to – said it'd be awright. And I wanted it as well. I love 'im so much. And I never knew, Poll – honest. I thought it took an age to catch for a babby!'

'Well—' Polly turned away, face twisted with disgust. 'Now yer know better, don't yer?'

'Ow can 'er carry on like that right on top of church!'

The address she'd got out of Sally was in Highgate, close to St Alban's church.

'I'll 'ave to carry the shopping after,' Polly said. 'You'll be in no state.'

It was Saturday, late night shopping in the Bull Ring and lots of bargains. The two of them went most weeks,

144

staggering back with knock down meat, bruised fruit, all they could carry.

'Won't I?' Jess said nervously. She was completely ignorant of what was going to happen. She was just doing what Polly said. Letting her take charge.

'I'll never carry it all,' Polly was complaining, voice shrill with nerves. Both of them had a handy carrier in each hand, loaded down.

Tucked in Jess's pocket was the money she'd got from pawning Louisa's quilt.

'Oh no – not that!' she'd protested. 'It's the only thing of Mom's I've got!'

'Yer can get it back later, before our mom starts on about it. Yer might get five or six shilling for it, it's that nice.'

Jess walked along feeling desperate. She was very frightened, but at the same time, knew she was being given a way out. Things could go back to normal. Life had got knocked out of balance and had to be put back. Anything not to cause trouble and disgrace.

But shamed as she was, Jess still wanted to resist. Inside her was their child, the result of their love. Whatever the disgrace of it, she had something of him growing in her.

'Down 'ere,' Polly elbowed her down Conybere Street. It was cold, foggy, the edges of everything uncertain in the smoky gloom. The streetlamps provided pools of smudged light. They walked down past the almshouses, the church, a gloomy, hunch-shouldered edifice looming over the pavement.

They turned into Stanley Street and Polly slowed, trying to get her bearings. There were dark entries, leading off into the back courts, and all around the sound of human life, children playing, babies crying, doors open along the street to let in some air. They could see into some of the houses, hear the sounds of families carrying on their lives inside: knives and forks, raised voices, children in and out. Normal, Jess thought enviously. A sick feeling grew inside her.

Further on, Polly stopped. 'I think this is it.' Her voice was shaky.

It was a bigger house on the corner of Catherine Street, and even in the murky light its state of decay was obvious. The bottom windows were boarded up, and, blind-eyed to the street, the house looked secretive and forbidding.

'It can't be 'ere, can it?'

'This is it awright.' Polly's voice became hard and practical.

'How d'yer know?'

'I just do. Come on.'

Now she'd seen the place reality really hit Jess. 'Oh Lor', Poll – what's she going to do to me?'

'Yer'll see soon enough. Just think what'll happen if yer don't do it.' Polly had only the sketchiest idea herself. She had to keep her feelings at bay. This had to happen, didn't it? What choice was there: putting things to rights, or bringing a bastard child into the world. 'Come on – round the side.'

The door was not locked, and after knocking and getting no reply, Polly pushed it open, clutching hold of Jess's wrist as if she thought she might run away. The hinges whined. Darkness, and a fetid smell greeted them. The building's decay mixed with something else, cloying and rancid. Jess held the door to the street open. In front of them, very dimly, they could see a long hall and stairs.

'She said it was upstairs . . .'

146

'Who said?' Jess was only just managing to control her voice, her heart going like a hammer. The smell made nausea rise in her to the back of her throat. She had to swallow hard so as not to retch.

'Never mind.'

Polly edged forwards to the stairs. Broken tiles clicked underfoot.

'Hello!' she shouted. 'Is anyone there?' After the second time she called they heard creaking upstairs and a slow, ponderous movement across the floor. Eventually a door opened and dim, reddish light appeared.

'Who's that?'

'It's—' Polly was thrown for a moment. 'Is that Mrs Bugg?'

Silence, then, in a wheedling tone, 'Is that a wench needing my 'elp? Best get up 'ere. I won't come down to yer.'

The smell had grown stronger, a gust of disgustingly malodorous air wafting down to them.

'I can't . . .' Jess started to say, but Polly wouldn't let go of her, fingers digging into her wrist. Jess's legs were shaking so much she could barely climb the stairs.

They could hear Mrs Bugg's laborious breathing before they reached the top. At the sight of the woman in her dim room, Jess felt her legs begin to give way altogether, and she grabbed at the door frame. The large room was crowded with heavy, dark furniture. At one end, was a ramshackle kind of kitchen, where cooking was done over the fire. Near it was a table on which stood a candle in a red glass jar, like a church sanctuary lamp. On another small table to one side, two more candles burned on saucers. In the thick, blood-coloured light, crouched at the table, was the fattest human being Jess had ever seen. She had turned to look at them, and

147

her eyes were like two stab wounds between her fore-head and the welling dough of her cheeks. She spilled over the sides of the chair as if poured there like thick custard.

'Which one of yer is it then, dears?'

She stood up, pulling on the table, grunting and wheezing. It startled them both. The woman had appeared stuck to the chair.

'It's 'er, my cousin.' Polly pulled Jess into the room.

'Ow far gone are yer, bab?' Ma Bugg shuffled, pant-ing towards them, stringy hair dangling each side of her face. The floorboards groaned beneath her. Jess had gone rigid. Couldn't bring any words out.

'Not all that. Eight weeks at the most – ain't it, Jess?'

As the woman moved towards her, Jess recovered her ability to move and, yanking her hand from Polly's grip, ran back down the dark stairs. Outside, she heaved, bringing up teatime stew into the gutter. The breeze felt cold on her sweating face. She stood gulping and shuddering.

'I can't go back up there. The stink . . .' Polly had followed close behind.

'Oh yes yer can. You're going to or you'll be out on yer ear.' She sounded cruel, brutal. The place, the woman appalled her just as much and she was trembling all over. But she had to be strong. Had to get Jess through this.

'Come on, or she'll think we've done a bunk.'

The woman cleared the table, gave it a rough wipe and made Jess lie down on it. She shuffled to and fro, coughing. Her lungs sounded in a poor state. A kettle murmured on the range and a pot of something was bubbling which was the chief source of the vile smell.

'Just let's see 'ow far yer on. Yer don't look no size

148

but that's no proof. Don't want yer dropping a big'un on me . . . Get yer frock up, there's a good wench.'

Jess moaned at the sharp discomfort as Mrs Bugg prodded her stomach with her slabby fingers.

'I can start yer off. Should 'appen tonight or tomorrer when I've 'ad a go. Five shilling I can do yer for as it's not far on. Shall I crack on?' She held her hand out.

Jess saw Polly give her the money, making a low sound of agreement. She could just see Poll's face, white and pointed in the gloom. Mrs Bugg counted the money. She looked pleased.

'Get yer bloomers off then. And you—' She nodded at Polly, chins quivering. 'Lay the *Despatch* out for under 'er.'

Jess stood up, feeling as if all her bones had been taken out. Her teeth were chattering and the room began to spin, lights appearing at the edges of her vision. She could hear Polly rustling the newspaper. Old Ma Bugg lifted the steaming kettle with a grunt and poured water into a blackened pan.

'Just boiling up a few mutton bones in 'ere—' she pointed at the seething pot on the range.

Just as Jess blacked out she registered the sound of something metal, rattling. Polly broke her fall as she slithered to the floor.

She came round feeling terrible, to find she was lying on the table once more. It was not very big and her head was close to the edge, the knot of her hair pressing on it uncomfortably. Her legs were bent up, heels caught at the other end and she could feel someone's hands holding her ankles. Her knees had swung wide apart and she was naked between her legs and it felt cold.

With no warning, the woman's fingers jabbed

between her legs, pushing up between her lips, cork-screwing round. She whimpered.

'Just a bit o' lard, 'elp it in like.'

After more of the woman's elephantine movements, there was another little clinking sound. Jess rolled her head to one side, saw Polly put her hand over her mouth to stop herself crying out. She raised her head off the table and saw Mrs Bugg had pulled a long meat skewer from one of the saucepans.

'Soon be done, bab . . .'

'No . . . no!'

In a movement that tore at her guts she was off the table, holding out a hand to fend off Mrs Bugg, and reaching for her bloomers.

'Jess!' Polly wailed. Her protest lacked all conviction.

'Don't touch me, yer filthy stinking old witch! I'm not letting yer within a hundred mile of me with that! Come on, Poll. For Christ's sake let's get out of 'ere!'

'Please yerselves,' Mrs Bugg said, throwing the skewer back into the pan. She'd got her money, after all. 'You know where I am if yer 'ave second thoughts – only don't leave it too long.'

Outside, it was Polly who burst into tears, so over-wrought and hysterical that Jess had to hold her on the dark street corner, trying to calm the emotion erupting from Polly's shaking, gulping body.

'Oh, I'm sorry, Jess,' she said, over and over. 'I'm sorry, I'm sorry.'

Sixteen

Rain had been falling hard as Jess woke. There was very little light and it was a bitter day outside. She came inside, coat over her nightdress, still feeling wobbly after bringing up her guts over the lav.

It was only half-past six but Olive was down, stoking the range, empty coal bucket on the floor beside her. She turned as Jess came in and the look she gave her was unmistakably hostile.

'So – what've yer got to say for yerself?'

Jess shut the back door, shaking drops from her hair. Her hands started to tremble and she broke out in a sweat. She couldn't tell Auntie yet! Why was she being so angry? Surely she couldn't have guessed? She looked down, wiping her feet on the old mat.

'What d'yer mean?'

'I mean yer've put no jam-rags in the pail for two month and you're sick to yer stomach of a morning – don't think I ain't heard yer. And you're not shifting from that spot 'til I get the truth!'

Jess felt herself start to shake even harder. The one thing she'd dreaded the most was her auntie finding out! Without looking up, hugging the edges of her old coat round her, she whispered, 'I've just been feeling a bit poorly, Auntie.'

Olive stood with her legs apart, her hands, black with coal dust, clamped on her hips like a wrestler waiting to fight. She was already dressed, sacking apron on top.

'I'm not a fool, Jess, nor blind and deaf. It's no good trying to palm me off with some tall tale. I want the truth, and I want it now!'

She was going to have to tell her. Jess's knees went weak. Eyes fixed on the mucky scrap of mat at her feet, she murmured,

'I might be having a babby, Auntie.'

'Yer don't say.'

More silence. Only when Jess looked up did it dawn on her that her aunt was in as bad a state as she was, white and shaking, having to hold on to the edge of the range to support herself.

'Oh Auntie—' Jess stepped forward.

'It daint get there by itself, did it? Some Factory Jack up an entry, was it, full of blarney?'

Miserably, Jess shook her head. Now her aunt knew, the full enormity of what had happened fell on her like a lead weight. She felt utterly humiliated, but worse, seeing her aunt in such a state she was frightened of what she had caused.

Olive moved closer. Jess looked up to see a terrible expression on her face. For a moment she wondered if her auntie was really mad, she looked so peculiar. The look of her made Jess tremble all the more.

'Spit it out then.'

'It wasn't just – anyone. I love 'im and 'e loves me. I want us to stay together – live somewhere, like.'

'Live somewhere! Stop talking bloody rubbish, wench! Yer don't just go and "live somewhere" with a babby on the way! Yer make 'im marry yer and do it proper. So who is 'e – and where is 'e? What's wrong

152

with 'im that yer've never brought 'im 'ome, eh? 'Cause I'd 'ave a thing or two to say to 'im, that I would.'

'There's nothing wrong with him. It's . . .' She could only whisper his name. 'It's Ned, Auntie. The babby's Ned's.'

The blow her aunt dealt out to her knocked Jess to the floor. She reeled backwards, face stinging with pain, and jarred her lower back as she hit the floor. She sat up, moaning, rubbing it with her hand. Dimly, she saw that Sis had come down and was watching aghast from the doorway.

'Don't lie to me, yer scheming little bitch! Now you tell me the truth before I 'ave to beat it out of yer!'

'I am telling yer the truth, Auntie. I'd swear to yer on the Bible. Ned's the father of this babby and it's me 'e loves, not Mary. He wants to be with me!'

Olive's distress had transformed itself into pure fury, and it frightened Jess so much that she cringed, encircling her knees with her arms and leaning her head on them as she thought Olive was going to hit her again.

'Just like yer mother – no thought for anyone.' Olive's voice hectored at her. 'Ned wouldn't . . .'

'Oh yes 'e would, Mom.' Polly appeared in the back room. 'You may not want to face it, but that's the truth. 'E's the father of Jess's—'

'Keep out of it!' Olive turned on her. 'Ned's a good lad – 'e's got a wife and a babby and I won't 'ear it of 'im. And I won't 'ave 'er in the house – carrying on like . . . like . . .' She couldn't seem to think of an evil enough word. 'I'm not giving 'er a roof over 'er 'ead – she can get out and fend for 'erself and good riddance!'

There was a shocked silence. Then, in a low voice, Jess said,

'So 'ow did Ronny come about then?'

She thought her aunt was going to have a fit. She was quivering all over, her face twitching with uncontrollable emotions. She grabbed a blouse of Jess's that had been drying by the range and hurled it at her. 'Get out! Now! Go on!' Her voice went high and shrill. 'Yer can take everything that's yours and go. I don't want yer coming back tonight!'

'Mom!' Polly cried. Sis started to cry.

'But Auntie!' Jess wailed. 'Where'm I gunna go? There's nowhere for me. I've no one else to turn to!'

'Yer can turn to the real father of that bastard child yer carrying – see 'ow 'e likes to take care of yer. I'm washing my hands of it. Go on – clear out.'

Stunned, Jess dragged herself up off the floor and Polly and Sis stood back to let her pass. She heard Polly trying to calm her mother, to plead with her.

'I'm not 'aving it in the house,' Olive was shouting. 'Not with the blood she's carrying in 'er veins!'

'What're yer talking about, Mom!' Polly was desperate. 'I know Jess's done wrong, but where's 'er going to go?'

Jess was shaking so much from weakness and emotion when she got upstairs, that she could only just manage to pull her few clothes out of the worm-riddled chest and bundle them together. She reached for the quilt, Louisa's quilt, to wrap them in, and remembered they had pawned it to pay for the visit to Mrs Bugg's stinking slum. She sank down on the bed and wept, sharp, dry sobs, pressing her knuckles against her eyes.

Polly and Sis ran up and sat each side of her with their arms round her, both crying too.

'Oh Poll – what'm I going to do? Where'm I going

to find a roof tonight? I'll be on the street! And what'll I do when the babby's born?'

'She'll come round. What did yer go and tell 'er for, eh?'

'I didn't. She guessed. And she'd've 'ad to know sooner or later. I know I've done wrong, Poll – I shouldn't've gone with Ned, even if 'e wasn't married and that. I know it ain't right. But I love 'im so much and 'e loves me. It's all wrong, I know. But I didn't think Auntie'd turf me out like this. I thought she was going to kill me!'

Sis was still sobbing against Jess's shoulder, and Jess slipped her arm round her.

'We'll 'elp yer, won't we, Poll,' Sis said. 'Til she calms down and comes to 'er senses. You can 'ave the two bob she lets me keep every week, and Polly'll give yer some too, won't yer?'

'Course we'll help . . . every way we can.'

Jess was so touched by their loyalty that she cried even more.

'Look—' Polly dragged a hand across her eyes. 'You want to get ready and go to work, or you'll lose yer job an' all. After work, find yerself a room to rent. Yer not showing yet so you'll be awright. And it'll give yer a bit of time to get sorted out. She says she don't want me seeing yer – but don't worry. I won't desert yer.' She squeezed Jess's arm and stood up. 'You're like a sister to me and I'll stand by yer. Meet me after work tomorrow – outside the Market Hall – and you can tell me where yer staying.' Polly stood up, went to the door. She turned, trying tearfully to smile. 'Go on then – get on.'

When Jess came slowly, heavily, downstairs, Sis was

waiting, looking round cautiously to see her mom was out of the way.

'This come for yer.' Sis looked, then handed Jess a letter when she was sure the coast was clear.

Jess looked at the envelope blankly. She had never had a letter before in her life. The handwriting was looped and a bit untidy. She hid it in her bundle.

'Get yer breakfast and go,' Olive said. Her face wore an odd, hard expression which brooked no pleading.

Jess left the house with Polly and Sis. There were no goodbyes from Olive. She turned her face away as Jess tried to speak to her.

'Ain't yer going to open that letter?' Sis was full of curiosity.

'Take this.' Jess handed her the small bundle of clothes and slit open the envelope. She read, slowly.

Nov 4th, 1914

Jess—

I've got to make this a short letter or my feelings will take over and I shall change my mind. I wouldn't have written to your aunt's house normally but I've got to risk it.

Jess – I've got to make up my mind to say goodbye to you. I'm a father as well as a married man, with responsibilities. Being here, away from everything, I've had a chance to think and see how wrong I've been acting the way I have. I can't help what I've felt for you. I couldn't say this to your face. If I saw you I wouldn't have the strength. But you can't carry on with two people at once. It's not right or fair and it's turned me into a liar – and you, and I hate myself for it. I don't think that's what we want and I don't see how else we can carry on.

156

I know I feel more for you than Mary. I'll say that, to be true. That's the worst of it. But she's my wife, mother to my daughter, and I want to find courage to be a better man than I have been.

Goodbye, Jess my love. Don't take this too bad, please. The war will take me away and you can forget me if you will. Don't write and try and make me change my mind. This has to be the way things are.

Yours – maybe in another life when things are different.

Ned.

Seventeen

'You awright, Jess?'

Evie peered at her in the gloomy passage at Blake's, when the two of them were clocking off. She stood back a moment as a large woman pushed past her.

'Blimey – mown over in the rush! Only you're looking down in the mouth today, and I thought ... Well what's so funny?'

Jess leaned against the wall, laughing weakly. Down in the mouth! That was one way of putting it! The most endless, miserable day she could remember: pregnant, sick, unmarried, thrown out of home and nowhere to sleep. And worst, by far the worst, Ned's letter. She felt as if her heart was taking up the whole of her body: she was one grieving, aching agony.

Yes, I'm down in the mouth awright! she thought. The only place left for me's the canal! Her laughter became hysterical, tears rolling down her face.

'What's up with 'er?'

She felt harsh slaps, first on one cheek, then the other, and abruptly her laughter stopped. Three women, Evie and two others, gathered round her, staring.

'Eh, Jess—' Evie's arm slid round her shoulders. 'This ain't like you.'

'I'll be awright.' She kept her head down, wasn't going to talk in front of the other two.

When she and Evie were alone outside, she said, 'Oh

158

Evie – I 'ad such an argument with Auntie, and she's turned me out. I've nowhere to go and I don't know what to do!'

'Oh my word – can't yer go and make it up with 'er? It can't be over much, can it?'

'She won't 'ave me back. She says she never wants to see me again. I . . . I . . .' She was on the brink of telling Evie the truth, but she couldn't. She was far too ashamed. It sounded so bad – her and a married man doing what no girl was supposed to do until she was wed! What had seemed so right when she was with Ned would look disgusting and wrong to everyone else. Evie would never speak to her again.

'Look – come on over to ours. Our mom'll put yer up 'til yer get yerself sorted out.'

Jess seized on this with hope for a moment. She'd visited Evie's family a couple of times over the summer and found them warm and friendly. It'd be so nice to accept, to be able to go and rest somewhere where there would be a welcoming face or two. But she quickly dismissed the thought. Evie's mom, Mrs Cotter, was no fool, and their place was so crowded. With her sick as a dog every morning, Evie's mom'd soon guess what was amiss and Jess couldn't bear Mrs Cotter to know her shame.

'That's nice of yer, Evie – but I'm going to look for lodgings. I've got to get somewhere so I might as well start now.' Jess wiped her eyes on her stiff serge coat sleeve. 'I'll let yer know 'ow I get on tomorrow.'

Evie looked doubtful. 'I'd come with yer, only I said to Mom I'd shop for 'er – look, if yer don't 'ave any luck, yer know where we are.' She squeezed Jess's hand. 'Yer shouldn't 'ave a problem round 'ere. Lots

159

of folk in need of a few bob, and you looking so respectable!'

Carrying her bundle, Jess walked out of the Jewellery Quarter feeling sick and exhausted. On the way she passed Albion Street, and hovered for a few moments outside the fire station. Seeing the place set her off crying uncontrollably. How could he have written to her as he did? She felt destroyed by his words.

Just two weeks ago she'd gone to watch him march with the other lads, all soldiers now. Ned was in the Second City Battalion, the 15th Service Battalion of the Royal Warwickshire Regiment. The three City Battalions were made up primarily of the more educated young men of the city: office workers, accountants, librarians, and Ned had said he felt like one of the nobs! The lads were given a grand send-off with church services, parades, and Jess waited among the crowd along the road to watch them march from the General Hospital to Edgbaston Park, their Commanding Officer on a fine dappled grey horse. Everyone cheered and shouted, their breath white on the air. Jess had stood on tip-toe, straining to catch a glimpse of him as the body of men streamed past, still dressed in civilian clothes and singing a new song, 'It's a Long Way to Tipperary'. He passed quite close to her and she called out to him, saw him look round, just catching sight of her as she blew him a kiss.

She sobbed bitterly at the memory, there in the dark, head pressed against the rough side of the building. She felt as if her life was over. There was no hope in anything. Nothing but trouble, fear and shame.

Come back to me, she found herself begging. Please,

Ned. She wanted rescue and shelter from being abandoned and alone. But of course he wasn't there: he had no idea of the state she was in and now he didn't want to know either. She was alone, and alone was how she would have to cope. Scarcely knowing where she was going, tears half blinding her, she walked on.

She had decided to look for lodgings on this side of town, because it was nearer work – and nearer, somehow, to him. His place. His area of town. Polly had slipped her ten shillings to help her out. Jess tried to argue: she knew the money was from Polly's savings for her life with Ernie.

'Take it – don't be so daft. It's now we need to worry about. The future'll come when it comes.' She told Jess to let her know as soon as she'd found somewhere. Polly'd be over to see her, whatever Olive thought.

She walked out along the Dudley Road. On one side there were houses, and she kept peering at their dingy windows in the poor light to see if any of them had 'Room To Let' signs up. Across the road were high walls, and when she came opposite the gates she saw it was the Workhouse, a huge building which seemed to loom towards her in the dark. Jess felt the hairs on her skin stand up and a shudder went through her. If she wasn't careful she might end up in there! Fallen girls went in there and sometimes never came out! What made her different from any of them in anyone else's eyes? And even if she wasn't thrown into the Workhouse, what in heaven was she going to do after the babby was born? She certainly couldn't hide it then. All the problems she faced swirled in her head like a leaf storm until she was rigid with panic.

She gripped her bundle tighter. Just think about today, she told herself. *Sufficient unto the day is the evil thereof.* Sarah used to say that. *Sufficient unto the day . . .*

She turned back. I ain't looking for lodgings facing over the Workhouse, she thought. Along a side street men were coming out into the slate-grey evening from the factories, a rolling mills, a varnish and colour works. The road crossed over the canal. Jess stopped and looked down at the sludgy line of it. It appeared solid, more like dull stone than water.

How many girls like me have ended up in there? She started to imagine it: turning off the road down that path there, under the bridge, all dark and echoing. Feeling the water first over her boots, fitting close, like freezing stockings sliding up her legs, then her waist, neck . . . Lying down in it, taking it into her and everything would be black, and there would never be anything else but black, and nothing more of her. She found she had been holding her breath and took in a gasp of air as if she really were drowning and hurried over the bridge. No – not that. Not while she had strength and Ned was somewhere in the world. She had to try and survive.

Further on were houses, close-packed little terraces. She knocked at the first one with a sign in the window, where a man appeared, snarled, 'It's already taken,' and slammed the door shut again. In the window of an end terrace squeezed in beside a chapel, she could just make out a card in neat, but shaky writing. 'Room to Let. Single Person. Female Pref.'

She waited such an age after knocking that she was about to move on, but then the door opened a crack. Peering at her was a thin face, wrinkled as an old paper bag, with long white hair straggling down either side.

Jess could tell there was a candle burning in the hall behind. A frowsty smell seeped out.

'Yes?'

'I saw the sign,' Jess said fearfully to this witch-like creature. 'I'm looking for a room to rent.'

The door opened further, and Jess saw that the old lady was supporting herself on a crutch. Her left leg hung, severed off at the ankle, a useless stump with a sock on the end of it. She looked Jess up and down.

'Well, it's not much, I'm afraid.' Her voice was soft, surprisingly well spoken and polite, with a trace of Black Country. 'I can't get about very easily, you see, to keep the place as it should be. But if you'd like to go up and see . . .'

She lurched backwards to let Jess in. 'Have you work round here?'

'Blake's,' Jess was tearful with relief at being treated at least kindly. 'In the Jewellery Quarter.'

'Ah yes. Not far. Well look, dear – take this candle. I shan't come up – takes me too long. My bedroom is at the front – left at the top. If you turn right you'll see it. It hasn't been used for a few months since my last lodger left.'

The lady stood watching as Jess climbed the stairs. A thin runner of green carpet covered the middle of the staircase which creaked loudly at each step. The paper in the stairwell was hanging off the walls and the place smelled of damp and mildew. In the spare room, Jess saw a bare floor, uncurtained windows, an iron bedstead and a wooden chair. The walls were painted white and though it was icy cold and cheerless, it was not unpleasant.

This'd do, Jess thought. And the lady seems kind enough.

She went back down into the front room, which was also sparsely furnished with a table, two wooden chairs, and a small, glass-fronted cupboard. Apart from that was only a little blue and green rug by the unlit grate, and some faded pink curtains. But the old lady, despite her ragged grey frock which hung limp and shapeless on her, and her obvious poverty, had an air of gentility about her which made Jess feel both shy and respectful.

'How much is the rent?'

'Five shillings a week.' She said this with some awkwardness, as if it pained her to talk about money. 'With an evening meal. But not tonight, I'm afraid.'

'I'll take it then.' Jess handed her a week's rent in advance.

'Thank you.' The gnarled hand closed over the money with a slow dignity. 'Now we had better know each other's names.'

Jess hesitated. 'Jess. Jessica Green,' she said. 'My husband and me we're – well, hanging on 'til we can afford a proper place like. 'E's joined up, you see, doing 'is bit – 'e's away at the training camp.'

'I see.' The woman's pale eyes stared back at her. Jess sensed she didn't believe her. There was a kind, homely look to her wizened face, Jess saw. It was her hair made her look like a madwoman.

'Pleased to make your acquaintance,' she said grandly. 'My name is Miss Iris Whitman.'

Once she had taken her things up and unpacked them, Jess was almost fainting with hunger. She found Iris Whitman sitting in her back room, which was as bare and chill as the front.

'I'm going out to get some chips,' Jess told her. Even

164

if she hadn't been hungry she'd have had to get out. The thought of sitting in that freezing room all evening, when she was a bag of nerves, was terrible. 'D'you want me to bring yer anything back?'

Iris's face brightened. 'Yes, a penn'orth of chips would be very nice, dear.'

Iris told her the nearest place to buy chips, and when she came back, her newspaper parcels smelling of hot vinegar, Iris said, 'Perhaps you'd like to stay down and eat them with me, dear?'

The back room was barely warmer than it had been outside. Not a spark of light or warmth came from the range. Jess was longing for a cup of tea, but it was obvious there wouldn't be any on offer. Miss Whitman sat on her hard chair huddled in a shawl which draped her sufficiently to hide her bad leg. Jess wondered whether she was unable to get down and see to the range.

'Would you like me to build a fire?' she asked timidly.

'I would,' the woman said, in her measured way, 'if I had anything to build it with.'

'Oh.' Jess had not met anyone so poor before that they didn't even have a few handfuls of slack to burn. 'Well maybe tomorrow . . .?'

'Yes.' The lady smiled suddenly. 'Things will look up tomorrow, dear. You'll see. They have a way of doing that.'

Jess suddenly had the oddest feeling that Miss Whitman knew all about her, could see into what she was feeling. But there was no nosiness, no sense of judgement. She asked no questions, but ate her chips, delicately from the newspaper as the smell of them filled the room and warmed both of them.

'If you look in the bottom drawer there, you'll find a little bedding.' Miss Whitman pointed at a battered chest of drawers. 'I'm afraid it's not aired.'

How could it be, Jess thought, in this dank room?

'Not to worry.' She was relieved just at the thought of lying down, never mind aired sheets. But she was grateful to Miss Whitman for the company, for distracting her from her own misery.

She found two sheets and a blanket in the drawer. Turning, she dared to ask,

'Miss Whitman, don't you have no one to 'elp yer – get coal and food and that?'

'Oh yes – there's Miss Davitt from next door—' Iris nodded in the direction of the chapel. 'They're very good people. But I believe she's ill this week. I haven't seen her. And I haven't been any too well myself. Things aren't usually quite so cheerless as you see today.'

Jess was relieved to hear it. 'I was thinking – I could fetch in coal and some groceries on my way back from work tomorrow if yer like.'

Iris Whitman was pulling herself awkwardly to a standing position. She looked across at Jess, as if assessing her.

'Well, that's a kind offer. I believe you're a good girl, aren't you? A little help tomorrow would be very nice, I must say.'

Jess looked into Iris's pale eyes for a second, then lowered her gaze. She could feel herself blushing.

'I'd be glad to help yer if you need it. Goodnight then.'

Upstairs, she made up her bed by candlelight. There were no curtains, and the windows were solid rectangles of black. She laid her coat and other few garments over the blanket for a minuscule bit of extra warmth. She wondered what Iris Whitman had to keep her warm Precious little no doubt.

Once in bed, she took out Ned's letter again. The pain and confusion of her feelings overwhelmed her. Grief, hurt, but also a sense of injustice and frustrated anger.

He loves me, he told me so, and I'm never to see him again! It was madness, all of it! She wanted to run to him, pour out everything to him, about the child, their child she was carrying, that she'd been thrown out of home and all her troubles. Have him say he belonged with her, not Mary and Ruth. It was *her* he loved ... But then an awful chilling thought ran through her mind. He doesn't love me at all – he was only saying that to let me down gently, to get out of seeing me again. He was just using me the way Olive says men do. I've no sense, none at all – I've been living in a dream! Of course he wasn't going to leave her and come to me. He was always going to stay with Mary, that was the harsh truth of it. And even if she wanted to see him she couldn't: how could she go to him, force him to come to her when he had a wife and he had rejected her? And when he wasn't even here? Choked with emotion she lay down still holding the letter. She couldn't think clearly about anything, the future, the reality of it. Sleep came down on her suddenly, like a blind.

Eighteen

Polly was already waiting for her the next afternoon, after work. She saw Jess coming and ran to her.

'Oh Jess – I've been that worried. I 'ardly slept a wink thinking about yer last night – I should've come with yer, that I should!'

The tears Jess had been suppressing all day welled in her eyes. Everything felt vicious this evening, the hunger in her belly, a cold wind grating on her face like sandpaper. 'I'm awright. Look – 'ere's the address where I'm lodging.'

Polly squinted at the scrap of paper. 'Crabtree Road? Where's that?'

'Near the Workhouse – off of Dudley Road.' She told Polly about Miss Whitman. 'Poor soul. She's quite nice really, I think. Got hardly two farthings to rub together, and she ain't nosey or particular like.'

'So yer set for a bit? Oh thank God for that. Now yer mustn't worry, Jess.' Polly felt the hollowness of her words. If she was Jess she'd be more than worried. Scared half to death more like. 'We'll see yer awright, and we'll try and talk our mom round. I don't know what's got into 'er. She wouldn't treat a dog the way she's turned on you. I can't seem to get through to 'er. I kept on at 'er to change 'er mind, and Sis has, but she won't even listen. Kept shouting at me, telling me she didn't want you anywhere near 'er, and if I didn't keep

168

quiet, I could go an' all!' Jess could see Polly was in almost as bad a state as she was. 'She ain't going to stop me coming to see yer though. I'll come round Friday, awright? Bring yer a few things.'

'Thanks, Poll. Evie said she'd come an' all. But yer don't need to worry yet – I've still got my earnings. Auntie needs yer money, to look after Ronny and that.'

'Oh she's getting 'er usual. I just can't stand to think of yer all alone the way you are—' Polly started to cry. 'It's just not like our mom, Jess. I don't know what's going on. I don't know who I'm most worried about – you, her or Ernie!'

Through those dark days of November and December, Jess went to work at Blake's every day, secure at least in the knowledge that her pregnancy was not yet showing. The sickness left her and she had more energy, but not having the wretchedness of feeling ill to distract her, the full misery of Ned's absence overcame her. She lay in bed at night crying for him, for what they had had before. It had not been much, after all, but to her it seemed like the world now that her existence had become a lonely, dragging round of drudgery and unhappiness, with no hope to lighten it, no love from him to see her through.

Every evening she spent in Iris Whitman's spartan little house. But she did make sure a fire was lit and that they had food. Miss Davitt, the kind lady from the chapel, came to help Iris with her shopping, and Jess would fetch any extras which were needed, so the house was never quite as wretched again as the night when she first arrived. Sometimes Evie came to see her for a while, and Polly and Sis, who Jess introduced as friends of

169

hers, and Iris Whitman let them sit downstairs if they wanted to, to keep warm. They'd tell her any news about Bert and Ernie, who were both still safe training in England. Of course, with Iris about there were things they couldn't say, so sometimes after a cup of tea they'd go up to Jess's room for a private talk. Sis was very sweet, always bringing a little something – a chunk of cake, a couple of apples – and saying, 'It ain't the same at home without yer, Jess.' But so far, nothing they'd said had been able to shift Olive. Jess was still an outcast.

After a few weeks, she got to know more about Iris Whitman. Iris did not have visitors, except for Miss Davitt and Beattie, another elderly woman across the road who looked out for her, when she was well enough to venture out herself. Iris was not able to move far outside the house on her crutches without completely exhausting herself.

Iris was lonely and liked Jess to sit with her, and Jess felt sorry for her and was glad of the distraction of company. Now the evenings were bitterly cold, they sat close to the range cradling cups of tea in their hands, Iris in her shawl, hair straggling round her face so that Jess itched to get the scissors and give it a good cut. She found Iris a strange, disconcerting woman. For days on end their talk consisted of trivial detail about the weather, food, little incidents about Miss Davitt or Beattie, Jess's work, the state of the house ... Iris hopped from subject to subject like a sparrow. Jess never asked her leading questions, hoping Iris would not ask any of her. But one evening, after a long silence, Iris said,

'I was a schoolteacher, you know.'

Jess looked across at her, startled out of her own miserable thoughts. For a second she nearly laughed. Miss Whitman looked so unlike the neat, strict teachers she had had at school! But the well-spoken voice, the gentility of her, once you looked past the eccentric way she was dressed – yes, you could imagine it, almost.

Cautiously, she asked, 'Were you?'

'A trained teacher of young infants, I was. Always liked children. Taught in several schools across Birmingham – one in Sutton Coldfield. Until this.' She straightened her damaged leg, the stump poking out from her shawl, dressed in a sludgy green, handknitted sock. 'They wouldn't have me back afterwards. Said I wasn't fit to be associated with small children.'

Jess tried to control her expression of astonishment.

'Hand to mouth I was, after it. That's why you find me in these straits. Hand to mouth all these years is how I've lived. Faith, hope and bread. That's life, dear. And thoughts. Must have your own thoughts.'

Iris looked very directly at her. 'I'll tell you what happened. You must've wondered, Jessica, although you're too polite to ask.'

Jess nodded, blushing.

'I was engaged to be married, aged thirty. Over the hill, some would say.' She stroked one venous hand back and forth along the thigh of her gammy leg. 'Quite besotted I was. I thought I'd found the only thing in life, pinned all my hopes on him. Anyway, to keep it short: a month before the wedding was due to happen he took off. February it was. Left his lodgings with everything – no letter, nothing. I was told he'd gone to Stafford. Whether that was true now, I don't know, but I was in a desperate state, you see. How I felt about

171

him, I mean. Fit to do myself in – though I don't hold with that, it's irreligious. So, what to do but go to Stafford. Well, it was snowy – inches of it settled for days, banked up in places – and Stafford's a long way to go. By the time I got there this one foot was frozen. They had to have it off at the ankle. Frostbite, you see. I was in hospital in Stafford for weeks. I'd left my school – never said where I was going. They wouldn't have me back – said I wasn't a responsible person. Walking to Stafford like that.'

'But—' Jess sat up straight, appalled. 'Why didn't you go on the train?'

'I was in love, dear. Madly in love.' Iris's pale eyes looked back at her. 'I wanted to show him, you see, what I'd do for him. Find him, wherever. Of course he never knew. I don't even know if he was really in Stafford. Silly young thing, wasn't I? I never saw him again. Thirty years ago now, all that.'

Jess stared back, thinking her way into Iris's life. A life wrecked by love. She was so shocked by what she had heard that she felt as if she'd been punched in the chest.

'So – you never found him?'

Iris shook her head.

'And you never worked again?'

'Oh I did. Of course. Had to, dear. But not as a teacher. Odd jobs here and there. Factories. A bit of private tutoring once or twice. Enough to keep body and soul together. What a fool, you're thinking, aren't you? Everyone does, I know. Mad old Iris. Lost everything for a man. I did – and I regret it. My old life was all gone, of course. But I did *have* love for a time, or thought I did, and that came to the same thing. Had some of the strong stuff for a bit – more than the everyday bread and water of keeping alive and breathing. 'That's more than some.'

Jess's heart was beating hard, she could hear the pulse of it in her ears. She looked down into her lap. Am I the same: ruined for love? Soon, she thought, the babby's going to start showing and she'll know. Whatever Iris felt for this man of hers, she didn't have a babby ... But she thought of Iris's leg. A severed leg and a babby came to nigh on the same thing for a woman without a husband.

'I've heard you having a weep up there at nights, dear. I don't know what your trouble is. As soon as I saw you though, I knew there was something. I know a frightened face when I see it.'

Jess couldn't answer.

'Whatever it is, you're a comfort to me, Jessica. I'm not for convention and stoning people for their misfortunes like the woman taken in adultery. No, no. "Let he who is without sin cast the first stone." I could be bitter, but I'm not. God's love and man's – that's all that matters. Loving kindness and seeing into people as they are, that's me. You'll have a roof over your head, my dear, whatever your trouble, have no fear about that.'

'Thank you.' Jess could barely speak, so close was she to pouring out all her woes. Without looking up at Iris, she whispered, 'I'm going up now.'

She managed to control her tears until she reached her room and buried her face in the bed, trying not to make a sound. The blanket was scratchy against her face and smelt mouldy, but it absorbed her sobbing.

Oh Ned, Ned, *please* ... Over and over again the

begging words spilled from her, whispered into the mattress. Iris's story affected her deeply. It was too late for Iris, but the idea of ending up like her filled Jess with horror: unwanted, disgraced, alone with a child. All because of her love for a man. Are men different? she wondered. Don't they feel? How could he just leave Miss Whitman like that if he'd said he loved her? Perhaps he was married as well? Had a wife and family that Iris never knew about. And hadn't she fallen into the same trap? She curled herself up tight on the bed, lying on her side, banging one hand hard on the mattress as she wept, again and again so that the springs squeaked. How can I go on? she sobbed. How can I live like this, without him, without anyone?

Nineteen

'Mom – you'll let our Jess come 'ome for Christmas, won't yer?'

Polly spoke to her mother's back. Olive was sitting at the table. Sis looked round, watching them both.

There was no reply.

'I don't mean for good, but won't yer let 'er come for the day with us? We can't just leave 'er there all on 'er own! Ernie'll be back Christmas Eve, and Bert ... family all together like ... Please, say summat! Why're yer being so cruel to 'er?'

Olive stood up and tipped slack into the range, face turned away from them. The fire flared and crackled. She put the pail down and wiped her sooty hands on her apron.

'Mom!' Sis couldn't bear the silence any longer.

Olive ignored the pair of them. Face blank of expression, as if she was shutting out them and all their words, she took the bucket out to the back yard, went into the privy and banged the door shut.

Polly slammed her cup down on the table. 'I can't stand much more of this. One way or another summat's got to give!'

Jess pulled up her vest and looked down at herself. No doubt about it: it was beginning to show. Not enough for anyone else to notice, but that wouldn't take long now . . . Her nipples had darkened, and there was a little bulge to her stomach that hadn't been there before. She reckoned she'd caught for the babby in August, that time in the park, she remembered bitterly. So she was nearly four months gone. She was starting to feel tiny movements inside her, wrigglings, flutterings, different from anything she'd felt before. She pulled her clothes on, pressing her hand to her stomach. No – no one'd notice for a little while yet. But it was frightening, having something control you from inside, knowing it was getting bigger, spreading.

'I wish I could run away too, just move on and start again.' She buttoned her cardigan with cold fingers. 'But it's done now – there's nowt I can do about it.'

The week before Christmas, she walked home from work, alone as usual. It was dark, with a thick, swirling fog, the lamplight smudged and dim, and the dark walls seemed to close in on her. She was forced to walk more slowly, feeling her way along, able to see hardly a yard in front of her face.

When she reached the fire station in Albion Street, she paused, putting a hand out to touch the cold bricks. Everything else was invisible in the fog. It was not far from here that Ned had told her he loved her. For a moment she leaned back against the building, breathing in the rank, sodden air, and closed her eyes. If only it was June still! How strong and happy she'd felt then, believing in the strength of his feelings for her!

'Yer doing business?'

Jess opened her eyes. A burly man, not much more than her own height, stood just in front of her. His collar was up and his cap pulled low over his eyes. In the gloom she could make out that he had a thick beard.

'What?' She stood up straight, alarmed.

He spoke in a murmur, through the side of his mouth.

'You doing business, are yer?'

'I don't know what yer mean.' She sidled further along the wall.

'A shilling. All I can spare.'

Jess stared at him for a moment, until it dawned on her. That woman in New Street, drenched in perfume!

'No – oh my God, no! I'm just going 'ome, that's all. I'm not what yer think!'

She stumbled away from him, terrified he'd follow. After a few moments she stopped, peering back at the invisible street. She couldn't hear anyone following and she slowed to a walk again, feeling shaky. That'd teach her to stand and dream in the street! It was a horrible feeling, being mistaken for a sordid, fallen woman. The man's words wormed through her mind. A shilling, he'd offered. Just like that. Money for a job. If she did it say six times – even ten times a week . . .

'I must be going mad,' she muttered frantically as she strode along the Dudley Road. 'Right off my 'ead, even thinking such a desperate thing! Never – however bad things get – not in a million years!'

By the time Christmas Eve came there was snow on the ground. For a few hours it made the city look clean and newborn, until the wheeltracks and footprints shovelled it into tarnished heaps and the factories belched their filthy breath all over it.

The lads were due home that afternoon, those with leave. Bert came home from Tidworth, new blue uniform and all, full of himself.

177

'Awright, Mom—' Bashful, he gave her a peck on the cheek and for a moment Olive's face relaxed with pleasure. Ronny was wild with excitement, pulling at Bert's coat until his big brother took notice, picked him up and dangled him playfully upside down.

'Yer looking well, son,' Olive said.

'In better nick than when I left, no doubt about that.' Bert threw himself down on to a chair and Ronny jumped on top of him, laughing. 'Knocking us into shape good and proper, and some of 'em could do with it, I can tell yer!' He grinned, looking round the room. 'It's good to be 'ome for a bit though, Mom, 'stead of sleeping in a leaky bloody hut ... 'Ere—' He dug into his bag. 'I've brought summat for yer.'

From a paper bag he unpacked a row of brass ornaments and stood them along the table. Olive came nearer, peering at them. Each one was a man's head, moulded in brass, about four inches high. Bert pointed at each of them.

'That one's Kitchener—' Olive smiled 'Oh yes!' recognizing the moustache. 'Then yer've got, let's see – Joffre, Jellicoe for the navy, and Beatty, and that's Sir John French ... They're to go on the mantel – look.'

He helped her line them up, seeing she was pleased.

''Ow is everyone – awright?' he asked as she made tea.

'Ar, they're awright.'

'Poll?'

'Going along. She'll be in soon.'

'And Sis? And what about Jess?'

Olive tinkled a spoon round inside the teapot. 'I've told yer – they're all awright.' She turned, her harsh expression softening again at the sight of him. So like

178

Charlie he was getting! 'You look as if yer could do with a good sleep, you do.'

'I could an' all. Plenty of time later. After a couple of pints . . .'

There was a knock on the door soon after Polly and Sis got in. Polly dashed to open it.

'Ernie – oh love, it's you at last!'

Ernie was pink-cheeked, bursting with health, though he did look a little thinner in the face, and younger without the beard. He and Polly flung their arms round each other and stayed for some time out in the dark street, hugging and kissing, before going inside.

Polly rested her head on Ernie's shoulder. 'Oh love – I wish you was 'ere all the time, I've missed yer that much. I don't want yer to go away again.' She squeezed him tight.

'Eh – come on, I've only just got 'ere! No need to talk about me going yet.'

Later, the two of them walked out together, to get away from everyone else, holding tight to each other so as not to slip in the street. It had started snowing again, small, dry flakes, falling skittishly.

'I feel I want to hold on to every second,' Polly said. 'The time's going to go in a flash and yer mom's going to want yer over there too . . .'

'Roll on the time when we've got our own place.' Ernie stopped and pulled her close to him, licked a snowflake from her cheek. ''Aving tea and a chat's awright, but it ain't the thing I've been looking forward to all this time, I can tell yer!'

'Ernie!' Polly giggled. 'Cheeky thing – eh, stop it,

not 'ere! There'll be time for that later!' She removed his hand from her bottom. 'Mom says yer can stop over, and turf Sis out of 'er bed tonight.'

'I don't know as I can wait 'til then . . .' He ran his hands over her, feeling for her breasts. 'Oh Poll, I've missed yer.'

'I've missed you too – like anything. But listen, let's walk on a bit. Before we go 'ome I want to talk to yer about summat. It's Jess . . .'

Walking down the Moseley Road, she told Ernie all that had happened. He was far from impressed.

'Stupid bloody fools, the pair of 'em – 'e's got a wife and a nipper! What the 'ell does 'e think 'e's playing at – and 'er! That's disgusting that is.'

'But she's having 'is babby and our mom won't let 'er anywhere near – she's all on 'er own and she's pining and worried sick! She's got no one else, Ernie, and she loves the bones of 'im, 'owever much she shouldn't! I think Ned ought to know. Why should Jess put up with all of it and 'im do nothing? And if 'e knew, maybe . . .'

'Maybe what?' His voice was harsh. 'If you go telling 'im it'll only cause trouble and you'll be caught up in it. It ain't up to you to go interfering. If a woman goes behaving like that she has to count the cost. It's 'er own bloody fault. I must say, I'd never've thought it of 'er, but she's made 'er bed and she'll 'ave to lie on it. Unless – I mean, there's ways yer can get rid of a babby, can't yer, some'ow? Why don't she do that and 'ave done with it?'

''Ere—' Polly's tone became sharp. 'Don't talk to me in that voice – it's horrible! We thought of that. Went to this woman. But oh Ernie, if you'd seen – it frightened the life out of both of us. Yer wouldn't do it to an

180

animal. But someone's got to sort it out. She won't tell 'im 'cause she's shamed and frightened . . .'

'No, Poll – it ain't on. You keep out of it. It ain't your business or mine, and I daint come 'ome to argue with yer. Come 'ere, wife, and give us a kiss!'

For a moment Polly didn't look up at him. She bit her lip. He's wrong, she thought. I've got to interfere. She didn't want to go against her husband, but he couldn't see things the way she could. She didn't want to spoil their time together though. Looking up she smiled.

'Come 'ere then, yer big 'andsome soldier boy!'

Jess spent Christmas with Iris Whitman. She turned down Iris's invitation to go to church with her because she didn't feel like going out, and having people asking questions about her to her face. If they wanted to gossip behind her back, then that was their business.

'You go,' she told Iris. 'And I'll cook us a bit of dinner.'

She hadn't had the heart to do anything about decorating the back room, and the house seemed so dismal in the harsh white light from the snow outside. She didn't want to be reminded that it was Christmas at all, except that somehow it had to be lived through. They did have a small joint of beef as a Christmas treat though, and Jess prepared it for roasting with potatoes and parsnips, sprouts and carrots alongside. But she did so with such a heavy heart. How small were the amounts she had to cook, and how lonely the little cut of meat looked! She thought of everyone in Oughton Place, the family all together. The fact that her aunt hadn't caved in and let her back just for a visit hurt her so much. And there'd been nothing in the way of a Christmas greeting sent from Budderston either. She cried, peeling the three potatoes, scrubbing the few carrots. Of course she was in the wrong: a disgrace to the family. But she'd thought that Olive, after she calmed down, might find it in her to forgive. She would have had her first Christmas with a proper family in such a long time. She knew Bert and Ernie were home on leave, and ... and ... She dragged her mind away from the thought of Ned. He'd be on leave too – going home to Mary, loving her, being a family ... And of course that was the right thing because she was his wife, and whatever Jess felt for him she had no right ... She, and all her deepest feelings and yearnings, were wrong in the eyes of everyone. Worst of all, in his eyes too ... It was a grim, despairing morning, and when Iris came back it took her an enormous effort to conceal her misery.

On the morning of Boxing Day, Ernie went to his mom's for a bit and Polly said she was going out. She looked defiantly at Olive.

'Please yerself,' Olive didn't look up. She had a darning mushroom pushed into one of Bert's socks. She was having to sew again now Jess was gone.

'Shall I come?' Sis asked.

'No!' Polly spoke too sharply. 'Er, no, Sis – not this time. Maybe later, awright?' She gave her sister a wink as she put her coat on and Sis was appeased. They had told Bert Jess was away visiting her father.

She set out across the quiet city, asparkle today in its

new coat of white, screwing up her eyes against its brightness. St Martin's Church seemed made of sugar Polly felt well in herself. She had had food and rest over Christmas, and her husband home. But the deep breaths she breathed in were as much from nerves as contentment.

'I 'ope I'm doing the right thing,' she said. 'God alone knows – but someone's got to do summat, the way things are!'

Late that night, Jess lay in bed, trying to get warm before she could sleep. She tucked her feet into the bottom of her nightdress, curling up tight, arms folded, hugging herself. It would be a relief to go back to work, get back to the normal routine.

She tucked her nose under the covers, smelling the damp sheet. Nothing in this room ever felt warm. She imagined looking down from outside herself, the sight of her body lying covered by the cold sheet and her black coat, legs bent up trying to get warm. Her body: where she began and ended, the limits of her, so small, so minutely insignificant compared with everything outside. The muffled city, the huge sky flecked with stars ... what did any of it matter? She lived, she'd die: just like a lump of meat in a big pot of stew. She'd be gone, and none of her problems would matter. Comforted by this, her mind drifted and she was beginning to doze.

The cracking sound seemed loud as a bullet from a gun. She sat up, wide awake again, heart beating like mad. Silence, then it came again. Someone was throwing things at her window. There was a third rap on the pane as she crept across the floor.

She could make out nothing through the pane, and, pulling at the sash, was surprised when the window opened easily.

'Jess?'

She could barely find the breath to answer. His voice, low and cautious.

'Ned!'

'Can yer come down?'

'Wait – I'll come to the back . . .'

She fumbled into her cardigan, fingers almost useless, breath coming in snatches, whispering frantically to herself. 'Oh my God, oh please . . .' It was like a dream, speeding down the stairs in her bare feet, noticing nothing, neither the cold nor the dark. She unbolted the back door and saw the shape of him, faintly silhouetted in the doorway against the snow-covered yard. They both stood quite still. Jess could think straight about nothing, why he was here, what she might say, could only see him standing there where she'd never expected to find him.

'Can I come in? Is it safe?'

'The lady's asleep – ages ago I s'pect.' Jess stepped back and he stamped the snow from his boots as gently as he could before coming in. She took a candle from the cupboard, lit it and stood it in a holder on the table. Across its light they looked at one another in silence.

At last he said, 'Is it true?' His face was fearful, tender.

'Who told you?'

'Polly. She came this morning.'

'*Polly?* Why did she . . .? I daint ask her to come and see yer, honest. I weren't going to force yer . . . to interfere with your life when yer'd said yer didn't want me . . .'

184

'Jess – for God's sake, tell me.'

Slowly, she nodded.

'A babby . . . you . . .' He went to the back window, staring, for long moments, though there was nothing to see in its opaqueness. Softly, behind him, she started to cry. Eventually he turned round and stood watching her.

'God, Jess – I feel like doing that too.' Gradually, he came over to her. 'I'm frightened to touch you because if I do I shan't be able to let go of yer. What can I do? I can't go on like this any more. I hate myself for it.'

Not understanding, she looked up at him. 'Why did you come then?'

'Because I couldn't stay away. When Poll came and told me . . .' His voice trailed off. 'For heaven's sake – come 'ere.' He pulled her to him so fiercely she gasped, and feeling his arms round her, sank into them, crying wildly. He held her close, rocking and soothing her, one hand in her thick hair, pressing her head close to his chest.

'It's no good.' He was near to tears himself, the tension inside him near breaking point. 'I can't go on with Mary – trying to be a good husband to 'er when all the time my mind's with you, all the time I can think about you and nothing else. Being away and that – away from you – I thought I'd come to terms with it. But I can't. I love yer so much, want yer so much, I'm frightened to death by it, and that's the truth.'

She looked up into his eyes, quieter now, almost forgetting to breathe when she heard what he said, the strength of feeling in it.

'What . . . what d'yer mean?'

'Mary's got 'er mom. It'll be bad for 'er, but she'll

manage. That's if yer still want *me*, after what I've writ to yer . . .'

'*Want* you!' She pulled away from him, standing back, afraid. 'You mean you're going to . . . to . . .?'

He gave a great shuddering sigh, afraid of the words he was about to say. 'To leave Mary and come to you. I'll have to tell 'er. Soon. Before I go. I don't know what's right any more except being with you. I know I love you, Jess. I can't stay away from yer. I married Mary when I didn't know how it was possible to feel, though I can't blame 'er for that. But I've got to be with you. I knew if I saw yer again it'd be like this.'

Jess moved close to him.

'D'yer mean it? You'd really . . .'

'Yes, love, I do. It's all I can do, loving you.'

'And me,' she whispered. 'It's all I can do.'

She put her arms round him and they held each other close, awed by what this meant, by the feeling between them which wouldn't die, however hard they'd each tried to stamp it out.

Twenty

A week later, at work, Jess began to be troubled by low, grumbling pains. On the walk home they became agonizing, and before reaching the house she had to stop, bent over with the cramps in her body and a sudden wetness. Looking down, she saw blood on the ground. Doubled up with the pain, she tried to make sense of what was happening to her. The red stain spread, melting into the snow. She made it home in fits and starts, legs soaked with blood.

Inside the house she fell to her knees at the foot of the stairs, arms pressed into her as the pain tore across her. She heard herself moaning, as if it was someone else.

'Jess?' Iris clumped along the hall. 'Whatever's the matter, dear? Oh, my word ...' One hand went to her mouth.

Jess was sobbing with pain. 'The babby ... it's ... I'm losing—' She broke into an anguished moan. Whatever use was Iris going to be? 'Oh help me!'

But Iris Whitman, in her odd way, couldn't have been a better person to be present at this time, Jess acknowledged after it was over. Unshockable, somehow detached from social conventions, she was calm and practical.

'Miss Davitt will know – I'll just be a moment, dear.' She pulled herself to the door. It closed behind her with a waft of snowy air. There was a moment's lull in the pain. Jess pressed her cheek to the cool lino. She couldn't think about anything, only try to get through those moments, fighting the pain.

Miss Davitt helped Jess up to bed. She was more flustered than Iris, but kindly.

'Poor little thing,' she kept saying. She pressed a pad of soft, folded cotton between Jess's legs. 'I've sent for the doctor – soon be here, dear. Oh you poor young thing . . .'

Jess lay on her side, knees drawn up, biting on a folded corner of the sheet as the pains came and went. Sometimes it was so bad, she cried out. Iris sent Miss Davitt up with warm water for her to sip, but it made her sick. The two women hovered round. Jess heard them talking in low voices outside the door. She felt helpless and completely humiliated.

'Ned,' she whispered. 'Oh Ned – our little babby . . .' Her tears ran on to the pillow. For all the trouble and anguish the pregnancy had caused her, its failure was terrible. She could not give him a child, as Mary could. Mary was a proper woman. He'll go back to her now, she thought. She has a child and I'll have none. He won't stay with me now . . .

She managed to stop crying when the doctor came in, a thin, tired-looking young man with a sharp manner. Iris appeared behind him, which later, Jess saw, was a true act of friendship on her behalf, though at the time she gave it no thought.

'So – miscarrying, then?' The doctor didn't look at her, but put his bag down on the end of the bed and opened it. 'Let's see if we can deal with it all here, shall we, not have to send you into hospital?'

Jess nodded, frightened.

188

'Much bleeding?'

She nodded again. Miss Davitt had twice had to find replacement strips of stuff to stem the thick flow of it.

The doctor examined her. His fingers prodding her stomach made her moan, she felt so tender.

'So . . .' he eyed her ringless finger. 'Miss er . . .'

It was Iris who spoke up. 'Mrs. Mrs Green. Her husband's in the army.'

Jess felt a kind of love for Iris at that moment.

'Well, Mrs Green. By the looks of what your losing, the miscarriage is a thorough one. You'll need rest – several days, after the bleeding stops. Any problems – your temperature going up, or if the bleeding gets heavier, call me again. Otherwise you should be back to normal.'

Miss Davitt saw him out and, Jess realized, must have paid him as well.

Iris stood by the bed looking down at Jess's white face. Her pale eyes were watery.

'Sad,' she said. 'Very sad. Whatever anyone else might say.'

Jess's eyes filled with tears again. 'Thank you, Iris,' she whispered.

She lay in bed for a week, looked after by Miss Davitt, who prayed at her bedside, and Iris. Miss Davitt was a quiet presence in her flat, silent shoes. She was kind, effective and utterly reserved. Jess never got to know her any better, nor did she know what Miss Davitt believed to be the truth about her situation. One morning she placed on the chair by Jess's bed a little glass containing a few snowdrops.

'Surprising what grows, even in the depths of winter,'

189

she said, when Jess thanked her. She was touched, tears welling again, as they seemed to so easily in her low state. For hour after hour she looked at the flowers' delicate white, their shading of green underlying the petals. Her mind was hazy and unfocused. The bleeding slowed, but she was weak. She felt scoured and empty.

Iris was much noisier, unable to climb the stairs without the rhythmic thump of her crutch, sometimes an exclamation of 'Ooops – oh dear me!' as she almost lost her balance, or a little argument with Miss Davitt about her going up there when there was someone else to help.

But Jess liked it when Iris came up and sat with her, found her smell of old wool comforting. She didn't say much, often, but she gave off a sympathy of the sort that didn't tut and cluck about how sorry she was, which made Jess just want to cry again. It was something more fundamental. A feeling that she understood about Ned, about love and loss. She went straight to the heart of things.

'Anyone else would have put me out on the street,' Jess said to her one day. Iris sat on the chair by her, holding the glass of snowdrops. Her crutch was propped against the wall, and a wedge of winter sunshine was brightening the room. Outside, the snow was beginning to thaw.

Iris was silent, just held her head to one side in a considering way.

'People are cruel,' Jess said.

'God sent you to me.'

Jess thought about this. Iris said odd things. But it felt true.

'Cruelty is part of life, remember,' Iris said. 'What about his wife? She must feel life is cruel.'

Iris had met Ned, the day before his leave ended. He had gone to Mary, to tell her. When he came back he was in a bad state, agitated, full of shame. They explained to Iris, but even then, hadn't told her about the child. Perhaps she had guessed in any case.

'The way it feels, it should just be between me and him,' Jess said. 'But nothing's like that, is it? Not really private. Things always bring in other people.'

She thought a lot about her father during those long, dreamlike days. His love for Louisa which, as she understood it, had been so strong, so exclusive that it could scarcely encompass the love of a child as well. For the first time she really wondered what her mother had felt for him. That embrace, that private moment she had come upon that time. It was his face she saw, which wore that expression of completion, of bliss. Louisa's face had been turned away from her.

Gradually she felt stronger. She could sit up and eat, then go downstairs. Going outside seemed a possibility.

I'll have to write and tell him about the babby. The thought weighed on her, filling her with dread.

When Polly came, she was full of remorse.

'Oh Jess – if we'd only known! You going through all that with no one round yer!'

'I'm awright.' Jess patted her hand, trying to smile. 'Iris and Miss Davitt have been good to me. And I feel better now.'

At first Polly was wary with Iris.

'No need to worry,' Jess told her. 'She knows every-thing and she's been ever so kind.' She saw Polly watching Iris when she came into the room, could tell she was thinking how odd she was, wondering how Jess

191

could confide in such a person. Seeing her through Polly's eyes, Jess noticed again what a mess Iris looked, how peculiar and badly fitting her clothes were, her patched old skirt like a sack on her, the enormous, stained blouse and garish blue shawl. Jess had simply got used to her, her looks and strangeness, and grown fond of her.

When they were alone Polly said, 'Mary's been round. If she sees yer she'll kill yer, the state she's in.'

'You didn't tell 'er . . .' Jess half got to her feet in alarm. The thought of Mary turning up on her doorstep on top of everything else was too much.

'No. Even Mom kept quiet. But yer can't blame 'er, Jess. She's got a child to bring up and you . . . Well, you ain't, now, 'ave yer? I mean 'e should really do the right thing and go back to 'er.'

She looked across at her cousin. Jess's hair was loose, lying thick on her shoulders. She had folded her arms, hugging herself, and was crying quietly.

'Oh Jess!' Polly went to her, kneeling to hold her close. 'You don't 'alf get into some messes, you do! Why don't you think for 'alf a second before yer do things?'

'I dunno,' Jess sniffed. 'I never meant – I mean I just . . .'

'I know.' Polly smiled into her face. 'Yer just can't help yerself. I don't know – I'll go grey early having you around! At least though . . .' She hesitated. 'You 'ain't got the babby to worry about no more.' Seeing that this made Jess cry even harder, she said, 'I'm sorry, but you know what I mean, and eh – maybe our mom'll let yer come home now?'

*

Ned sat at a scratched table, a thin pad of blank paper in front of him. For their leisure time they had been given the use of the Parish Rooms in Boldmere, a suburb near Sutton Coldfield, and around him was a buzz of conversation from the other lads, someone plinking out a tune on the old piano. He sat with one elbow on the table, cheek resting on his upturned hand, staring across the room, seeing nothing.

'Yer coming out for a pint?'

There was no response.

'Eh, Ned? A pint – yer coming?'

'Oh–' Ned roused himself. 'No, ta Jem. Not tonight.'

'What's up, pal? Not bad news? Your missis ain't playing you up, is she?'

'No. No – you go. I'll stop 'ere tonight.'

'Awright – please yerself.'

Ned watched his two pals go, joking together, to the door. He picked up his pen.

Dearest Jess,
    I'm so sorry to hear . . .

He tore the sheet of paper from the pad, screwed it up, sat twisting the pen round between his fingers. Had it been true? Doubts nagged at him. Had she told him she was expecting to make him leave Mary? But no – no. That night, the night he'd gone to her and they'd lain together she'd taken his hand, placed it on her belly, and he'd felt it, the unmistakable little rise in it, spongy but definite. And that wouldn't be like her, to lie to him. A wave of tenderness passed through him.

16.1.'15.

Dear Jess,

I got your letter today. Your news about the baby has knocked me for six and I'm sorry you've been so poorly. I hope you feel better now. Don't feel badly about it, love. It's not your fault, you've been under a lot of strain. We'll have other children, you and me, won't we?

I know why you're frightened of what I might do now you're not in the family way, but don't be. I love you with all my heart and I'm coming back to you. I said so, didn't I? It wasn't just the baby that made me decide. It would've happened in the end because I can't do without you.

No time to write more. My mom and dad deserve a letter. But I wanted to tell you not to worry, because you're everything to me, whatever else.

Your very loving,
Ned

16.1.'15.

Dear Mom and Dad . . .

Again, he sat for a long time, turning the pen round and round. Imagining his parents at their table, eggs in front of them, the morning post propped by the teapot. Reading his letter. His father's incomprehension, his mother crying. Slowly he began, honestly, trying to explain what to them would be inexplicable.

'Jess – there's someone to see you.'

Jess had been lying down upstairs. It was Sunday afternoon and she was gathering her strength to go back to work next day, worrying in case she'd lost her job from being off sick. She hadn't even heard the knock on the door.

From the top of the stairs she saw Olive looking up at her from the hall. Jess stopped and laid a hand on her chest.

'Oh – Auntie!'

'Go in the front room, dear,' Iris said, clump-clumping her way through to the back.

Jess led her aunt into the chilly front room, and they stood looking at one another in the grey light from the window. Olive was wearing her best Sunday frock. She still had her hat on.

'So. Yer better then?' Her voice was gruff.

'Yes, ta.'

Olive walked to the fireplace, stood on the little mat, eyeing the ash in the grate. Jess looked at the thin twist of hair low on her neck. For a moment the only sound was Olive's harsh breathing.

'I didn't want yer bringing a babby into my 'ouse.'

'I know, Auntie.'

'No – yer don't. Yer don't know, and yer don't need to.' She turned, her expression terrible. 'I could spit on yer, Jess, that I could, for what yer've done. Ned ... were a good lad before you come along.' Her mouth twisted bitterly to one side. 'I s'pose 'e'll go back and patch things up with 'er now, if 'e's got any sense, though that seems to 've flown out of the window from what 'e used to be like. You're a – a – disgrace, the pair of yer. I can't even say what you are ...' She made a despairing gesture with her hands, holding them up, then letting them drop.

Jess stood with her arms tightly folded. She didn't say anything.

'I came to say, as there's no babby, yer can come home if yer want. I won't have 'im there. You're bad enough but you're family. I don't want to clap eyes on 'im though. I thought the world of him and 'e's – well, 'e's beyond redemption in my eyes now. I won't 'ave it. Is that understood?'

'Yes,' Jess found she could only manage a humble whisper. She cleared her throat. 'Yes, Auntie.'

Part III

Twenty-One

November 1915

'Jess? Wakey wakey – time for a break!'

The other girls were already moving out of the shed but Jess was oblivious to them all, peering into the neck of a grenade, checking it was full of powder. She jumped violently as Sis tapped on her shoulder.

'Oh my word, yer gave me a fright!'

She went with Polly and Sis outside to the canteen shed where they were given a cup of milk and a bun. Polly pulled off the mob cap they were all obliged to wear and shook out her hair before replacing it again. All of them wore khaki, uninflammable overalls over their clothes.

'Flaming milk again,' Polly complained. 'I'd rather 'ave a good strong cup of tea.'

'S'posed to keep us from getting bad from the powder, ain't it?' Jess said. They'd been told that the better their diet, the less they would be affected by the TNT in the grenades.

''Ere – sun's out for a bit,' Polly said. 'Let's drink it out in the yard, eh – get some air?'

All year, with more and more munitions equipment needed to feed the war, factories had been going over to armaments production, and new ones springing up. A friend of Polly's had told them about this one in Small Heath when it was recruiting workers, and offering good wages.

'Why don't we all go?' she said. 'We could work together. 'Ave a bit of a laugh. I could do with a change, and on money like that . . .'

Jess had been very pleased to move away from the Jewellery Quarter. She had seen Mary, more than once, in the street where she worked, and run guiltily away to avoid her. She didn't want to be anywhere where she might meet her again.

The new factory consisted of a collection of wooden buildings built on a piece of waste ground, and they'd spent the summer in the TNT sheds, six or seven girls to each shed. They were moved about: some days they worked together, some not.

They stood out in the weak winter sun amid the clattering from the packing shed behind them. Across the yard, boxes of the grenades were stacked on wooden staging. Some of the other girls came to join them, their faces a sallow, yellowish colour from the powder.

Jess stared into her milk, not joining in the chatter round her. The other girls' eyes followed the foreman, Mr Stevenson, as he walked across the yard. He was tall, slim and dark, in his mid-thirties. He called, 'Morning!' to them abstractedly as he passed.

''E don't look too 'appy,' one of the girls remarked.

'Never does, does 'e?' Polly had downed her milk and was dangling the cup from one finger by its handle. 'Ole misery guts.'

Jess became aware of Sis's freckled face peering round into her own with a grin which was so irresistible, Jess found herself smiling too.

'Cheer up!'

'I'm awright.' Jess roused herself, giving Sis a look of caution. At work she never spoke of Ned or her circumstances. Didn't want to have to explain, or have people judging her. But her thoughts were with him more than ever. Today his battalion was leaving for France. All year the news of the fighting had been so grim, from Ypres and Loos, from the Dardanelles. She dreaded the thought of Ned being sent into it. She still felt he was so close to her after his leave last week. Now she had no idea when she would see him again.

Polly gave her arm a squeeze as they went back in to work. Ernie had been gone since July, and Polly sometimes got very down about it.

'I dunno – 'ere I am, still at home with Mom like a child. I might just as well not be married at all.'

But there had been a big change for her: she was expecting a baby the following spring. There wasn't much to show yet, but the pregnancy had already filled out her face a little, softening the angles of her pointed cheekbones. Ernie had been over the moon at the news, and Polly too, although true to form she worried and fretted. 'When will Ernie ever get to see the babby? This is a rotten time to be expecting. Why does there 'ave to be a flaming war – they said it'd all be over by now!'

They returned to their steady, monotonous work. The women filled the grenades, ramming the powder down inside with an aluminium mallet fixed to a wooden handle. Jess's job was first to check the boxes of twelve to see that each was properly full of powder. Then she inserted an aluminium screw into each, securing it with red sealing wax, and checked the safety catch was in position before they were taken away. She could do the job almost automatically, leaving ample space in her mind for her own thoughts. And those thoughts today were poignant ones.

*

201

'Jess—'

The day Jess left, Iris had stood forlornly in the gloomy hall watching her come downstairs with her small bundle of belongings. The sight of Iris brought tears to Jess's eyes but she tried to smile.

'I'll come back and see yer, Iris. I hope you get a new lodger soon.'

'Jess—' Iris continued as if no one had spoken. 'What are you going to do?'

'Well – I'm going back to Auntie's.'

'But you and your – and Ned? You say she won't have him there?'

'I – I don't know, yet ... There's been so much to think about.' After the enormous mental adjustments she had been through, first to the knowledge that she was carrying a child, then to its loss, Ned leaving Mary – then Olive coming to her ... She didn't feel up to deciding anything. She was nervous about going back, though she wanted to. That Ned loved her, had come to her, had seemed enough. She hadn't, yet, faced all the consequences or made plans.

'You don't think ahead a great deal, do you, dear?'

Jess couldn't help thinking this was quite a criticism from someone who had run off to Stafford in the snow after a man who might or might not have been there, but she looked chastened. 'No – I s'pose I don't.'

'Well,' Iris made a twitching motion with her shoulders, pulling her shawl closer round her. 'I'd like to say this. You'll have difficult times ahead of you, dear, any way you look at it. Now, I shall look to rent out your room up there. I have to keep going, you see. But there's the front room. Never gets used very much. I'd like to offer it to you whenever you need it.'

'Oh Miss Whitman! You're so, so kind!'

'Don't go all weepy on me, dear, please. That's the last thing . . .'

'We'd pay you – to use the room, and . . .'

'Pay me or not. No, pay me – then you won't feel obliged. Keep it as business.'

'But what about your lodger – what would people . . .?'

Iris waved a hand dismissively at this. 'Oh – people. You soon find out who's worth anything.' There was a pause. With dignity, she added, 'You will come and see me?'

'Of course. As often as I can!' Jess almost went to kiss her, but stopped. Iris was somehow untouchable. But her lined face lit into a smile and for a moment she was transformed, like an angel.

Jess kept her promise and visited Iris almost every weekend. Once she was earning better she took her little presents: fruit, or flowers, or a nice cut of meat, now things were becoming scarce in the shops. By February Iris had found a new lodger, a typist working in one of the firms nearby, a stodgy, very private woman.

'Not much to say for herself,' Iris whispered to Jess, raising her eyes to the ceiling where the woman remained silently in her room. 'No trouble though.'

Jess was glad to be back with the family, but life over these past months had been full of tension. Living with Olive had become a difficult, delicate business. The woman was so wound up that the slightest thing made her lose her temper and Jess still felt she was an irritant to her by her very presence. Bert had sailed for the Dardanelles with the 9th Warwickshires. Ernie was gone, Polly pregnant, all things to make Olive tense and worried. Her sense of betrayal by Jess and Ned seemed to underlie everything that was said and no one dared mention his name.

Now and then, Mary appeared. She came twice, when Jess was out: both times when Ned was still in Sutton Coldfield and was back on weekend leave. Jess was with him at Iris's, her snatched, brief taste of life with Ned, and the family did not tell Mary where they were. Then one spring day Jess opened the door and there she was, with Ruth sitting up in the pram. Her face was very thin, those arched eyebrows giving her the look of a frightened animal. Jess thought her heart was going to stop. Seeing Mary, her bereft sadness, her hurt and anger, she knew that what she and Ned had caused was terrible.

'Oh God.'

She expected Mary to leap on her, swear at her, scratch her face. But whatever fury had possessed her for weeks on end, it seemed now to have burned itself out. Now the moment had come, she didn't seem to know what to do with it.

For a time she didn't speak. She and Jess stared into each other's eyes, until Jess had to look away.

'Yer bitch! I don't know how you can even . . .' Mary started to say, but burst into tears before she could finish. Slowly, weeping, she pushed the pram back along the road. Jess saw her shaking her head from side to side as if it was the only thing she could do. Horrified, she watched Mary walk away.

That weekend was the last time she saw Ned for a while, and it was an emotional one. He went, once more, to his family, to talk to them, to try and explain himself, and it left him distraught and tense. It was some time before he would talk when he got to Iris's.

Eventually they made a makeshift bed on the floor with a few covers, and lay holding each other in the strained light through the net curtains.

'I've done the worst I could do – to everyone.' He lay on his back, one arm round her, one bent to rest his head on. Jess fitted beside him, head on his chest. 'I've been a good son to them – the favourite really. Our Fred'd say that if yer asked 'im. 'E was always more trouble. But me – I've done what I'm told, gone on awright with my job. Married the way they wanted me to. I mean Mary was just ... she was chosen for me before we'd thought really – either of us. And now, when I do the one thing I do for myself, out of ... of *desire* for it, they don't want to know – can't see it. I don't know, Jess.' He looked back at her. 'What're yer s'posed to do – stick with things even if yer know they're not right?'

'We've done wrong,' she said gently. 'We have.' Mary's face haunted her, though she hadn't told Ned she'd seen her. She couldn't bear to talk about that and see his eyes fill with longing to see Ruth. She couldn't face hearing how much he was missing his daughter.

Ned's expression froze. 'Are yer sorry – d'yer want out of it?'

Jess put her arms round his neck, pulling him close. 'No ... no,' she murmured. 'I don't want anything 'cept you.'

'Come 'ere.' He rolled over and looked into her eyes, then laid his cheek against hers, taking in a deep breath, smelling her skin, nuzzling against her. 'I don't know how long it'll be before we can ever be normal – live without worrying.'

She knew he was thinking of his marriage, how long it would take to end it.

'Don't think about it,' she said. 'Just be here, now, that's all.'

He moved his head down, seeking out her breast. They made love carefully. He waited until the pleasure mounting in him became impossible to contain, then, with an enormous effort of will, pulled himself from her, burying his face in her, gasping. She held him, kissing him tenderly. There must be no more babies – not now.

That week his battalion were transferred to Wensley-dale. He wrote to say they had at last been issued with khaki uniforms, although there were still very few rifles. And to say he loved her, that he did not regret it. The letter made her ache for him. Throughout the summer he was moved around: Wensleydale, Hornsea, then in August, to Codford Camp on Salisbury Plain. While he was away, things were less tense at home, but Jess fretted, not knowing when she would see him again.

He had some time away on embarkation leave. Once more a difficult visit to his mom and dad who were begging him to heal the breach with Mary, to go back to her.

'They talk as if you don't exist – like I've left Mary for nothing, for a ghost. I can't seem to get through to 'em.'

At the station, when he left, Jess couldn't help her tears. The war was real now. Casualties had been coming in from Loos – one of the Bullivants from next door, a lad of seventeen, had been killed. She and Ned stood looking into each other's eyes, then hugged, closely, in silence, for as long as they had.

'I'm with you,' she said, as he left. 'Everywhere you go.'

He smiled wistfully, waving.

That was the picture of him she carried in her head. The uniform – not a black-clad fireman any more, but a soldier, smart, dignified, yet somehow passive: waiting for what was to come. There was nothing she could do about any of it except wait too, and hope, just the same as Polly waited for Ernie, the two of them making bombs day after day.

She tightened the screw hard into the neck of the grenade in her hand and sealed it up. There you go, she thought. One more for the Hun.

Twenty-Two

A new brick building was put up at great speed, some distance from the wooden work sheds, and shortly before Christmas 1915, a Lieutenant Michaels from the Woolwich Arsenal visited the works and announced that there was to be a new process for dealing with detonators.

Soon after, one morning while Jess was working, she sensed she was being watched, and looked round to find the foreman, Mr Stevenson, observing her.

'I've a new job for you,' he was softly spoken, polite, not like the cocky sods you found in some factories. 'Would you come with me, please?'

Polly, who was in the same shed that day, winked and pulled her mouth down mockingly as Jess was led out, as if to say, 'Well aren't we the lucky one!'

Jess and two other girls followed Mr Stevenson as he led them with long strides into the new building.

'You can hang your outdoor clothes here when you come in,' he told them. He stood with his hands pushed down into the pockets of his overall while the three of them moved into line, facing him. Jess was rather in awe of him. He was so tall she had to look up to see into his face which was a handsome one, she realized, with dark eyes and strong black eyebrows. But she thought how tired he looked. Even the way he talked seemed to imply an infinite weariness. 'And you'll need to wear these over your ordinary shoes.' He freed his hands from the pockets and turned to reach for pairs of rubber overshoes which he handed to them, and the three of them bent to put them on. Jess's felt rather big and floppy.

'This is dangerous work you'll be doing. I've picked out you three because so far you've been sensible, and good workers. I'm going to take you through each stage and you must listen very, very carefully, for your own safety. Now – come through here.'

The shed was divided up by two brick walls. A doorway led through to the next section, with a high brick barrier that they had to step over. Jess followed, walking awkwardly in the oversized rubber shoes.

'If you look, you'll see only three walls are brick,' Mr Stevenson pointed to one side. 'That one's plywood. In the event of an explosion . . .' He finished the explanation with a gesture which implied that one wall, at least, would rip off like paper. The three girls looked at one another.

'You two will work in here,' he told the others. 'This is where they're varnished, then heated in the oven. So – you wait here, please, and you . . .?'

'Jess,' she said shyly.

'Jess – come through here.'

Behind another wall, in the third section was nothing but a large metal drum, attached to a spindle which passed through the wall, allowing it to revolve at the turn of a handle. Above it a clock hung on the wall and nearby on the floor stood piles of boxes. *White and Poppe, Coventry*, Jess read on the side of them.

She listened carefully as Mr Stevenson explained that she was to put forty detonators – 'no more than that, all right? There're forty in a box but I still want you to count' – into the drum, which was full of sawdust. 'That'll polish them up in there. You'll be surprised at the difference when they come out.'

He showed her how to rotate the drum. Jess watched his long fingers close round the handle, became mesmerized by the circling motion. She imagined writing to Ned about this. So many of her thoughts were a commentary to him in her head. I've a new job finishing the detonators for your grenades, so I'm doing it the best I can. I have to wear shoes that make me feel like a duck . . .

'Are you listening?'

She jumped. 'Er . . . yes.'

Mr Stevenson looked at her in silence for a few seconds as if reappraising her and Jess found herself blushing. 'I said turn it for three to four minutes – look, you've got the clock up there. D'you think you can manage that?' He wasn't being sarcastic, she realized. He spoke with a kind of detachment, as if his mind was partly elsewhere. She found herself wondering what he would look like if he smiled.

'Yes, Mr Stevenson.'

'Then you count them out again – carefully. You don't want any left in there. They go through next door then for varnishing. You might as well come and hear what I tell them – you can't start 'til we're all ready.'

Jess didn't take in much of what he told the other girls. She felt how cold it was in the shed and stood hugging herself, hoping the work would warm her up. The varnish smelt strongly of methylated spirits.

'. . . heated for ten hours,' Mr Stevenson was saying. 'When they've cooled they'll be picked up from here to have the fuse caps fitted. Now – have you got all that?'

The detonators went into the drum looking dark and

tarnished, and emerged as if reborn, a shiny copper colour. Next door the girls varnished them and stood them to dry on racks. Jess rather liked the new work, the fact that she was alone, the rhythmic rumbling of the drum.

When they got home that evening, a letter had arrived from Bert. The Dardanelles had been evacuated earlier in the month and he'd been reposted to Mesopotamia, had had a bad dose of fever but was feeling better. Olive seemed as if a weight had been lifted from her, and was in a good mood. When Jess told her about the new work, she made a face.

''E put a dreamy so-and-so like you on doing that? Heaven help 'em – I just 'ope yer don't send the whole place sky high!'

Jess laughed, happy at her aunt's warmth towards her.

She settled into the work, in the 'Danger Shed' or what quickly became known as the 'Rumbling Shed', and managed it without mishap. She was happy in the job. But even working alone, she soon picked up the fact that there was discontent growing among some of the other women, through murmurings during the breaks or through Polly and Sis repeating the gossip.

One morning when they got to the factory they found a group huddled round the entrance, arms folded, their faces defiant.

'We've come out on strike,' one of them said importantly. Vi was one of the older women at the works, the sort you didn't tangle with and a natural leader. 'We reckon we'd all be better off on piece work, so that's what we're asking 'im for, when 'e comes in.'

Jess and Polly hesitated, but by the look of it, with

everyone else out, they didn't have much choice but to join in. The morning was damp and very cold. They stood in groups, their breath billowing like smoke.

'Are they right?' Jess asked Polly. She didn't know what to think about it, but most of the women had years more experience of factory work than she did. 'D'yer think we'd be better off? We don't seem bad off now, compared with before.'

Polly hunched her shoulders to raise her collar higher round her ears. 'I dunno – it's worth a try anyhow. They could've chosen a better day for it though.' Her nose was pink with the cold, eyes watering in the chill wind and her skin yellow. Although among some of the 'canaries' the yellowness was a sign of pride, a sign of what they were doing for the war effort, Polly loathed it. 'Makes me look really poorly and ugly,' she complained sometimes, looking in the mirror. 'Blasted TNT. I'm all sore and itchy round me collar from it an' all. Maybe I should look for another job.' But it suited them all for now, going off to work at the same place.

Sis looked round at the crowd filling the yard. 'Oh well – this makes a change from being in there, don't it?' she said cheerfully. 'Ooh, I wonder what old Misery Guts is going to say when 'e gets in!'

A few moments later Mr Stevenson came round the corner, the collar of his black coat up to keep the wind out, hat pulled well down to stop it blowing off. Though a quiet man, he had a strong presence and the women fell silent as he approached, all watching him. Jess felt her stomach tighten. It was only then it occurred to her that Mr Stevenson was a nice man and she liked him, didn't want to make him angry.

'O-oh,' someone said. ''Ere we go!'

Seeing them all standing there by the sheds he faltered

for a moment. Jess saw the surprise, then concern register on his face, eyes scanning the sheds as he hurried towards them.

'What's wrong?' He looked over at the Rumbling Shed. 'Has something happened? Is everyone all right?'

He didn't sound furious at all. Jess had expected him to lose his temper at the loss of time and order them all back to work. But then she saw by the way his gaze swept over the sheds that he was worried there might have been an accident.

'It's nothing like that.' Vi moved forward, arms folded. She was a broad, muscular-looking woman with black hair on her top lip almost like a 'tache. 'We've come out to ask yer to put us on piece work, like they've got over at Dalston's. We ain't happy with it being a fixed wage, like, and we're all fast workers. We think we'd do better on piece work.'

'Oh, I see.' Mr Stevenson took his hat off and looked down, obviously considering this, his dark eyes scanning the muddy surface of the yard. His black hair blew boyishly down over his forehead. After they had stood waiting for a couple more moments he looked up at them.

'The thing is, ladies—' He spoke in a reasonable tone, and rather quietly so that some of the women moved closer to hear, leaning towards him. 'I know every one of you is working very hard here – not much in the way of holiday time and so on . . .'

'None at all, yer mean,' someone mumbled behind Jess.

'Sssh,' Jess turned to them, without thinking.

'Oi – who d'yer think you're telling to shoosh? Think yer above the rest of us now yer over there, do yer?'

213

Jess blushed, and stared straight ahead of her.

'I do want to do what's best,' Mr Stevenson was saying. 'But the problem is, we're going to find that the amount of work coming to us varies from time to time. Sometimes you might be right about earning more on piece work – fractionally more anyway. Other times when things're slower, it'll be less. So if you stay on the regular wage . . .' He looked round at them with genuine, disarming concern. He knew, and they knew, that they were now earning better than most of them had ever earned in their lives before. 'You'll be guaranteed that coming in every week instead of it going up and down – especially down.'

There was silence for a moment as the women digested all this.

'So 'ow come Dalston's do it the other way?' Vi didn't want to give in too easily.

Mr Stevenson shrugged. 'Up to them, isn't it? I'm just telling you what I think's the best for you. So – that's my point of view.' They could tell that, for all the gentleness of his tone, he was not going to be argued with. 'Are you in agreement?'

Again Jess's mouth leaped ahead of her. 'Yes!' she cried.

Mr Stevenson almost smiled. The corners of his wide mouth twitched as Jess's face went even pinker.

Vi, after conferring with her neighbour, gave a nod. 'If that's the way it is, we'll stick with the wage.'

'Thank you,' Mr Stevenson said. He put his hat back on firmly and turned towards the shed that served as an office. 'Good morning, ladies.'

This was his way of telling them to get to work.

*

A card had come from Ned to Iris's saying he'd arrived in France and would write properly soon, and Jess tried to fill her time so that it would pass more quickly, keeping herself as busy as possible.

On Christmas Day she went to see Iris Whitman, who was under the weather with a cold. Jess stoked up the fire for her, making her tea and pampering her as much as possible. She'd considered buying her a little bottle of brandy to help warm her up, but thought the better of it because of Iris's religion. Iris had no desire to possess knick-knacks of any kind, so instead, Jess found her a nice second-hand blanket for her bed, and bought a few groceries to go with it.

'Ooh,' Iris was childlike with delight, her face rearranging itself into one of her rare and beautiful smiles. She spread the blanket over her lap, stroking the soft wool. 'My goodness, they must be paying you well nowadays.'

'They are,' Jess beamed, warmed by Iris's pleasure. 'When I got my first wage packet I went and got my mom's quilt back.' She'd told Iris long ago that she'd pawned the quilt, though not the full reason why.

'Well—' Iris said, holding up her teacup as if it was a champagne glass. 'Here's to happier times. Pity we haven't got something a wee bit stronger to toast ourselves.'

Jess grinned. 'I thought you'd most likely signed the Pledge.'

'Oh no—' Iris was spooning extra sugar into her tea from the bag Jess had brought. 'Why should I want to do that? Do you think of me as an immoderate person – someone who wouldn't know when they'd had enough?'

She seemed rather indignant.

'Er – no, I don't.' Jess raised her cup too, to change the subject. 'Different from last year, eh?'

'Yes,' Iris gulped the tea. 'Yes indeed, dear. Best to be friends with your family, if you can manage it. Though that Ned of yours...' Iris had taken to this particular phrase for talking about him. 'He's used to approval, isn't he? Not easy, if you have to become a fighter all of a sudden. Rather different for you, of course. Seems to be more of a habit for you.'

Jess laughed at Iris's sharpness. 'It's one I wouldn't mind breaking though, Miss Whitman.'

One evening they were all sitting round at home. Ronny was asleep upstairs, Olive at the table thumbing through the paper, and Jess was sewing a soft little nightshirt for Polly's baby, squinting in the poor light. Polly had her feet up on a little stool, yawning frequently. She didn't have the energy to do anything much once she got home from work. Her belly was like a neat little football now and she sat stroking one hand over it. Jess looked at her, wistfully.

'Is 'e kicking?'

Polly nodded. 'Got 'is feet under my ribcage and 'e don't half thump about.'

'Let's 'ave a feel...' This was one of Sis's favourite pastimes at the moment. Polly took her sister's hand and laid it in the right spot. Sis waited, leaning forwards solemnly, long hair falling over one shoulder. She looked sweet, and was always the most carefree of them, although her young man, Perce, had now joined up as well.

'I can't feel... ooh yes, there! Oh, and again! Blimey, Poll,' she laughed. 'Getting a belly like a cow on yer – I

216

'ope it goes down after!' Sis had the kind of laugh that made everyone want to join in and even Olive looked round and smiled rather dryly.

'You just shurrup—' Polly whacked at her and Sis dodged. 'Wait 'til it's your turn.'

Jess watched, forcing herself to smile, but her feelings were very mixed. How did it feel when the baby grew that big? When you could really tell there was a robust life in there? She knew things were infinitely easier for her than they would have been with a child of her own, that her loss was really for the best, but that little person who had inhabited her was like a shadow that still followed her. An unseen ghost. Who would it have been?

Polly gave another huge yawn.

'Go to bed, why don't yer?' Sis said.

'When I'm ready.'

Polly sat back with a disgruntled expression. She was used to being the bossy elder sister: she wasn't having Sis telling her what to do. And she felt tired and vulnerable. Her ankles were swelling up in the evenings and her back ached. She wanted Ernie. Sometimes, just for a second, she envied Jess. Losing a babby was a terrible thing, but at least she didn't have to have it and bring it up on her own with a war on, not knowing if its father was ever coming home. She tried to push away such wicked thoughts, but she hadn't reckoned with the way carrying a child made you feel so tired and uncomfortable and at the mercy of everything. So old, suddenly.

'I s'pose I'd better get up there before I end up spending the night down 'ere.'

She was just hoisting herself out of the chair when Olive made a strange, involuntary sound. A gasp or moan, it was hard to tell. Her back was to them, head bent over the paper. Everyone looked at her.

'What that, Mom?' Sis looked over her shoulder at the paper.

Olive had one hand over her mouth, as if to stop any further sound escaping.

'Deaths . . .' Sis read. 'What's up – is it someone we know?'

Polly and Jess both moved in closer.

As if reluctant, Olive slowly moved her finger to a name on the page.

'Arthur Tamplin, seventy-two, of South Road, Erdington,' Polly read, slowly. 'January the ninth. Leaves wife, Elsie and four children. Well who's that then?'

All eyes were on Olive. Without meeting their gaze she said, 'Your grandfather.'

Polly straightened up, wincing at the pain in her back.

'But we ain't got a grandfather – I mean, we never have had one. They're dead, you've always said – ain't they?'

'Well they are now,' Sis said.

Polly frowned furiously at her.

'Four children,' Olive murmured. 'I don't s'pose 'e ever knew about Louisa passing on . . .'

'But why . . . whose . . . ?' Polly couldn't get a whole sentence out.

'My father, that was. Gone now then. Well, well.'

The loathing in her voice was barely concealed. Jess's eyes never left her aunt's face. Their grandfather.

'But I thought 'e'd been dead years. Didn't you think 'e was dead, Jess?'

'I s'pose – yes,' Jess said. There'd never been any

218

mention. But then she'd barely managed to get Olive to talk about the family at all. It was just as if they'd never existed. 'Yes, I did.'

'So 'e was living just nearby and we never even met him! Why the hell not – didn't yer get on or summat?'

Olive stood up, closing the paper, pressing her hands down on it.

'After our mother died – Louisa's and mine – our father remarried. 'E didn't want us and 'e threw us out. It were his sister, Bella, brought us up, in Sparkbrook. So no – I never went and saw 'im after that. Why should I? I weren't wanted.'

Jess watched her aunt, full of pity.

'Well, how old were yer when she died?' Polly's tone was still harsh, as if she felt cheated.

Olive's expression became guarded. She seemed to calculate in her head. 'About twelve or thirteen, I think. Yes, thirteen. Louisa would've been ten or eleven.'

'So were there any more of you? Any other cousins or missing relatives we ain't been told about?'

'Poll—' Sis said softly. She had tears in her eyes. 'Don't be like that.'

'No. No others.' Olive moved from behind the table and thrust the newspaper into the fire. Jess saw that her hands were shaking. Sis went and stood beside her as the paper caused a brief blaze, but didn't touch her.

'It wouldn't've gained yer nothing if yer'd met 'im.' She turned, including Jess as she spoke. 'None of yer. Some things are best left dead and buried. Now I don't want to talk about this no more.'

'But—' Polly began, but was silenced by the look on her mother's face.

Twenty-Three

Polly worked all the day her baby arrived. That morning she was flushed in the face, the picture of health in fact, even with her jaundiced skin. She was also very restless and talkative.

'You got the chats today, ain't yer?' one of the older women said, grinning at her. 'That's a sign the babby's on the way, that is.'

'I 'ope so,' Polly grimaced at her swollen belly. 'Be glad to get shot of it now, that I will.'

The timing was perfect. Soon after she got home the pains started.

'Oh Lord,' Olive said, ''Ere we go.'

Jess saw that despite her gruff attempts to seem matter of fact about it, Olive was nervous, and flustered. Jess felt her own stomach turn with dread at the sight of Polly as she sat by the window, face screwing up with pain. She remembered that pain, the agony which had spelt loss for her. It was going to get a lot worse. They had to keep Ronny away from Polly as he kept worriting at her.

'Come 'ere,' Jess said, feeling sorry for him. He couldn't understand what was happening. To Olive she said, 'Shall I take 'im to fetch Mrs Cooper?'

'D'yer think yer need 'er yet?' Olive was laying the table, the forks all upside down.

'No, I'll be awright for a bit. You 'ave yer tea. I don't

220

fancy none just yet.' Polly sat back with a sigh and Jess went and rearranged the cutlery, getting Ronny to help her. His freckly face, topped by the carroty hair, was only half visible above the table.

'I'll go and 'ave a lie down for a while.' Bent forwards, Polly carefully went to the stairs.

'You shout if yer need anything, won't yer?' Sis said. She touched her sister's shoulder nervously. 'Never mind, Poll – soon be over now, won't it?'

None of them had much appetite, except Ronny who tucked into pie and potatoes, oblivious of what was going on. Olive tried to behave as normal, but after a few mouthfuls, laid her fork down. They were all quiet, listening for sounds from upstairs.

'Ooh Mom – it's exciting!' Sis said, all aquiver. 'I can't eat – shall I go and see if she's awright?'

'Leave 'er. We'd soon hear if she wasn't.'

As they finished there was a wail from Polly and Sis and Jess rushed upstairs, Olive panting behind them.

'I must've gone and wet myself!' she cried, mortified. 'I dunno how – I never meant to – oh!' She was seized by a severe pain.

'That'll be yer waters,' Olive said, nodding her head at Sis to run down the road for Mrs Cooper. 'Yer awright – that's natural. Should get yer on the way that should. Jess and me'll give yer a clean bed. We'll get Ronny down for the night after.'

From then on things happened quickly. Mrs Cooper was a cheerful little lady with fading blonde hair who talked non-stop, so much so that at the height of her pain, when Mrs Cooper was gassing unstoppably on, Polly croaked,

'Can't yer just bleeding well shurrup for a bit?'

The lady seemed not the least offended.

'Everyone likes to curse a bit when it comes on bad,' she said. 'They don't remember a thing about it after.'

'Well I bloody sodding well will!' Polly yelled.

Jess watched her cousin writhing around. It was all so ungainly and undignified and she trembled at the odd sounds of pain she made. She wondered if Polly minded them all in and out but she didn't seem to care. They took it in turns to keep an eye on Ronny downstairs. He was wide-eyed and full of questions. Sis had a hard job getting him to go to sleep as the night wore on.

But soon after three in the morning, the baby arrived, long, mauve and shrieking.

'Another lady of the house!' Mrs Cooper told them. 'Yer got a healthy little wench there, Poll – 'ark at 'er!'

Jess cried. They all cried, standing in a snivelling ring round the bed until Polly, who was now quite composed, looked up and said, 'What the 'ell's got into you lot?' and they all started laughing and crying at the same time.

Mrs Cooper washed the baby in a basin and wrapped her carefully.

'There yer go—' She handed her over to Polly who took her confidently as if she was born to it. Her face was transformed – exhausted, dark under the eyes, but smoothed out and happy.

Once Mrs Cooper had gone they sat round in the candlelight, listening to the baby's tiny, fluttering breaths. Their sense of wonder filled the room like incense. Jess saw that Olive's tough face softened at the sight of her first grandchild.

'I wish Ernie was 'ere to see,' Polly sighed tearfully.

'Yer've good news to write and tell 'im anyway,'

Sis said. 'And p'raps 'e'll be home soon. Yer never know.'

Polly smiled down at the little one nestling close to her. 'I think I'll call 'er Alice . . .'

'No!' The harshness of Olive's tone cut into the serene mood, making Jess jump.

'Mom?' Sis looked round, startled.

Olive lowered her voice. 'No, Poll – not Alice.'

'Why not for goodness sakes?'

'Just not Alice. It's . . .' For a moment she couldn't speak, as if the words had to be found from somewhere deeply buried. 'Your grandmother was called Alice, if yer really must know. It's unlucky . . . I won't 'ave yer calling 'er that.'

She sounded really upset at the idea. Jess's eyes met Polly's. Another of those areas of knowledge about their family that had been kept from them, about which Olive refused to speak, and almost violently resisted their asking.

'Well awright – not Alice then,' Polly said carefully. 'It's just I know Ernie likes it. What about Grace?'

'That's pretty,' Jess said.

'Lovely,' Sis added.

They looked at Olive. She nodded, reclaiming her dignity.

'That's a good enough name. I've nothing against Grace.'

'Grace Violet – after Ernie's mom. That'll please 'er.' She leaned down and kissed the child's head. 'So soft,' she murmured.

'D'you know what?' Sis said. 'I'm starving.'

Polly looked up. 'So'm I! My belly's gurgling like mad!'

They ate bread and jam in the bedroom at four in the morning, laughing like children on a forbidden picnic.

Jess had the job of relaying the good news at work. The other women were overjoyed for Polly.

'Tell 'er to stay home as long as she can,' one of them said. 'Old Stevenson's quite good about that sort of thing.'

That week, they had another inspection visit from the Woolwich Arsenal. A party of officers would arrive every few weeks to check the work, explode a few detonators and, as some of the women put it, 'hang about poking their noses in everywhere.'

Jess was hard at work rotating the handle on the drum when they came. She got quite a sweat up doing it now spring had arrived, and she wasn't looking forward to the summer heat. The elastic holding her cap rubbed, making her forehead itch. She finished turning and stopped the machine, breathing hard, and wiped her face on her handkerchief.

She heard voices in the varnishing section of the shed. She didn't think much of this and carried on emptying the drum of the last of the detonators, when there came a bang from next door. She ran through to see what had happened.

'Oh my God!' she heard one of the other girls cry.

One of the inspectors, a woman, was standing, stunned, blood pouring from the end of her finger down into her sleeve.

Jess pulled out her handkerchief and gave it to the woman who wrapped it round her finger.

'I'll go for Mr Stevenson!'

She ran out of the Rumbling Shed, her feet slapping

across the yard, trying not to trip over the rubber overshoes, and wondering whether Mr Stevenson would be in the office or in one of the sheds with other inspectors.

She knocked softly on the office door and immediately pushed it open. Mr Stevenson was sitting side-on to her, bent over on the chair, and for a moment she thought he was searching for something in the bottom drawer of the desk. But as he straightened up on hearing her, she saw that she had disturbed him sitting with his head in his hands.

'What is it?' He looked dazed, she thought, as if trying to remember who she was.

'There's been an accident. One of the inspectors.'

He ran ahead of her, his long stride far outstripping her, the First Aid box clenched under one arm.

The woman was still standing, ashen-faced, trying to staunch the flow of her blood.

'A chair – please,' she said. It was only as Mr Stevenson examined her that Jess saw the tip of her finger had been blown right off.

The girls told Jess afterwards that the woman had been examining one of a new range of tiny detonators which they had been processing of late, which was placed in a fuse cap to explode a larger detonator.

'She picked up this one, and she must've seen summat on it – looked like a hair. Anyroad, she went and took off this brooch she 'ad on and started prodding at it to get it off – I mean I should've stopped 'er, but I couldn't believe my eyes! The thing just went up in her hand!'

Afterwards, when they'd gone, Mr Stevenson came and spoke to Jess. 'I should've been there myself really. I'd've been able to stop her.' He shrugged. 'But there it is. I can't think why she started messing about like that. You did well fetching me so promptly.'

'That's awright.' Jess smiled shyly.

Something resembling a smile fleetingly passed across his face as he walked away.

'Oh—' he turned. 'Those overshoes'll need a clean up.'

That evening, when Jess thought back on the day she remembered the expression on Mr Stevenson's face as he looked up at her in his office. She sensed, without knowing the cause, that what she had witnessed was a moment of private desperation.

10th Royal Warwicks
2.6.1916

Dearest Poll,

I'm happy to hear you're recovering well and our little Grace is coming along. We've drunk to her health a few times, I can tell you! I'm sad at the thought of how long 'til I see her but what you've said gives me a picture. My eyes, has she? Quite a thought that. Give her kisses from her loving dad for me.

Weather's warm here – a nice change from sleeping in the wet and snow. The mud's drying out at long last. We're still as lousy as a load of old rooks – one favourite pastime is burning the so-and-so's off our clothes with a candle! Good bunch of lads here though.

We moved on again in the last few days and much talk of build-up to what's ahead. Not sure what we're in for but it feels like high time to give them a good pounding – we're ready after waiting all this time.

I'm being used as a delivery boy at present, better than all the waiting. You know me, I like to be on the go. Up and down the trenches with supplies day and night. We bought a pig off one of the farms nearby a couple of days ago. What a feed that was, I can tell you. One nearby's got a cherry orchard. Next it'll be . . .

The door flew open and Polly jumped. Grace stirred at her breast.

'I won, I won – I got the Lucky Potato!' Ronny shrilled into the room with the natural ecstasy of a three-year-old who's just acquired a stick of sugar-pink rock, no charge.

Polly swallowed her irritation at being interrupted and smiled. 'You get the Lucky Potato number? Lucky old thing, ain't yer?'

Ronny already had the wrapping off and was going at the end, cheeks hollowed with sucking.

'Keep yer quiet for a bit any'ow.' She looked across and saw Olive's face, felt a moment's terror clutching at her innards. Ernie! No, it couldn't be – she had his letter in her hand . . .

'Kitchener's dead. Drowned. Ship went down off the Orkneys.'

'Oh—' Polly sighed with relief, then saw it was indeed awful news. General Kitchener, hope of the nation. 'Oh Lor',' she said.

Olive went to the mantel, picked up the brass moulding of Kitchener's head and leaned it face to the wall.

Ned had passed some of the winter of 1915 on a quiet part of the Western Front, firstly around Suzanne, camped in the grounds of the Chateau, but also later spent a month in the appalling trench conditions of the front line at Maricourt. Now summer was here and the war had moved on once more. Jess still collected his letters from Iris, who said, 'Here you are dear,' with some pleasure whenever there was one. Jess was touched by her loyalty to her and Ned, when she could have been bitter on her own behalf.

15th Royal Warwickshire Battalion
10th June 1916

My dearest Jess,

   A few days' rest and clean-up once more, so time to write. I hope you're all right, all of you, and Polly's little one?

   Things got very lively here Sunday. Such a pounding the trenches in parts are all knocked for six and quite a few losses of our lads. At the same time it made you feel full of it, somehow. Never felt anything like it before. Shook me after, when I thought about it and roll call was—

There was a sharp jerk of the pencil, scraping a line across the page.

   That's some silly sod in the barn behind me. Shooting rats, I'd take a guess, made me jump. Anyway – we've had a memorial service. Poor lads. But don't worry about me. Everything's all right and it's very pretty round here now spring's come. Birds in the hedges. Larks over the fields, rooks. A couple of the lads are good on naming birds so I'm picking up some knowledge. I wish I could show it all to you – without the company we've got

228

watching out for us in the trenches over the other side, of course.

Did I tell you they've made me a Corporal? Going up in the world, me. I wouldn't mind being a Sergeant and giving some of the orders for a change.

There's talk of us moving on soon. We're being trained up for something big though none of us know exactly what yet. There's a feeling about. I suppose we'll find out soon enough.

I've been wondering, when I get home leave, whenever that will be, if you and I should go and see my family together and try to put things right a bit. Let them see you as you are. It'd be an ordeal for you but let's plan to do it. Or am I mad even to think of it? If the war wasn't on we'd have had to sort it out somehow and we can't just go on as we are forever.

Will close now. I think of so many things to tell you but when I come to write them I can't remember. Send my regards to Miss Whitman – and Polly and all. To you my love, as ever, missing you,
Ned

Jess folded up the letter, gazing at the pale grey lines on the cheap paper. His hands had touched it, sealed the envelope. She pressed the paper to her face and breathed in, searching for some trace of him. She felt as if she was always living in the future when he'd be home, all her energy directed towards that. Now she was earning better she was saving a little money every week so that month by month it grew: her nest-egg for their future life together.

She sighed walking home from Iris's house in the

warm evening, the letter in her pocket. It was hard to admit to herself but she also felt a bit disappointed. The parts of his letters which she longed for, apart from his news, were his expressions of affection for her, his feelings pouring out. They warmed, fed her. But they were never enough. He felt so distant and she needed to see him, to be reassured constantly of his love. It seemed to her he was being drawn farther and farther away into the companionship of men, the clutches of the war, and she even had to strain to see his face in her mind.

Just let this war be over soon, she thought. Let them all just come home. Let us be able to live properly, not wasting our days waiting for life to begin.

Twenty-Four

That morning, the first weekend in July, Jess and Polly said they'd take Grace and Ronny out while Olive went to church. Perce, Sis's sweetheart, was home on leave and she was spending every moment she could with him.

The two of them set off for Calthorpe Park, both in summer frocks, Ronny skipping back and forth along the pavement. Mrs Bullivant had let Polly use her old pram, which had served for most of her children and she hadn't parted with it. It was a deep, clattering contraption which had come to them with patches of mould on the hood and dirt and cobwebs inside, but Polly had cleaned it up as best she could.

Jess smiled as the wheels went clunking round. 'She don't seem to take any notice of the noise.' Grace's tiny, mauve-tinged eyelids had fluttered closed almost the moment they started moving.

'Nah,' Polly peered over adoringly at her. 'It rocks 'er to sleep. Any'ow, she was playing about that much in the night, she ought to be tired out!'

They decided to cut through the back, past the sweet factory on Vincent Parade. Further along, outside the houses, a man had wheeled out his hurdy-gurdy and they stood with the crowd, letting Ronny go to the front to watch the monkey on top of it, with his little fez falling down over one eye, prancing along the top

231

on his bony legs to the tinkling tune. Ronny giggled and jumped, copying the monkey's old man gestures.

'Bless 'im,' Polly said. There was a wistful note in her voice as she watched him.

'Poll – don't snap my head off – but who *is* Ronny's dad?' Jess spoke nervously in a low voice, wondering if she'd get an answer this time.

Polly carried on staring ahead, eyes on her little brother. 'Hand on my heart, Jess, I don't know for sure.'

'But – I mean, the colour of his hair . . .'

'I've told yer, I dunno. I can't think of anyone we've ever known who it could be. It was a mistake, that's all. I don't dare ask.'

'There's a lot of things none of us dare ask.'

'She's ashamed of it. She ain't that sort of woman . . .' Polly trailed off, turning red, as she realized what she was saying, and to whom. She called Ronny to her and they walked on down the road in the sun.

'Sorry, Jess – I daint mean . . .'

'I know what yer meant.' Jess was stung, her cheeks flushed pink. 'I know what yer all must think of me. But it's as if there ain't nothing yer can ask Auntie about. She's a closed book: the family, our grandmother. Why shouldn't we know about 'er? I mean, I barely had my mom for any time – I want to know about everyone else.'

'Well *you* try asking 'er then!'

'I can't; can I? She's funny with me all the time – nice as pie one minute, huffy the next. I only have to do one thing wrong . . . Yer never know where you are with her at the best of times, but after what I've done – sometimes I think she can't stand the sight of me, and other times she's awright . . . But Polly, ain't she *ever* talked to you about our grandma?'

Polly's brow crinkled. 'The only thing I can remember is, she was marvellous at baking – bread and that. Mom used to say that sometimes.'

Jess took Ronny's hand as they crossed the road into the park. 'Well there must be more to know than that.'

Polly breathed in the flower-scented air of the park. 'We ought to come in the afternoon. There'll be a band.'

'I'm going over to Iris.'

'Yes – course. Oh Jess...' Polly linked an arm through her cousin's, both of them pushing the pram together. 'Never mind our mom. She don't seem too bad at the minute. Let's just make the best of today, eh? It's lovely in 'ere.'

They chose a place to sit, legs stretched out comfortably, and Ronny found another little boy to play with, tumbling on the grass together and chasing one another. Jess and Polly turned their faces up to the sunlight, talking intermittently. Nowadays their favourite talk always began, 'when the war's over...'

'I want to go and live in the country.'

Jess snorted. '*You?* That's a laugh!'

'Get a little house, bring our family up where the air's better. Cleaner, like where you grew up. Don't you want to go back?'

'Yes, I s'pose so. All I can think of at the moment is getting Ned back safe.'

Polly watched her cousin's thoughtful face, her brown eyes fixed on the trees at the far side of the park. Jess's sweet looks, her tendency to stare dreamily ahead, gave her an air of vulnerable impracticality which sometimes made Polly want to shake her. But she knew that Jess was much tougher and more determined than she looked.

'I reckon you'd do anything for 'im though, wouldn't yer?'

Jess nodded. 'I feel ever so bad about Mary, though. I think about 'er a lot, how she's getting on. She must hate me so much.' She was silent for a moment, looking at the pram. 'Mrs Bullivant carried nearly all her babbies in there, didn't she?' Their neighbour had had nine children. 'Now there's five at the Front, Stanley already dead. What was 'e – seventeen? It's frightening, Poll.' She turned, looking her cousin in the eyes. 'Life's like paper on the fire – gone, fast as that. I could've married Philip if I'd wanted just an arrangement, no feelings to speak of. If we've done wrong, me and Ned – well there's no if about it, we have – it's because we love one another and we want to spend our lives together. Is that wrong? *Is* it?'

A few nights later Polly lay in bed with Grace tucked beside her. Grace had finished feeding and was sleeping in the crook of her mother's arm, Polly curled beside her so that her face was close to the child's, hearing the sweet sound of her breathing.

Polly was in the half-wakeful, alert sleep of early motherhood. She stirred, moving carefully to ensure Grace's safety beside her, and woke, opening her eyes suddenly in the dark. A moment later a sensation passed through her as if an icy wave had sluiced over her body. She pulled herself up and sat hugging her knees, teeth chattering, her hands and feet as cold as if she had walked the streets in midwinter. But worse than the cold was the terror that took possession of her, a fear that made no sense but which turned her body rigid, filling her with a terrible certainty.

She got out of bed, covered Grace and stumbled next door to where Jess and Sis slept. Jess woke to find icy fingers clutching at her hand.

'Poll?' She sat up immediately. 'What's up? You're freezing! Is everything – Grace . . .?'

'She's asleep – I just . . .' Polly sank down on the bed, still shaking. 'Summat terrible's happened.'

'What – what's the matter?' Hearing the fear in Polly's voice Jess could feel herself beginning to panic.

'I was just lying there, and I just went cold, and it was then I knew. I'm so scared, Jess!' She began sobbing. Jess moved beside her, wrapping her in her arms. 'It's Ernie – I'm sure that's what it is, summat's happened to 'im.'

'Oh Poll – how can that be? You've likely caught a chill and yer imagining things – you know 'ow yer get delirious when yer poorly. All them bad dreams you had last winter when you was bad—'

'I'm not sick,' Polly interrupted. 'Jess, there's nothing wrong with me. I was perfectly awright when I went to bed. It's a message from Ernie – he's calling out to me, I can feel it!'

A letter arrived that Saturday. Olive brought it to her. One of Polly's hands went to her throat. She didn't say a word, and her hand shook as she reached out to take the envelope.

> *10th Royal Warwickshire Regt.*
> *B.E.F.*
> *July 6th, 1916*

Dear Mrs Carter,

It is with deep regret that I have to inform you that your husband Pte Ernest J. Carter 10/612 died of wounds last night.

His Company showed great bravery and he was a gallant man who will be missed by his comrades.

Please accept my very sincere sympathy for your loss.

The letter was signed by the Captain of his Company.

Polly's legs went from under her and she sank groggily to the floor. Gently, Olive helped her up on to a chair.

Ronny stood staring, not needing to be told he must keep quiet when Polly, who was usually full of jokes, was sitting absolutely still, her face stony with shock.

Grace was crying upstairs and Jess fetched her down. 'She wants yer,' she said, holding her out to Polly who took her, automatically latching her on to feed, hardly seeming to notice she was there.

'Oh Polly, bab...' Olive whispered, watching her. Her own legs were trembling, but she forced herself to be practical: get the kettle on, hand Ronny a finger of crust to keep him quiet.

'I knew...'

'What's that?' Olive was putting cups out.

'I knew summat had happened. I had a message, the other night, from Ernie. 'E were trying to tell me...'

'Don't start talking like that,' Olive said sharply. She didn't mean to. Her daughter's suffering was unbearable to her. It made her hands shake so she could barely put out the cups. She wanted to take that agony on herself and knew there was nothing she could do. Polly had had just a few days of proper marriage with Ernie, and now it was over.

For a second, as she went to the hissing kettle to warm the teapot, another loathsome thread of recall from the past forced its way up through a crack in her mind as if one cause for distress brought back the memory of another. Images chasing one another, the staircase, sound of footsteps on the bare stairs, that dark room, the woman with her back to her at the window . . . but there were curtains drawn, closed, she was staring at nothing. And there was a smell . . . that smell . . .

She found she was shaking her head hard from side to side – forget, forget . . . don't let it come back, keep it down, down . . . It was Polly she must think of now.

'What're yer doing, Mom?' Ronny said.

'Yer mom's upset, darlin',' Jess told him. 'Don't you worry.'

'I'm so sorry for yer, love.' Olive left what she was doing and went and stood by her, pressing Polly's head to her and stroking her hair with her rough hands. 'So sorry. I don't know what to do for yer.' Polly began to cry, high sobs like a little girl. Ronny came to her, his eyes full of sorrow, and stroked her too.

'I'd just sent him them nice things,' Polly sobbed. 'And now 'e won't get 'em. Oh Mom, I want 'im back – I hadn't even seen 'im, not for ages. And now I shan't ever see 'im again. Never!'

Polly had been thinking about weaning Grace early and going back to work, but now she didn't want to be parted from her. Jess had to tell Peter Stevenson what had happened.

She stood in his office, feeling as if she was going to teacher for a telling off, her cap held in front of her, aware that her hair was sticking out in wayward wisps. Mr Stevenson's face looked bruised with exhaustion. He listened quietly as Jess explained what had happened.

'There's no need for her to worry, tell her.' He spoke kindly, but it seemed somehow an effort for him to bring forth the words. 'We've almost more work than we can manage all the time. I'll happily take her back when she's ready.'

'I'll tell her,' Jess said. 'That's nice of yer.'

He shook his head with such a sad expression in his brown eyes that Jess was touched by his sympathy. 'Not at all. Poor thing – with the child to look after as well.'

'Yes, she's upset 'er husband never saw Grace – that's the babby. It's been a terrible shock for all of us. You don't think it's going to happen to yer 'til it does.'

'That's true, you don't. Terrible for her.'

There was an awkward silence during which Mr Stevenson seemed to sink into his own thoughts, and Jess wondered whether she should be gone.

'Well, thank you,' she said, turning away.

'Oh, Jess?'

She turned back.

'Is everything all right out there?' He nodded towards the Rumbling Shed.

'Yes, thank you. I think so.'

'Good. That's good,' he said distractedly. Jess went back to work, grateful for his genuine sympathy.

She was full of sorrow for Polly, and of unease. The Big Push everyone had been talking about on the Somme had begun on the first of the month, and that was where Ernie had been with the 10th Warwicks. Jess felt sure that was where Ned must be, and as the Casualty lists poured in, taking up more and more column inches in the newspapers, she became increasingly frightened and uneasy. Death had already come to the heart of the family: sudden, arbitrary, final. The

238

image of Polly sitting at home, so numb and bereft, haunted her all the time. They were helpless, unable to argue with anything that was happening. Nothing could be done to change the fact that they would never see Ernie's chubby, cheerful face again and Grace would grow up without her father. Jess's eyes kept filling with tears thinking about it. It touched on her own deepest feelings, her memories of Louisa's death, and her desperate longing to have Ned home, safe, loving her and alive.

Twenty-Five

Weeks passed. Casualty lists kept on and on coming from the Somme. Each day they looked at the newspapers in silence, the long columns of names, seeking out, in dread, any that might be familiar. Polly had kept the little cutting of Ernie's name, had stuck it into the frame of their wedding photograph. In August the name Bullivant appeared twice: this time Frederick, who had been the youngest to go, a bright-eyed, muscular sixteen-year-old, and their oldest son John, who was wounded. Olive steeled herself to call next door and see Mrs Bullivant.

'I'll come with yer,' Polly said.

'Oh no – yer awright. You stay 'ere with Gracie. I want to go now while '*e*'s not there.' She was none too keen on Mr Bullivant, a sullen man who was working in munitions.

'I'll bring the little'un with me – I want to come.'

Polly had scarcely been out since the news of Ernie's death. Olive eyed her pinched face. She didn't want to inflict any more misery on her, but thinking it might do her good to give sympathy to someone else, relented.

'Awright. But none of that clap-trap you've been on about.'

Polly carried Grace next door, where they found the lady with her younger children. The house smelt of cabbage water. Mrs Bullivant was a quiet, stoical lady,

240

broad in the beam, with a ruddy complexion and a mound of thick, dusty-looking hair fastened into a bun. She was trying to be brave, admiring little Grace and sitting them down while she made tea. But she was clearly not far from tears, and their sympathy started her off weeping.

'I should never've let 'em go,' she sobbed. 'Not the two young'uns. Fred never said 'e was joining up, not before 'e'd gone and done it.'

'You couldn't've stopped 'im,' Olive said, reaching over to pat her hand. 'Not once 'e was signed up. And 'e thought 'e was doing the right thing ... There's no telling 'em, not at that age.'

Mrs Bullivant mopped her tears with a large crimson handkerchief.

'Has 'e tried to get in touch with you at all?'

'*Don't*, Poll,' Olive seemed to swell with anger. 'I told yer not to ...' Her eyes flashed fury at Polly, who ignored her. Since Ernie's death she had started coming out with some notions which filled her mother with horror and distaste.

'What d'yer mean?' Mrs Bullivant sat turning the handkerchief round, kneading at it.

'The day my Ernie died 'e tried to tell me – get in touch with me. I know 'e did.' Polly spoke with great intensity. 'All them boys dying out there – their souls don't just disappear, you know. Not when they can't rest. They're all out there, round us, trying to find a way back to us ...'

The woman stared hard, as if stunned. For a moment Olive thought she was going to lash out and hit Polly. But she said, 'D'yer really think ...?' Mrs Bullivant wanted to believe it. She wanted desperately for her sons not to be gone from her forever.

'I do,' Polly sat with Grace in the crook of her arm, a fact which somehow increased the impact of her earnestness.

'Stop it,' Olive hissed at her. 'I've had more than enough of yer nonsense and yer carrying on. You'll only get 'er all upset!'

'She ain't upset, are yer, Mrs Bullivant? Least, not about that. Whatever you think, Mom, it's a comfort to know we might not've heard from the ones we love for the last time. You wait and see, Mrs Bullivant, if your Stan and little Fred don't send you a sign from where they've passed on to.'

Olive held on to herself until they got home. She closed the door and stood leaning against it as if in need of support or containment for her feelings.

'Don't you walk away from me, my girl!'

Polly turned by the door of the back room, still holding Grace. Her face held a kind of blank defiance.

'You've got to stop this – stop it now! I can't stand any more of it. You're making yerself bad with it.'

Polly sensed the suppressed fear and panic in the way her mother was talking. What was the matter with her? Why couldn't she see how simple, how beautiful it was that Ernie was taken from her but was still here, still loving her, watching over her?

'I'm not making myself bad, Mom.' She tried to sound reasonable and calm. She moved back along the half-lit hall. To Olive she looked like a ghost herself, her face long and white in the gloom. Olive shuddered. 'I don't know why yer getting in such a state. I just know Ernie's still 'ere, somewhere, trying to get through to me.'

'I wish *I* could bloody well get through to yer!' Olive summoned her last shreds of patience and tried to speak gently. 'I'm worried for yer, Poll. Girls sometimes turn funny after birthing a child. And now Ernie going too. Yer need to try and get hold of yerself, Poll, or people'll start talking if they see yer acting peculiar . . .'

Polly gave a bitter laugh. 'That's a good'un coming from you!' She backed away down the hall. 'I'm not the one who's peculiar, don't you worry . . .'

'Yer not the first woman to be left on 'er own, yer know!' Olive couldn't hold back her feelings any more, felt that if she raged and screamed loudly enough she could batter some sense into her daughter's head, make her put a stop to all this nonsense. 'I lost my husband and I weren't going on the way you are! You 'ave to keep going – put it behind yer, or yer going to end up in the nut house, that you are!'

Appalled to find she was bawling along the hall at the top of her voice, she pressed a hand over her mouth to stop anything else escaping from it. Would they have heard next door? Her breath rasped unevenly in and out.

There was no response from Polly. As Olive stood there trying to collect herself, the door opened behind her and Jess and Sis came in.

'What's going on, Mom?' Sis asked cautiously.

Olive tried to pull herself together. She jerked her head in the direction of the front room.

'I was having words with Poll. More of 'er carry-on about spirits and ghosts and such. Came out with it to Mrs Bullivant. It's got to stop.'

*

243

The atmosphere was uneasy as they sat down for tea that night. Polly had Grace on her lap.

'Why don't yer put 'er down while yer eating,' Olive suggested brusquely.

'She's awright. She'll only blart. It's quieter keeping 'er here.'

Olive pursed her lips, carrying a pan to the table. In it were pieces of pig's liver, onions gleaming in thick gravy, a great treat nowadays when things were short.

'Ooh – liver!' Sis cried. 'Did yer have to queue long for it, Mom?'

'Long enough.'

Jess took a potato to go with her liver and gravy, not looking at her aunt. She didn't dare say anything about the latest row with Polly. Over the past weeks Olive's temper had been even more uncertain than usual. Jess felt she had to be secretive about so many things so as not to provoke trouble: her visits to Iris, letters from Ned. One day, the week after Ernie was killed, Olive said to her, 'So 'e's awright, is 'e?'

Jess was startled. She had had a letter from Ned, but had not breathed a word about it.

'Er – who?'

'Who d'yer think?'

Somehow neither of them could speak Ned's name in front of the other.

Olive was looking at her, waiting for an answer.

''E's awright, Auntie, yes. Says he's . . .'

Olive held up a hand.

'Yer can keep the detail to yerself. I don't want news of adulterers in my 'ouse.'

They all ate in silence for a time, until Jess said,

'We heard some sad news today, didn't we, Sis?'

'Oh ar – I'd forgotten . . .'

'What?' Polly was always interested to hear gossip from the factory.

'Mr Stevenson's wife died,' Sis said.

Polly looked surprised. 'I never knew 'e had one.'

'Nor did we,' Jess said. 'Never thought about it, I s'pose. Apparently 'er's been bad for months. 'E's got a little lad an' all, only two years of age, poor little lamb.'

'Oh *dear*,' Polly said, with genuine sympathy. 'What a shame for 'im.'

'No wonder 'e's always looked so miserable,' Sis said. 'Poor thing. 'E's probably quite a nice man really, under it all.'

Olive shook her head. 'Bad thing, that, a man left on 'is own with a child. With all them dying over there you forget people're still dying here like normal.'

Jess had felt shocked by the news, suddenly seeing her employer as a real person with a whole life outside the works.

'He must've been going through hell, and never said a word,' she said. She had found herself thinking about him all day, seeing him in a quite new light and moved by the sadness that she'd felt from him.

Two nights later, when Jess came home Polly beckoned her to go upstairs, peering round to see whether Olive was listening.

'Go and see Mom for a minute,' she whispered to Sis. 'I've summat to say to Jess.'

Jess hung up her hat and went up to the room she shared with Sis. Polly slept in Bert's room now, with Grace, and through the wall at night, they often heard Polly sobbing. Sometimes she went to her and tried to comfort her, other times just left her alone. Polly's loss aroused strong, conflicting feelings in her: sorrow, help-lessness that there was nothing any of them could do or say to ease her suffering, but along with these emotions also a tangled mix of relief and fear. Relief because she felt, superstitiously, that if death had come to them once, then Ned was the safer for it. Death should spread itself out fairly, should strike somewhere else. But fear also at the danger Ned was in, and at the violence of Polly's grief and loss. Polly had crossed the black river into the land of mourning and it made her seem older and separate.

'You awright, Poll?'

'I'm awright. More than Mom thinks. Look, I wanted to ask if you'd mind Grace for me tonight. I want to go out.'

'Course. Why're you asking me though?'

'I don't want Mom knowing about it – not 'til I get back. I'm going to a meeting – she won't like it.'

Jess sat down on the bed, her face serious. 'What is it?'

Polly hesitated. 'Look, I'll tell yer if yer don't start on me. They call themselves Spiritualists. There's some-one there, a Mrs Black, can get messages from – you know, the other side. Mrs Bullivant told me – she's going as well.'

Jess looked closely at her. She knew Olive was worried Poll was going off her head, but Polly seemed calm enough.

'Poll – after Mom died, for a long time after, I used to talk to 'er. I mean, there wasn't anyone else I could talk to, 'cept sometimes Mrs Hunter at the farm. I used to tell 'er how I was feeling and that. And it felt as if she was still there, some of the time, close to me. I mean, I never heard her voice or nothing like that, but I thought she

246

could hear me. So I know 'ow yer feel. It's natural to feel like that. But d'yer really need to keep on about it so much – going to meetings? They're most likely all barmy and if Auntie finds out you'll be for it.'

'I'm not going to hide it from 'er – I'll tell 'er when I get back in. I just want the chance to go, find out. If I say beforehand she'll kick up one 'ell of a fuss. I'm just going to slip out – tell 'er later. So will yer, Jess – please? If I give Grace a feed I'll be back before she's ready for the next one. It's just if she cries . . .'

Jess could feel herself giving in. Polly didn't seem any madder than the next person, she just wanted comfort. Who was she to stop her going out?

'Awright then. But for 'eaven's sake watch what yer getting into.'

After tea, Polly slipped out into the light, warm evening, without announcing she was leaving.

'Where's Poll?' Olive said after a while. 'She still in the lav?'

'I think she went out – said she was going to see someone,' Jess said, her heart thumping hard. She saw Sis frown. Polly hadn't been out to see her friends for weeks.

'She didn't say.' Olive wasn't sure whether to be encouraged or worried. 'What about Grace?' Jess saw her aunt's expression change and Olive was on her feet and across the room. 'Grace – where is she? Has she taken the babby?'

'No—' Jess was bewildered. 'She's upstairs, asleep.'

They heard Olive's frantic tread on the stairs.

'Well where's she gone?' Sis demanded. 'What's all the flaming fuss about?'

'To a meeting,' Jess hissed. 'Some Spiritualist thing or summat. For God's sake don't say nothing.'

Sis rolled her eyes to the ceiling. 'Oh blimey – there'll be all hell let loose.'

Olive came back, her face relaxed again, having found Grace splayed peacefully on the bed upstairs.

'So why'd she go out and not say then?'

Polly came in at half past nine, her cheeks pinker than they'd been in weeks, and a slight smile on her lips.

'Is Gracie awright?'

Jess smiled, holding Grace, who was staring mesmerized up at the sputtering gas mantle. 'You can see.'

'Well – where've yer been?' Olive asked fairly cheerfully, but Jess and Sis eyed each other, both holding their breath.

Polly leaned over and lifted Grace off Jess's lap. ''Ello, my pet! How've yer bin – awright?' She rubbed noses with the baby and kissed her. 'Ooh, I've missed yer, I 'ave!' She turned to her mother. 'I'll tell yer, but yer not to bite my 'ead off.'

'Oh yes?' Olive said suspiciously.

Polly looked at Jess as she spoke, as if feeling that was safer. 'There was this meeting – just in this woman's house, down in Balsall 'Eath. She's got a special gift like, she can get messages from people who've passed away . . .'

This was an immediate red rag to a bull. Olive was tutting loudly straight away.

'It's awright, Mom – really. Mrs Bullivant came with me, and they were all very nice. And I got a message from Ernie . . .'

But her mother got up and walked out of the room. They heard her going upstairs.

Polly looked at Jess with desperate appeal in her eyes. ''E said 'e's in the pink where 'e is and I'm not to worry and that 'e loves me and is looking out for me . . .' As she spoke her voice cracked and tears ran down her cheeks. 'I know it ain't much and Mom don't want to hear about it, but it's everything to me, to know e's getting on awright and 'e's still with me! I hadn't seen him for such a long time and it felt as if 'e'd gone forever without us being able to say goodbye . . .'

Jess felt a lump rise in her throat, seeing the pain Polly was in, the joy that this simple message had brought to her, whether it was real or not. She got up, saying 'Oh Poll—' She and Sis went to her and took her in their arms.

Twenty-Six

Monday morning. Jess stepped into the Rumbling Shed and exchanged her cardigan for the overall and cap. It was going to be a hot day. Work started at eight and even on the journey she had felt almost too warm. As she slipped the rubber overshoes on, the other two girls came in saying 'Morning, Jess!'

She greeted them absent-mindedly and stepped through into her section of the shed at the end. The other two exchanged looks which said, 'What's up with 'er?'

'Yer never know with people from day to day nowadays, do yer?' one of them said. 'Anything could've happened.'

'It could. Or maybe she's just mardy 'cause she is.'

'Nah – she ain't like that.'

In the few moments before work was due to start, Jess leaned her back against the brick wall of the shed and pulled Ned's latest letter from her pocket. She had collected it from Iris's the evening before. Each time she read it hoping she'd missed something. A postcard fluttered to the floor and she bent to pick it up. It was a view of a French town, its church spire standing tall and noble. Small grey print on the back said, '*Albert – la basilique*'. He had enclosed a second card of the same view, but this time most of the buildings were wrecked, heaps of crumbling brickwork: the spire of the basilica was smashed away at the sides, its statue at the top lurching sideways at a right angle to the spire

She read Ned's letter again, urgently trying to find in it the warmth of the man she loved from this foreign country which felt so far away. Her eyes moved quickly over his sloping hand and settled on the end of the letter, needing his parting words which always meant so much to her. But they were so brief, matter of fact almost. And things he said in the letter: '*bombed it to hell,*' . . . '*we were dead beat . . .*' It didn't sound like him. It was almost as if it was written by another man.

She folded the letter away and went to work, counting the detonators with half her mind, distracted. She turned the drum fiercely, feeling her cheeks turn pink with exertion, pounding all her misery and frustration into it.

For a while she fought against giving in to her emotions, mechanically doing her job. But after a time, going to re-load it she turned too sharply and caught her elbow hard on the edge of the drum.

'Oh sod and damn it!' She doubled up nursing her elbow and gave in to her feelings, tears running down her cheeks. 'Oh Ned, I want you – I want you here now, just to see you!'

She was barely aware of the door opening.

'Jess – are you all right? What've you done?'

She straightened up immediately, rubbing her elbow, then quickly wiping tears from her face. 'Nothing. I just caught my elbow. I'm awright.'

Peter Stevenson looked closely at her. He had dark, sleepless rings under his eyes. The kindness in his expression, when she knew the loss he must be suffering, made Jess fill up with tears all over again.

'It's not just that, is it? Has something happened?'

'No—' Jess pulled out her hanky and mopped her eyes. She felt very stupid and her hands had gone all clammy. 'No – not really. I mean . . .'

Peter Stevenson hesitated, struggling to overcome his natural shyness. 'Perhaps I shouldn't be asking, but do you have a young man at the Front?'

'Yes . . .' She was in an agony of indecision and embarrassment. Mr Stevenson catching her in this state – but she could hardly tell him anything about Ned! Yes, I've got a young man at the Front who I love like crazy and he's married to someone else and he's left her and his child for me and everyone thinks we're wicked . . .

'Nothing's happened, I don't think. It's just I had a letter and . . . and . . .' Her cheeks were on fire. She had no idea how lovely she looked, face glowing, her eyes wet with tears. 'I just want the war to end,' she added lamely. 'It's silly of me. And compared with what you must be going through with your wife and everything . . .' Then she wanted to bite her tongue out. She shouldn't have said that! They'd all put together a card for him, from the works, but she'd never imagined saying anything to him. It'd never've happened before the war, she thought. So much was nearer the surface now.

'Oh . . .' Peter Stevenson looked at the floor. Oh God, Jess thought, don't let him start breaking down or carrying on as well because I shan't have the first idea what to do.

'Her name was Sylvia.' He looked up at her again. 'Everything feels pretty grim, at the moment.' Jess felt her heart contract at the tender sadness in his voice. Ned was alive – what did she have to complain about? 'But you know, although I miss her a great deal, what was worse almost was when she was very sick and we didn't know how long she had left. How much she was going to suffer. Not knowing is terrible – the waiting.' He tried to give a rueful smile but it reached no further than his lips. 'So I do understand. There're so many people waiting at the moment . . .'

'I'm sorry.' She didn't know what else to say.

'Thank you.' For the first time she saw him really smile, a wide, rather melancholy uplift of his features, but wholehearted. It reminded her of the way Iris's smiles transformed her face. What a lovely face, she thought. He's a nice man. His kindness warmed her and she felt better for having let out her emotion.

Peter Stevenson's tone changed, became businesslike again. 'I really came to say – to warn you – that there's another group here from the Woolwich Arsenal.'

He rolled his eyes half comically to the ceiling.

'What, again?'

'I'm afraid so. They're over in the filling sheds at the moment so I thought I'd pop in and let you three know.'

'Oh well – I'd better get to work then.' Jess paused. 'I'll do my best, don't you worry.'

Peter Stevenson turned away, smiling faintly again. 'I know.'

That night, Jess lay in bed listening to the rain. The day had been intensely hot and close. Her temples throbbed and her body felt clammy and heavy. It was an effort to move.

The atmosphere at home was fraught. Polly had sloped out again, and though Olive didn't say anything, the strength of her feelings seeped out in the way she slammed pans down on the range, chewed at the edges of her fingers when they were sitting together after tea. The sense that she was charged, ready to explode with some fearsome emotion, increased daily, making all of them nervous of her, not just Jess.

Jess and Sis had carried pails of water in from the tap and poured them into the tin bath so they could all have a wash to cool down. Ronny always loved it when it was bath night, and chuckled as they stood him naked in the tub like a little white freckly fish, to pour water over him. Their splashing and activity relaxed the atmosphere a little, and afterwards, Sis bundled Ronny up in an old shirt of Bert's and rubbed him dry. Jess sat by her aunt twisting the long, wet skein of her hair between her hands. She liked the summer: they had bare legs so she didn't have to keep darning stockings every night.

'Yer know, Auntie—' Jess reached out and dared to touch Olive's hand for a second. 'Poll's awright. I know she's picked up a few odd notions for the moment, but . . .'

Olive jerked her hand away and Jess retreated, chastened.

'She said she'll come back to work if Grace can stop with you and Ronny.'

'She knows she can,' Olive snapped. 'I've said enough times, ain't I?' She was keen for Polly to get back to work, thinking it would help restore her to normality.

Polly got in just as the first growls of thunder echoed round the sky.

'It's flaming dark out there already!' She sounded cheerful enough.

Don't say nothing, Jess pleaded with her eyes. Don't tell us about messages you've had from the 'other side'

254

for goodness sake. Just keep them to yourself for now
'cause we need that like a hole in the head.

The storm distracted everyone. The strange quietness,
as if the whole city was waiting for each lightning flash,
for the loud wrenching of the thunder, as a release from
the fetid stillness which had settled over everything.
They sat in the gloom, not even lighting the gas. Their
horizon was limited by the row of houses opposite,
only a thin border of sky visible to them, but they
watched, sometimes glimpsing the lightning across the
thick swirl of clouds. At last the rain came in force, a
hissing, sighing sound sweeping over the rooftops,
swelled by the wind. Grace slept on despite the noise,
but Ronny was too excited and frightened to go to bed
and sat cuddled up on Sis's lap, cowering when the
thunder came.

They went up for the night when the worst of it had
passed, but Jess could not settle. She lay for a long time
with her eyes shut but no closer to sleep, feeling stirred
up by the force of the storm outside. Storms visited
themselves on you, powerful and out of your control,
and it brought to her mind sharply the other events
going on beyond them all, yet touching them, over
which they had just as little influence. People said the
guns sounded like the thunder. The feeling of her own
insignificance which sometimes came over her at night
filled her now. Sometimes that was comforting, but
tonight her nerves were on edge with worry and longing
and she felt small and frightened.

All she could hear was the steady fall of rain. But a
few moments later there came a cry from the other end
of the house, so agonized that it made her skin come up
in goose pimples. She jolted upright, her heart banging,
and found she was drenched in cold sweat.

Sis stirred, her bedsprings creaking as she half sat up. Jess could see her, dimly, across the room, hair hanging dark each side of her face.

'What was that?'

'I dunno. God, it was horrible. Sshh.'

They both sat absolutely still. The cry was not repeated, but gradually they heard the sound, at first low and intermittent, then louder, of anguished, unstoppable weeping.

Sis gasped. In a small, frightened voice she said, 'I think it must be our mom.'

Twenty-Seven

The two of them tip-toed along the landing, sliding their hands along the walls in the dark. As they passed Polly's door it opened and Jess and Sis jumped, clutching at each other.

'Poll!' Sis whispered furiously. 'Yer nearly made my heart stop coming out like that!'

Polly was holding Grace, who was awake. 'That ain't just Ronny, is it?' She sounded frightened. The crying was childlike and utterly desolate.

'I think 'e's blarting as well now,' Sis said. 'She must've woke 'im and set 'im off.'

'What're we going to do?' Polly held Grace close, the baby's head tucked under her chin.

'God only knows. Let's get Ronny out of there anyhow.'

Sis pushed open the door of Olive's room and felt around in the darkness for her distraught little brother, lifting him into her arms. He sobbed into her neck and she stroked him, murmuring comforting things to him. Olive was still weeping, more quietly now, sounding tired and defeated.

Jess, the only one with her hands free, knelt down by the bed.

'You ain't going to wake 'er, are yer?' Polly said, alarmed. She moved Grace who was rooting around for milk and began to feed her.

'She sounds so sad. What's the matter with her?'

'I don't know. Honest I don't.'

'Sis – fetch us a candle, will yer?'

Sis persuaded Ronny to get down and in a couple of moments they were back with a lighted candle.

'Auntie.' Jess's hands were shaking as she very gently prodded Olive's shoulder. 'Auntie, wake up.'

Olive's eyes opened but at first it was as if she couldn't see them or make sense of their presence in the room and she was still crying. After a moment she sat up, knuckling her eyes like a child. Her arms were bare and she had on an old vest which was tight across her slack breasts. Sitting close to her, Jess could feel the moist heat coming off her body.

Gradually she quietened and sat with her head in her hands. Minutes passed. At last, more composed, Olive spoke quietly through her fingers.

'What've I been doing?'

'You were crying out, Mom,' Polly said gently.

They all waited. Jess expected Olive to say she was all right now, it was nothing, just a dream and what were they all mithering round her for in the middle of the night. But instead she continued to sit there, rocking gently back and forth, her breathing still ragged from crying. Jess thought how vulnerable and broken she looked in her yellowed old vest, her hair hanging down, no longer on her dignity, the fight gone from her. She wanted to embrace her, but didn't dare.

After a time Olive wiped her eyes. 'I can't keep on like this.'

'Auntie—' Jess dared ask. 'What're yer so sad about?'

Olive's hand went to her mouth as her emotion began to well up. Tears spilled from her eyes again.

'I can't stop crying,' she shook her head helplessly.

'Don't know what's got into me. I've tried never to think of it, never burden anyone with it, but lately I can't . . . it keeps . . . I keep remembering.'

'What, Mom?' Polly moved closer. She sounded near to tears herself. 'Why don't yer tell us – get it off yer chest, 'stead of bottling it all up. Is it summat about our granddad?'

Olive shook her head. 'No – not 'im. Not exactly.'

'If yer tell us,' Jess at last found the courage to touch her aunt's arm. 'Maybe it'll make yer feel better.'

'I worry I'm going off me head, that I do.'

'We've worried about yer an' all, Mom,' Polly said.

'And then you started on about all this . . . after Ernie died and I've been frightened to death you was – poorly . . .'

'I ain't, Mom. I just miss him so bad, that's all.'

Olive looked at the stricken faces of the girls gathered round her. They're not children any more, she thought. None of them.

'If I'm coming out with it it's now or never. By morning I'll've changed me mind.' More in command of herself, she beckoned to Sis who was still holding Ronny's hand. 'Bring 'im here.' She gave the little boy a kiss. Jess was touched. She'd seldom seen her aunt show the boy much warmth.

'Get 'im into bed, I don't want 'im listening. He'll soon be off to sleep and we can go in the other room.'

Sis settled Ronny back in bed and kissed him too, and they went into Jess and Sis's room, and Olive got into Sis's bed.

'It was your grandmother,' Olive began when they were all gathered round her. 'My mother. Ours, Louisa's and mine.'

Jess's attention was fixed so absolutely on her aunt's

259

face and her voice, that she was conscious of nothing else. If another storm had taken the roof off she might not have noticed.

'Alice, she was called. Alice Tamplin. Louisa favoured 'er but—' Jess felt her aunt touch her hand for a second. 'You're the image of 'er, Jess. When I saw you again, that night you turned up 'ere, I thought you was a ghost. It was you coming seemed to set it all off. I'm not blaming yer – 'ow could you know? All the things I kept down, didn't want to think about ever in my life again. I'd be standing there one day, getting on with things, and summat'd come flooding into my head, just for a second ... And then it'd be gone. But it'd be so strong – like the past coming back, as if it's still 'ere. You know – if you've got memories, people who're dead're still alive like, in a way, ain't they? Almost like it's still happening to yer.'

Jess saw Polly was about to speak, but she silenced herself. None of them wanted to stop Olive talking.

'Our mom, Alice, had us – there was about two years between me and Louisa. I'd've been four – so that'd make Louisa two – when she had another babby. I don't remember much before the babby came. Just odd things. But then there was three of us. Another girl, Clara. Our mom liked fancy names. She was bad after Clara. Louisa was taken away to stay with Auntie May. She was always the pretty one, see, the easy one, and the aunts liked her. I was plain and quiet. They never liked me as much.' She pressed the large mole on her cheek with her finger. 'They used to say it was a shame, me 'aving this. Said it spoilt me looks. But Louisa'd dance for them, like, and sing, even at that age. Queer how different sisters turn out when yer think of it. I was the older one who had to be responsible, even then.'

Olive spoke looking down into her lap, hands still moving restlessly on the sheet, alternately twisting and smoothing it.

'I don't know exactly what was wrong with 'er in the beginning. She was really sick like – poorly in herself. Lay in bed all day, feverish. Whiteleg or summat, I s'pose. Our dad came in and out, carried on going to work – 'e had a good job then, in a Japanning works. She got better so's she could get up but she was still bad. Course I didn't know. Not at that age. And then . . .'

Her breath caught. Until that point she'd been telling the story calmly.

'All I remember is, she was carrying the babby about with her. Not just in the 'ouse. She'd been down the 'orse road carrying her in 'er arms. And she'd gone up and said to people – it just shows 'ow bad she was – showed 'er to people she met before she came home. What she'd done. She was upstairs – I was up there . . . just standing . . .' She stopped, unable to speak. All that came from her was a moan of distress. Her need to speak battled with a terrible fear, swelling and filling her until she was gulping for air, couldn't breathe. She threw back the covers and tried to climb out of bed. Jess moved quickly out of the way—

'Auntie, where're yer going?'

'Oh God!' Polly cried. She tried to restrain her but Olive flung her off.

'I can't!' Olive gasped. 'Oh that smell – I can't stand it!' She wanted to go to the window, to fling it open and get some air she was so hot, so desperate to breathe, to escape this mounting pressure inside herself. But as soon as she stood up she was dizzy, the room swaying and lurching round her. Sis and Jess caught her as she

261

began to fall. She was both heavier and softer than Jess would have imagined, and hard to keep a hold on. It took all their strength to ease her back on the bed.

'Get 'er head down!' Jess instructed.

While Olive recovered, Sis went down and put the kettle on.

'Auntie?' Jess sat beside her, supporting her, stroking her shoulder. She felt more able than her cousins who found it harder to face all this emotion locked away in their own mother. 'When you feel a bit better shall we go down and have a cuppa tea? Then you can tell us . . .'

They sat round the table downstairs with the candle in the middle. Jess looked round at them all: Olive, her face washed with tears, and Polly and Sis, both looking like little girls with their hair loose on their shoulders. The storm had long passed over but there was still the soft sound of the rain outside.

'Will yer tell us, Mom?' Polly said. 'Did she do summat to the babby?'

Olive was able to speak more calmly now. 'We was upstairs. I don't know why. It was later on and I followed her up there. I was stood behind her and she had Clara in her arms. We had curtains on the upstairs windows, made out of this thick mustard-coloured material they were, and she was stood by them. Not looking out the window. They was drawn closed. She was holding this bottle of smelling salts to Clara's nose, and the smell of it was all in the room . . . She must've thought it'd bring 'er back . . .

'They came to get her. I don't know 'ow long it took, 'ow it happened exactly. I heard 'em coming up the stairs. Two coppers. There was one of 'em, very tall, said to me, "Are you all right?" And then one of them

262

took her arm and she walked down the stairs with them . . .'

She was crying again, but quietly, the tears simply flowing as she spoke. Polly and Sis were crying too. Jess reached over and took her aunt's hand as tears poured down her own face.

'See, it weren't like – yer know, one or two you hear of get desperate, nowt to feed another babby on, roll over on it and say it were an accident. And there's some'll guess what might've happened but no one can say for certain. But our mom – Alice – she walked round the streets telling them what she'd done, pressed a pillow over 'er babby's face 'til she went blue, and she weren't newborn, she were a good four month by that time.

'They wouldn't leave us alone. Everyone knew. They were that cruel. Stones through the windows, shouting and making a display of us when we went out. Not everyone, but enough of 'em. And at school, because I'd just started going by then. My mom was a murderess so far as they was all concerned. She'd killed her child. Never mind that 'er mind was disturbed. Oh you don't know what people can be like. Course, Louisa wasn't there, she was still with Auntie May and Uncle Bill and they hung on to 'er after it happened. Louisa never remembered any of it too well. By the time she started at school we'd moved on. But in the beginning . . . They copped 'old of me once, bunch of kids held me down there was this pothole in the road on the way back from the school, a real big'un, and when it rained, course it filled up with filthy water. They shoved my face in it and held me down. I thought I was going to drown. Yer can drown in a teacup, our dad used to say. 'E moved

263

us on a few times – just nearby to begin with, but there was always someone found out where we'd gone. There was two of 'em, Doris Adcock and a Mrs Dobson. Doris 'ad these peculiar eyes...' A shudder passed through her. 'They daint 'ave one black bit in the middle like normal – there was two, sort of double. Looked more like a cat's eyes and she frightened the life out of me. I don't know why they did it, why they wanted to be so cruel, tormenting a man and his children. But Doris always found us, after a time. To this day I don't know 'ow. She'd come and leave a note through the door, "I know where you are..." At first we'd not move too far. Round Saltley or Bordesley. I saw her once, in the street after we'd moved on, and I wet myself I were that terrified of 'er—'

'Mom—' Polly interrupted suddenly. 'Is that the woman you saw, that day when you went shopping?'

Olive hesitated. 'If it was her she'd be well into 'er eighties by now. I don't know, Poll. It might've been her and it might not. Anyroad, in the end we went and lived the other side of town. Our dad only went back over that side when we was growed up. Once 'e thought everyone'd 've forgotten. Louisa ran off and got married the second she was asked.' The bitterness in her voice was unmistakable. 'Left me to it as usual.'

'Where did they take our grandmother ... Alice?' Jess asked softly.

'They put 'er in the asylum. In Birmingham first, and after we was told she'd been taken out to somewhere in Staffordshire. I don't know why that was. I never knew any of the ins and outs. We just wanted 'er to come back to us. She was our mom. But we never saw 'er again, Louisa and me, although I think our dad went out there a couple of times. We never saw the babby, little Clara, again neither. Never 'ad her to bury so what they did with 'er I don't know. And I never knew how our mom carried on or what state she were in after. Seven years she were there. She died in there, never came out. Pneumonia, our father said. 'E'd moved 'is new missis in with us by then, not that they was married or anything. Not 'til after Mom died.' She seemed to notice then that she had been crying again, and wiped her eyes.

'Oh Mom,' Polly's face was blotchy from her own tears. 'What a terrible thing. Why didn't yer tell us all before? We'd've understood – what yer went through and that.'

Olive gave a deep sigh. 'I tried to put it all out of my mind once I was older – then married to Charlie. Past was past. And what good would it've done yer to know a thing like that? 'Specially when you was having bab-bies yourselves. When you turned up–' she looked at Jess. 'And then when you said you was expecting, out of wedlock – never mind who the father was – I just . . . It did summat to me nerves. I just couldn't 'ave yer in the house. It was as simple as that. I know you thought it was just 'cause you was in trouble, but it weren't that, though I was angry about yer leading Ned astray. But God knows, I've made mistakes in my time. You'll've worked out that Ronny's father was one of 'em. But you're the mirror image of 'er . . . I thought history'd start repeating itself and I couldn't even bear to look at yer, not knowing you was carrying a child. You'd come back to haunt me, that's what it felt like. And I've been that frightened for you as well, Poll. I never 'ad no trouble after I had all of you, not being bad like, and I was scared of 'ow things would go then. But I had Charlie then and I was safe with 'im – solid as a rock, he was, whatever 'appened. When you started on all this talk about spirits and ghosts I thought yer mind was going . . . Don't get that upset, love—'

Sis was sobbing. 'But Mom, why did she do that to 'er little babby?'

'She weren't 'erself. Sometimes it does summat to a woman's mind 'aving a child. And our Dad was no help to 'er. Took no notice. I s'pose 'e daint know what was happening, what to do. No one else could understand it – t'ain't a natural thing to do and that's why they were so cruel. But she weren't a wicked woman—' Her voice caught as she spoke. 'She were our Mom and we loved 'er. And she was your grandmother.' She looked across at Polly whose eyes were fixed on Grace. The baby had finished feeding and was sleeping snuggled close to her, a tiny fist curled by her face.

'I know what yer thinking,' Olive said. 'Clara would've been about that age. But yer grandmother needs yer sorrow, not you condemning 'er.'

'That was what I was thinking, Mom,' Polly said. 'With Ernie gone, Grace is all I've got. I'd kill anyone to protect her, that I would. Someone should've helped our grandmother and taken that babby off 'er for a bit.'

'They didn't know she were that bad. Not 'til it were too late.' Olive looked round at them. 'So now yer know.'

'You should've told us, Mom.'

'I didn't think it'd do yer no good.'

'No, but it might've done you some.'

'It might.' Olive sat up and let out a long, tremulous sigh from the depths of her. 'Ar, I think it might.'

Twenty-Eight

'I tell you what, Auntie,' Jess said a few days later. 'If you'll look after Gracie, I'll go with 'er and see what this Spiritualist business is all about.'

'Can I go too?' Sis asked.

'No,' Polly retorted. 'You'll only get the titters, I know you.'

Mrs Bullivant was not going tonight as she was visiting her son John, who had lost his legs on the Somme and was now in hospital in the city. Jess and Polly set off along the road in the smoky dusk. As they passed a bus stop on the Moseley Road a bus drew up alongside, letting a passenger off.

'Yer getting on or what?' the conductorette shouted.

'What does it look like?' Polly snapped at her. The bus chugged off in a cloud of fumes. 'Think they're the Lord God Almighty, some of 'em, once they've got a ticket machine over their shoulder.'

Jess laughed. 'You sound more like yerself.'

Polly smiled faintly. 'I'm up and down. Natural though, ain't it?'

'Auntie's better in 'erself too.' Over the fortnight since Olive had told them about Alice she had been emotional. Sometimes she'd start crying unexpectedly, and was bewildered and embarrassed by it, but she was more relaxed than Jess ever remembered her and somehow softer. It had been a release.

' 'Ow's Ned?'

'Awright, so far's I know,' Jess said carefully. She kept her feelings to herself, the worry that was constantly with her. All that year there had been little news but that of slaughter: the French at Verdun, now the Somme, day after day.

'Come on—' she changed the subject. 'How much further to this barmy Mrs Black of yours?'

'It's no good thinking like that,' Polly was on her high horse straight away. 'Nothing'll ever happen for yer if yer think that way about it.'

Jess nudged her. 'I was only kidding.'

'Remember what they said after Mons? There was that queer light in the sky, like an angel watching over them?'

Not the Angel of Mons again, Jess thought. 'Yes, you 'ave mentioned it before – just a few dozen times.'

'Anyway – 'er lives on Runcorn Road. Nearly there.'

Runcorn was a road of respectable terraces, intersected every half dozen houses with little avenues leading to houses behind, all bearing the names of trees.

'I wouldn't mind living here,' Jess found herself talking in a slightly hushed voice, even though there was plenty of neighbourhood noise from children playing out in the avenues and on the pavement. They walked a good way down the road. As they passed under the railway bridge a train thundered over their heads. The loud sound brought Jess's arms up in goose pimples.

'Lilac, May, Myrtle . . .' Polly read off the names. ' 'Ere we go.' She knocked on the door of a house between Myrtle and Vine Avenues and it was opened immediately by an elderly man with a drinker's complexion, who must have been standing just behind it.

There was no hall and they stepped straight into the

front room, which was gloomy and sparsely furnished, with brown lino on the floor, and obviously used more as a passage than a room.

'Evening, Mr Black,' Polly said respectfully.

'Oh – Polly, it's you! 'Ow are you then? And who's this you've brought with you?'

'This is my cousin Jess.'

Jess shook Mr Black's sinewy hand. He had a quaint, gentlemanly way, but it didn't seem to come quite naturally, as if he'd trained himself in this rather starchy new way of behaviour.

'Have you had a loss, my dear?'

'Er . . . well, no,' Jess said. 'Least, not for some time.'

'She's just come along to keep me company,' Polly said. She handed over the money and Mr Black stowed it in a jar which had once contained barley sugar.

'Go inside,' Mr Black pointed to the back room and returned to his post behind the door. 'There's a few waiting.'

Three rows of upright chairs had been fitted in at the nearest end of the room, and several of them were already occupied. Facing them was another more stately seat with arms, built solidly in oak. At the far end an upright piano stood against the window, but Jess's eyes were immediately drawn to a strange, pavilion-like construction in the other corner. A wooden frame was draped in white sheeting, creating a shrouded oblong area which Jess realized must have covered the door to the stairs. On the long wall beside them was a painting depicting the afterlife. As well as lots of swirling cloud and what looked like a vivid blue lake in the middle, there were crowds of people in white, flowing clothes, and small, plump angels hovering above their heads.

Jess squeezed into the middle row between Polly and

269

a middle-aged woman in black, who had apparently dozed off to sleep. Everyone else was very quiet and a rather resigned, gloomy atmosphere hung over the place which was stuffy and smelt overpoweringly of mothballs, although this didn't overcome the stale odour coming from the lady on the other side of Jess. The woman behind them kept coughing. Jess felt self-conscious and not very trusting of what was going to happen. She nudged Polly, pointing at the sheets.

'What're they for?' she whispered.

'Mrs Black always comes out from there. I s'pect she's upstairs getting ready.'

Jess jumped violently as the lady on the other side of her roused herself and laid a hand on her knee. She greeted Polly, then said to Jess,

'My name's Irene Crawford. 'Ave yer suffered a loss?'

'No.' She felt almost guilty at this admission. 'I've just come with Polly.'

'My 'usband and my son have passed on to the other side. Only me and my daughter left now. My son William was killed at Suvla Bay.'

'Was your husband killed in the fighting too?' Jess asked.

'No, bab, 'e fell off of a roof on the 'agley Road. The two of 'em keep in touch though. Always were good to me, both of 'em.'

As they waited a few more people arrived, all – with one exception – women, who seemed to know each other at least by sight, and there was a low murmur of conversation.

At half past seven on the dot, Mr Black disappeared into the white, tent-like structure and they heard him calling up the stairs,

'Yer ready now then, Dora?'

There came a muffled reply, then they heard what sounded like at least two pairs of feet on the stairs. Jess, in a slightly hysterical state, found herself picturing Mrs Black having four legs like a pantomime horse and had to force down the powerful urge to laugh which swelled up inside her.

Mr Black held the sheet aside, closing it behind his wife as she appeared. She was a small, neat woman, quite a bit younger than her husband by the look of her, dark-haired, with bold, shapely eyebrows. She was also dressed in black, and her hat was trimmed with black net. There was a stiff elegance about her movements.

'Good evening, everyone,' she said, looking round at them with composure.

'Good evening,' they all muttered.

'We shall start with our hymn.' She moved to the piano and began to play it rather well, but there were not many voices to make a swell of sound and their efforts at singing turned out as more of a mumbling,

> 'Jesus lives! no longer now
> Can thy terrors, death, appal us;
> Jesus lives! by this we know
> Thou, O grave, canst not enthrall us.
> Alleluia!'

By the end of the first verse, Mrs Crawford and Polly were both crying and some of the others soon joined in. It was so sad it set Jess off crying too, thinking of Ernie's sweet, friendly face and how happy he and Polly had looked together and now they'd never see him again. And it called to mind the day her mother died and she found she was crying for her too, and for her

271

grandmother and baby Clara, until she was at least as upset as everyone in the room, and needed something to blow her nose on. She had to borrow Polly's handkerchief.

They all sat down. The room was rather shadowy now, although there was still some silvery grey evening light coming from the window. Mr Black lit the three candles in a brass candelabra and placed it on the piano. For a moment they all sat quietly, except that Jess heard someone give a sniff and she frowned. It sounded as if it had come from in front of her, but that would mean someone who they couldn't see was waiting behind the screen of sheets. The thought was rather spooky. She wondered at Polly coming here on her own: she must truly have been desperate.

Mrs Black sat down on the rather grand oak chair and took several deep breaths. Her little round tummy seemed constrained by her frock, and her full bustline looked fit to erupt out of it too. She closed her eyes.

'I can feel the spirits are close to us tonight.' She kept her voice low, intoning in a rather posh voice so it didn't seem like natural speech. Despite her unease, Jess found she was reluctantly full of curiosity. If it was real it would be very nice to hear from Ernie again.

'Who has grief pressing on them at this moment? Who shall I summon from the spirit world, the land of blessed light? Those on the other side are only gone before: they are watching over us, and they are still needful of our love and our communion with them.'

'I . . .' Polly sniffed. 'I'd like to 'ear from Ernie . . .'

'Ernie . . .' Mrs Black said meditatively. Then opened her eyes and said in a normal voice, 'You mean yer 'usband?'

Polly nodded. 'Ernest Carter. Same as last week.'

'Ernest Carter . . .?' The eyes closed again. 'Your wife would like to hear from you Ernest, come to us: cross back from the other side to where your wife waits faithfully for you . . .' Her tone turned incantational, like someone pretending to be a ghost.

'I'm here,' a voice said.

Jess nearly jumped out of her skin. She gripped Polly's wrist.

'Oh Ernie!' Polly whispered.

'I've come to see yer again . . . er, wife. I'm awright. It's very nice over 'ere. Very comfortable and er, pleasant. Wish you could come and join me . . . well, when yer ready and that, I mean. I hope everything's going along at home. Don't worry about me. The wounds don't hurt any more. Well – love for now then . . .'

The voice seemed muffled during the last sentence, in a way which sounded to Jess as if the person speaking was backing away up the stairs.

''E sounds different,' she whispered to Polly.

'Dying does that,' Polly said tearfully. 'Mrs Black told us that. They've gone to another place. They have astral bodies.'

Irene Crawford, next to Jess, was asking about her husband and son.

'I'd 'specially like to 'ear from my son if you can manage it again. I know the Dardanelles is a long way.'

Mrs Crawford's son William did want to speak to his mother and he seemed to be having a quite similar experience of the other side to Ernie. Jess found, after several encounters with the spirit world, that life over there didn't seem to be any more varied or interesting than existence in this one and she began to lose interest. Until a thought struck her.

When there was a gap in the proceedings she said,

'I'd like to call someone.'

Polly's head whipped round. 'Jess – what're yer doing?'

'I'd like to talk to my grandmother. She was called Alice Tamplin.'

She heard Polly gasp.

'How long has she been gone from this world?' Mrs Black asked in her strange, sing-song voice.

'Er . . .' Jess looked uncertainly at Polly. 'Oh, at least twenty years.'

'I see.' Mrs Black was sitting with her eyes closed, obviously concentrating. There was a long silence. Jess was torn between amusement and nervousness. This would be a tough one for the man behind the screen! But still she found she was tingling with a strange sensation. Everyone was silent. An atmosphere of intensity had come over the room.

She'll have to give up on this, Jess thought. She's not asked me anything about her. How's he going to know what to say?

She was looking expectantly at the little sheeted box, when Mrs Black abruptly put her head back, her body went rigid and she gave a long, horrifying howl. Jess felt her limbs turn to water. The howl was followed by a high keening of grief and distress and Mrs Black's body jerked about as if in pain. Then they heard the sound of a woman sobbing as if her heart would break. There was nothing going on from behind the screen: it was all coming from Mrs Black. Jess couldn't see her moving: her lips and throat were still, the noises shrill and disembodied. She and Polly sat rigid, gripping hard on to each other's hands.

The desolate weeping went on for a short time, then

stopped abruptly. Mrs Black relaxed into the posture she had been in before.

'She is not quiet.' She spoke softly. 'She is not at peace. She cannot speak to you.'

'Oh my God,' Jess whispered. She was shaking all over.

Both of them were sober and shocked on the way home. Polly tried to talk. 'You see? Marvellous, ain't she? It does me so much good to know I can hear from Ernie.'

Jess didn't reply. Away from the confines of the Blacks' dark house she was struggling to make sense of what had happened. She had felt frozen in there, although the night was not chill. All the grief and sorrow and desperate hope congregated together seemed to cast a cold pall over the atmosphere. But she didn't really believe in all that sort of thing, hadn't until tonight. She'd been certain they hadn't really heard from Ernie. It was clear as anything that there was a man behind the sheet doing all the voices. Why could none of them see it? Was it because they needed so badly to believe what Mrs Black told them, because they were so bereft and lonely? And if that was the case, did it really matter that she was a fake if she brought comfort?

But Alice . . . Had Mrs Black taken over the act of being Alice because she'd only got a 'ghost' who could do men's voices? But how had she known what sort of person Alice would be? Was it luck? But the sound of that weeping, when Mrs Black had been sitting so still, not apparently moving a muscle . . . The sound of it was locked, echoing round in Jess's head. What if it was real, if their talking about her had somehow brought her spirit closer to them? Poor, unquiet Alice. Was she still out there somewhere, mourning, needing them in some way? With all these thoughts turning in her mind Jess was silent almost until they got home. At the end of Oughton Place she turned to her cousin.

'Well Poll,' she was trying not to show how uneasy she felt. 'I'm glad I came with yer, but I shan't come again.'

'What'll yer tell our mom?' Polly stopped her for a moment. 'You won't make things difficult for me, will yer?'

Jess shook her head. 'Course not. But Polly – what about Alice?'

'We'll 'ave to do summat to help her rest in peace.'

'But what?'

Polly frowned. 'I dunno. We'll 'ave to put some thought into it. P'raps we could find where she's buried, when we get the chance. But Jess – don't let on to Mom. She's been in enough of a state lately. Knowing this won't help 'er.'

When they got home, Olive said, 'Well – what was it like?

'Oh,' Jess managed a grin at her. 'It weren't too bad. Nice enough people, no madder than most. I don't suppose it can do any harm.'

PART IV

Twenty-Nine

June 1917

'Right, girls – come on over 'ere and gather round – I've got summat to say to all of yer!'

Vi, who was still the unofficial gaffer at the factory, was out in the yard, waving her brawny arms to get their attention.

It was a bright day, with a feeling of warmth and promise peculiar to early summer. It had rained in the night and there were puddles dotted about, but now they could hear birds on the waste ground beyond. Pigeons were muttering on the roof of the Rumbling Shed.

Sis winked at Jess as they met outside the office on their way to the canteen.

'What does she want then?'

Jess shrugged. 'Soon find out.'

There was already a crowd of women round Vi, and a sallow, jaundiced-looking lot they were, a number obviously full of cold even though the winter was long over, some with red, itchy skin from contact with the powder. They were all squinting, coming out of the sheds. Quite a few were coughing, including Sis who complained continually of having a sore throat. In the bright light Jess saw she was thin and tired-looking. Perce had been posted now and she had joined the ranks of the permanently worried.

Someone handed Vi a chair and she stepped up on to

it, wobbling and flailing her arms before standing upright as it creaked under her.

'To my mind,' she bawled across the yard, 'we're all in need of a bit of a day out.'

Jess and Sis looked at each other and raised their eyebrows. 'We've had a long, hard winter,' – murmurs of agreement – 'and yer all looking like yer've bin locked up in the cellar for six month—'

'Feels like it an' all!' someone shouted.

'So 'ow about a picnic out somewhere Sunday? Bring some grub—'

'That's if yer can get 'old of any!' There was laughter.

'—and we'll go over the park . . .'

A discussion broke out about where it should be. Some wanted more of a day out, right out of town, and eventually it was decided that they'd go across to Sutton Park.

'Ooh—' Jess said. A quiver of pleasure went through her. 'How lovely. It's s'posed to be real nice up there.'

'Poll could come, couldn't she?' Sis said. Polly was back at work, but had decided to find another job nearer home so she could pop back at dinnertime and look in on Grace. She found it difficult enough to be separated from her for even an hour or two.

'I should think so,' Jess said. 'And Ronny'd love it.'

She went up to Vi. 'Can I bring me cousin – 'e's five?'

'Bring who yer like, bab, so long's yer can get 'em on the bus.'

As they dispersed to go and fetch their daily cup of milk, Peter Stevenson was standing watching, leaning against the wall by his office door. Jess saw Vi go up to him. A few moments later she came in to the little canteen.

''Ere – guess what. 'E wants to come along an' all.'

'What – Mr Stevenson, on a picnic with us lot!'

'Blimey – 'e must be lonely.'

'Did yer say 'e could?'

'Well I could 'ardly tell 'im 'e couldn't, could I?' Vi grunted, lowering herself on to a chair, the enamel cup in one hand. 'Oh me legs! Flamin' 'ell, I'm old enough to be 'is mother! Now there's a thought.'

It had been a dismal winter indeed. The cold and shortages of food, the queueing, the triumph of finding a potato in the shops when there was such a scarcity of them, the long, grinding hours at work day after day made nearly every aspect of life a struggle. Added to that was the yearning for loved ones, some had now been absent so long, and the constant gnawing anxiety for their safety.

My life, Jess thought sometimes, is made up of work and Ned. She dreamed about him as she worked, hour after hour, her arms and back aching. Of their future, when the war was over. Some days she burned with optimism, others she was full of fear and insecurity. He might be killed. He might change his mind. Perhaps already he'd decided he didn't love her any more but couldn't bring himself to tell her? On days like that she felt low and hopeless and tried to put him out of her mind. It was too unbearable to think about. If he was taken from her, her life would be empty. It would have no meaning.

She was comforted though, with regard to his safety, by his letters throughout the winter. He was at a quiet part of the Front, he told her. It was bitterly cold for a large part of the time, frosts which broke French records, but there was little in the way of shooting and shelling.

She tried not to ask more than to know he was all right. In the April his Company were involved in the fighting at Arras, helping to capture Vimy Ridge. Soon after he wrote and told her he was safe. Just occasionally he managed to say more to her than the facts and these parts were the greatest treasure to her.

Sunday started off cool and misty but they had hopes of finer weather. Jess, Polly and Sis piled on to the bus with Ronny. Polly had Grace in her arms.

'You can come too, yer know,' Jess had said to Olive. 'It don't matter who goes so long as they make their way and bring their food.'

Olive smiled. She was sitting back comfortably in anticipation of a day on her own. 'Nice to be asked, but I'm going to 'ave a day's peace without them two.' She nodded at the two little ones. 'No one keeping on at me or causing trouble.' She fixed Ronny with a dire look.

There was a festive atmosphere on the bus as quite a few of the other workers had caught the same one. Ronny sat on Jess's knee and Polly was next to her with Grace. Ronny had lost all his baby fat and was now a thin little thing with white, stick legs and knobbly knees, hair a vivid carrot colour and freckles all over his face. And he was trouble in motion, despite the innocent expression.

'You're not going to run off and be a nuisance, are yer?' Jess spoke close to his ear over the noisy rumble of the bus.

Ronny shook his head absent-mindedly, knowing this was the right answer.

'I wish this one'd get up and run about,' Polly nodded at Grace. She was over a year now, and despite the limited amount of food about, was a rounded pudding of a child with thick brown hair and big blue eyes, who was barely showing any inclination to walk. 'Tires me out lifting 'er, that it does.'

They'd got no sense out of Sis who sat reading and re-reading a letter she'd had from Perce and grinning to herself.

'From the look of yer I take it 'e's awright,' Polly said.

''E's being trained up to work in them tank things,' Sis said proudly. 'In the Tank Corps.'

'Blimey,' Polly made a face. 'Well p'raps 'e's safer inside one of them.'

As the city fell away and they moved towards the old town of Sutton Coldfield, things started to look more cheerful. The sun found a chink in the clouds and shone in a determined sort of way. When they got off the bus and walked into Sutton Park, the smell of the grass rising to meet them, Jess suddenly felt her spirits lift further than they had in a long time. She wanted to drop everything and run across the open expanse of green, over to the fresh spring trees at the other side, but knew she couldn't leave Polly to carry the bags as well as manage Grace.

They strolled across among a crowd of other women from the works with their families around them, calling out noisily, the children chattering with excitement. Ronny, for the moment, seemed awed by the space round them.

Vi was there with two of her daughters, and a carrier in each hand, swaying from side to side as she walked across the grass. As usual she took charge.

'Best stay in the sun,' she squinted up at the clouds. 'There ain't much point in sitting in the shade when the sun's hardly shining.'

Jess, Polly and Sis settled with a group of others. There were more arrivals from another bus and gradually the group grew, snaking across the grass, everyone close together but gathered into smaller clusters here and there. Some laid out mats and coats on the damp grass. Behind them, a short distance away was a row of trees edging a stream which ran through the park, and in front stretched the wide swathe of grass.

It was only mid-morning and too early for dinner, although that didn't stop a few having a nibble of the food they'd bought. At first Ronny sat quietly between Jess and Sis as the women chatted, enjoying the freedom to loll on the grass and talk for as long as they wanted without having to go back to the sheds and fill grenades. Then a set of identical twin girls, both about seven, with ash-blonde hair and freckles, went up to Ronny and pulled him to his feet, each hoicking him by the hand.

'We'm gunna play tag,' they commanded. 'So come on with us.'

Jess smiled over at the twins' mom. 'No saying no to them, eh? Bet they give you the run around?'

'Not 'alf.' The woman smiled wearily.

'Eh—' Vi said. 'Look – 'e's come an' all!'

Peter Stevenson was walking towards them, a little self-consciously, Jess thought, one long arm raised in greeting. He was dressed casually in grey flannel trousers and a dark green sweater, with a jacket over one arm. Beside him, holding his spare hand and walking with stolid, rather uncertain steps, was a young boy.

'Oh look,' Sis said. 'His little lad. Poor little bugger.'

'Oi,' Vi said. 'Watch yer mouth.'

'Morning!' Peter Stevenson put his bag down. They all replied, cheerfully though with a shyness that his own reserve brought out in them. He wasn't like some of the men they were used to, full of lip, and they weren't sure how to talk to him.

The whole group must have numbered about sixty or seventy people, and now they were closer, the little boy was overcome and turned away, pressing his face into his father's thighs.

'Now, Davey – there's no need for that, is there?'

Peter Stevenson gradually prised the boy away from him and squatted down to look into his face. The child tried to move close again and hide his eyes.

'These are the ladies from the factory and their families,' he said gently. 'They all want to see you, and we're going to have a picnic together, remember? Maybe have a game or two.' He turned, smiling. 'He's always been shy, but recently . . .' He stopped. They all knew what he meant.

Jess watched the careful way he looked into his son's face, reassuring him. But David's eye was caught by a movement beside him. Grace had crawled across the grass and was looking up at him with her mouth open, drooling. The boy squeaked with alarm and clung to his father again.

'She wants to play with yer!' Polly said. Grace moved closer, kneeled up at the side of him, wrapped her arms round the boy's legs and started sucking experimentally on one of his kneecaps. He started to giggle.

All the women laughed too, and for the first time Jess could remember, so did Peter Stevenson.

*

By the time they ate dinner the sun came out, coats and cardigans came off and everyone relaxed visibly in the warmth. Jess lay back, straw hat on the grass beside her, feeling the sun on her eyelids, warming her stiff limbs. She stretched like a cat. It was so nice to lie still! She knew in a while she'd have to give Polly a rest and take her turn traipsing round after Grace who wouldn't sit in one place for a second. But for now she felt drowsy, half detached from the shrieks and laughter around her, the distant chug of a bus on the road. She could hear women talking lazily round her, and mixed with their chat, the occasional low sound of Mr Stevenson's voice which she found reassuring. She remembered the tender way he had looked at his son and for a moment a great longing filled her. When had her own father ever looked at her like that? The sunlight and country smells of grass and earth took her mind back. The orchard at Budderston, the hayfield, Louisa ... And Alice. She recalled Olive's sudden, so far as she could see, unprovoked anger that day. Had it been out of bitterness at all Olive had endured, when Louisa had escaped so much of it? The three women haunted her. Even though Olive was part of the present, the past felt mysteriously, nudgingly present. But shortly the actual present crashed in on her.

'Oh, take 'er off of me for a bit, will yer, Jess – she's running me ragged!'

Jess sat up drowsily. Polly was clutching a beaming, grubby-faced Grace whose arms and legs were pedalling frantically in her eagerness to be off.

'Come on then, Gracie.'

It was a little later, while Jess was trailing round after Grace as she half crawled, half staggered holding Jess's hand, ferreting into people's bags and picking up odd bits of soil and leaves to eat, that some of the older children tired of games and discovered the stream.

There were four boys all about Ronny's age, including David Stevenson. Ronny, who had quite recovered from his quiet moments of awe and wonder, was the undoubted ringleader. Jess saw them hurtle down into the shade which shrouded the low banks of the stream. After a second or two's uncertainty they pulled their shoes and socks off and their shrieks of agony and delight could be heard at the coldness of the water.

'Let's go and keep an eye on 'em,' Jess said, picking Grace up. 'Ooh, you're a lump. And don't go thinking you're going in with them 'cause yer not.'

When she reached the stream the boys were all bending over something they could see in the water, prodding at it with their fingers. She stood watching, Grace struggling in her arms. In a moment Sis came to join her.

'They awright? Not getting into any mischief, are they?'

'Not so far, but there's no telling.'

A couple of other women were looking across towards the stream, but seeing Jess and Sis there, sunk down again thankfully. Peter Stevenson had got up and was also walking towards them.

'Is David in there?' he called, sounding anxious.

Jess nodded. 'They're all awright.'

He had taken his hat off and his black hair was blowing waywardly about. He seemed aware of it and tried to smooth it with one hand but it sprung up again. When he reached them, Jess felt small again beside his tall, rangy figure.

'Don't get your clothes wet, will you?' he called to the boys.

287

They ignored him, their eyes fixed on the water in search of tiddlers.

There was silence for a moment. Jess felt self-conscious beside Peter Stevenson. He was staring across the stream, out through the trees the other side, to the grass beyond. His face was sad and her heart went out to him.

'Who's looking after Davey?' she asked. 'I mean when you're at the works.'

'Oh – I've got a housekeeper. Very kind lady. And sometimes my mother comes – she's been very good too. Things could be worse,' he finished valiantly.

Could they? Jess wanted to ask. Instead she said, ''E's a lovely little lad. Got your eyes.'

She saw him smile. 'He's a good boy. We help each other along.'

Ronny spotted them watching and grinned.

'Oi, Jess, Sis – come on in 'ere with me, it's bostin'!'

'No ta, Ronny,' Jess said. 'I've got to hold on to Grace.'

'I'll take her if you like,' Peter Stevenson offered.

'Oh – no, yer awright. I'm not keen on cold water.'

'Oh—' Ronny pleaded. 'Go on!'

'I'll go in with them.' Sis had been rather hoping for a paddle. She slipped her shoes off and slithered down into the water. 'Oh my God – it's flipping freezing!' She laughed, holding up her skirt, trying to tuck it between her knees, and waded unsteadily over to the boys.

'You're close, you and your sisters, aren't you?' Peter Stevenson observed. He stood in a relaxed manner, hands loosely clasped behind his back.

'Oh we ain't sisters,' Jess laughed, rearranging Grace in her aching arms. 'Well, Sis and Poll are – I'm their cousin. Their name's Beeston – well, Poll's was before she was married. Mine's Hart.'

'Oh – sorry. Too many names to take in. But I thought you all lived together . . .' he trailed off, afraid of seeming too nosey.

'We do. I came to Brum to live with my auntie just before the war. She sort of took me in when I . . .' She had been about to say 'ran away' but it sounded bad, she thought. Flighty. 'I er, didn't get on too well with my stepmom so I thought I'd just get out of 'er way. Auntie's been good to me.'

'That's a hard thing to do. Your mother . . .?'

'She died years ago. Only Sarah – that's my step-mother – well, the older I got the worse we got on.' She spoke matter of factly, not thinking she gave away any of the pain of the situation, but Peter Stevenson could sense it in the way she looked away at the ground, touching her cheek against Grace's.

'I lost my father when I was ten,' he told her, his eyes on Sis who was holding hands with Ronny and Davey, larking about with them. 'Changes everything, doesn't it? If he'd lived I'd've stayed on at school, but as things were, it was out to work as soon as possible. Still – could be worse,' he said again. He smiled, and Jess smiled back shyly.

'I'll have to move back and put this one down,' she said, looking at Grace. 'My arm's'll drop off else.'

As she spoke, there was a great yell from Sis. The two lads had been pulling playfully on her arms and Sis had slipped on one of the rounded, slimy stones at the bottom and was now sitting down, laughing and shriek-ing at the same time.

'Oh my – oh flippin' 'ell, it's icy cold! Oh, you little perishers . . .' She struggled to stand up, water pouring from her clothes.

Jess started laughing, but Peter Stevenson said, 'Oh

goodness – let me help you.' And stepped into the stream, wading along without even rolling up his trousers.

Sis was still trying to get to her feet, splashing about almost hysterical with laughter.

'You've still got yer shoes on!' she cackled, pointing at Peter Stevenson, seeming to find this the funniest thing of all. 'Oh my word, look at that – they'll be ruined!'

Peter Stevenson took a couple of strides then looked ruefully down at his feet. 'Oh dear!' he said. 'What an idiot!'

Jess and Grace walked back up the grass with Sis and Peter Stevenson dripping alongside them, all of them unable to stop laughing. Ronny and David, having expected a serious ticking-off, were laughing as much from relief as anything.

Polly looked at them with amused incomprehension as they approached, holding out her arms to take Grace. 'What in the . . .?'

Having all been released into laughter, none of them could seem to stop.

Jess and Peter Stevenson's eyes met as they laughed, each enjoying the other's mirth. As he looked at her pink cheeks and wild, wispy hair, the thought came to him, what a lovely girl she is, that Jess. Somehow sad, but lovely.

Thirty

France, October 1917

The hospital train approached the railhead at a shrieking pace, smoke puffing out into the chill blue sky. As it drew nearer it slowed, with an intermittent screech of brakes, eventually to ease its way alongside the platform with a glide which barely suggested it was moving, and halt with a final swooshing climax of steam.

The orderlies awaiting its arrival were working against the clock, each carrying a clipboard, making their way back and forth along the tightly packed rows of stretchers, several deep, which occupied the length of the platform. The wounded men on the stretchers were covered with grey blankets, only their faces visible, some appearing swaddled like babies and just as helpless. They had been assembled from the Casualty Clearing stations and many were deep in post-operative shock, glassy-eyed, silent. But amid the terse calls of the orderlies and the hiss of the engine, low groans and an occasional cry of pain cut through the cold air.

By and large the orderlies treated the wounded men with gentleness and respect. Just one or two were brusque, unable or unwilling to see into the extent of their shock and incapacity. The embarkation details had to be completed before their patients could be entrained and they were under pressure, so that for the less sensitive of them the prostrate men became a mass of spiritless items with which they had to deal.

'Name?'

A ginger-haired orderly stood over one young man with full lips and cropped wavy hair who was one of those evidently suffering from shock, his face deathly pale. The lad stared up at him with a frozen gaze, straining to make sense of the question.

'Can you tell me your name, chum?'

His licked his lips. 'Jem . . .?'

'Jem? Jem what?'

'No . . . not . . . My name's . . .' He frowned desperately. 'Green. Ned . . . Edward Green. 15th Warwicks. D Company . . .'

'That's a good lad. Now – what's your address?'

After a moment he managed to say, 'Oak Tree Lane, Selly Oak, Birmingham.' His childhood address was the only one that came to him.

'Right. District Three. That's it then. Soon be on your way to Brum, chum.'

The train rumbled along at a more careful pace with its full load en route to Boulogne. The men lay trussed up three layers deep along the sides of the compartment. Ned was on a middle berth. He was aware of what was going on around him only in a dreamlike, distanced way. Nurses moved about the carriage, holding on where they could as they went about their duties to keep from lurching over. One of them, seen sideways on, had a pale, sharp face and when she turned, Ned was convinced in his delirious state that it was his wife. She must have come on the journey to look after him, he thought. Despite everything. He was filled with enormous shame and humility. Who was looking after Ruth, he wondered, and supposed Mary had left her with her mom so that she could be here to look after him,

There was a ghastly smell in the compartment, the suppurating odour of gas gangrene. He heard groans, the sound of retching, a shout here and there. He didn't know how far apart the cries came but they seemed to clang into his brain, unbearably loud, making him moan quietly. The stench seemed to intensify with every mile, even though the nurses, sickened, slid windows open. It mingled itself with the fractured images in Ned's head.

'Gas!' He tugged at the bed covering, trying vainly to find his respirator.

'What is it? Are you in pain?'

Mary's face loomed close, level with his, wearing a nurse's veil. She was so young, so sweet. 'Is it your leg?'

'I'm sorry,' he sobbed. 'I'm sorry, Mary, sorry . . . sorry . . .'

'Sssh.' Accustomed to incomprehensible outbursts of woe, the young woman squeezed his hand, the other going to her nose and mouth at the smell of decompo sition. The gas gangrene case was below him. 'Try and sleep. We'll soon be there.'

During that autumn, John, the oldest son of the Bulli-vants, had come home to Oughton Place after months in hospital. Olive saw him arrive. She was coming up the road with a bag of shopping when the ambulance pulled up and saw them bringing a wheelchair out of the back. The rest she watched from inside, standing a little back from the window, the handles of the bag still cutting into her hand.

Mrs Bullivant stood in the road holding a bundle of clothes in one arm while the other made nervous gestures as if in an attempt to help, but there was nothing she could do. They lifted him out and placed him in the chair. No legs, or at least, two bits of legs which ended mid-thigh and stuck out a little bit over the seat. His trousers were folded up at the bottom and pinned. As they put him down he cried out, and Olive saw the bones of his skull move under his skin. Her hand went to her mouth. Almost more shocking than the legs was the sight of John Bullivant's face which had once been solid, almost bullish, with a thick, black moustache, and was now clean-shaven, cadaverous and twisted with pain.

There was a low step up into the house, and they had to manoeuvre the chair up over it while John clung, obviously petrified, to the arms. They disappeared inside.

Olive went through unsteadily to the back, put her bag down and reached for the kettle, overcome by the pity of it. She found her lips were moving, praying for her own, for Bert, for Sis's Perce, for Ned ... Her bitterness towards him seemed petty, horrible, when his wrongdoing was set against the disfigurement she had just seen. Her heart ached for Mrs Bullivant. Two sons dead, one maimed, how much more was there for her to bear?

It was quiet for the first few days after John arrived home. Mrs Bullivant told Olive he was starting to get used to things at home. Her face was strained and she looked exhausted.

'Mr B's not finding it easy seeing 'im like this, yer know,' she confided. 'John used to be such a big strapping lad.'

'Look, Marion,' Olive said, drawn to her neighbour by her staunchness. 'I'm always 'ere. Anything yer need 'elp with. You know that. I mean if yer wanted to get him out for a bit of air and that – when yer ready. You'd need help shifting the chair out, wouldn't yer?'

'That's good of yer,' Mrs Bullivant said resignedly. 'It's nice to have a good neighbour and I'll let you know when 'e's ready. But 'e's dead set against anyone seeing 'im.'

Not long after, when they were all home having tea, they heard shouting from next door. Polly paused, a spoon halfway to Grace's mouth.

''Ark at that – is that . . .?'

'Well, 'e sounds back to normal any'ow,' Sis remarked. John Bullivant always had been a mouthy so-and-so before the war.

'No,' Jess said. 'Listen.'

It was a man's voice all right, but the way it was raised, the rage and anguish registered in it was that of a small child or a lost soul. None of the words was comprehensible, but the emotion was. Jess had not seen John since he was home, but the sound of his distress, the softer sounds of his mother trying to comfort and quiet him brought tears of pity to her eyes.

'Poor, poor man.'

''E's twenty-four,' was all Olive said.

As the days passed, there were more outbursts next door. Olive thought about how Bert had been when he had left: strong, upstanding, full of physical confidence. So far as she knew he was still full of life, although having suffered bouts of fever. He wrote her short letters full of wry details about Mesopotamia which he summed up as 'flies, beggars and s—t'. The thought of him coming home in the same state as John Bullivant was almost beyond imagining. But then she thought of Mrs Bullivant's other sons. At least John had come home.

She took courage one morning when she knew the younger children would be at school, and went next door and knocked. The step was newly scrubbed and Mrs Bullivant came out calmly to her, but didn't invite her in.

'I wondered if John'd like visiting,' Olive ventured to say. 'You know – stuck in there all the time. Would 'e like a bit of young company? The girls'd sit and chat with him for a bit if 'e'd like?'

Mrs Bullivant began to wring her hands in an agitated way.

'It's nice of yer, Mrs Beeston, but I don't think . . . I mean, I don't think 'e's up to it. 'E's still in a bit of a state, and . . .' Her emotion flooded to the surface, and she was fighting back tears as she spoke. 'I really don't know what I'm going to do with him!'

Trying awkwardly to offer comfort, Olive said,

'Yer going through a bad time, I can see. It's terrible for yer. But 'e'll get adjusted to it by and by, won't 'e? Things'll get better.'

'They will, will they?' Marion Bullivant's eyes blazed with sudden, bitter fury. 'How? You tell me that!'

Thirty-One

Jess was growing more and more worried and despairing. She hadn't heard from Ned for three weeks.

She went over to Iris's every other day now, each time full of hope, only to be greeted by Iris sorrowfully shaking her head. The third Sunday in October, a lowering grey afternoon, she hurried over there, sodden leaves underfoot and a bitter wind in her face, in such suspense that she could barely contain herself as she ran alongside the Workhouse wall, past the factories and into Crabtree Road. There had to be a letter from him this time! Perhaps he'd been too busy. The news was full of the fighting at Ypres. If that was where he was he most probably hadn't had the chance . . . But then if that was where he was . . . Never had there been a gap in their communication this long before. He had to have written by now – had to!

Iris was expecting her, and the door opened almost straight away to let her in. Jess didn't need to speak.

'I'm so sorry, my dear. Still nothing.' Iris looked upset.

'Oh Iris, I can't bear it!'

They went through to the back room where a meagre fire was burning. The coal shortages had become acute and now the cold weather was drawing in it was increasingly hard to get hold of any. Iris, being Iris, dealt with the shortages imposed by the war with equanimity. Her life had long been one of privation. She stood watching Jess with her arms folded.

'I know there's summat wrong!' Jess paced the floor, wringing her hands. She found it impossible to keep still these days, her body full of restless agitation. 'Anything could've happened.'

'Not the worst, necessarily, remember,' Iris reminded her.

'But it could be, Iris. Oh it's so horrible – never knowing, not being able to *do* anything!' Her anxiety and frustration, which she tried to keep in check at home, poured out now.

'In any case, if anything's happened to 'im, I'm going to be the last one to know. They'd send word to his mom and dad, or Mary, but they're never going to tell me. So far as they're concerned I don't even exist.'

She sank into a chair, looking woefully up at Iris, arms wrapped tightly round herself as if to contain her emotion. 'I'm sorry, Iris – my troubles always seem to land on you one way or another.'

'His family really should be the ones to be told in the first place if anything's happened,' Iris pointed out. 'It's only natural.'

'I know. But how am I ever going to find out if I don't hear it from Ned?'

'Well . . .' Iris hesitated. 'I suppose if the worst comes to the worst . . . and God forbid,' she added. 'You'll have to go and ask them.'

'But I can't – they'll never speak to me! They think I'm the *devil* – or worse!'

*

The next day, Jess bought an evening paper as she had all the week before, and scanned frantically through the columns of names.

Sis peered over her shoulder as they walked home, just as anxious not to see Percy's name among the casualties.

'Nothing there,' she said.

Jess closed the *Mail* and tucked it under her arm. 'But I could've missed it. It could've been in earlier.'

The days were torture. Fear and dread seemed to swell inside her like a physical sensation and she found it difficult to get any food down her. Her emotions ran out of control: at home, snapping at everyone, bursting into tears and running upstairs to hide her emotion, and at work she was a bag of nerves, jumping at any sound. While before she was glad of her solitary job so that she could think her own thoughts, now she wished she could be in the filling sheds again among the chatter of the other women to help keep her mind off it. Apart from the breaks, the only people she saw from one end of the day to the other were the two girls next door when she took batches of detonators through for varnishing, and Peter Stevenson when he popped in to check on things, which he seemed to do more often nowadays. She was glad of the interruption. She found his strong, kind presence soothing, and was always aware that while she felt sorrow and dread, he was also grieving and had plenty of problems of his own.

By the time another few days had passed with no news, Jess's nerves were ragged to a point where she was beyond fear of any reaction from other people. Whatever it took, she had to find out if something had happened to Ned.

'I can't live like this,' she said to Polly. They were sitting on Jess's bed, Grace lying kicking behind them. 'It's like Mr Stevenson said to me – not being sure's almost worse than knowing . . .'

Polly looked round at her. Jess's usually rosy cheeks were white and drawn with tension, her eyes dull from exhaustion and lack of sleep. Pitying her, Polly put her arms round her shoulders.

'How much longer's it all going to go on for?' she sighed. 'There's hardly anyone yer meet not grieving, or in a state. I mean, look at 'im—' She jerked her head towards the wall which they shared with the Bullivants. 'I hear 'im nights, sometimes. Crying. Sobbing like a child. Must be the pain. They say it's worse at night.'

Jess shook her head. 'Poor bloke. Auntie says 'e's not been out since 'e come home.'

'I'd go and call . . .' Polly said hesitantly. 'Only his mom said he don't want anyone round.'

'Maybe you should. Leave it a bit though. See if 'e settles in.' Jess wiped her face, sniffing exhaustedly.

'What is there you can do?' Polly asked.

Jess bit her lip, staring at the floor, then roused herself and stood up with sudden purpose. 'I'm going to his mom and dad's. They may hate my guts, but the least they can do is tell me what's happened.'

'What – now? But we haven't had tea!'

'It'll keep. If I don't go straight away I'll lose my nerve.'

Riding the tram out along the Bristol Road, Jess felt calm, resolved. Courage in the face of the hangman, she thought. After all, Ned's mom and dad were only people. What could they do except shout and curse at her? She thought she could manage loathing: her childhood had given her practice at that. And she knew it was no worse than the fear and worry she was living with now.

But climbing down from the tram in the tranquil suburb of Selly Oak, with its genteel High Street, she immediately felt out of place and very frightened. She hadn't even changed out of her work clothes! What a mess she must look. She wanted to get back on another tram straight away and go home. But she just couldn't go back to waiting, dreading, still with no idea where Ned was.

Ned had told her his family lived in Oak Tree Lane, but she didn't know the number. A lady was coming towards her as she turned into the road and passed the Oak Inn. Jess quickly tucked some loose ends of hair under her hat.

'Excuse me – do you live along 'ere?'

'Yes,' she replied pleasantly, and Jess was momentarily reassured. When she asked for the Green family the woman laughed and said,

'It's yer lucky day – I live a few doors up from 'em.' She pointed. 'On the left there – the blue door.'

Once she'd knocked, Jess felt as if her chest had caved in, she was finding it so difficult to breathe. As Mrs Green came round the door she took in a great gulp of air.

She found herself observed, scrutinized in fact, by Ned's mother. She was a little taller than Jess, a gently rounded woman dressed in a soft, brown wool frock with a cream collar and brown leather shoes. Her hair was thick and fastened back into a soft, dignified pleat.

Jess could see immediately where Ned had inherited his clear blue eyes from. Her face had a natural gentleness, and in the seconds that they looked at each other, Jess felt a pang of great sorrow. If she had married Ned, if this woman was her mother-in-law, she sensed instinctively that she would have felt great fondness for her.

'And who are you?' Mrs Green's tone was polite, but already held suspicion, as if she guessed or was beginning to.

Jess saw herself through Mrs Green's eyes: young, unkempt, a stranger on her step, but not one who was nothing to her. She was much more than nothing: she was an object of loathing. She opened her mouth to say her name, finding it as hard as coughing up a chicken bone.

'I'm Jessica Hart – please...' Seeing the hostility provoked by the mention of her name she reached out to put her hand on the door so Mrs Green couldn't shut it on her. 'I know what you must feel about me, but just tell me where 'e is and how 'e is! I ain't heard a thing from him for weeks and I've been nearly out of my mind worrying. Just tell me 'e's alive, Mrs Green, I beg yer...'

The woman folded her arms tightly across her chest and stood back.

'Step inside. I don't want the whole neighbourhood watching.'

Jess walked into the narrow hall. It was covered with brown linoleum and there was a nice, homely smell of cooking, apples and onions mixed.

'He's alive,' Mrs Green said, hoarsely.

'Oh thank God!' Jess put her hands over her face and sobbed, unable to stop herself. For a few moments there was no sound but that of her weeping. Mrs Green watched her.

'Do you have any idea,' she started speaking quietly, but her voice rose until it was shrill with emotion. 'Of the trouble and pain you've caused? To all of us? His family, his wife and child?'

Jess took her hands from her face and looked into Mrs Green's eyes, unable to reply. Whatever answer she gave would be offensive, and the truth, the most honest answer of all was no. No she didn't know. Hadn't wanted to know because she'd believed she loved Ned with all her heart and that had been all that mattered. Guilt, consideration of the consequences to others had been there, had lain constantly between them, but nothing, not even those things had been enough to quell the power of attraction, the passion she felt for him which dictated that they had to be together whatever else.

Mrs Green took a step towards her and Jess cowered.

'My son was married – happily – to a girl he's known most of his life. They made their vows in church. He had a child, a good job. He'd never thought of anything else. Why should he? What more could a mother ask for her son? And then *you* came along. Have yer thought for one second what it's been like for his wife, for Mary, to be deserted with a child to bring up? Have yer?'

Jess hung her head, unable to meet the woman's eyes. 'Yes,' she whispered. 'I have, course I have, but . . .'

'But what?'

There were more footsteps from the back of the house and a man appeared who Jess saw was Ned's father.

'What's all this?'

Mrs Green gestured towards Jess. 'This is – the girl. The one – Jessica. Look, you deal with it. I can't . . .' Hands over her face she went into the front room and Jess heard her weeping.

Faced with Mr Green, Jess could feel the fury emanating from him. He was quite a tall man, though perhaps an inch or two short of his son in height, his hair still mostly brown, though greying round the temples. Jess saw Ned's chiselled features, the generous mouth.

'So you're the one.'

'I know what you think of me. I just want to know he's all right. I hadn't heard . . .'

Mr Green was by nature a mild, gentle man, qualities Ned had inherited from him. But he was outraged at what had happened to his son's marriage. Mary had been a sweet girl as a child and the two had been friends for such a time. The arrangement had felt safe and right. Everything had been well sorted out until Ned went off the rails like a weak fool. How could he admit what had happened, his son running off with some factory bint, deserting his new family and asking for a divorce? As well as this reservoir of anger and disappointment, his emotions were twisted further by the sight of this pretty, distraught girl in front of him. For a second, before he repressed the feeling, he understood his son's desire, his wish for this lovely girl who was crying so passionately for him and he found himself speaking more harshly to her than he ever had to anyone in his life before.

'How can you dare even set foot in my house?' He paced the floor in front of her, trying to steady himself. He fished around in his pocket for his pipe and took

refuge in lighting it. 'After what you've done. You're a
. . . a bloody disgrace!'

Jess almost had the impulse to go down on her knees.
'All I wanted was to know if 'e's alive. I didn't
know . . .'

'Well of *course* you didn't know, yer stupid girl.
You're not family. You're nothing to us!'

'*Please.*' She wrung her hands.

Mr Green held a match in the bowl of his pipe,
puffing at it to get it lit up. The sweet smell of tobacco
curled round the hall.

'He's wounded.' Ned's father spoke as if against his
own will, without looking at her. 'Smashed up thigh – a
shell caught him.'

Jess's hands clawed at the air. More, tell me more.

'I'll tell yer, and then you're to go for good. D'you
understand? And I mean for good.'

She nodded. Anything. Just tell me.

'He's home – in hospital, at least. Things haven't
gone any too smoothly – infection set in. It was touch
and go at one point. He's coming out of it now but for
a time he didn't know us. His mother's been worried to
death. They think it'll be a good few months in hospital
– then home, and who knows. It may all be over by
then.'

Jess was listening with absolute attention, quite still
now.

'He's going to be all right?'

'Depends on how the leg heals. There may be a limp.
But he's going to live, yes.'

'Thank God,' she gasped. 'I thought . . . oh . . .' She
was weeping again, quietly. 'Thank you,' she said softly,
then looked up. 'Where is he?'

305

He jabbed the pipe at her. 'He doesn't need disturbing – what 'e needs is rest and settling back down with his family where he belongs!' Mr Green looked down into the bowl of his pipe, evading her eyes. 'I'm not going to tell you where he is. His wife's going – that's all he needs. You're to keep away. Ned's married. He and Mary can . . . well, this is a chance for them. Patch things up and put the mistakes behind them. He's finished with you. Is that clear?'

He looked across at her with a terrible sternness that made Jess shrink inside.

'I've told you what you want to know. Now, if you've any real consideration for him, for all of us, you'll keep away. You've done enough harm to us all already.' His voice became ever sharper. 'Keep away – you're not wanted. By anyone!'

Thirty-Two

That same night, Peter Stevenson sat staring into the grate in his back sitting room. He had drawn the chair in close to catch the last of the heat from a smouldering log and was hunched forwards, elbows resting on his knees in a sad, sagging posture similar to that in which Jess had once come upon him in his office. Mrs Hughes had long since put David to bed and the house was quiet except for the fire still hissing quietly and the clock on the mantelpiece with its slow, mellow ticking. Either side of it were arranged framed photographs: a small, oval, silver frame held a picture of David as a baby, and the other, a rectangular frame wrought in silver-plated filigree, was a portrait of Sylvia. She had had a soft, reassuring beauty, long fair hair brushed back and fastened elegantly for the photograph. Every so often his gaze moved up to take in that picture. Even now, so many months after her death, he had to stop himself expecting to see her seated opposite him on the chair by the fire, legs comfortably crossed, with sewing or knitting for David in her lap. When he looked at the photograph the day it was taken always came to mind, how she couldn't stop laughing: for some reason the sight of the photographer disappearing under the black hood of the camera tickled her, seeming absurd in some way, and they had to make several attempts. Even in the finished portrait her face had a look of repressed mirth.

Peter Stevenson put his hands over his face and rubbed his eyes. At last he sat back in the chair, crossing one long leg over the other. The eyes of the picture seemed to watch him relentlessly, as if she were seeing into his thoughts, and with a sudden movement he stood up and picked up the frame.

'You know I loved you, Sylvia, don't you? Always . . . I wish I still had you here, God knows I do. There's nothing I wish for more.' For a moment he held the picture over his heart, smoothing the back of it with his hand, then replaced it, turning it away from him towards the wall. He went to the glass door which looked out over the bleak little garden, but in the dark, could see only his own, long reflection, and he pressed his forehead against the window, shocked for a second by the coldness of it.

He had expected grief to go on, undiluted, forever. The extent of his anguish when Sylvia first fell ill, then lay dying and was finally taken from him, leaving him with a motherless child, was so acute that he could not then imagine life without the agony of it inside him. The early mornings were the worst, waking alone, and these silent evenings. Sylvia had liked music, would sing to herself, and the house had felt full of life. The pain of losing her had been his one certainty. It was still present, waves of loss and bereftness building and receding within him. But already he found that other feelings could exist mingled with grief: he could begin to move on without her, and this made him feel guilty and ashamed of his disloyalty. Chiefly these emotions were directed towards Jess Hart. At first he simply noticed her, the way some people in a group stand out while others fade. Her presence drew his eye, her prettiness, her shape. And he liked her, enjoyed the way their brief conversations seemed to fit with each other's, her smile which had become, along with seeing David, the main thing which could brighten the day. She could make him laugh. More lately, she had aroused his tenderness, finally his desire.

He found himself looking for opportunities to talk with her. He wondered now at his decision to put her in the 'Rumbling Shed' as the women called it. At the time it had been nothing whatever to do with being able to see her alone. But had some deeper instinct, riding ahead of his knowledge of his own feelings, prodded him to do it? Whatever the case he was thankful daily that he had placed her there, and found himself looking for excuses to visit the shed.

'Is there bad news?' he had asked her again, cautiously, earlier in the week.

It was clear to everyone that Jess was in a state. Of course, so were a lot of people, but it was her that he particularly noticed. Her expression was tense and she looked pale and drained. He knew there was something – someone – for whom she worried and suffered constantly, yet she would say nothing about him except that he was on the Western Front. He wanted to know who it was that took up her thoughts and feelings, but why should she tell him anything about her private life? He was only her boss, and he must seem like an old man to her!

But when he asked, she turned to him with such a look of desperation in her eyes that he wanted to take her in his arms.

'No – no news at all. That's the thing – I just don't know.' Her eyes, already pink from crying, filled with tears.

'Oh dear,' he said. 'I'm ever so sorry.' He wanted to

add some platitude about no news being good news but it felt the wrong thing to say. 'I hope you have some good news soon.' The words sounded hollow. He turned to leave.

'Mr Stevenson?' She was hurriedly wiping her eyes. 'Is there anything the matter with my work?'

'No!' He sounded too emphatic and corrected himself. 'No – not a bit. Why?'

'I just wondered if you was feeling you had to check up on me.'

He cleared his throat, finding himself reddening a little.

'Not at all, Jess. You've been doing that job more than satisfactorily for a long time now. I – er, just like to keep tabs on things . . .' He knew he was not bound to explain but found himself doing so anyway.

'Oh,' Jess gave him a wan smile which simply jerked at her mouth and didn't alter the rest of her face. 'That's awright then.'

She turned back to the drum, already oblivious to him. He watched her, the sturdy determination of her movements. Finding he had been standing there too long, he hastily moved away.

Staring into the fire he went over what had happened. Had he made a fool of himself? She wouldn't have noticed, he told himself. She was so worried she barely even saw him. But all evening he was full of longing thoughts of her.

Jess walked through the gates of the infirmary, the blackened brick building on the Dudley Road next to the Workhouse and near Iris's house.

She still had a sense of disbelief that she had found

out so quickly where Ned was. When she left his parents' house her emotions were in such turmoil that no single one seemed able to master the others. She had expected the anger and bitterness they felt, but she was taken aback by how much this bruised her, made her feel worthless and rejected.

What did you expect? she ranted at herself on the way home. Considering what you've done they could've been a lot worse! But still she felt winded by it, and tearful. However wrong she and Ned had been in what they'd done, however much they had hurt and betrayed Mary, she had wanted them at least to understand the strength of her feelings for Ned and his for her. That her love was enduring and genuine. But while this seemed so important to her, in their eyes it counted for nothing.

But with the pain of this, there was also her enormous relief after the tension of the last few weeks, and she was full of joy.

She burst in through the door at home, her face alight with the news.

'Ned's alive – 'e's awright! 'E's home!'

Everyone stopped what they were doing immediately.

'Oh Jess!' Sis said. 'Thank God for that!'

Polly smiled bravely at her and Jess saw Olive's face relax. Though she seldom ever mentioned Ned, the war's months of slaughter had softened her attitude. Life was too short to bear grudges. Just getting those lads back alive, that was all that mattered.

'So 'e's out of it?' she asked.

'Yes!' Jess was dancing round the room. 'He's been wounded – one of his legs, they said. He's in hospital.'

'Who said?' Olive frowned.

311

'Mr and Mrs Green.'

'*You went to their 'ouse?*'

Jess's face fell. 'I had to find out, Auntie.'

Olive sank down at the table. 'Well, what did they make of you turning up?'

'They were none too pleased.'

'I'm not surprised! Oh Jess, how could yer've done it?'

'I couldn't stand it. No one'd ever've told me, would they?'

'So where is he then?' Polly said, eyeing Grace, who was walking now, round the room.

Jess shrugged. 'I don't know. Yet.'

At first she almost despaired, realizing the number of hospitals in Birmingham, and especially the additional mansions and private houses which had been converted for nursing the war wounded. She'd have to go round every one and ask. She might never find him!

But luck, in this instance, was on her side. The next evening she went to tell Iris the news. When she described her visit to the Greens, Iris seemed to withdraw from her a little, as if the reality of Ned's situation, of his parents as live flesh and blood people, had impinged on her properly for the first time.

'You must be careful,' she cautioned. Her injured leg was troubling her and she leaned down, massaging it as she spoke. 'You've upset people badly, the two of you, and you must think seriously of what you're going to do next.'

Jess was in no mood for a sermon from Iris.

'But you've always stood by us, up 'til now.'

'I know, dear. I am standing by you, but the facts don't alter. Happiness should never be at other people's expense.'

Jess moved restlessly about the room.

'It's a bit late for that, Iris. Look, I've got to see 'im. I can't think of anything else until I've seen how he is, what he feels. Can't you understand that?'

'Yes. And I know what you've suffered on his behalf . . .' Iris sighed. 'But it's all looking rather a mess.'

'I don't even know where to start – he could be anywhere.'

'Well,' Iris said simply. 'Why not try the nearest? It's a big hospital. There's a good chance he could be there.'

Before going home Jess went into the hospital to enquire and was told that a Corporal Edward Green of Oak Tree Lane, Selly Oak, was indeed in the hospital. Visiting, she was told, was for close relatives only.

'That's awright,' Jess smiled. 'I'm 'is sister.'

So now she stood looking at the brightly lit windows of the infirmary, wondering which of the high rooms contained him. A thrill passed through her. He was here, so close after all this time! She could see him, touch him! She knew there would be very little time, and was terrified of meeting a member of his family, but her determination was absolute. If she had to come every day, waiting for a chance to slip in and see him alone, she would do it. Nothing was going to stop her.

She pulled the belt tighter round her coat. She had on her close-fitting hat with the cream band, and under the coat a purple velvet skirt which she had made, with a white blouse and a little blue waistcoat. She knew she was looking her best, her hair brushed and tied back.

As soon as she was inside the hospital, her excitement faded and was replaced by terror. Her heart was pounding, hands horribly clammy. In these long, echoing corridors there was very little place to hide and she expected any moment to find Mr and Mrs Green walking towards her. But she had to see him . . .

Ned's ward was upstairs. Every bend of the staircase, with people moving up and down, was a source of fear for her. She felt like a criminal about to be arrested at any second. By the time she'd reached the door of the ward she thought her heart was going to give out on her.

The door was open and she stepped in. A nurse near the door seemed to be in position to direct visitors.

'I've come to see Mr Green.' Jess found that she could sound calm. 'Ned Green. I'm his sister.'

The nurse looked confused for a moment. 'Oh – er, I see.'

'Is there anyone here – my mother and father may have beaten me to it?'

'No one's come in yet.' She leaned back and looked along the ward. 'He's alone. He is very tired today though. Still very up and down. Not too long a visit, please.'

'Yes of course,' Jess said. 'I'll just pop over and say 'ello.'

Her heels sounded to her like hammers as she walked along the long Nightingale ward, wishing she was invisible. Some of the lads were sitting up talking quite cheerfully to their visitors. One or two lay quiet, some with one or both arms bandaged. One, who smiled at her, had lost most of his right arm, and was nursing a short, bandaged stump. She found this less shocking than she would have expected, and realized that knowing Iris had accustomed her to such sights. She smiled back as she passed. On some beds there was a frame under the bedclothes holding their weight off the injured legs beneath like a tent, and there was one on Ned's bed when she reached it two-thirds of the way down on the right.

He was propped in a reclining position on his pillows, his eyes closed, head tilted a little to one side. Jess stopped. Seeing him was a shock: she didn't know whether he looked different or the same. She was not used to observing him in a lifeless position like this, unaware that she was there. For a moment she did not want to speak, afraid of what he might say when he saw her. But she longed to move closer, to touch him. And there was no time to delay. She glanced behind her, terrified his family might be bearing down on her, then moved quietly to sit beside him.

'Ned.'

He opened his eyes at once, and she saw his face register who she was. 'Jess . . .' Immediately he tried to push himself up, wincing at the pain he caused himself. To her horror, she saw his eyes fill with tears and his face, at first startled, crease with anguish. Supporting himself on one elbow he covered his face with his other hand, trying to hide his distress from her.

'Oh Ned!' She leaned close, putting her hand on his shoulder, tears running down her own face. She would never have believed she'd see him like this. 'What is it? Oh Ned! Look, my love, I can't stop 'ere long – if your mom and dad were to come . . .'

Hearing what she said he managed to control himself, wiped his face and looked up at her almost as if he was afraid of her.

'Does it hurt?'

'My leg?' He lay back, grimacing for a second. 'Sometimes, now. Didn't at all when it happened. Just

315

like a little knock. And all the way back from France. Not a thing. But now – at night mainly. Oh God, Jess . . .'

'I was so frightened . . .' It was she, now, who couldn't stop crying. 'So frightened for you!' She leaned down and kissed him, stroking his hair, his face. 'I love you so much and now you're safe, back with me.'

He looked back into her eyes with a bewildered, hungry look, as if hanging on every word, needing to hear what she said.

'I saw your mom and dad—'

He started to speak, but she held up her hand.

'It's awright. But they mustn't find me here. Are they coming today?'

'I don't know . . .'

'They said you and Mary are going to start again . . . Is it true, Ned?'

She saw panic in his eyes. 'No, Jess. No! They've not said a thing . . .' He grasped her hand, and to her confusion said with strange intensity, 'You're good – a good, good thing. You are.'

'Tell me you love me, Ned. Please. It's been so long . . .' She felt and sounded plaintive.

He began talking fast, a desperate note in his voice. 'I do. I love you. Oh Jess, I just want to get out of here – away from them all. To come out with yer. You're my love, you are. Let's go somewhere where none of them can find us.' He gripped her hand so tightly that she gasped.

'Are you still feverish?' she felt his forehead. It was overhot, but not extremely so. But she knew he wasn't himself, and could see how ill he'd been, this odd excitement in him. He lay limply now, as if he'd exhausted himself. Jess kept her hand on his forehead.

'Never mind, my love. You'll soon be better. It'll be awright, I promise you.'

'You mustn't come in here again, Jess.' She was terribly hurt by the sudden aggression in his voice. He was becoming agitated again.

'But why . . .?'

'I've told yer – yer mustn't – it'll cause trouble. I've hurt them all enough and I can't face it, not stuck lying 'ere like this. Please – stay away. Wait 'til I'm better and then I'll come to you.'

'But what can they do to me?' She felt burningly defiant.

'Nothing – not to you. I just – I'm a coward, Jess. I don't want it going on in here. Fighting, arguments.'

She understood. He was too weak, too low to have conflict going on around him.

'It's ain't just them, it's Mary . . .'

Jess had a sensation like a cold hand closing round her heart.

'Has she been to see yer?'

'Not yet, but she will. They'll make sure she does. Look, just keep out of it for now – please. Don't make it any worse, Jess.'

She swallowed. There was desperation in his plea. 'Whatever you want, Ned. Whatever'll get you better sooner. As long as I know you love me I can put up with anything.'

Ned looked stricken. 'I *know* yer can . . . oh God.' He was sobbing again, clutching at her.

She held him close, kissing him, pressing her cheeks against his, trying to will all her strength into him. 'I can't stay now, Ned – just remember, I love you. You get better – that's your job. I'll be waiting, however long it takes yer. I promise.'

317

She felt him nod as she kissed him goodbye.

Jess left the hospital with the image of his face in her mind as she left him, pale, but calmer. When she turned back to look, he had already closed his eyes. She was disturbed by the state of him, one moment calm, the next distraught. What in God's name had they done to him over there? But she was so full of resolve now, that she felt unbreakable. If she couldn't see him for a time now, until he was healed, if that was what he needed, she could bear it. Knowing he was safe, away from the trenches, and that he still loved her, those were the main things. For their own good she would keep away until they could be together. She would wait. She had borne so much for him already that this seemed only a small thing.

Later that week, Olive pointed to a few lines in the paper which said that Lance-Corporal Edward C. Green, had been awarded a Military Medal for courage under fire.

'Oh Auntie!' Jess cried. She burned with pride for him. 'See how brave 'e's been – oh ain't that summat special!'

And she could see that, though she tried to hide it, there was also pride in Olive's eyes.

Thirty-Three

December 1917

'When're things ever going to get better?' Sis groaned, eyeing the evening meal Olive was dishing up, which consisted of a thin broth with a few bits of vegetables in stock made from boiled up chicken bones and a bit of bread and cheese. 'We'll be starving hungry again an hour after tea!'

'I was in the line for some stewing beef today,' Olive ladled out the broth, glowering round the table in a way that dared anyone else to complain. 'Stood there over an hour I was, and then they shut up shop and said it'd all gone – and that was with *her* mithering at me the whole flaming time.' She nodded at Grace. 'Half the morning gone, nothing done back 'ere, and it'll all be the same tomorrow. 'Ere – save some of it to go with yer broth!' She rapped Ronny's hand gently with the ladle as he went to cram his share of bread into his mouth.

'Ow, Mom!'

'Eat slower – it'll last yer longer.'

It was a couple of days before Christmas and everyone round the table looked sunk in gloom, exhaustion, or both. The fighting on the Western Front had ground to a halt for the winter months. Everything felt as if it was everlastingly stuck: the grim news, the grief and worry, the sheer drudgery of war seemed set to go on and on.

This evening was pitch black and wet. Jess and Sis had been soaked through by lashing, ice-cold rain as they came home from work, and even after they changed into dry clothes, sat shivering for ages before they felt warm again because there was barely enough fuel to keep a fire going. Now Grace was toddling, Mrs Bullivant had her pram back and it had found a new role as a coal cart for both families so they could at least get some warmth in the house.

But day-to-day living had become even more tiring and gruelling than usual. And everyone had the worry of a loved one on their mind: Sis was fretting about Perce, Olive and the girls worried for Bert, Polly was still grieving and Jess waiting for Ned to be released from hospital, on tenterhooks, longing to know how he was and what was happening. Through an old acquaintance of both Olive and the Greens, Olive had heard that he had been moved out of Dudley Road to a convalescent home in Bromsgrove, which would have been difficult for Jess to get to even had she been allowed. But she was tormented by the thought of Mary being able to see him. It was terrible to be banished, pushed into the background, a dirty secret in a corner of Ned's life. Almost daily she was tempted to go against what he had asked of her, and try to travel over and see him. She didn't even know the address to write to and she had not heard from him. She understood that while he was convalescent and needing help, he was at the mercy of his family, but his weakness frustrated her when she felt so strong. She was caught between jealousy and worry and shame that she was being so selfish when he had fought and suffered. He needed his leg to mend, she told herself, to get his strength back. Then they would face everyone and fight them together. The two of them could overcome anything. And every day she was thankful that he was at least home, alive and safe.

The rain was still pelting down. Jess looked at the clock. Normally Polly would be on her way out by now. It was her night for going to Mrs Black's.

'Not going out tonight, Poll?' Jess asked, wiping the bread round her dish.

'No—' Polly had Grace on her lap and was dipping little bits of bread in her broth, feeding them to Grace on a teaspoon while trying to feed herself and keep her daughter's inquisitive hands from tipping the bowl over. 'One soaking's enough. Hark at it out there! I'll leave it for this week.'

She still clung to her messages from Ernie as one of the few things that kept her going. Jess once asked her whether it might be a good idea to stop, try and put his death behind her for good.

'I can't, Jess,' she said. 'Not yet. It's too much for me on my own. I need him to help me – I know that sounds like nonsense to you, but it's true. It'd be different if we could bring his body home – have a proper burial and a funeral and that. But being out there – I know 'e's gone really, in my heart. But it ain't finished. There's too many of 'em all just to go like that, for good.'

Jess half understood Polly's need, although she'd never gone back to the Blacks' spiritualist sessions with her. The experience of going once had been unsettling enough. Most of it was a trick, she was sure: so obvious to anyone who didn't desperately want to believe it wasn't.

'It gives them comfort,' she told Olive. 'You can feel it. Everyone's so sad, and it makes 'em feel better.

I think it's harmless enough.' But what about what happened when she'd asked to hear from Alice? What if that had been real? It had certainly seemed convincing at the time. She hadn't mentioned the incident to Olive.

Sometimes, usually in the dark of the night, she found herself wondering about Alice, fancying a plea, a cry coming from her, something unfinished that it was her responsibility to act upon.

That's just daft, she'd say to herself when daylight came. Getting the heeby-jeebies in the night! But she knew instinctively that she wanted to know more, as if her grandmother's fate was a key to something in herself. She found nowadays that she could ask Olive more about the family. A dam had been breached and she would try to remember details about Alice, about Louisa. Jess was hungry for the information, was beginning to understand more fully her aunt's contradictory feelings towards her sister: the great protective love for a younger sister, mixed with enormous bitterness and resentment that Louisa had been absent through so much of the grief and trouble they'd endured, that in marrying first, she had escaped it again. Jess was watching her aunt, thinking about these things, when Polly looked up, her chin close to the top of Grace's tufty head.

'I thought I might pop in next door again – a bit later on like. When the younger ones've gone up.'

Olive paused, spoon halfway to her lips. She looked concerned. 'Why don't yer leave it for a bit, Poll? Yer said 'e daint take too kindly to yer going last time.' She was worried about Polly's preoccupation with John Bullivant.

'I hear 'im – the way 'e keeps moaning and carrying

on. It's terrible, Mom. Heartbreaking. No one should 'ave to suffer the way 'e is. 'E was a big strapping bloke before. And she's at 'er wits' end. I know 'e'll most probably tell me to get out. But how's 'e ever going to have any sort of life again if all 'e does is sit there?'

Polly leaned in close to the Bullivants' front door, trying to shelter from the rain. Mrs Bullivant opened it cautiously, unused to visitors at this time of night, and hurried her quickly into the hall out of the wet. She held a lamp in one hand and they stood in its arc of light.

'Anything the matter?' She sounded tense, had guessed why Polly had come. Polly's hands had gone clammy. He's only a man, she told herself. An injured man, that's all. What was there to be so nervous about? But she was frightened: at the same time she felt compelled to be here.

'I just thought I'd pop in and say hello to John again. Wondered if 'e'd like a bit of company? I know it's late, only I'm at work again now.'

'Well, I don't know . . .' Marion Bullivant kept her voice low. ''E's not been too good today.' She worried at her lower lip with her teeth. Polly's heart went out to her.

'I'm ever so sorry.'

'Oh, you've got yer own troubles, Polly. I know that. Look, come in, but I don't know what sort of welcome you'll get.'

Through the back, Mr Bullivant, a dark, stocky man, was asleep in a chair beside the same sort of puny fire that burned in their grate next door. The room was cold, although it had a cosy atmosphere, plates and cups tidy on shelves and the range and little ornaments on the mantelpiece. Close to Mr Bullivant sat Lottie, who was twelve, fiddling with a tangled skein of wool. She looked up at Polly and smiled, but also glanced anxiously across at her brother.

'Awright, Lottie?' Polly greeted her. ''Ello, John.'

There was no reply from John Bullivant, seated in his wheelchair which was pushed up close to the table. The way he was sitting you couldn't see his injury. He just looked like a man reading the paper, elbows on the table, hands making a frame round his face. For a second Polly imagined him getting up, walking across the room, like before.

She pulled up a chair to sit down by him. As she did so she saw him wince as if she had hurt him, or he was afraid she would.

'For Christ's sake watch it!' He bellowed so loudly that Polly jumped. Mr Bullivant stirred, opening his eyes. John's face was contorted with rage and pain.

'I'm sorry,' Polly stood gripping the back of the chair. 'What did I do? Did I hurt yer?'

She knew she hadn't touched him. It was as if pain surrounded him like a magnetic field.

'What do you want?' he said, more quietly, but with such contempt that Polly cringed.

'John—' his father warned.

'I just came to see yer. Thought you might like a bit of company.'

'Come to have another look at the cripple, 'ave yer?' he propelled himself back from the table. 'There yer go then – 'ave a good look.'

'I didn't come to . . .'

'LOOK, I said!' Again, a loud bawl, which sent his

mom and dad into protests that he should stop it and calm down, Polly was trying to be kind.

Polly clung to the back of the chair and did as she was ordered. John sat with his shoulders thrown back in an awkward, helpless posture. Polly thought, you don't see how much the legs do, even sitting down, until they're gone. She looked down, past his strong, barrel chest to the thick stumps, sawn off mid-way between knee and groin. There was nothing repulsive in the sight, barely even shocking. He was covered, dressed. It was unnatural to see, but the full horror of it came when she slowly moved her gaze upwards, over his thin, taut face. He had grown back his moustache, but when their eyes met, she felt herself go cold at the expression in his.

'Now get out.'

'Oh don't, John!' His mother stood over him, her hands squirming round each other. 'Polly's just come out of friendliness – to see if yer'd like a chat.'

'A chat! What in hell's name does she think I've got to chat about? Go on – out. Bugger off out of 'ere!'

'Awright—' Polly shifted towards the door. Her knees had gone weak. 'I'm going . . .'

'I'm sorry,' Mrs Bullivant said in the hall. 'I did warn yer. I just don't know what to do with 'im for the best, that I don't . . .'

'It's awright.' Polly was shaken by the intensity of John Bullivant's self-loathing. 'I s'pose I shouldn't've come.'

'No – I'm sure it's what 'e needs. It's just – well, it's taking a bit longer than we thought . . .' She trailed off, her voice desolate.

'Any news of the others?' Polly asked.

The woman nodded. 'They're awright, for the moment. Look—'

Polly stopped with her hand on the door handle.

''E won't see anyone – pals of his, nothing. Course, most of 'em ain't home anyhow. But the couple that are've given up . . . I hardly dare ask this, but . . .'

'I'll come again,' Polly promised. 'In a while.' She squeezed Marion Bullivant's hand. ''Ave the best Christmas yer can manage, love.'

Thirty-Four

Ned was let out of the convalescent home at the end of February 1918. His leg was healing reasonably well, and the doctor said he should soon be able to progress from walking with a crutch to a stick. Eventually, perhaps barring a very slight limp, he should be back to normal. He didn't say 'fit for duty' but Ned knew that was what he meant.

'You'll be able to come and stop with us, son,' his mother said. She was looking forward to having him there, he could tell. His brother Fred was in France, and she had at least one of her sons where he belonged – at home. She was longing to look after him, fuss round him.

He felt like a stranger in his parents' house, although every inch of it was disconcertingly familiar. He spent the first few days resting, waiting to feel normal, to find himself again. More mobile now, he soon became restless. He couldn't concentrate on anything, and found himself wandering without purpose from room to room, looking at things. There was the table at the back where he had eaten breakfast and tea every day of his childhood. His bedroom – also at the back – overlooked a short strip of garden where his mother grew marigolds and pansies in neat beds, though now she had taken some of them up for vegetables. He saw the same old wooden bedstead, the faded hazelnut brown eiderdown, the little table where he had done his homework with scratches and ink marks and in the top right-hand corner, a hardened patch of glue. His father's chair with the round patch worn thin and oily where his head rested. Things from which he now felt cut off: a past when he had been innocent of both love and war.

'How d'yer feel today?' his mother asked every morning, carrying him up a cup of tea on a little tray. Even the cups and saucers were unnervingly familiar.

'Not too bad,' he'd say. 'Better.'

In truth he felt nothing, or rather could not find the place in himself where feeling should be. But he couldn't say this. It was too strange and difficult to make sense of this state he was in.

In the hospital there had been the other men, the ones who knew the Front, had seen the same sights, the commonplace horror, the things impossible to describe – or perhaps possible if anyone ever asked, which they did not. They avoided the subject as if it was personal and embarrassing. It was too far from them. Back here he was supposed to put it behind him, to forget: he protecting them and they him. Here at home, he reverted to the state of a child, sitting for hours at a time in the back room, watching thin winter sunlight etch the bright, distorted shape of the window on the carpet. His mother brought him food on invalid trays. She would come and sit opposite him with her own dinner balanced on her knee, and he learned, watching her hold her knife and fork, that her knuckles had begun to swell and she told him they ached. She looked much older than when he'd left, her hair steely grey, the white catching the sun from the window. She talked about the neighbours, snippets of amusing or reassuring – never bad – news. In the evening his father came home. Sometimes they went down to the pub together where Ned went through the motions of talking to people, being modest when they called him a hero because of his medal, being cheerful and grateful to be alive. He *was* grateful – of course he was. He was also thankful for their affection but he could barely breathe at home. He knew he had to get away.

The pressure they put on him was gentle at first. It started in the hospital, after the delirious days of fever had passed and he was cooler, weak, but able to talk.

'We thought, in a day or two, Mary could come in and see you,' his mother said.

Ned looked into her face. At that moment he didn't care who came. 'What good will that do?'

'Well – she wants to see you. I don't think they'll let Ruth in here, but all in good time. It'll give you two a chance to have a talk together, won't it?'

'But Mom '

'She wants to see yer.' In a sterner voice she added, 'She's your wife, Ned. Of course she's going to visit yer.'

He had started to cry.

'There, there.' His mother kept patting his arm. 'Oh dear, never mind, love, never mind. Least said soonest mended.' She interpreted his tears as those of remorse. They had decided to act as if Ned's behaviour before he went away had been a few weeks of madness, an aberration so offensive to their respectable social standards that they could ignore it and treat him as if it had never happened. They wanted their son back from years before: a good lad, biddable, settled.

Jess's visit now seemed like a kind of dream. Her lips on his cheek, her face ... One small crack which had opened in him, letting emotion crowd through. But now that too was distant from him. He couldn't seem to rouse any emotion towards any of them.

Mary came dressed sweetly in a sea-blue skirt gathered at the waist, a white blouse with an Eton collar tucked over her navy coat. She was still painfully thin and obviously very tired. Ned saw how much she was coming to look like her mother.

'Hello, Ned.' She tried, uncertainly, to smile as she sat beside him. He realized as he answered, that she was fighting tears, but she won against them, looking down for a moment, controlling herself.

'How are yer – the leg and that?'

'Oh – coming along, you know. I weren't myself for a while I think.' He tried to move the leg and clenched his teeth at the pain which shot through his thigh. 'But they say it'll be awright.'

There was a long silence, before he remembered to say,

'And how're you?'

'We're getting on awright,' she spoke carefully. Everyone seemed in a conspiracy to spare him any feeling, to pretend everything in life was smooth and quietly contented.

'You wouldn't know Ruth now,' she said. 'She's ever so pretty. Got your eyes. I'd've liked to bring 'er in but they don't want children in 'ere. She'll be four before long.'

Ned nodded. 'Yes. I know.' He licked his dry lips.

'Would yer like to see 'er?' There was a tremor in her voice.

'Yes, awright,' he agreed, dismissively. 'Mary?' He looked into her face.

Mary kept her expression calm. 'What is it?'

'I'm sorry.' He knew he should be sorry, that he *was* sorry. He had the memory of sorrow and knew it was for her. 'What I did ... you and Ruth. It was terrible ...'

Tears welled in her eyes again. 'Yes it was.' She pulled out a handkerchief. 'It bloody was, Ned.' She sat waiting for him to say more.

'I don't know—' he hesitated. 'I don't know what else to say to yer.'

She shook her head, wiping her eyes. 'One minute you was there – Ruth's dad, my 'usband. And the next you'd just gone – with *her* ...'

She was really crying now, unable to control it. 'I wanted you to die,' she said bitterly, through her tears. 'For what you'd done to us. I thought if I couldn't have you then neither would she. How *could* you've done it?' She clasped her handkerchief over her mouth for a second. 'Oh – I said I wouldn't ...'

'It's awright – I deserve it,' he said dully. He watched her, trying to enter into the situation. It must be because I love Jess, he thought. I can't pity Mary as much as I should.

In a short time she stood up. 'I'll come again. Let you know 'ow Ruth's getting on. I'll bring a picture of 'er.'

As she left he turned his head away, exhausted, and closed his eyes. As soon as he did so the ward vanished and he was back there, as ever among the dead, standing completely alone, it seemed, heat hammering down on him. The only sound he was aware of was the roar of thousands of flies moving over the scorched waste of No Man's Land.

Mary walked out to catch a tram on the Dudley Road, back to her mother's house where she had lived with Ruth for the past three years. As Ned's wife she had received her share of his army pay, but it had made no sense to rent two houses next door to each other and she could barely afford it anyway.

When Ned left she had felt disbelief for a long time, then anger and jealousy. If she thought back now to that time, to what she had suffered, she could still get herself worked up into an almost hysterical state of bitter fury. But after three years of bringing up Ruth on her own, yet being also back in the position of child in her mother's house, her emotions now included a shrewdness towards the practicalities of life.

I don't want to spend the rest of my days like this, she thought. I've got the worst of all worlds. I want a house of my own and a husband. She knew that Ned's mom and dad had always been on her side when he left, and when he came home, injured, it was they who told her of it and suggested she should be beside him in his weak state to tell him how his little daughter missed him.

'Take it slowly,' Mrs Green said. ''E's been ever so poorly since 'e's been in hospital. But if you're prepared to make a fresh start with him, now's yer chance. Be gentle with 'im and I reckon you'll soon win him back.'

I was gentle enough, she thought. Gentle as I could be, when I think of some of the things I might've said to him! And I'll be back, so he'll have to get used to me. Seeing him lying there helpless, she knew she could still feel for him, despite the hurt he had inflicted on her. He's still mine – my husband, the only one I'm likely to get now. I want him back and I'm going to see I get him!

Every week throughout the winter, Mary travelled out to visit him in the convalescent home. She brought in photographs of Ruth, with her hair waving round her mischievous little face. He smiled when he saw them, a little uncertainly, but when she said,

'She's a lovely little thing,' Ned agreed, yes she was. She talked lightly to him, getting him used to her being there, herself getting used to him again, told him about what Ruth had been doing, things she'd got up to as a baby, and as an older child, toddling around. She told him news of her mom, the family, as if he was still part of it, and he seemed to listen with interest, pleasure sometimes. She was, she thought, being as saintly and patient as it was possible to be, in the circumstances. She knew Jess had been to see his family, had been told to keep away. So she, Mary, was the one with a chance. He would come to his senses and come back to her.

As the weeks passed though, she began to get impatient. It would take time, she knew, but as 1917 turned into 1918 and she was still visiting Ned in the convalescent home, nothing seemed to change. He smiled when he saw her, listened to her, talked a little about his injury, the ward routine, all little everyday things. But never did he show the emotions she'd hoped for, the remorse, the begging her for forgiveness and asking for her to have him back. And she was afraid to ask, for fear of his reply. She was in fear of him, a little, for all that he was wrong, because he had the power to hurt her so badly. At least though, she thought, he's not turning me away. He's used to me being around.

Soon after he came out of the home and was at his parents' she went to see him. She found him sitting bent over the table in the back sitting room, writing. He looked different. He had been to the barber's and his hair, which had grown in hospital, was now cropped short again. Startled, she realized it was the first time she had seen him fully dressed since his return and suddenly felt intimidated. Before, sitting there in pyjamas, he had been defenceless like a child. She'd stood over him and been able to pity him. Now he was fully a man again: tall, stronger, a soldier, the man who, in spite of his dutiful nature, had felt such overwhelming desire for another woman that he had left her, his wife.

He turned as she came in and she saw him swiftly close the pad of paper he was writing on and arrange a smile for her on his face.

'So – yer out,' she said, stupidly. She felt gawky and awkward, like a young girl asking to be wooed.

'Yes.'

'That's – well – it's good, ain't it?'

His hand was spread on the writing pad as if he was afraid of her looking into it.

'I've brought someone to see yer,' Mary said softly. She stepped out into the hall where Mrs Green was holding Ruth's hand. She was squatting down with her finger pressed to her lips and Ruth was copying her game of being quiet, keeping her presence there a surprise.

Ned's mom led the little girl into the room.

'Now, love – this big man here is *my* little boy – yes, he is! And you won't remember him because he's been

334

away fighting in the war. But this is your Daddy, Ruth.' Eyes on Ned's face, she led the child over. 'Come and say hello to Daddy.'

Ruth came over to him, led by Mary, one finger in her mouth, walking with a child's shy, dragging steps until she was right up close. She was a leggy child with wide grey eyes and thick, wavy hair cut level with her chin. Ned thought of the night she was born, remembered that he had had strong, protective feelings towards her and Mary and he tried to summon them up in himself now.

He told himself he should smile at her, and commanded the muscles of his face to bend for him. The smile was achieved and now he knew everyone was waiting for him to speak. Ruth was standing, wide-eyed, at his knee.

'Hello, Ruth.' She rocked slightly from side to side, body half-rotating, feet planted firmly, plucking at the back of her skirt with the other hand

She removed the finger and said, ''Ullo.'

Suddenly he could no longer stand the child's stare, the naked enquiry in her eyes. Unlike the others she was not careful with him, not in a conspiracy to keep him calm. She gazed right into him, looking for a father, wanting to know from him the meaning of 'father'.

Ned put his hands over his face. 'Please. I can't. Take her away.'

He heard her being taken out of the room, pacifying promises of cake and 'never minds' and 'Daddy hasn't been very well – you'll see him another time when he's better . . .' His hands were trembling. When he moved them away from his face his fingertips were moist from the cold perspiration on his forehead.

He pulled his chair close to the table again and with desperate haste opened the writing pad. With fast, hard strokes of the pencil he finished the note.

Dear Jess—
    I'm out of hospital and at home. I've got to see you – please. Can you meet me Sunday p.m. – at Iris's? No – I'll wait in town, by Nelson's statue, from 2 p.m. Please come – please.
    Ned

Before they could come out of the kitchen he limped quickly to the hall, pushing the note into an envelope. The door slammed behind him.

'I'm ever so sorry, Mary,' Mrs Green was distressed at the scene she'd just witnessed. She stroked Ruth's hair as the child sipped a cup of milk. ''E's just not 'imself. I thought 'e'd be over it by now.'

Mary dried her tears. 'I dunno what 'appened to 'im over there,' she said. ''E's like a different person. But I've waited this long, Mrs Green. I want him back and I know he can be a good father to Ruth – like the Ned I used to know. I'll stand by 'im. After all *she* soon vanished out of sight as soon as there was any trouble, daint she? 'E's got no one else now – 'e's got to come back to me.'

Thirty-Five

That Friday, Peter Stevenson woke to hear a bird singing outside his window. There were only a few days of February left and that morning felt light and springlike. Sunshine came strained through the thick weave of the curtains. It was early and the house was quiet, David not yet awake. He closed his eyes again, still half inside a dream, a pleasing one, though he couldn't remember it now, its images flickering elusively in his head. He turned on his side and out of old habit stretched out his arm to the left to embrace Sylvia, hard with desire for her. The cold of the empty bed shocked his hand. Sleep tricked him so often. Waking alone, no warm female body beside him, still gave him moments as raw and terrible as in the early days after her death. He brought his outstretched hand up and laid it over his eyes, letting out a low groan.

By the time he had eaten breakfast and Mrs Hughes was there, bustling round David, insisting he ate all his boiled egg because her chicken had laid it especially for him, Peter felt better. Light was pouring in dust-laden bars through the window and his early morning phantoms receded. But there was still the thought of Sunday, long and empty before him. Often he and David went to see his mother, but today, somehow he couldn't stand the thought. He longed for other company, something difficult to achieve for a rather reserved man so

337

busy working long hours, and with a young son to care for. But today the need of it was on him like an itch.

'Tell you what, Davey—' He was excited suddenly. 'How would you like to see Ronny again? D'you remember – the little lad you played with on the picnic, in the stream?'

David smiled slowly, and nodded.

'I'll see if he'd like to come out with us on Sunday – how about that? Just for a play in the park. That'd be a change, wouldn't it?'

Cycling to work, the idea grew in him. He could ask all of them if necessary – Sis, Polly, Grace. So long as Jess could come. He'd be grateful for the others being there. He knew she was spoken for, and nowadays he felt nervous in her company, afraid his own feelings towards her were obvious, that he would make a fool of himself. He hoped the difference in their age would stop anyone suspecting how he felt. She could bring a whole crowd if she liked – so long as she was there and he could see her and be near to her. He found himself whistling as he came closer to the works. She'd be on her way too – he was moved by the thought of Jess and himself travelling towards the same spot.

'Silly fool,' he said to himself, wheeling his cycle round to its spot by the wall. But the very thought of her made him happier.

As he turned to go and start work he saw Jess and Sis turning in through the gate and his heart began to thud rapidly. Her expression caught his eye, because she was laughing, looking pink and radiant. She always stood out among the other women, not just in his enamoured eyes, but because it was a long time since she had worked in the filling sheds and her skin had returned to its natural, healthier colour. And today she

338

was all smiles. She leaned towards Sis and another of the girls and said something and they all laughed.

He didn't speak to her until later, enjoying the anticipation of seeing her, but all morning the thought of asking her made his stomach flutter with nerves, however much he told himself he was being ridiculous. Eventually he told himself, casually, it was time to have a look in the Rumbling Shed, see everything was working as it should be . . .

He found Jess filling the drum with fresh sawdust and humming to herself. She didn't notice him for a moment and he stood watching her profile, the upturned mouth, pink cheeks. She looked animated, happy, even working here on her own. Her expression was no longer drawn and tense as it had been over the past months. She seemed to glow.

Something's happened, he saw, and had a sudden cold sense of foreboding. Whatever he felt for her, however much tenderness, however much he would do anything for her, he saw in that moment that it was hopeless. Her mind, her whole being was centred elsewhere. He was invisible to her.

Somehow this enabled him to speak to her more calmly.

'Er – Jess?' She turned, smiling.

'I just wondered if you and the girls – your cousins – would fancy a walk out on Sunday. My David's a bit short of pals and he and little Ronny got on so well – I wondered if you'd all . . .?'

'Sunday?' Her forehead wrinkled for a second, then a smile of vivid joy spread across her face. 'Oh no – not Sunday. Sunday's busy. Sorry . . .' She spoke abstractedly and he sensed enormous excitement pent up in her. 'Maybe another week?'

'Yes, course,' he said with overdone cheerfulness. 'It doesn't have to be this week – any time'd do.'

Jess could barely contain herself on Sunday. She didn't give the others a chance to ask where she was going, though she knew Polly would guess. Once dinner was over she tore along the road into town, setting off far too early, but unable to sit still any longer. Ever since Ned's note had arrived – at Olive's house this time – she'd moved round in a cloud of happiness and anticipation. He was out – free! He was asking – begging, almost, to see her. He'd written 'please' twice at the end of the letter. She was moved by the urgency of this. Her body quivered with excitement and longing for him.

The Bull Ring, usually teeming and loud with the raucous shouts from the market stalls, was a peaceful place to meet on a Sunday, when instead, it became a place for people to go to church at St Martin's, its spire a landmark at the lower end of the street. The statue of Nelson was a little further up and usually attracted hawkers and street musicians trying to earn a few pennies, and was a meeting place for lovers and friends. Today though it was deserted, except for an old man, asleep with his mouth open, leaning against the railings.

Jess waited. Pigeons toddled round her, some making half-hearted attempts to take off and fly. Mostly they just stalked aimlessly back and forth across the filthy cobbles pecking at odd leftovers of food on the ground. Jess looked up at the church clock. A quarter to two. Despite the plea in the letter she was so afraid he wouldn't come.

*

Limping, with his stick, up Spiceal Street, Ned saw her before she caught sight of him. She was dressed much as she had been that time she came to the hospital: black coat, a glimpse of her rich purple skirt showing where it fell open at the bottom, white blouse at the neck. Her neat little felt hat. He stopped. She was looking down at her feet. He willed her not to look up for a moment, to give him time to locate his feelings, to gather himself. Again there came the sense of utter familiarity, her wide, pretty face, the shape of her, her way of standing. How lovely she was! She was the one, if anyone, who could restore him, bring him properly back to life.

Help me, was his silent plea to her. Please help me.

And then she saw him, moving slowly towards her, supporting himself with a stick, dressed in the blue uniform issued to soldiers recovering from wounds, with a coat over the top. His eyes were fixed on her and she walked forward a couple of paces, her breath catching, unsure for a moment. Then she saw the corners of his mouth turn up.

'Ned! Oh Ned!'

She ran down to him, her arms held wide to embrace him. He dropped the stick, his arms came round her and she was laughing, crying, nuzzling against him, so starved was she of the feel and smell of him.

'Oh Ned, at last – at last!' She turned up her face towards him and closed her eyes as his lips met hers, the moment she had waited for all these months, years. They stood locked together.

But she was eager to talk, beaming up into his face. 'You're here – oh God, you're really here!'

She saw him smiling back at her, as she drank in the

sight of him, his face, thinner now, the thick, wavy hair, the eyes that she so loved looking down into hers, flecked pebble-grey in the sunlight.

'It's so good to be out of that hospital, and out of 'ome too for that matter.' He bent to pick up his stick, then took her arm. She was relieved to hear that he sounded more normal, more like the old Ned.

'How's yer leg now?'

'Pretty good.' They made their way slowly up the road, no particular destination in mind. The light was hard and bright, casting sharp shadows. 'I reckon it'll be just about back to strength before long.'

She looked up at him sharply. 'You mean . . .? They ain't going to send you back, are they?'

'Dunno. S'pect so.'

She tried not to feel deflated, chilled inside by the offhand way he said it. So much time has passed, she told herself. I don't know what it's been like for him out there. It takes time to get used to someone again. She squeezed his arm, smiling up at him.

'Saw about your medal – in the paper. Ooh, we was ever so proud of yer! "Courage under fire." So – does it feel nice to be a hero?'

'No!' He spoke more harshly than he intended. As he did so, an image of his friend Jem, the dead Jem, sitting beside him in that trench with a bullet hole in his head, flashed through his mind. He closed his eyes for a second. 'No,' he said more quietly. 'It weren't like that, Jess.'

This conversation seemed to be turning into a quicksand. She struggled to say the right thing. 'I'm sure you were brave though.'

'No,' he insisted. 'There ain't no heroes and there

ain't no cowards. Yer a coward one day, a hero the next and yer never know yerself which it's to be. I just didn't notice I'd been hit.'

She was silent for a moment. 'I've missed you so much,' she appealed to him.

Ned stopped. They were at the bottom of New Street.

'I'm sorry, Jess. I didn't mean to be short with yer.'

Ignoring passers-by, he pulled her to him and kissed her hard on the mouth, and Jess responded, full of relief and desire for him. Her young body came alive at the feel of him close to her. She ran her hands up and down his back. Then he released her.

They strolled round town arm in arm, talking of this and that, unsure where to begin.

'It's a long time since I've been in 'ere,' he said. 'Bit of a mess, ain't it? Any bombs come down here?'

'No. They bombed a few times but they missed – kept dropping 'em out in the fields.'

By the cathedral they sat on a bench with their coats pulled tight round them and Ned's arm round her. Small clouds moved across the sun. Jess did most of the talking, told him about how things had been at home since Ernie was killed, and about Alice, about how upset Olive had been.

'She's forgiven you, yer know.' She turned to face him. 'Give 'er a bit of time and she'll be back to letting yer come round again.'

'That's good of 'er,' Ned said, but his voice sounded flat. There was silence for a moment.

'Has Mary been coming to see yer?'

Ned sighed. 'Yes.'

'She still want you back?'

'Seems that way.' There was a pause. 'I didn't think she'd – well, after all this time . . . forgive me like she has.'

Jess froze. She forced the words out. 'Are you going back to her?'

Ned pulled her close to him with a fierce, hard movement. '*No!* No, of course I'm not. Christ, look I ain't got no words – just come 'ere . . .'

Again he kissed her so hard she was gasping, his arms almost crushing her. She tried to pull away.

'Ned, you're hurting . . .'

'Sorry.' He relaxed his grip. His intensity, his need of her, filled her with desire.

'I began to think I'd never feel like this again,' she pressed herself close to him. 'I needed you to come home and wake me up!'

His lips moved close to her ear. 'God, Jess, it's more than waking up I need.'

She went weak at the urgency in his voice. 'Iris'll let us go to hers—' Their eyes met. 'We can't just turn up today. I'll have to ask 'er . . . Next week.'

He closed his eyes. He wanted her now, here on this bench, as if it would sort everything out.

'Seven days is too long.'

'I know.' Jess laughed. 'But it'll come round.'

Thirty-Six

When Peter Stevenson asked Jess again that week whether she and her family would like to meet him, she tried to drag her thoughts away from Ned and take a little more notice. This time he came in late in the day, just as she was in the outer room of the Rumbling Shed, unbuttoning her overall. The other two women always left in a great rush and he had waited until they'd gone.

Jess hung her overall on the peg. Peter Stevenson felt ludicrously bashful just asking if she and her family wanted to take their children to the park, but this was not evident to Jess. To her he seemed calm and dignified.

At the thought of Sunday Jess felt a blush spread right through her and wondered if Mr Stevenson had noticed.

'Oh dear, I'm sorry – this Sunday's not much good either.' She pulled off her mob cap, releasing her hair down her back. Peter Stevenson watched, longing to step forward and take her head, with the long, soft hair, between his hands and turn her face up to him to be kissed. Emotion twisted in him, an actual physical pang. She was so lovely, and she didn't even see him: had no idea how he felt.

'You having a busy time then at the moment?' he asked carefully.

Jess put her head on one side. 'To tell you the truth, Mr Stevenson, I've got my . . . my friend home from the

Front. He was wounded before Christmas and 'e's just out of hospital. Sunday afternoon's the only time we've got.'

'Oh I see,' he said brightly. 'Well of course you're busy then. That's nice for you – you should've said, then I wouldn't't've kept pestering you.'

Jess frowned, puzzled. 'But you ain't. And it'd be nice to take the lads out. Ronny and David got on like a house on fire, daint they? Tell you what.' She shouldered her coat on, pulling her hair out over it at the back. 'As soon as there's a free Sunday I'll tell yer. When it gets warmer, we could have another picnic or summat like that? I enjoyed the last one ever such a lot.'

'Yes, me too.' He hesitated, bathed in her smile. 'To tell you the truth, Jess, Sunday hangs very heavily for us now. David misses his mother. It's good to have some company.'

Jess saw suddenly how thoughtless she'd been, how lacking in imagination. Mr Stevenson looked so sad and dejected sometimes, and he was such a nice, kind man. She wanted to cheer him up. But nothing could stop her seeing Ned this Sunday, and any other Sunday she could.

'I'll talk to Sis and Polly,' she said. 'And we'll plan an outing as soon as we can, shall we?'

Peter Stevenson smiled. 'It'd be a treat.'

Iris gave her a surprisingly disapproving look when she went one evening and asked if she and Ned could come and be together in her front room on Sunday as they had used to do when he had leave.

'Well you did say we could,' Jess protested. 'Like before.'

'Yes – yes I did.' Iris clumped along the hall and flung the door of the room open. 'You do what you like – light a fire if you can find anything to light it with. Nothing to do with me.' She stood back leaning on her crutch and sniffed. 'I think my morals have slipped.'

'Iris—' Jess tried to appease her. Miss Davitt's been on at her about us coming here, she thought. 'We're not here to plan a bank robbery. We just want somewhere we can be on our own for a bit.'

'Well, as long as you both know how to behave . . . I shall probably go out to see Beatt. As for her—' She rolled her eyes up in the direction of Hilda the stodgy clerk's room. 'You won't have any trouble. You'd barely know the woman's alive.'

Jess tutted at Iris's contrariness and looked round the room. It was bleaker even than she remembered, but she and Ned had made do there before, barely noticing their surroundings in their hunger for each other. But now she felt more effort was needed. The floor was bare boards except for a little woven rug by the grate and the only furniture was two upright chairs and a worm-ridden chest of drawers in the corner. The window was shrouded by an old net and there was also a pair of limp curtains which had once been pink but were now almost grey.

I'll have to do better than this, she thought. This has got to be as cosy and nice as I can possibly make it.

That Sunday morning, Ned agreed to go to church with his mom and dad. His father was a sidesman and Ned had grown up well known by the regular congregation. Still dressed in his convalescent's uniform, he hobbled into the familiar building, taking in the smell of the place, a mixture of polish and old books and stone which had stood, unaired, for many years. His father, after he had shown people to their seats, sat at the end of the pew dressed in his Sunday suit and well-polished shoes, the green and gold collection pouches on the seat beside him. Ned sat between him and his mother. He felt like a child sitting between his mom and dad, but this time the feeling was welcome, as if all responsibility was taken from him, no decisions or commitments expected.

As they sang the first hymn: 'Oh for a faith that will not shrink, though press'd by many a foe', he felt his mother glancing anxiously at him. Her worry and concern had increased since he had come home. She had thought he would immediately be restored after so long in hospital, but he was withdrawn, silent. Perhaps it was only to be expected. It was his reaction to seeing his daughter which had really distressed her. She had thought at first that he was going to break down, but he had simply gone quiet again. Mary had brought the little girl a number of times since and the first time Ruth screamed and said she didn't want to see 'Daddy' – she didn't like him. But on these occasions he had been calmer, if not animated. He had talked to her, shown her a little wooden puzzle, tried to befriend her. Mrs Green and Mary had given each other nervous looks of relief.

'It'll take time, son,' Mrs Green said to him afterwards. 'It's hard for her as well, the little lass. Growing up without yer. Not that that's your fault,' she added quickly. 'That's the war, done that.'

Ned could see their pain, their anxiety: his mother's worn face and her constant fussing, his father's attempts to have conversations with him, heart-rending in their awkwardness. He asked about France, but in such a sidelong way that Ned deduced from it that he didn't want to know.

'I s'pose you got through the winter all right there? They looked after you?' Such questioning demanded the reassuring answer 'yes'.

'They gave us leather jerkins,' Ned told him. 'And goatskin jackets.' He could not tell him how impossible it was ever to get warm day after day on an inactive part of the front where the ground was either stone-hard with frost and snow or thigh deep in water, and any careless raising of your head too high could result in your being shot.

But he recognized his parents' agitation, their need to see things put to rights, for him to be well and back with his wife and daughter. He heard barely a word of the service, thinking of these things.

Afterwards, he was greeted like the conquering hero by the parish. A soldier, wounded, with a medal: he was their pride and joy. He smiled and shook hands. By their questions he saw that none of these people had any idea that he was the object of shame and trouble who had deserted his wife and child. Of course, his mom and dad had kept it to themselves. Partly the shame, partly because they believed it would not last, that he would come back to Mary and things would be smoothed over. To everyone else, things were as they had been before.

The church warden, a jolly, elderly man with a red face, pumped his hand up and down.

'Very good to see you, Ned. I hope when all this is over you and your wife'll move over closer to home again. We've missed seeing you – and the child.'

Ned nodded and smiled, murmuring, 'We'll have to see.'

Deeply ashamed, and desperate to escape, he edged to the door.

As they finished dinner later on, his mother said, 'I thought we'd go and see Auntie Joan this afternoon.'

'Oh – I can't,' Ned said. 'I'm off out.'

'Are you. Where?'

'Just – out.'

He knew they wouldn't ask. He saw the way they exchanged worried glances, and a great weariness came over him. He stood up and forced a smile. 'See you later.'

Jess spent the morning at Iris's getting ready for his arrival, dressed in her old work clothes, a black skirt worn so threadbare that it was grey, and a scarf tied in her hair to keep the dust out of it. Her best clothes lay folded on a chair ready to change into later.

First of all she swept the front room out and dusted it. During the week, on her way home from work, she had bought a couple of bundles of kindling from a half-starved looking boy. They were obviously chopped up bits of orange boxes, but beggars couldn't be choosers. She'd managed to scrounge a few small pebbles of coal and wrapped them in a newspaper which she used when she arrived, to twist into fire lighters. She swept out the grate and laid a meagre little fire.

With her she had also brought Louisa's quilt and another blanket and she laid them on the floor, the colourful quilt on top. She took two candles and brass candlesticks from her bag and stood them on the mantelpiece. She'd also brought a twist of paper with some tea in it, and a bag of buns – one extra for Iris.

As she worked on the room she hummed to herself, imagining, as she used to do before, that this was her own house and she and Ned were soon going to live together and make it their home. Soon, she thought, please God. If only the war would end, we can all get sorted out and start our lives over again, together, where we're meant to be.

She stood by the window for a while to get her breath back, hugging her arms across her chest, looking out at the pale blue sky. She pretended to herself that she was already married and was waiting for Ned to come home from work, his dinner in the oven. That's all I want, she thought. Husband, babbies, just normal. Bring 'em up right. Family life, not like my childhood. Excitement bubbled in her, her pulse racing. Soon he'd be coming along that road, she'd see him, the tall, wondrous shape of him, be able to touch him, lie beside him . . .

'Come on,' she said to herself. 'Daydreaming all morning ain't going to get the babby bathed.' She went to fill a bucket of water and wipe down the windows, singing 'Keep the Home Fires Burning' at the top of her voice.

Jess waited. An age seemed to pass. He's got a long way to come, and there's not a lot of trams on a Sunday, she said to herself, trying to contain her impatience. She'd waited so long to be reunited with him that these last minutes, once Iris had taken herself off across the road, were suddenly unbearable. She kept going to the window to look down the street, which remained sunlit but stubbornly empty.

She was becoming desperate when at last she saw him and ran to open the door. There he was on the doorstep, tall, handsome, here at last. Her first impulse was to throw her arms round him but she cautioned herself to be careful, and she stood aside to let him in. Once the door was closed they stood in each other's arms.

'So—' he said eventually, looking about him. 'Back 'ere again.' Their eyes met for a second, each remembering other afternoons here, and the night he had come to her in the snow and they had lain upstairs, clinging to one another. 'Not changed much, has it?'

'Not at all, I shouldn't think,' she laughed.

For a few seconds they were at a loss.

'Come on in – to our room.' Jess opened the door. The colours of the quilt seemed to leap out at them in the bare room. 'I can light a fire, but it won't last long, so I thought we'd save it.'

Ned nodded, looking round the room.

'What's up?'

'Oh – nothing much. It's only that it's still a bit hard for me to sit – on the floor like. I can lie down, or sit on a chair. I don't think I could manage sitting down there though, that's all.'

'There're chairs—' she pulled one out from behind the door, wanting everything to be right for him. 'Look – shall we see if we can breathe enough life into the range for a cuppa tea?'

Ned nodded. 'That'd be nice.'

He followed her out to the kitchen, his presence seeming to burn through her back. He felt so distant from her. They needed time to get back to where they were again. She longed just to hold him, to lie with him and get back to the closeness they'd had.

They talked a little as she made the tea, the sort of polite, careful conversation she might have had with anyone.

'Where's Iris?' he asked.

'Over at Beatt's.' She decided not to mention that Iris had turned a bit sniffy about the two of them being there. Before she would have told him and they'd have laughed about it, but the situation felt delicate enough already.

'How're things at home?' she asked.

'Oh – awright.' He was staring out through the back window. 'Mom's carrying on as if I'm made of bone china. With Fred out there an' all she's always worrying. I'll be glad to get out though. Gets a bit much after a while.'

Jess tipped some of her precious tea into the pot. She looked at Ned's pale profile by the window, the face she loved so much. She longed to know what he was thinking. There were so many questions buzzing in her head that she was afraid to ask. Where did he want to get out to? Had Mary been, and how often? Were they all trying to force him back to her, and if so, what chance did she stand in the face of all of them? And how did he feel – did he love her as she so desperately, devotedly loved him, so that he was all of her life? Tell me, tell me! her thoughts screamed, so that for a moment she felt choked by panic. She fought to speak calmly.

'Must be nice for 'er though – being able to look after you.'

There was a long silence as she brewed the tea, that

353

neither of them seemed able to break, and the tension grew until the very air between them seemed brittle with it. Jess fiddled with spoons, cups and saucers and poured the pale tea. He still stood at the window, hands in his pockets.

'Ned?' She held a cup and saucer out to him, but the tone of her voice asked him so much more.

As he took the cup and saucer from her his hands were trembling so much that he couldn't hide it. He had to put them down. He stood by the table, pressing his palms against his thighs to try and control the tremor.

'Ned – love?' She stooped to look into his face. 'What is it?'

He shook his head, unable to find words for the confusion inside him.

'I so want to make things better,' she said. 'I want to be close to you.' She took one of his arms and firmly helped him stand upright. He couldn't look into her eyes. He was breathing hard, in panic, distress.

'Love, oh my love – don't! There's nothing to worry about.' Overwhelmed with feeling she pulled him to her, felt his trembling. Into his chest she said, 'Let me love you . . .'

She looked up at him, needing reassurance herself, needing him to desire her. 'I'm bad, I know. But I want yer so much – all this time I've waited and I love you more than anyone, anything . . .'

He seemed to relax, and smiled properly for the first time, gently kissing the tip of her nose. 'I like your badness. Oh Jess, you're what I need.'

'Come with me.'

She led him into their front room and closed the door. As he stood watching she knelt by the grate to light the knotted twists of newspaper. The flames bit into them and soon they could smell smoke. She turned, and saw how intently he was watching her, his eyes moving over her.

'That'll help – for a little, anyhow.' She drew the curtains, then sat on the quilt, her legs stretched out, hair falling over one shoulder. 'Can you get down 'ere with me?'

He managed it, slowly. Once he was comfortable he reached out for her. 'You're so lovely.' His voice held a desperate mixture of longing and regret.

They bunched up the edges of the quilt and blanket to rest their heads on. Ned eased himself down beside her, settling on his back, where he was most comfortable. It was only after a moment that he realized his body was so tense that he was holding his arms and legs almost rigid, and he tried to relax and let them sink closer to the floor.

'You awright?' she moved her hand across his chest.

'Yes – just stiff.'

Jess leaned up on her elbows beside him and looked down into his face. She reached round and pulled the ribbon from her hair and it fell in long, thick waves over her shoulders. Teasing, she took an end of it and tickled his nose.

He shook her off, still taking deep breaths, trying to calm himself out of a sense of panic that he didn't even understand. He looked into her face, seeing the love in her dark eyes, a tiny freckle on her left cheekbone, her soft, radiant skin. She leaned down and kissed his lips and her hair hung over him, further darkening the room.

'I love you,' she said, her face close to his.

'I love you too.' He searched inside himself for the meaning of the words.

'You lie still,' Jess said. 'And I'll make it better.' She

knelt up and simply took charge of him. Stroking, circling her hands, she moved over his body – his shoulders, his neck, arms, smoothing and kneading with her palms over his clothes, stopping often to turn and kiss his face. She felt him watching her, submitting to her, waiting. When she reached his injured leg she softened her caress to a light, fluttering stroke. She confined her touch to parts of his body which showed she was not impatient to arouse him. She simply loved him with her hands, her face intent. At first he felt foolish, passive. Then, under the warmth of her hands, sensations flooded through him.

She heard his breathing change and smiled into his eyes.

'Oh God, Jess,' he whispered.

Seeing the longing in his face, Jess unbuttoned her blouse and took it off, then her vest, with neat, graceful movements. Her skin was naturally slightly sallow across her shoulders and down her outer arms, but her breasts were very white, the nipples pink.

Clumsily, he pulled off his clothes, then reached out to touch her, heard her gasp as his flesh met hers. She clung to him, laughing, lips, tongue, hair moving over his flesh. Seeing her desire for him increased his own and he urgently pushed her down on to her back. She looked up into his eyes, giving her wide, delicious smile.

'I don't think there's much wrong with you, is there?'

He pulled away after, leaving her abruptly cold after the heat of their lovemaking, drew his knees up and sat with his elbows on them, hands supporting his head.

'I shouldn't've done that. Not the full way. You should've stopped me.'

'I didn't want to.' Jess hugged her arms across her breasts, shivering, inching herself closer to him again.

'You could 'ave another babby.'

'I don't care.'

'Well yer *should* care. Christ!'

She had thought that he was with her, that they were back where they used to be, and then it was lost. She had let him make love to her, holding in the back of her mind a tiny hope that she might carry his child again, perhaps be able to lay to rest the phantom of the one she had lost.

His mind was in turmoil. With her, he had experienced the first real depth of feeling, wholeness, that had come to him since he came home. For those moments he had at least had the physical evidence that he was well. He was a man again. He had been able to perform with a woman. But then the desire was replaced by remorse. This was wrong. Since he had met Jess his life had buckled out of shape. It was all wrong. He thought of his mom and dad and Mary and Ruth: he'd let down and betrayed every one of them. He thought of all the good, weary-faced people who had greeted him that morning at the church, who all thought so well of him. Ned Green, the splendid lad they all knew. And this Ned here now – who was he?

He looked round the rotten little room, feeling as he did so, Jess's caress on his back. He leaned away from her. What was this life with her? Lying and squalor and turning everyone against him. No it was impossible. It couldn't go on. The thought came to him, *I want to be safe*.

He got up, with some difficulty, and started to dress. Jess watched him uneasily, her teeth chattering with cold. The feeble little fire had gone out. When they were both dressed she could no longer bear the silence, the way he had closed himself against her so completely. She went to him and held out her arms, her face appealing to him.

Slowly, with infinite regret, he held her close for a moment.

'I've got something to eat,' she said, trying to be cheerful, to tell herself it was early days. He had been so passionate for her while they were making love. Things would get better.

They had more tea with the buns in the kitchen, huddling close to the range.

'We need time to get used to each other again, don't we?' she said. 'Will you come here – next week?'

Ned swallowed. He could think of nothing else to say, not in the right words, so he said, 'Yes.'

Thirty-Seven

'I don't want yer pity. Get out of 'ere and don't come bloody mithering round me, woman!'

John Bullivant had shouted these words, and variations on them, at Polly through the winter as she continued to try and visit him. At first she had gone tentatively, once a week, her heart pounding, frightened of him, but somehow unable to keep away.

'Leave 'im be if 'e don't want to see yer,' Olive said. ''E'll have to get over it in 'is own way.'

'I can't leave it, Mom,' Polly said. 'If you'd heard 'im like I do, and seen the state 'e's in . . .' She couldn't easily explain how John had touched her heart, how she felt she couldn't just abandon him to suffer like an animal in a cage, never going out and seeing the sun. And his family couldn't get anywhere with him and didn't know what to do for the best.

'When yer come down to it,' Polly said to Jess, 'that's all the war'll amount to when it's over and done with. Widows like me left to grieve or a wheelchair in the corner of a room. There's nowt we can do except help each other.'

'I think yer brave,' Jess said. 'I don't think I'd have the courage to go in there and have 'im shouting at me. I wouldn't know what to say to him.'

'I think I'll go more often,' Polly smiled ruefully. 'Get 'im used to the idea that I won't give up!'

She'd call in and sit beside John. The rest of the family got on with their lives around them, timidly, obviously afraid of John, his suffering and his moods. He was so down in himself that he barely ever answered her, sitting with his dark head sunk on to his chest. Mrs Bullivant whispered to Polly that she couldn't get him to do anything. He wouldn't even sit and read a newspaper. After a time, instead of shouting at Polly he seemed to realize that it would do no good so instead he sat quiet, seeming indifferent, just tolerating her presence.

Polly talked to him about all sorts: the news, work, what happened when she went to see Mrs Black, Ernie and how they'd got the news about him, where he was when he died. She asked him how he was keeping, never really expecting to get an answer.

The week before Jess met Ned though, John had seemed particularly low. Polly sat beside him, chatting away. John didn't answer her, although she did feel he was listening. After a while, running out of news and gossip, Polly said,

'D'you know, your moustache has grown nice and thick again now – and yer face ain't so thin as it was. You look more like yer old self.'

To her bewilderment, John's shoulders began to shake and she thought he was beginning to weep, but instead she realized he had been overcome by a desperate mirth. He put his hands over his face, the dry laughter escaping from him.

'What've I said?'

Eventually he looked at her.

'My old self? Oh that's good, that is! Look at me! A man with no legs, who can't walk, can't work, can't even dress or get out to do me business without someone seeing to me. I'll never be any use to anyone ever again, so for God's sake, woman, leave me alone – why d'yer keep coming, carrying on and on at me?'

Something had broken through the rage, the bitterness. The face that Polly saw before her showed all his agony, his vulnerability.

'John—' Polly spoke softly, laying a hand gently on his arm. She could tell Marion Bullivant was listening, but she didn't care. 'I lost my 'usband on the Somme. You know that. My life'll never be the same again now. Grace'll never know her father and I'm so sad and lonely that sometimes I don't know what to do with myself. Many's the time I've thought of finishing it altogether, to tell yer the truth. But I've got Grace to bring up – and I've got a life to live the best I can. And you've got one too, John. It'll never be the same again for you neither, but it's still a life. You know – if yer'd just go out of the house for once you'll see there's lots of boys on the streets with one leg or both missing. You're not the only one. But I still reckon if it was me I'd sooner be 'ere with no legs and all my family round me, than buried in French mud.' Her voice was fierce as she finished.

He didn't say anything, just continued to stare into her face. A nerve in his cheek twitched. He was in a tumult of confused emotions.

'Maybe . . .' Polly said. 'If you was to get out and see some of the other lads – you know, a trouble shared . . .'

He tutted, suddenly furious, and looked down at his lap. 'I'm finished . . . I'm not a man . . .'

Polly hesitated. Very quietly she said, 'You are to me, John.'

*

On the Sunday he agreed, at last, that she should wheel him out for a walk.

'Shall we all come?' his mother said nervously. 'Make a bit of an outing of it?'

'No!' John protested sharply. 'I'm not being taken out with yer all like a freak in a fairground. Just Polly on 'er own. That's all I want.'

'It'll start getting him used to the idea,' Polly spoke to Mrs Bullivant quietly in the hall, hoping she wasn't offended. But she was only relieved.

'It's marvellous him agreeing to go out of the house!' she said gratefully. 'Where'll yer take 'im?'

'Cannon Hill Park.'

'Oh no – that's too much for yer, Polly – it's a hell of a walk, and pushing that chair! You've no flesh on yer bones as it is!'

'I'll manage,' Polly said determinedly. 'I'm feeling strong today. And I want to take 'im somewhere really nice. Get some fresh air into 'im and summat pretty to look at. There might be a few daffs out by now.'

The two of them manoeuvred the wheelchair down the step, with John clinging tensely to the arms, cursing at them as they landed it rather joltingly on the pavement. They'd wrapped him up in blankets over his coat because although the sun was shining weakly, it was still a bitter day.

'Have a nice walk,' Mrs Bullivant said, then looked as if she wanted to cut her own tongue out. 'I mean . . .'

'See yer later.' Polly smiled ruefully, waving at her.

They didn't talk much on the way, as Polly needed to concentrate on learning to steer the chair and she could sense that John was having to get used to all sorts of sensations. All these months he had not been outside for more than a few moments. He screwed up his eyes, which watered in the bright winter light. The air felt strange on his pallid skin, everything felt so wide and spacious, even in the streets. And above all, he was not the man who had left Birmingham, full bodied and vigorous. He had to face meeting people outside, being seen for what he was: a man who had been mutilated, changed forever on the battlefield.

'There at last,' she said, and saw him nod.

She pushed the chair into the wide, green space, and along the path which led to the pond, pausing to look across the water. As they did so, both of them caught sight of a young man and woman, arm in arm together. But instead of moving with the easy strides of a young couple in love, the man was taking tiny, shuffling steps, and clinging to the girl's arm as if terrified that a great crevice was about to open in the ground in front of him. His free arm waved in front of him, feeling the air like an antenna. It was immediately apparent that he was newly blind. As the two drew painfully nearer, Polly saw that while the girl was holding his arm, talking to him calmly, reassuring and guiding him, tears which he could not see ran ceaselessly down her face. Polly and John watched silently as they passed.

She wheeled him to the far side of the pond, so that the water was to their right, the park on their left, and it presented a beautiful sight.

'No daffs yet,' Polly said. 'But just look at that.'

Planted in huge numbers, in great patches across the grass were crocuses, all flowering at their perfect best in purple and mauve, rich golden yellow and the purest white. The thin sunlight caught them, illuminating the perfection of their shape and colour as if they were jewels scattered across the green.

John had been looking round, taking everything in,

but suddenly Polly saw him lower his head and clasp his hands to his face.

'John?' In concern, she leaned down, her face close to his. She stood up and gently laid her hands on his shoulders. After some time he reached round and clasped one of his hands over hers.

Thirty-Eight

Sunday came at last. As before, Jess made preparations for Ned. She took time over it, arranging a few sprigs of forsythia in a jam jar, brushing out the room, singing and humming. She took a warm, caressing pleasure in the homely activity. Soon she'd be doing this properly, in a place of their own.

I'll talk to him about it today, Jess thought. Tell him about the money I've been saving for us. But then she changed her mind. The war wasn't over. Ned had said they'd most likely send him back once he'd recovered fully. Though she longed with all her heart for the love and security of marriage to Ned, of a home, it would be tempting fate to start planning now. There were still so many hurdles in their way.

She was lost in thought, kneeling by the grate, sweeping out the ashes from last week, when she heard Iris come and stand in the doorway and turned, smiling. Iris had washed her hair that morning and got Miss Davitt to cut it, and it hung just below her ears, severely chopped, but clean and almost pure white. Once again she had promised to pop out for a bit, although Jess told her there was really no need.

'This can't go on forever, you know.'

'I know that,' Jess stood up and came over to her. 'Of course I do. I was only thinking that myself. But the war . . .'

365

Iris just sniffed.

'The man you loved, Iris – d'yer think *he* was married?'

'I don't know, dear. Quite possible. I expect he was lying to me all the time. I was such a foolish, innocent little thing. I just wonder . . .'

'What?'

'How serious your young man Ned is after all, carrying on in this hole in the wall sort of way.'

'Oh 'e is!' Jess didn't feel she could say, you should see his face, the way he looks at me and loves me! 'It's only that he's living with his mom and dad and they don't approve of me. But when we're together, there's nothing to worry about there!'

She was expecting him at two o'clock. We'll go out, she thought. They'd walk arm in arm round the park, close, loving, stopping to kiss. Then come back to the house. As the time approached she went through to the back and put a kettle on the fire. Between them, Iris's helpers seemed to be making sure she had enough fuel, and Jess had paid her a few pennies for the use of some of it. She had put the lid back on the kettle and was brushing soot off her skirt when she heard him rapping on the front door.

She danced along the hall singing out, 'I'm here – I'm coming, my love!'

She flung the door open with a flourish, a smile of joy and welcome on her face. In a second the smile froze. Jess felt as if she had been punched. Her breath seemed to get stuck in her chest. It took her a couple of seconds for her mind to process what was in front of her eyes.

'What're *you* doing 'ere?'

Mary stood before her, thin as a park railing and

366

dressed in grey. The arched eyebrows which before had made her look friendly and enquiring now gave her an expression of superiority and triumph.

'I'm 'ere to give you a message.' Jess could feel her enjoyment, the way she was savouring what she had to say, almost delaying the moment. 'A message from *my husband*.' Mary gave a knowing, calculated smile.

'Ned and I have been spending a lot of time together over the past months. With our daughter. I don't s'pose he told you all this? Anyway, he sent me to tell yer that he's decided to come back to me. He's come to his senses and he's coming back home for good . . .'

'No!' Jess's hand went to her throat. 'It's not true!'

'He never really left me in the first place,' Mary said spitefully. 'After all, he's been away fighting like everyone else so yer've never really 'ad 'im at all, have yer? Don't go getting any ideas that you can go changing his mind – 'e says 'e wants to live a decent life now with his wife and family – 'stead of with a whore like you . . .' She spat out the word.

'I don't believe yer – he wouldn't . . .' Jess could barely get a sentence together.

'Oh wouldn't 'e? And you think you'd know, do yer?' She came up very close so that Jess could feel the woman's breath on her face as she spoke. 'You know nothing. And yer'd better take my advice and keep well away from us. Keep out of our lives – yer not wanted!'

She began to turn away, then looked back. 'I'd tell yer 'e said 'e was sorry – but come to think of it, 'e never said that.'

Mary stalked off down the road without looking back, her head held high.

Jess shut the door and leaned back against it. Her limbs seemed to have turned to water, her shocked mind telling her she had found herself in a crazed dream. Here, where he'd come last week, loved her, held her ... suddenly everything was shattered.

She hugged herself, trying to force from her mind the memory of Ned's back turned away from her after their lovemaking. It couldn't be true! Mary had wormed out of him where she was meeting him, had come to spin her a pack of lies ... Ned would never do this to her, he loved her! She shook her head, moaning gently to herself.

'He loves me – just me ...' She couldn't stand the pain of what she had heard, nor would she ever believe it unless she saw Ned herself. She had to hear the truth from his own lips.

Afterwards she couldn't remember the journey to Selly Oak. It was as if she had done it in her sleep and wakened to find herself outside the Greens' house, wondering how she got there.

She hammered on the door, past caring about anything: that it was Sunday afternoon and that his mom and dad loathed and despised her, that Mary might well be there as well by now ... In her desperation none of this mattered and only one thing in the world did: she had to see Ned and talk to him.

It had begun to spit with rain as she walked up Oak Tree Lane and the wind was getting up. As she waited for someone to open the door she thought, we'd've got wet. We couldn't've gone for a walk in the park after all.

Ned's mother opened the door. She gasped when she saw who it was.

'You've got some nerve coming here! Don't you

think you're coming in because you're not. Clear off and don't you ever come near this house – breaking up families. You're nothing better than a common little tart!'

She went to shut the door, but Jess ran against it with her full weight, making sure she got her foot wedged in the doorway.

'I've got to see him!' She found she was right out of control, shouting at the top of her voice. 'I'm not going away 'til I've seen 'im and 'e tells me the truth with his own lips – 'stead of sending a cowing messenger round – if 'e did send her! Ned – Ned!'

'Mom—' She heard his voice, very tense sounding in the hall behind.

'Disgusting little trollop, coming round here!' Mrs Green's face was contorted with anger and disgust. The sight of it made Jess feel dirty and sordid. Something in her shrivelled and died, knowing so clearly and brutally what they all thought of her.

'I don't care what you think – I love 'im!' she sobbed, distraught. 'I want to see 'im!'

Ned pushed past his mother, gesturing for her to go inside. Jess heard him say, 'Let me deal with this.' Being referred to as 'this' wounded her more than anything else had done so far. She found herself weeping uncontrollably in the street as Ned seized her arm, leading her away from the house as the rain began to come down in earnest.

'Tell me it's not true. Tell me yer love me! Yer love me, Ned!'

But he didn't speak. He pulled her along by the arm, the rain pelting into their faces, turning down towards the Infirmary, walking very quickly until they passed the gates and reached a green space under the bare trees at the end of the road where there was more shelter. Then he stopped and faced her. Jess, her face wet with rain and tears, looked up into his eyes.

'Oh God—' she put her hand over her mouth, feeling for a moment as if she was going to retch. She swallowed hard before she could speak. 'It's true – what Mary said? You're going back to 'er?'

For a moment Ned seemed frozen, as if in those seconds he had to make the decision all over again. They heard the rain falling through the trees. He looked away from her, down at the rotting leaves under their feet, and nodded.

'And you – you—' Jess was panting, so beyond herself she could barely get the words out. 'You sent *her* to tell me – of all people. You come to me, you tell me we're going to have a life together, you come and love me as if I'm the only woman in the world, *use* me – and then you—' She ran out of words.

'Jess—' He went to touch her shoulder.

'Don't!' she screamed. 'Are you going back to Mary? I want to hear it out of your own mouth.'

'Yes.' He sighed resignedly. 'Yes. I'm going back to Mary. She's my wife.'

'But why? You don't love her – you love me!'

He spoke dully, but she could tell from his tone that the decision had been made. He was unshakeable. 'I do love her – in a sort of way. She's always been there. There's a lot in that, Jess. And there's Ruth . . .'

A man appeared, cutting through the trees, shaking the wet off his cap, but she was too overwrought to wait until he'd passed.

Scalding tears stung her eyes again. 'You're a coward, Ned! You're the worst sort of coward there is. You didn't even have the courage to come and speak to me, after all this – all that's happened. I've devoted myself to you. I carried your babby – or have you already forgotten that? And I would've kept quiet and suffered bringing it up alone to spare you, so's not to force yer into anything because I loved yer that much! I was turned out of home for you – on the streets, with no one. I turned Auntie against me, I've waited for you and lived for you. You're my life, Ned! I would've done anything for yer – and you send Mary to me. You treat me like ... like *nothing*, and you didn't even have the guts to come and tell me yourself ...' She could say no more, she was crying so uncontrollably.

'I didn't come because I couldn't – can't you see that? I couldn't do it. Not after last week – seeing you. I just wouldn't have been able ...'

'Because you're a bloody, sodding coward!' she screamed at him. 'I hate you – hate you for being so weak that you can't stand up to them all!'

'Yes—' he held out his hands helplessly. 'Yes – I am, I know. But Jess, I've got a wife, a daughter – there're my mom and dad to think of. Everyone – everyone we know – it's like my whole life falling apart if I leave it and go with yer. You're so good, so beautiful ... That's the thing. Choosing between good and bad's not the hard thing – but how d'yer choose between two good things? Things which both feel right? When either way the choice hurts someone – lots of people.'

Jess stood quiet, feeling despair come over her like great weariness. Because for all her hurt, her anger, her love for him, she understood what he was saying, and that cut her more than not understanding.

'It's like the war.' He looked at her again. 'You kill them or they kill you. Which is better?'

'Oh, you have to kill them.'

'That's where we're different. You're a born survivor. I don't know how I've lasted this long in life.' He looked into her eyes and she saw his, at last, fill with tears.

'God, Jess – this is the most horrible thing. I hate hurting people, you more than anyone.' He reached out for her but she kept back, standing stiffly. She could not bear for him to touch her. She felt as if she would go crazy, thump and kick and scratch him if he came nearer, to release her pain on to him.

'I should've known I could never have you,' she said. Her voice sounded strangled. 'Not really. Not a proper life, happy ever after. It's always been a dream. Just a dream.' She paused looking up at him. 'You won't change yer mind – not even now? We could just go ...'

He was solemn. 'No. I've got to stay. No more lying and letting people down. I want to live decently.'

These words winded her as if he had punched her. Decently. He wanted to live decently. For a moment she closed her eyes. When she opened them he had stepped closer to her. 'Jess – I'm sorry ...'

'I know.' She looked down, tears running down her cheeks. She pressed her hands over her face to shut out the sight of him. 'Ned – go away. I can't stand seeing yer.'

'I can't just leave yer here ...'

'Why not? You're leaving me anyhow. Just get away from me – leave me!' At last she was screaming.

Ned paused helplessly for a second, then walked away under the trees without turning to look back. Jess watched through her fingers, saw the strong shape of him darken further for a moment in the shadows. Then, with his head down, moving slowly and sorrowfully, he stepped out into the rain, taking himself out of her life. She wondered if she would ever see him again.

She gave way then, her legs folding so that she crumpled forward on to the sodden leaves and twigs, sobbing in anguish. She curled into a ball, incoherent cries of grief tearing from her. Her forehead was pressed against the wet earth as she wept, arms clenched tight round her body as if to hold within herself a heart that was shattering apart.

Thirty-Nine

The fighting began again in earnest in March with a German offensive, once more on the Somme, and through the summer of 1918 the numbers of casualties on the Western Front soared again to the highest they'd ever been.

It was Sis's turn to spend her life in a state of acute worry about Percy. Tanks were being used more and more often in the fighting to try and break through the Hindenburg Line. In parts the Germans had dug trenches so deep and well defended that the line seemed impregnable. And in the early spring it was the Germans who were pushing west, forcing a bulge in the allied front. By April though, they had still not broken through. The war had taken on a terrible, unresolved permanence and everyone was worn down with it, sickened, exhausted.

Jess did, after all, see Ned again, and quite soon. One Sunday in May, he and Mary arrived at the house, Ned carrying Ruth in his arms. It was Olive who opened the door.

'Oh. It's you.' She stood firmly on the step. 'What d'yer want?'

The cousins heard her voice from the back room and looked at each other. Ronny ran through to see.

'We wanted to come and see yer, Auntie,' Ned said, hesitantly.

Mary was obviously eager to take over the talking. 'Only – Ned knows what yer've thought of 'im over the last years, and 'e wanted to try and patch things up, for the best like.'

Jess seemed turned to stone. For the last two months she had felt like a dead person, full of leaden despair, and her cousins were helpless in the face of her misery. For a moment, hearing his voice, hope sparked in her. He had come back for her. It was all a mistake and he loved her after all, couldn't live without her as she couldn't without him! But then she heard Mary speak too.

'Dear God, no!' She got up to escape upstairs, but it was too late. Olive had stood back, grimly, and they were already coming along the hall.

'They've got a bloody nerve coming 'ere!' Polly said, enraged. Although they had always known Jess was wrong to go with a married man, her obvious love and devotion to Ned, the suffering they had witnessed in her since, had drawn all of them, even Olive, on to her side.

As Ned and Mary's footsteps came closer, Jess stood behind the door, arms tightly folded, trying to keep her emotions closed down. As soon as Ned came into the room he shot her a look of apology, but Jess wasn't looking at him to intercept it.

Olive didn't ask them to sit down, though she greeted Ruth kindly enough and let her perch on a chair by the table.

'So – what've yer got to say?'

The smug look on Mary's face dropped a bit. She could feel Polly and Sis's eyes boring into her with loathing.

'Me and Ned want to say a few things to yer,' Mary said. There was satisfaction in her voice.

375

'Oh yer do, do yer? Why should we care, yer smug little bitch?'

'Poll—' Olive shushed her and looked at Ned. 'Yer've made a right mess of things, my lad.'

'I know . . .' he looked round her and spoke to Jess. 'I didn't come to upset yer – I wouldn't've come . . .'

'What're yer talking to *'er* for?' Mary snapped. 'Don't go crawling to 'er!'

Jess couldn't look up or answer. Her cheeks were burning. Just go, she prayed. Please. Leave me in peace.

'I wanted to say to you, Auntie, that I'm sorry for all I've done to upset you, and your family—'

'It's not as if things were easy for me,' Mary interrupted, unable to keep quiet. 'Having *my husband* stolen by some common little—'

Ned laid a hand firmly on her arm. 'Mary, you said we was coming to make our peace, so just keep out of it, will yer? Auntie—' he looked appealingly at her. 'Can yer forgive me?'

'You've got a bleeding cheek!' Sis exploded. 'Coming 'ere, trying to make everything awright for yerself! That's all you ever think of, ain't it? Never mind all the misery you've caused . . . you just want to go off thinking you're bloody marvellous Ned Green again . . . Well you ain't, I can tell yer – your name's muck around 'ere.'

Olive waved an arm to shut Sis up. Jess seemed to shrink further into herself. There was a silence as Olive stared at him so intently that Ned had to look down.

'I might be able to forgive yer,' she said slowly. 'In time. But not yet. There's too much heartbreak round here for me to wave you off with my blessing. It takes two, Ned, and you was every bit as much to blame for all that's 'appened. So you can put up with a heavy

376

conscience for a bit. I ain't handing out my blessing just on your say so. It's Jess yer should be talking to.'

'Well 'e ain't doing that,' Mary said. She looked round at them all, then announced, 'Ned's been redrafted.'

This stopped Olive in her tracks. Less harshly, she said, 'You going back to France?'

'No.' Ned spoke quietly, almost shamefully. 'In the Reserves. My leg's not fit. They're sending me to Dover.'

'Well you ain't going to get killed there, are yer?' Sis said.

Mary looked as if she was about to say something that would have started a slanging match, but she thought the better of it.

'Come on,' Ned said quietly. 'I think we'd better go.'

As they were shown out, Polly said, 'I think we did well not to 'ave a proper old ding-dong with 'er. How I didn't put my fist through 'er cowing smug gob I'll never know!'

Jess sank into a chair, trembling like someone who's been in an accident.

Those last months of the war were a time of mourning for Jess. She felt hollow, lost. Sometimes she confided her feelings to Polly and Sis. One evening they were standing out in the little yard behind the house, catching the last of the sunshine. The sky was a pale yellow with a few sludgy wisps of cloud across it.

'I've spent four years thinking of no one but 'im. I feel as if life's empty and it'll be empty forever.'

'I know yer do,' Polly laid a hand on her shoulder. 'And I know 'ow yer feel. Even though I've got John to think about now, I still feel it's Ernie I'm married to. I can't help it. And every time I think about it I feel really bad inside. It's like 'e's not dead and buried – I don't feel I can ever believe 'e's really gone. I mean, if John and I was to ... well, you know – I'd feel like a bigamist.'

'Least Bert seems to be awright for the moment,' Jess turned to Sis. 'And you heard from Perce yesterday.'

Sis nodded despondently. 'But God knows how much longer they'll be out there . . .'

Jess squeezed Sis's hand. It was no good telling her everything would be all right. You never knew. They just had to hope.

As the months passed, the war began to turn. The Germans began many successful attacks, their artillery bombardment devastating the allied lines, but as soon as their infantry tried to move forward they lost the initiative. By September the whole Front was ablaze, and at last, the allies ruptured the Hindenburg Line. The newspapers began to trumpet successes. A breathless, almost unbelieving hope began to break through the gloom.

During that summer, Jess and Sis also honoured their promise to invite Peter Stevenson and David out with them. They spent several hot Sundays picnicking in Cannon Hill and Highgate Parks, the two boys scrapping on the grass like pups or playing ball, with Grace trying to join in and annoying them.

One hot afternoon in August they all went to Cannon Hill, taking a picnic of sandwiches and cake and some cold mutton contributed by Peter Stevenson. John Bullivant agreed to come. He was wary towards Peter

Stevenson at first: a man who hadn't been in the fighting, who was an outsider, a shirker even, so far as John was concerned. He was also mortified at his disability in the presence of a strong, able-bodied man, and it took some time to break the ice. John scowled when Peter offered to push the wheelchair and Polly indicated gently that it might be better if she did it.

They all set off, Jess and Sis with a bag each, Olive and Peter looking out for the boys and Grace riding in pride of place on John's lap in the wheelchair. She loved it sitting up there, with John tickling her and trying to remember little rhymes to sing to her. Grace thought 'Uncle' John was wonderful.

For a long time, Jess scarcely noticed that whenever they went out together, Peter Stevenson always seemed to gravitate towards her. Walking down to the park that day, he appeared at her side with David.

'Looks set fine, doesn't it?' he said.

Jess managed a smile. 'Yes, nice and warm,' she said absently.

David reached up for her hand. She transferred the bag to her left hand and took his.

'And how're you, young man? Getting big now, aren't yer? You'll be taller than Ronny, I reckon. You two can have some nice games.'

David grinned. 'Football.'

'You gunna play for the Blues when you grow up?'

'Yep—' Davey kicked an imaginary ball along the road.

'He's dead keen,' Peter said. 'Course, at that age you think you can do anything in the world, don't you?' Jess gave a little chuckle. Peter thought how long it was since he had heard her happy, full hearted laugh. By now he knew what had happened, or some of it, from Sis. That Jess had been let down badly, was rejected and sad. He longed to bring the smile back to her face.

They made themselves comfortable on the long sward of grass which sloped down to the pond. The grass was parched and worn from the crowds of people out enjoying the summer sun. Between them, Polly and Peter lifted John out of his wheelchair and on to the grass. He had to accept their help, but a distant look would come over his face as if to dissociate himself from what was happening. The children romped around and Jess and Sis kept an eye on them while Olive opened the bags and sorted out the food, her hat well pulled down to shade her eyes. Polly got up to chase after Grace.

Jess felt the sun pressing on her back as she sat on the grass and the warmth made her feel drowsy. She became aware that Peter was talking to John behind her, gently asking him questions. What had happened, how had he lost his legs. Did he mind being asked?

'I don't mind – there's not many ask as a matter of fact. They was blown off. A shell came down and the next thing I knew I were in a bed in a hutment hospital – that's what they call 'em – sort of makeshift places out there. Left the rest of my legs somewhere near Plugstreet – that's Belgium.' Jess could hear a kind of pride in his voice: he knew about the war first hand, Peter didn't. 'Lot of lads gone the same way. Nothing like them lads: bloody golden, the whole lot of 'em.'

'Sometimes I think I should've kicked up and gone. I was fit enough, after all.'

'No.' John was angrily emphatic. 'Oh no. Mind you, nothing would've kept me from joining up. Not at the time. But we shouldn't've been there – not a single one of us down to the last man. No – you're best out of it, pal. It's just one long f—.' He bit back an expletive. 'Scuse me, Mrs Beeston . . . It's a nightmare, Peter, that it is.'

'Yer awright,' Olive said. 'Any'ow – there's dinner ready now. Go and get the others, Jess, will yer?'

'I'll come and get Davey.' Peter was on his feet as Jess got up.

'No need,' she said. 'I'll get 'em.'

'I'd like to,' he smiled at her.

They wove through the lazing family groups on the grass. Polly and the children were at the edge of the pond watching the ducks.

'He's a brave man, your friend John,' Peter said. 'He must be going through hell.'

'Yes, 'e is brave,' Jess glanced round at John. 'But 'e has suffered such a lot and 'e feels useless. Polly was wondering if 'e could maybe get a job somewhere – get 'im out and keep 'im busy like. Otherwise 'e gets ever so down at home, thinking he'll never do anything again.'

'I'm sure he could. There's munitions factories crying out . . . Tell you what, Jess. I'll ask around.'

Fleetingly, she smiled. 'That's kind of yer.'

He wanted to say, I'd do anything for you, Jess. Instead he said, 'I'd be glad to. It'd help make him feel part of things again, wouldn't it?'

They helped Polly gather up the children and went back up to eat dinner. Jess was conscious of Peter striding tall at her side once more. She found herself noticing the warmth in his eyes when he smiled at her, and was suddenly cheered and comforted by his presence.

Forty

'It's over!'

Sis came tearing into the Rumbling Shed, bursting with the news, her face pink through the canary yellow. She threw her arms round Jess, jumping up and down in excitement.

'Oh Jess, I can't believe it – it's finished, over at last! And Perce can come 'ome!'

'Are you sure?' But she could already hear the shrieks of excitement from outside.

'Yes – definite – they signed this morning! 'Ere, come on – everyone's out!'

They pulled off their caps and overalls. All the other women had come out from the sheds and were hugging, laughing, shouting all at once in a great commotion. Jess saw Peter Stevenson among them, being grasped hold of and kissed by all and sundry, all of which he seemed to be rather enjoying.

'Go on!' Sis shouted down her ear. 'Go and give 'im a kiss – make 'is day!'

'What d'you mean?' Jess shouted back.

'You blind or summat, Jess? Ain't yer seen the way 'e looks at yer?'

Jess shook her head. 'No!' She'd been so wrapped up in her hurt, her misery over Ned, that nothing much else had got through. At the edge of the crowd with Sis she watched him, standing at least a head taller than the women, in his khaki overall, his eyes crinkling with laughter as a group of them milled round him. She saw he was looking round, searching, and after a moment his eyes rested on her for a second, with a questioning, uncertain look. Jess managed to meet his gaze, equally uncertain. Was Sis mistaken, and was she imagining the special tenderness in his eyes when he looked at her?

She saw he was coming over and she felt panic rising in her. But Sis saved her, launching herself at Peter Stevenson, throwing her arms round him and just managing to reach up and kiss his cheek.

'Ain't it *bostin*!' she cried. She couldn't keep still at all.

Peter laughed, pretending to stagger with her hurling herself at him. 'Yes, Sis – it's bostin all right – couldn't be better. Could it, Jess?'

'No.' To her annoyance Jess felt a heavy blush spread across her cheeks and hoped Peter Stevenson would think it was just excitement about the news. 'It couldn't, could it?'

'Why don't yer come round ours and help us celebrate later on?' Sis said irrepressibly.

'Sis!' Jess reproached her. 'Mr Stevenson's got his own family . . .'

'Well – Davey can come with him, can't 'e? The more the merrier!'

Peter Stevenson came round that evening to join in the celebrations, which spread out all along the streets, with singing and dancing, drinking and cheering. But the poignancy of the occasion, its combination of joy and grief, was too much for Polly and she broke down during the evening. The truth that Ernie would never come home now peace had broken out hit her even harder.

When they had all been out partying in the cold long enough, Olive suggested everyone go in for 'a cuppa tea and a nip of the hard stuff'. They crowded into the back room, Ronny and Davey both up long after their bedtime although Grace had given up the battle with sleep some time before and was tucked in upstairs. Olive poured celebratory tots of brandy, they had glasses of ale and later on, boiled up the kettle.

'It's nice to 'ave yer with us,' she said to Peter Stevenson. 'I 'ope you'll come and see us, even when the factory's gone and that – they won't be needing it no more, will they?'

'I s'pose not, no. I haven't had time to think yet, to tell you the truth!'

'Poor old John,' Sis said. John had got a job making Lee Enfield Rifles – now there wouldn't be much call for them.

'What'll you do then?' Jess asked Peter.

'Look for another job, I s'pose – even start summat up myself in the long run. I've always fancied that.'

It was a happy, if poignant evening, so much ending, so much lost, yet such an enormous relief still tinged with disbelief that it was finished. Eventually, when David was beginning to look glazed with sleepiness, Peter stood up.

'Come on, my lad. High time we were off.'

'Jess'll see you out,' Sis said, wickedly. Jess glowered at her, blushing, but stood up.

Once they had coats on, Peter picked David up and the boy leaned his head thankfully against his father's shoulder and closed his eyes. Peter carried him carefully out through the front door and turned to say goodbye.

Jess stood on the step. A candle was burning in the hall and against the soft light she looked so sweet, so soft and deliciously feminine. He could just see her face, her teeth gleaming as she smiled at him.

'Goodnight then,' she said softly. There was a wistfulness in her voice that he was unsure how to interpret.

'Jess?' Thank God I'm holding Davey, he thought, otherwise I'd be unable to stop myself taking her in my arms.

'Umm?'

'When the factory closes – I mean it's bound to be soon – I wouldn't want to – not see you – and the family, of course.' He paused, then added, 'But especially you.'

Jess was deeply touched by his care for her, but in her own heart there was still such hurt and confusion. She wasn't sure exactly what Peter felt for her, let alone what she could feel in return.

'I—' she swallowed. 'No – course not. You must come and see us. I'm glad you came tonight. It's hard to believe it's all over.'

'Yes—' All evening they had been saying things like this. 'Maybe tomorrow it'll sink in.'

'Well . . .' Jess pulled the door closed a little. 'Goodnight then. Give Davey a kiss from me.'

'Jess, I . . .' He saw her hesitate at the door. 'Goodnight.'

'Goodnight, Peter.'

His face didn't register his disappointment. He heard her shut the door gently behind her.

After all, what else could she say? he demanded of himself as he carried his sleeping son home through the streets still full of jubilant, carousing people. There were moments when he thought he saw her eyes respond to his, to his feeling, but so fleetingly that he wasn't sure.

I'm so flaming old, he thought. Maybe I'm just making a fool of myself. Why should such a lovely girl want a man more than ten years her senior? And when she's grieving for someone else? I ought to keep away. Leave her alone. But I can't.

He let out a groan of longing and frustration that got lost in the clamour around him.

God, I love her, he thought. I do – I just can't help it.

The following weeks were spent adjusting to the idea of peace after the long, dark years of war. The munitions factories closed or reverted back to pre-war production and all the cousins had to look for new jobs. Polly managed to get taken back on at Clark's Pens, Sis found a job at Wicker Carriage and Basket Manufacturers, and Jess found a firm needing experienced enamellers that was the right side of town, not in the Jewellery Quarter. She knew, guiltily, that if she'd gone back over there to work, she could have seen more of Iris. But fond as she was of her, she had avoided going over there too often. Iris was sympathetic about what had happened, but for Jess, Iris's house held too many memories of Ned.

As the weeks passed, the boys came home. First one of Mrs Bullivant's remaining sons, Ed. The other, Lol (short for Laurence), was wounded and in hospital in France, but would be following later.

The family were waiting on tenterhooks for their loved ones to come back. Perce was the first. There was a knock at the door one evening after they'd finished tea.

Polly led him through to the back crying out, 'Look who's here!'

Percy looked bigger and broader in the shoulders, blond hair cropped, a man suddenly, instead of a boy. He stood beaming in the doorway, arms outstretched.

'Perce!' Sis shrieked. 'Oh my God, Perce!' She almost flattened him, hurling herself on him with full bodied ardour and covering his face with kisses which he enthusiastically returned. Everyone else might just as well not have been there. Polly and Jess grinned at each other and even Olive's face softened at the sight.

'Sis—' Perce held her by the shoulders as soon as they both got their breath back, although Sis couldn't keep still.

'What?' She was tearful and giggly all at once.

He had been about to say something else but he stopped. 'Bloomin' 'ell! Yer've gone all yeller!'

Sis laughed, wiping her sleeve across her eyes. 'It's the powder goes in those grenades – it'll go in the end!'

'I should 'ope so, yer look like a flaming budgie! Anyroad, Sis you're my girl and I want to ask yer, 'ere and now – will yer marry me?'

'Oooh yes! Yes I will, Perce!' Her arms snaked round his neck again and she squealed with excitement, then burst into tears all over again.

''Ere – steady on,' Olive said. 'You've only just got through the door!'

'I know, Mrs Beeston – but it's been a long, long war and we've had time enough to think,' Perce said seriously. 'I spent hours sitting in them tanks, sick to me stomach from the stink in there, thinking, when I get out of 'ere, the first thing I'm gunna do ... I love yer daughter and we've lost enough time. I don't want to waste another second. That's with your permission, of course.'

'Oh Auntie!' Jess said, more animated than she'd

looked in ages. 'Of course you'll give yer permission – look at them!'

Olive, on her dignity, paused before nodding, though a smile was spreading over her face.

'I reckon the pair of yer are sensible enough after all this time.'

'Oh *Mom*!' Sis cried in delight. 'Oh Perce! When shall we fix the day for?'

''Ow about sitting the poor lad down and offering him a cuppa tea?' Olive said. 'After all – 'e's come a long way to ask yer!'

The next thing, a week later, while Olive was alone with Grace, was the door opening and a lean figure walking in, a greatcoat over one arm.

'Mom?'

'Bert?' For a second she didn't recognize him. 'Oh Bert, at last!' She flung her arms round him, more emotional than he'd ever seen her before. 'What's 'appened to yer – you're all skin and bone!'

'Oh I'll be awright, Mom, with some decent 'ome cooking inside of me.' He was in good spirits. 'Eh – I'm dying for a decent cuppa tea. You got the kettle on?'

As she heated up some food for him and brewed tea Bert sat at the table looking round, chattering to her, although his face looked grey and drawn with exhaustion.

'The 'ouse looks smaller, Mom. It's a queer thing but yer come home after all this time and everything looks the same but different some'ow.'

Olive was watching him, frowning. 'What's the matter with yer, Bert? Yer look like a death's head.'

'Oh I'll be awright. It were just one damn thing after

388

another out there. Poxy bloody place the east is – I never want to set foot there again, what with the heat and the flies – and I was sick like you'd never believe. Fever and dysentery and Christ knows what. Blokes dying all round – not just from the fighting, mind – from all the diseases out there. Terrible. Anyroad . . .' He sat back, breathing in contentedly. 'Home at last. I wouldn't go back in the army if yer gave me a fortune to do it, I can tell yer!'

PART V

Forty-One

Spring 1919

'You go,' Polly said to Jess. 'I'll stay and mind Ronny and Grace. Might cheer you up a bit.'

It was Saturday morning and Olive and Sis were off to town to choose material for a wedding dress for Sis. Polly stared commandingly into Jess's pale face. 'Go on with yer – get yerself out. I'll trust yer to get summat nice for Gracie.' Grace, now three, was to be Sis's little bridesmaid. 'You're the one that's doing the sewing anyhow. And you never know who yer might meet!'

Jess managed a wan smile. 'That's what I'm worried about.'

'Look, Jess—' Olive buttoned up her coat with her gnarled fingers. 'It's high time you put it all be'ind yer, instead of mooning and mooching round 'ere. Ned's gone and now 'e needs to be forgotten. You've got yer own life to lead. Get yer coat on and come and give us a hand.'

'Awright,' Jess said listlessly. She knew her aunt was right. They had all been nothing but kind over the winter. She owed the family everything. But she felt so low and raw inside, as if Ned had taken away her youth and energy, her capacity to love.

For Sis's sake she tried to put on a cheery smile.

'Two weeks!' Her cousin could barely prevent herself from skipping along the pavement. 'Two weeks and I'll have a ring on my finger and be Mrs Bolter!'

'An old married lady,' Jess teased her.

'With her own little house!' Sis hugged herself.

'Ar – and 'er own scrubbing brush and mangle,' Olive added.

Listening to Sis, Jess felt such a pang of longing. How close she had thought herself to a settled life with Ned, and how much joy the thought of that had given her. To be loved, to have a home and feel secure!

'You make the most of it,' she told Sis. 'Scrubbing brush an' all.'

Sis grinned gladly at her. 'Ta, Jess. I will. I know I'm one of the lucky ones.'

The three of them walked along companionably in the bright March sunshine. A few trees they saw along the way were coming into leaf and though the sunlight still had the thin, strained feel of winter, it was good to feel its warmth on their pale faces.

'I still can't get used to it,' Olive said. 'Having time to walk about and shop – not queueing for hours for everything. Just not 'aving the war on.' Things had returned, in so far as they could, to normal. Bert was one of the fortunate ones who had his old job back at the rolling mills. The three girls had all squeezed into one room to let him have a bed, although Sis would soon be gone, and the house had settled into a routine again.

'It's lovely, ain't it!' Sis was truly full of the joys of spring and everything else too. 'Ooh – this time in two weeks! Let's hope and pray none of us go down with the influenza.'

'There's a lot bad with it,' Olive said. 'No good thinking about that.' She made a wry face at Jess. 'Come on – let's go an' put 'er out of 'er misery.'

They spent a leisurely few hours combing through the rag market and along the shops, looking at bolts of cloth, hats and shoes, weighing up what Sis had already and what would need to be bought. When it came down to a choice between two materials, Olive favoured a plain lilac cambric.

'Oh no!' Sis protested. 'I'd look like a flaming nurse-maid or summat in that. Look – what about this? It's really pretty – for a spring wedding.'

She ran her hand over a soft lawn with a pattern of honeysuckle and roses on it. Jess smiled. Despite Sis's desperation to get married, she'd said she wasn't going to do it in December, oh no. It had to be in the spring with flowers and sunshine. Jess could immediately imagine Sis in the floral material, flowers, or perhaps even a little tulle veil in her hair . . .

'Oh Auntie!' she cried. 'That's Sis to a tee.'

Their eyes met for a moment and Jess knew they were both thinking the same thing: Louisa. It was just the pretty, romantic sort of stuff Louisa would have chosen.

Olive fingered the price label. It wasn't too expensive: Sis had made quite a simple choice.

'It'll be easy to work with, that will,' Jess cajoled her aunt. In the end, Olive nodded.

As the morning progressed, Sis chose a pretty straw hat which she could decorate with flowers, and settled for a pair of second-hand shoes, white, with a ribbon bow on the front.

'They're a bit scuffed.' She eyed the toes of them.

'We can stick some whitener on 'em,' Jess encouraged her.

'They're ever so comfy.' Sis was clearly delighted with them. 'Must've been pricey new.'

'I could do with a sit down,' Olive said, after all these deliberations. 'Let's treat ourselves to a cuppa tea and a bun.'

As they sat together chatting and sipping tea, Jess looked at her aunt. If there's one good thing, she thought, that's come out of Ned leaving me like he did, it's me and Auntie getting on again. That tension between her lover and her family which had torn at her for so long was gone now. She felt a great surge of affection for the stout woman in front of her with her worn face and hands. Her sad past. As Sis chattered on about Perce and the house they were going to rent together in Balsall Heath, Jess thought, she's been my only real family, Auntie has. I owe her everything.

'My treat today,' she said, handing over the money for the tea. 'Since you've got to put up with me about for a bit longer yet.'

'Oh—' Olive hauled herself up from the table. 'That's awright, bab. I shan't like an empty 'ouse, that I shan't.'

They ambled down along Spiceal Street and Sis, catching sight of the flower ladies, surrounded by their bouquets and all yelling in raucous competition, moved on to the subject of what sort of posy she was going to carry. Jess was just about to remark that she'd already have flowers in abundance all over the dress, when she noticed Olive was no longer walking beside her. She turned.

'Auntie?'

Olive had stopped and was standing quite still, one hand laid over her heart. Her eyes were stretched wide with an expression which Jess read as pain, and she hurried back to her.

'You feeling poorly, Auntie?' she asked, frightened. She took Olive's arm and her aunt didn't shake her off.

Sis came rushing back too. 'What's up, Mom?'

'Over there . . .' Olive was staring across towards a fruit and veg stall.

In that second Jess understood that her face was full not with pain but with fear. They followed her gaze and Jess saw a thin, stooped old lady in a black coat and hat. She was buying spuds and the stallholder was tipping them into her carrier for her. They could only see her in profile, but Jess made out a sharp face with a pointed nose and slack, yellowish skin.

'Oh God alive . . . It is – it's 'er . . .' Jess felt Olive sag as if she was going to collapse, and grasped her arm more tightly under Olive's, feeling her trembling. Her face had gone sickly white, perspiration breaking out on her forehead.

'Who?' Sis was staring across wildly, not under-standing.

'It's that woman,' Jess said. 'Doris . . .?'

'Adcock,' Olive added, her eyes still fixed on her. 'She's there – I ain't imagining 'er, am I? She really is there?'

'That lady in the black hat?' Sis frowned. 'You sure it's 'er?'

'Yes . . . oh . . .' Olive gave a moan, a hand going to her mouth.

'My God, Auntie—' Jess squeezed her aunt's arm fiercely. 'What in God's name did she do to yer?' She was appalled to see Olive, so strong, so brave, reduced to this by the memories of this woman's cruelty. She saw that no one has power like that of an adult over a child.

Olive shook her head. 'Just the sight of her . . . Oh, I feel bad.'

Sis handed her mother a handkerchief and Olive mopped her forehead.

Jess felt as if she was swelling inside with rage and indignation.

'We'll go and give 'er a talking to, that's what we'll do.'

'No!' Olive said faintly. 'I can't . . .'

'She's just an old woman,' Sis said.

'So what if she's old – what excuse is that?' Jess was on fire. 'You might be frightened of her, Auntie, but I'm certainly not. Come on – she's moving off. We'll lose 'er else.'

The old woman had begun to shuffle off with her walking stick along towards St Martin's Church, her lips seeming to move in an endless mumbling patter as she did so. Jess pulled the others along, following until they reached a less crowded little spot near the church gate, and released her aunt's arm.

'Oi – you. Missis!'

The old woman took no notice so Jess tapped her on the arm and she stopped abruptly. In that second Jess saw two watery eyes peering at her from under the hat brim with a steely hostility. Startling, horrible eyes with their double pupil, giving her the cold, glassy look of a cat.

'Doris Adcock?'

'Who're you?' She squinted at Jess.

'You deaf? I said are you Doris Adcock?' Jess experienced almost a sense of ecstasy rising in her. Her fury was so strong, so complete, her body so taut with it, there was a kind of perfection in it. It was the most soaring emotion she had felt in a long time and she was ready to knock the old crone into the day after tomorrow.

She saw the old woman nod reluctantly. The whites of her eyes were a sludgy yellow, lips mean and crinkled as pastry cutters.

'D'you know who this is?'

She heard Olive say, 'Oh Jess – no . . .'

Doris turned and looked at Olive with a vague bewilderment. Olive quailed under her gaze, gripping Sis's arm.

'This is Olive. Olive Tamplin, she was. From your old neighbourhood. Remember?' Jess had her hands on her hips. She wasn't speaking loudly, but she could hear the menace in her own voice. 'Had a sister called Louisa. Their mom was called Alice. Alice Tamplin. Bet you remember her awright, don't yer?'

There was a horrible moment as recognition seeped into the old woman's expression, a look of unguarded malice which narrowed her eyes and contorted her face.

'Yes.' She tapped the stick vehemently on the ground. 'The babykiller.'

Jess heard Olive give a whimper just behind her, and for a moment she had an urge to tighten her hands round Doris's scrawny throat and crush the life out of her.

'And you thought it was your business to follow 'er children and hound them, torment them until they was too frightened to live in that neighbourhood so they moved on, and even then yer'd still follow 'em and spread yer poison about them until life was hell for them. A worse hell than it already was without their mom because you saw to it she was locked up and the key thrown away!'

Jess had her face right close up to Doris's. She could hear the woman's whispery, agitated breathing, but her eyes looked back as cold as stones.

'Have you got children, Doris?'

'Yes.'

'Well you never should 'ave!' Jess spat at her. 'Nature should've dried your womb up before it let you breed any more of you. You're a cruel, vicious bitch and you made life hell for my auntie for no reason. You just had nowt better to do than be cruel and make life as rotten as possible . . .'

'She killed a babby,' Doris croaked. 'Murdered it with 'er bare hands. People 'ad a right to know what was living in their neighbourhood . . .'

'But you carried on when she weren't even there!' Olive spoke, crying, and Sis was holding her arm. 'On and on, never leaving us be. She was gone, our mom, and we never saw 'er again.'

'What's bred in the bone . . .' Doris said. The very sight of her filled Jess with horror. She had viciousness stamped through her like a stick of rock. 'I'd do it again tomorrer, that I would. She was a wicked woman, that Alice was . . . she walked the streets parading 'er crime. She were proud of it. Don't tell me that ain't evil in a woman.'

'She was sick,' Olive moved closer, sobbing. 'She was poorly, our mom was – after the babby . . .'

'Not half as poorly as you are though, Doris,' Jess snarled. 'Sick in the head, you are, ain't yer? This is who you've been afraid of all this time, Auntie: a broken down, mumbling old biddy so eaten up with nastiness towards other people you can read it in her face. Auntie—' Jess held out her arm and pulled her forwards.

Olive was trying to calm herself, wiping her eyes with the handkerchief. 'See – she ain't nothing to be afraid of. She's an evil old bitch who likes to make other people suffer.'

Doris tried to take a step back as Jess, Sis and Olive half encircled her, but there was a wall behind her. Olive stood staring into her face, taking deep, shuddering breaths. It was a moment before she could speak.

'You made life hell for us,' she said at last. 'It was wrong and cruel of yer. I 'ope you rot in hell for eternity for yer wickedness, that I do. But whatever happens, there ain't nothing more you can do to me. You're nothing. You're just a speck of filth and soon time'll sweep yer away and you'll've left nothing good behind yer.'

Doris was making vicious sounding mumblings, 'get away from me, yer bitches . . . get away!' Jabbing her stick at them, her head making little jerks which reminded Jess of her stepmother's hen-peck nod.

Olive straightened up. 'Leave 'er. Just leave 'er. I've seen 'er now and I don't want to look at 'er no more. Let's get 'ome.' She took Jess and Sis's arms and they turned away, Sis making sure they'd got all the right bags.

They had walked a little further on towards Digbeth when they became aware of a small commotion behind them. Nothing loud, but a ripple of different sounds at the end of the Bull Ring, and they turned. A couple of people were running and a little knot of passers-by was gathering round. The three of them stared for a few seconds at the little they could see of what was on the ground: what looked like a little pile of crumpled black clothing lying very still. A walking stick lay discarded nearby.

They looked at each other.

'We killed her,' Olive said. Her tone was of disbelief mixed with fear. Sis looked absolutely horrified. They stood stock still, watching as two of the crowd bent over Doris. A few moments later they saw she was being helped groggily to her feet.

Jess pulled on their arms, forcing them to turn away and walk on with her.

'She must've come over dizzy, we never killed her.' She squeezed each of their arms, certain, reassuring. 'But even if we 'ad, she'd've bloody well deserved it.'

All the way home Olive chattered, 'Oh Lor' – oh my, I can't believe it . . . And the way you carried on, Jess, I never knew you 'ad it in yer!'

'Well I 'ave – and the way I feel about 'er I could've broken 'er flaming neck, the evil old cow.'

They found Polly giving the children their dinner at the table and John Bullivant was there too. His face had filled out more and he was a calmer, slightly more cheerful man though still suffering times of deep depression.

Polly looked at her mom with concern.

Olive sank down on to a chair as if none of the rest of them was there.

'She awright?' Polly whispered to Jess.

'My legs,' Olive murmured. 'They won't hold me.'

'What's happened?' Polly demanded. 'Did yer 'ave a nice time?'

'We, er . . .' Jess looked at Sis who was still holding her bags of purchases, over her arm.

But Olive had put her face in her hands and burst into tears, crying with all the abandon of a young child.

*

402

Later, when they were alone, Jess said to Polly, 'There's one more thing for 'er now. For all of us. When the wedding's over, we've got to get things finished for 'er. We've got to find Alice.'

Forty-Two

'I now pronounce you man and wife!'

The vicar's thin face lit up as Sis and Perce flung themselves joyfully into each other's arms in the aisle of St Agnes' Church. Jess felt a smile spread across her own face. She wanted to clap but that wouldn't be right.

Sis, for all her passion to marry Percy, had been all nerves that morning. When they reached the church she'd come over wobbly and tearful and Olive had had to calm her down outside before they could go in, while Polly reminded an over-excited Grace that she was going to have to walk quietly up the aisle with her auntie Sis in their pretty dresses.

They'd all been on the edge of their seats as Sis and Perce took their vows. At the moment when the vicar asked did he, Percival James Bolter, take Louise Joan Beeston, Perce's head shot round to look at her in astonishment. He'd forgotten Sis's proper name – was he marrying the wrong woman? Little Grace had stood fidgeting and twisting round to receive encouraging looks from her mom, and they all thought Sis was going to get the weeps or the giggles again. But now she had got through it. She was married! She paraded back along the aisle on Perce's arm beaming at everyone.

As the rest of them turned to follow the couple out, Jess saw Peter Stevenson standing a couple of rows behind them, dressed smartly in black, following Davey out from the pew. He was turned slightly away from her and she had a couple of seconds to observe him, dark eyes fixed on his son, his tall figure stooped to guide Davey. The sight of his large, gentle hands on the boy's shoulders sent a sudden sensation through her, a kind of melting, a longing. What care, what kindness there was in the man, she thought. He didn't look round at her, and following him to the back of the church she thought how little they'd seen of him recently. Last summer he'd been round, or out with them almost every week, had been so often by her side, but she had been so preoccupied with Ned she had barely noticed, had taken his presence for granted, oblivious of the feelings which Sis said he had for her. She realized that until today they hadn't seen him for well over a month. Everyone was busy with new jobs and they no longer worked together. Peter had found another job as a foreman in a machine tool works. Perhaps he's feeling better in himself now, Jess thought. He just needed company then, that was all.

'Wasn't it lovely?' Polly was chattering down her ear. Grace, who had run to her the second the service was over, was in her arms. 'And didn't you look just like a princess, Gracie? You did them dresses lovely, Jess.'

Grace's yellow, flowery frock matched Sis's and the colours had looked warm and lovely in the dim light of the church.

'It was perfect,' Jess said absently. I miss him, she found herself thinking. Miss him being there with us.

After Sis and Perce had been duly showered with rice and congratulations, the families went down to the Ship Inn for a drink or two before going back to the house for some food. Jess hurried home with Olive to make sure everything was ready for them. Polly followed

405

them more slowly, pushing John, Grace riding on his lap and Ronny running alongside.

'Is, er – is Peter coming back?' Jess asked.

'Oh, I s'pect Sis'll bring 'im along,' Olive panted. 'God, it's warm today, ain't it? I 'ope we've got enough, Jess, I want them all to 'ave a good feed.'

The tables were chock-a-block with meats and pies, sandwiches and cakes, and a vase of spring flowers stood by the front window. Olive whisked the cloths off the plates and set out as many cups and glasses as she could lay hands on, Marion Bullivant having provided her with all hers. When Sis and Perce and the rest of them arrived from the pub, full of jollity, everything was looking ready and welcoming.

'Oh Sis!' Jess kissed her, then Perce. 'That was lovely. You look so beautiful, don't she, Perce?'

'Like my very own angel,' Perce said quaintly, and Sis, still clinging to his arm, said, 'Oh Perce, that's lovely, that is. I 'ope yer'll still be saying that when I'm an old lady and me teeth've all dropped out!'

Over their shoulders Jess saw Peter arriving. Her pulse picked up speed at the sight of him. I never thought this'd happen again, she thought, not for anyone. She waited for him to come to her, as he always had in the past, looking for excuses to be at her side. But instead he looked round the front room, his eyes skating over her, as if he was looking for someone else, and he went out, through to the back. Jess found herself feeling bereft.

Oh well, she thought. No point in me thinking about him. Sis was imagining things about Peter. He was just lonely. And anyway, I must seem almost like a child to him.

She moved round the room offering sandwiches,

406

chatting to Perce's mom, dad and sister, and his brother who had lost an arm on Vimy Ridge and had to stand next to the table to rest his plate on it or he had no spare arm to eat with. Jess liked Perce's family. They were all relaxed and friendly and full of jokes, but all the time she was aware of where Peter was in the house. He chatted to John, to Polly, to Sis and Perce. He played with the children, helped Olive bring in water from outside. Once or twice as they passed one another he nodded and said hello with a tentative smile. But not once did he come to her as he used to do, to talk and spend time with her. If Peter had ever felt anything for her, she thought, he didn't any longer. Now they were working apart that had changed. The chance was gone. By the end of the afternoon, happy as she was for Sis, she found herself feeling empty and disappointed.

They saw Sis and Perce off for their little weekend holiday with much cheering and kissing and good wishes. They were off into town to catch a train out to the country. Sis, her moods changing with great rapidity that day, was a bit tearful again as she embraced Olive.

'I'm not really leaving 'ome, am I, mom? I'll only be down the road!'

'Go on with yer and enjoy yerself,' Olive sniffed, giving her a watery smile. 'Time to worry about all that when yer get back.'

'Bye, Jess,' Sis hugged her tight. 'You next, eh, you and Polly?'

'Polly maybe,' Jess laughed. 'I don't know about me – I think I'm going to end up an old maid!'

'Poll?' John Bullivant called to her from where he was positioned by the table in the back room. Much of the afternoon he had been having a good chinwag with Bert and with Perce's brother, the other old soldiers present. Now things had quietened down a bit, the light was beginning to die outside and he wanted a few moments' privacy.

'Take us out the back for a minute, will yer?'

Polly, thinking he needed to use the privy and didn't like to say, tactfully opened the back door and manoeuvred the chair through it.

'Close the door, wench.'

Obediently she fastened it and went to push the chair closer to the door of the privy.

'No – I don't want that. I wanted to talk to yer, alone like.'

John found his hands were quivering and he gripped the arms of the chair. Polly stood in front of him in the half light, thin, kindly, waiting to hear what he had to say. For a moment he was overwhelmed by the sight of her. How could he even be thinking of offering himself to this woman: injured, useless, half a man as he was? How could he even dare think it?

'What did yer want to say to me, John?'

Best spit it out, he thought. Only way. 'Polly – I'll never be able to walk again. I can't work. I'm next to useless. But I love yer. I want to ask you to be my wife.'

There was a long silence as she looked into his face. For a moment John could barely meet her eyes, but he looked up to see her lips trembling and she turned away from him, putting her hands over her face.

'Yer can't face it, can yer? Being saddled with a cripple for the rest of your life! For all yer fine words that's what I am to yer – a lump of meat in a wheelchair, not a man!'

'No! It ain't that, John – truly!' Slowly she moved round to face him again, hands still held in front of her as if to replace them over her face at any moment. 'It ain't you. I love yer, John – I do. You're a lovely man and I'd give my life to yer with pleasure. But—' She couldn't put into words what was stopping her, was tearing her emotions apart. I'm still married: Ernie's still with me as if it were yesterday and until I can believe he's dead I can't marry you with a clear conscience. I'm haunted by him and he won't let me rest . . .

'But . . .' The grief and bitterness in John's voice as he echoed her made her distraught. She went to him, kneeling to take him in her arms.

'I do love yer – just give me a bit more time, sweetheart. That's all. I want to be yer wife. I just can't agree to it yet.'

John put his arms round her bony shoulders and his eyes met hers. 'Don't hide anything from me, Poll. I couldn't stand that. Is there someone else yer want more?'

'No! Oh John, no! I mean, not anyone like you mean. It's Ernie. I know it seems stupid to you but I can't marry yer 'til I've found a way to lay 'im to rest. Once and for all.'

Everyone looked up as they came back in. Perce's family had all gone and the rest of them were sitting round the back room looking relaxed and happy. As they came in, Peter Stevenson got up.

'Time we were off, Davey,' he said. 'I'm sure we've outstayed our welcome already.'

The little boy groaned. He and Ronny were playing together on the floor. 'Oh Dad – not yet!'

'Course yer staying,' Olive commanded. 'There's plenty more to eat and drink and we've 'ardly seen yer since Christmas. We'd thought you'd gone off us!'

'Don't talk daft,' Peter said, putting his hat down again. 'Course I haven't. I thought you might just want to be family . . .'

'You're almost part of the family,' Olive insisted, eyeing Jess meaningfully. 'How's that kettle coming on?'

'Slow,' Jess said. She was glad of something to keep her busy. All day she had felt an emotional pressure growing between herself and Peter Stevenson. She was sure now that he was not avoiding her by accident. But she hadn't approached him either. She didn't know how to be with him any more, what to say. She didn't know what he felt and was just as unsure of her own feelings. She found herself struck dumb in his company.

As John and Polly came in Bert got up to help. He took in Polly's emotional expression.

'What's up, Poll?'

Polly looked round the room, then down at John as if asking his permission. Jess saw him nod.

'Go on,' he said. 'Yer might as well.'

'John's asked me to marry him—' Polly held up one hand as the others began to exclaim at the news. 'But I've said to 'im I can't yet, things being as they are. You know 'ow things were for me after Ernie . . . after 'e were killed. I know you thought I were going off me 'ead, Mom. But it were the only way I could face things then. But the thing is . . .' She began to get emotional again. 'I still feel as if 'e's about. As if it's a mistake and 'e ain't really . . . dead. I know it sounds daft, but it's not knowing where 'e is or what happened . . .'

She stopped, looking round at them.

Bert spoke gently to her. 'You don't think 'e's not dead? Don't waste yer time thinking that, Poll. 'E'll be dead all right – you know that, don't yer?'

Polly nodded. 'I do really. It's just – if I could see his grave – you know, like you do with a normal death. I mean, even if we knew where 'e was, they ain't going to bring any of them back over 'ere, are they?'

Jess listened, one hand on the warm handle of the kettle. She thought of all her visits to her mom's grave, what strength she had taken from it. Things need finishing properly, she thought. For all of us.

Olive sat massaging her sore knuckles. 'Well there ain't no chance of that, Poll.'

'There might be, you know.'

Everyone looked at Peter Stevenson.

'What d'yer mean?' Polly said.

'People do go. Some even went before the war was over.'

'Well I know *some* do, like with money and that, but I mean it's right over there – across the Channel. It's *France*.'

Peter smiled. 'It's not the ends of the earth. People do go to France.'

'Not people like us.'

'Well I went,' John said. 'For a start.'

'But it'd cost the earth,' Olive said.

'There's a fund started up, I think.' Peter rubbed his forehead as if it would help him remember. 'Some feller at the works was talking about it. Look – I'll ask around, see if there's anything we could do.' He smiled suddenly, his gaze directed across at Jess who had not realized until that moment that she had her eyes fixed on him. It was as if each of them forgot for a second that they were not supposed to feel for each other. Shyly, she smiled back, instantly full of a warm sense of joy.

A few days later he called again, quite late in the evening, without David who was asleep at home. Polly let him in and Jess was startled at his sudden appearance, hat in hand, ducking his head to come through the door. For a second his eyes met hers, then he looked quickly away. Jess moved briskly across the room, finding things to busy herself with. He hasn't come to see me, she told herself. He's come out of kindness for Polly.

'There is a fund, like I said. Just starting up.'

Polly was watching him, her expression full of misgiving.

'If you go with a London travel company it'll set you back thirty-five pound – more even. If you go through the fund it's fourteen.'

'Struth!' Olive exclaimed.

Bert was shaking his head. 'Fourteen quid! The bloke's dead!'

Polly ignored him. 'That's still an 'ell of a lot of money.'

Jess moved over and put her hand on her cousin's shoulder. 'Poll – if you want to go that bad and put your mind at rest, we'll find the money for yer. I've got some savings – put away for a rainy day, like.'

'But I can't go to France on my own!'

Peter Stevenson cleared his throat. 'If you don't mind – I've got a suggestion to make.'

Forty-Three

May 1919

Jess leaned her head against the grimy window, feeling the rocking rhythm of the train as it chugged through the Staffordshire countryside. It was two weeks after Sis's wedding and she and Perce were home and getting settled into their tiny house on Sherbourne Road, though she was forever popping back to see them. She seemed happy and lively as ever, but missed the girls' company.

'Perce's lovely to me,' she said. 'But 'e don't *talk* all that much. I don't even know as 'e's listening to me 'alf the time.' She'd said she was too busy getting straight to come with them.

Polly and Jess sat side by side, each of them with their hats in their laps. Olive was opposite, dozing, mouth slightly open, hands slack. On the seat beside her was a posy of spring flowers. Outside was cloudy but dry, sunlight through breaks of cloud. They had started off very early that morning, taken a train up through the Black Country, seeing the red glow of furnaces in the grey morning, a pall of soot seeming to engulf everything, buildings, grass, trees. They changed at Stoke-on-Trent and were now on the branch line looking out at the fields green with young wheat, at tarnished churches, stone buildings. It's peaceful round here, Jess thought, and solid. She liked things to be solid. Sure. The nature of their visit filled her with a

413

great sense of poignancy. Travelling by train made her think of the passage of time, of life itself passing by in a way she seldom had time to do normally. She thought of Alice and Louisa. Her mother and grandmother, their lives cut short so young, and both, one way or another, because they were women. She found herself thinking of her own dead child. Ned's child. It came to her that every time a woman fell pregnant she took her own life in her hands, forever. Whether the babby lives or dies, none of us is ever the same again, she thought. And will there ever be any more children for me? Any more love for me?

Peter Stevenson's face came into her mind, the look he had given her that night outside the house, when he left with David asleep on his shoulder. She had been too frozen inside then, too full of grief to respond. Whichever way her mind turned it seemed to fasten on something sad: children, Ned, Peter. She turned to Polly who was looking across at Olive.

'Be there in a minute,' Jess said. 'It's no distance.'

'I hope this ain't going to upset her again.' Polly looked anxious. 'Mom's been through enough.'

'She wanted to come. Like you and France.' They were making arrangements, with Peter's support and help.

'I know it's the right thing to do. She should know where 'er own mom's buried. I think it's terrible our granddad never took 'er to see. I feel ever so churned up though, thinking about it.'

Jess nodded. 'I do an' all. Sort of touching the past. Gives yer a peculiar feeling.'

The train slowed and Polly leaned forward and gently prodded Olive's knee. 'We're there, mom.'

Olive opened her eyes, bewildered for a second as

414

the train braked abruptly. 'Feels as if we've been travelling for days.' She gathered her coat stoutly round her, picked up her bag and they hurried off. Polly had picked up the flowers.

As they stepped out on to the little station, a goods train made up of trucks full of sand rumbled past, the wind lifting a light silt of it sharp against their faces, making them blink their eyes.

'Ugh!' Polly said. 'It's windy up 'ere – let's get on.'

On the street, they stopped, at a loss.

'How do we know which way to go?' There was a tremor in Olive's voice. 'Oh Poll, we can't ask – not for that.' The terrible shame of it filled all of them. They would have to go and ask for the Mental Hospital. As good as admit that someone, one of their own, had been in an asylum, locked away from the world. For a moment they were completely at a loss.

'Maybe if we was just to walk round for a bit?' Polly suggested.

'No.' Jess pushed her chin out with furious defiance 'She was our flesh and blood, Alice was. I'll find out. I'll go back in there and ask.'

They had to walk out of the village, the stationmaster told Jess. He was a middle-aged, kindly sort who set them on the right road.

'You can't miss it,' he said. 'Look for the tower.'

The blackened, brick tower was the first they saw of the hospital. Once on the long drive the rest of it came into view, tucked in with hills behind, a low collection of buildings so desolate, so marked in its isolation from everything around it that the sight made the three of them reach for each other's hands. They had not spoken much on the walk out there, each of them too full of feeling. Jess breathed in deeply, trying to calm herself. Was this Alice's place? The walls behind which pretty, young Alice had lived out the rest of her days? She looked anxiously at her aunt and saw Polly was doing the same. How much more Olive must be feeling!

Olive showed no outward sign of emotion.

'This is it then?'

'Yes,' Jess said gently.

'I can't really take it in.'

'You awright mom?' Polly had a catch in her voice.

Olive's eyes moved over the collection of buildings. 'This is where they put 'er then. Where they took 'er. All that time . . .' She shook her head, beyond words.

When she had taken in the sight of the place for a time, Jess said,

'Shall we go and ask to see the graveyard?'

Olive seemed to steel herself for a moment, then nodded. As they walked along, arm in arm, she pulled the two of them closer to her. Jess looked round at her, remembering holding her aunt's hand the day they buried Louisa, when her head only reached up to Olive's elbow.

The main door was black with a small grille set in it which opened quite some time after they had pulled the bell. A man's face appeared, eyes narrowing against the light.

'We're expected,' Jess said. 'Mrs Beeston. We wrote to say we'd be coming.'

After a long process of rattling bolts and turning keys, they stepped inside, as if into another life.

'Follow me,' the man said. 'It'll be Mr Lang you want.'

416

He led them halfway along a deserted, echoing corridor and into an office where a dark-haired man with thick horn-rimmed spectacles sat owlishly behind a desk. Seated at another desk behind him, a woman was typing at high speed.

It was Polly, in the end, who did the talking. Olive found herself incapable and sunk down on to the chair opposite the desk. Jess found Mr Lang a little strange at first. He didn't look them in the eye, and he spoke slowly, as if unused to it, in a low, gravelly voice, but he was obliging enough. He searched through a pile of papers for Jess's letter.

'Let's see – you say you want to look for the grave of an Alice . . .' he strung out the words, 'Tamplin. Hmmm. Now I don't know anything about her, of course. You're certain she was here when she died? Good, well, I'll get someone . . . no, look, let me take you. That would be easiest.'

He stood up and put his coat on and a hat over his thin black hair. 'I shan't be long,' he told the typist.

To Jess's relief he led them, with loping strides, back the way they had come to the front entrance. She had been afraid they would have to walk through the labyrinth of the hospital, and the place appalled her. The man asked no questions, just kept walking, slightly ahead of them. Once they had walked out and round the side of the building he pointed and said,

'You can see the hospital chapel there.' The geometry of that part of the building differed from the rest, the roof curving up to a point, rather like the prow of a ship, with a cross on top, and the end wall, which jutted out, had crosses built into the pattern of the brickwork. 'We need to go just round behind there.' His tone was low and considerate.

'It's very quiet,' Jess said uneasily. 'Where is everyone – all the inmates, I mean?'

Mr Lang pulled out his watch as he walked and looked at it. 'They'll all be inside on the wards. Except a few who're out working in the grounds, but that's over the other side.'

The graveyard looked neglected, the grass long and full of clumps, and a riot of weeds and wild flowers had colonized all over it. Mr Lang explained that part of the hospital had been vacated for use as a military hospital during the war, the inmates moved elsewhere.

'Everything went downhill as you can imagine. Still recovering. I'm very new here myself, of course. Now – perhaps you'd like to have a look . . .'

He stood aside with his hands clasped behind his back as if to dissociate himself from their emotion as they began to wander up and down the rows of graves together, reading the plain little crosses and headstones, some of them wood, a litany of strangers' names, waiting for the words, 'Alice Tamplin' to be there, to jump out at them. Row by row they looked, reading along the fifty or sixty graves until they came to the last.

'Must be here,' Polly murmured. ''Ow could we've missed it? We can't've done, can we?' Jess felt she was studying each one more intently than the last, as if to force the name on it to be Alice's. When they reached the last stone, it read, 'Susannah Peters'. They looked up at each other.

'Well where is she then?' Olive said shrilly. 'What did they do with her?'

Mr Lang was beginning to sound weary of the whole affair. He led them back to his office.

'You say she died – when?'

'It'd have been eighteen eighty-four,' Olive said. She couldn't hide her distress. 'That's when my father told us. I was thirteen . . . She must be 'ere somewhere. I've always known of 'er being 'ere . . .'

'One moment Mrs – ?'

'Beeston.'

Olive sat, breathing audibly as Mr Lang went through a door at the back of the office and returned with two leatherbound ledgers which he opened on the desk and stood leaning over them like a carrion bird.

'What year was the lady in question sent here?'

Polly and Jess looked at Olive.

'Eighteen seventy-seven. August eighteen seventy-seven – no, 'ang on, that'd be Birmingham. She came out 'ere the following year. Eighteen seventy-eight, early on, about February.'

He replaced the ledgers with others, opening yellowed pages and running his twig-like fingers down inky lists.

'Ah.' He stopped. 'Yes. Here we are.'

Olive's right hand went to her throat.

'Alice Tamplin – from Birmingham? They brought her all the way out here?'

'Was that unusual?' Jess asked.

'Rather – but not unheard of. There are hospitals in Birmingham, of course. But if they were over-full, for instance . . . Or a request from the family. Now . . .' He turned over a few pages, musingly. Jess felt as if her eyes were trying to bore through the pages. Show us! she wanted to shout. Show us what it says!

Mr Lang turned another page and a sheet of paper fluttered to the floor. The woman who had been typing had stopped to listen, and she picked it up. Mr Lang peered with sudden attention at the page.

'Oh! Ah – now, here we are! Well well . . .'

'What does it say?' Jess couldn't keep quiet.

'No wonder we couldn't find her in the grave-yard.' He looked up at them over his spectacles. 'Alice Tamplin did not die in this hospital.'

They gaped at him.

'What d'yer mean?' Polly could barely do more than whisper.

'On the fifth of May eighteen eighty-seven, an Alice Tamplin quitted the hospital.'

'Quitted?' Olive said faintly.

'Yes, left. Was allowed to leave. Discharged.'

They looked back at him in sheer disbelief.

'But—' Jess said eventually. 'How could she just *leave*?'

'It seems that she was considered of sound enough mind, of no danger to others or to herself. It does happen occasionally. But someone must claim responsibility for any inmate who is to be released. In this case,' he looked down at the page again. 'The person named is a Mr Arthur Tamplin.'

Shock came so fast upon shock that they hadn't the time or capability of making sense of it. Olive sat quite silent, quite still.

'But where did she *go* then?' Polly asked. 'She never came 'ome, did she?'

'No,' Olive whispered. 'Never.'

'She may have gone to Leek to seek employment. Or even as far as Stoke. I'm afraid there's no record of that.'

'I think this might shed some light on it.' The woman at the typewriter was peering at the yellowed slip of paper which had floated to the floor. Mr Lang turned to take it from her, but she got up and handed it straight to Jess.

It was a cheap piece of notepaper with a few lines of looped writing on it. It was addressed to a 'Miss Harper'. Jess gave it straight to Olive and she and Polly leaned over her to read it.

1887

> I got to Whitall orite He got me a plase to live and Im making a start on the baking He said he'd see me orite wich he will in case i deside to goo back home wich he dont want I wont goo, too much water under the brige Ill get on here its nice and quiet
>
> Thankyou for waht youve dune for me ill niver forget you.
>
> sincerly, Alice Tamplin.

When she'd read it, Olive went very pale and her hands were shaking so much that she couldn't hold the flimsy sheet of paper. 'That's her writing,' she kept saying. 'Oh yes – that's her writing.'

Polly handed it back to Mr Lang and laid her hand on her mother's shoulder. She helped Olive lean forwards, supporting her as she tried to recover herself.

'D'yer think . . .' Jess's mind was racing. 'I mean, might she still be alive?'

The man shrugged. 'I'm afraid I have no idea. This was all before my time. I don't know the age of the woman in question, or her circumstances.'

'No – course you don't,' Jess said. 'Only this is such a shock for us, yer see. All these years . . .' She stopped, shaking her head. 'Where is Whitall?'

421

'Not far at all. Between here and Wetley Rocks. A couple of miles at most.'

She and Polly helped Olive to her feet and they left, thanking Mr Lang. The main door closed thunderously behind them.

Walking back down the long sweep of the drive, their minds were seething with all they had just learned. Olive, so silent before, couldn't stop talking, repeating over and over the anguish of the truth she had just learned, tears streaming down her face.

'All that time 'e knew our Mom was alive and 'e kept her hidden out of the way so 'e could live with that Elsie instead! Louisa and me'd 've done anything to have our mom back. Oh Poll – can yer credit it? She was out of 'ere and 'e never said. I can't believe 'e could be that cruel, that I can't. If 'e was still alive today I'd – oh, I don't know what I'd do!' She stopped, turning to look back at the hospital with its black, secretive windows.

'What if—' Jess said. She and Polly were nearly as overwrought themselves. 'What if she's still living there, in Whitall? I mean – she'd be what, seventy?'

'Nigh on. No – oh Jess, yer don't think . . . No, she can't be, can she? I mean, she ain't come to us in all this time. We can't – she daint want us . . .'

'Auntie—' Jess took Olive's arm and spoke gently to her. 'She'd been in this place for ten years. *Ten whole years.* Of course she wanted yer, but it must've felt like a lifetime she'd been away. And she knew she weren't allowed to 'ave yer.'

'Granddad would never've let 'er out if 'e thought she'd ever come near Birmingham again,' Polly said. 'She must've thought of you and Auntie Louisa with a new step-mom, all settled like . . . How could she just come back? She was dead to them and she had to stay dead even if it broke her heart.'

Olive's face crumpled again. 'Oh God, and it breaks mine just to think of it . . .'

Jess and Polly held her close to them. Jess felt the rough weave of Olive's coat under her fingers, and could feel her trembling.

'Mom,' Polly said. 'D'yer want to leave the flowers here somewhere? Where she was? I know she daint die here, but just in case?'

Olive drew back, tears on her face.

'I don't know.' She looked round. 'No. We can't leave 'em 'ere. I wanted somewhere with the feel of 'er in it, but I can't feel it. She ain't 'ere.'

Forty-Four

It took them nearly an hour to walk to Whitall. On the way they persuaded Olive to stop for a few minutes in a gateway by the road to rest and eat some of the bread and cheese they had brought.

'I couldn't eat,' she said.

'You must, Mom. It's hours since we had anything and we'll be dropping else. You need to keep yer strength up for this.' Polly handed round food from the bag. 'Ooh, I could do with a cuppa to wash it down,' she said.

The grass was wet and muddy underfoot so they stood up to eat. A horse and cart passed by on the road and a lad sitting at the back with his legs dangling down stared open-mouthed at them. Birds dived twittering in and out of the hedgerows and Jess breathed in the smells of grass and wet earth.

'Louisa took to the country,' Olive said, seeing Jess gazing round at the fields, a soft expression in her eyes. 'It were like she was born to it.'

'P'raps Alice liked it too,' Jess said.

The village of Whitall sprawled along the road which ran through it like a spine. They passed farms, then cottages, widely spaced at first, then huddling closer together, making a proper street. A few people were about, and some looked curiously at them. The road was muddy and churned up by cart tracks. At the heart of the village smaller lanes branched off the main road and to one side, and behind the cottages, they could see the square tower of the church, topped at each corner with little gold flags. They turned off down the lane to the church, hawthorn and young trees on each side of them. At the end the path widened and divided to run in each direction, forming an oval-shaped path round the graveyard.

Olive immediately began looking at the names on the graves. Watching her aunt's quest, her stopping, looking so intently, sometimes even tracing over the letters with her finger then straightening up, each time hoping, Jess felt suddenly that she couldn't bear it. Even if Alice was buried here, a stone would tell them nothing of her.

'That must be the vicarage.' She pointed at a large, gabled house behind the church. 'Let's ask, Poll, shall we? It's such a small place we must be able to find someone who knew 'er and could tell us summat.'

Olive began to protest.

'Please, Mom,' Polly touched her arm. 'We've come all this way.'

There were yellow climbing roses in the front garden of the vicarage and they could hear the sound of children from the back. The house was so big and grand that for a moment they hesitated. Then Jess lifted the heavy knocker.

The maid told them the vicar was in, and took them into a homely parlour evidently reserved for visitors. Soon they heard a voice in the corridor saying, 'Strangers, you say. Well, well. How exciting—' and round the door appeared the plump, boyish face of a man who appeared ready to befriend anyone in the world.

'Good afternoon – I'm Mr May. Archie May. Vicar of the parish.'

As he stepped forward to shake hands, it was immediately apparent that his left arm was missing, the sleeve of his shirt pinned up at the shoulder. Seeing their gaze immediately fix on this as they shook hands, he said,

'Yes – lost the other one. Ypres.' He pronounced it Wipers. 'Army chaplain – one of the Staffs battalions. Damn lucky it wasn't the other one, since I'm right-handed, eh?'

He indicated that they should sit down. 'Now – can I help you in any way?'

Between them, Jess and Polly began to explain, and the Revd Archie May listened attentively.

'I say—' he interrupted after a moment. 'You've travelled all the way from Birmingham! You must have a cup of tea – just a moment.' He went to the door and summoned the maid and in no time a tray of tea appeared. Jess felt like hugging him for his thoughtfulness. As they drank it, they explained that they were looking for a relative who may have lived in the village.

Archie May stroked his chin. 'Alice Tamplin?' As he spoke, Jess felt her innards contract. It was so strange hearing her name on someone else's tongue. It made her real. Out of the corner of her eye she could see Olive's hands tightly clasped on her lap. But the vicar shook his head. 'No – doesn't ring a bell. Thing is though, I've only been the incumbent here for a matter of months, so my memory doesn't stretch back all that far. Tell you what—' he jumped up boisterously. 'Soon as you've downed that tea – I've got just the chap for you. Just have a word with my wife – let her know I'm off out.'

He left the room for a moment and they heard his voice shout 'Darling?' distantly at the back of the house. They looked at each other in silence, sipping the hot tea from bone china cups as fast as they could manage.

'Now—' Archie May looked the sort of man who would have rubbed his hands together frequently had he been able to do so. 'Let me take you to meet Revd Chillingworth. He was vicar here for – oh, thirty-five years or more, and he still lives in the village, just across the green. If there's anything to remember about any soul in the parish, he's your man. Marvellous fellow.' He led them out of the front door. 'In his mid-seventies and still turns out to make up the Whitall eleven, cricket mad, all his life.'

Polly took Olive's arm and they followed Archie May's springy walk back along the lane to the road and along another short path running off from the opposite side, which led to the village green. Round it stood four cottages and he took them to one which had a riot of buddleia bursting out of its front garden, alive with cabbage white and tortoiseshell butterflies.

The Revd Thomas Chillingworth was, even at his advanced age, a magnificent-looking man. Tall, slightly stooped, with the bushiest white eyebrows Jess had ever seen, vivid blue eyes and a large, hooked nose. His face and hands were so lined and gnarled they made Olive's look quite youthful.

'Come in, come in!' He led them into a sitting room at the back looking out over a lawn edged with flowering shrubs. The three of them quailed at the sound of his loud, autocratic voice, but to Jess's astonishment,

Archie May turned round and winked conspiratorially at them. 'He's a proper old lamb in wolf's clothing,' he murmured. 'Very deaf though.'

They were invited to sit in this room, already so stuffed with books and papers that there seemed barely space to move. The wall was covered with pictures with leprous-looking mounts round them, mostly of cricket teams. Thomas Chillingworth sat grandly before them, a prayer book resting on the arm of his chair, and leaned forward to listen to what Archie May had to say, one hand cupped round his right ear to increase his chance of hearing.

'Alice?' he boomed. 'Oh yes – I remember Alice all right.'

All of them felt their hearts race violently, but intimidated by the old man they left the young vicar to question him.

'Alice Tamplin?' Archie May asked.

'What's that? Tamplin? No – no recollection of a Tamplin. But Alice – now I remember her. Could hardly forget her – practically lived in the church. Only one who came to evensong every night of her life . . .'

'But her name wasn't Tamplin?' Archie looked regretfully at them. No luck, his expression said.

'No – she was . . . Brodie. That was it. Alice Brodie.'

They all heard Olive's breath catch. Even Thomas Chillingworth seemed to sense the impact of his words.

'That was 'er maiden name,' Olive said, gripping Polly's hand. 'She was a Brodie – 'ad a brother, Joe Brodie all 'is life.'

'She's . . .' Jess hesitated. 'She's dead then?'

'Dead – oh yes,' he continued loudly. 'Died a good while back, poor old Alice. Before the war. She was taken with one of those wasting diseases and faded

428

away. Never would have any help from anyone. Baked bread – that was her living, you see – right up to the end. Always like that. Very reserved woman, very quietly spoken. Strong as an ox though, I reckon. She came to me two or three times—' His voice slowed, musing on the memory. 'Odd, it was – I thought so at the time. She'd look into my face as if she'd come to offload something particular, but in the end she'd never say anything much . . . In all the years she was here she barely ever said a word about herself. Not to anyone, so far as I know. I knew she'd been in the asylum over there—' He jerked his head. 'That was common knowledge. Heaven alone knows what effect that had. But she just went along, you know, lived a quiet life, no harm to anyone . . . that was all really.'

There was silence for a moment. He sat nodding, remembering.

'One thing I do recall, now I think of it. Early on – probably the first Christmas she was in the village though the Lord only knows now when that was . . . She was a very devout woman as I say, attended everything. But on that Christmas Eve she came to the midnight service. She was deeply upset by it. It sticks in my mind because she was in such a state when she came to take communion. Weeping, distraught. And upset at attracting notice to herself. It's a season which does heighten the emotions, of course. Especially these days . . . but I never saw Alice like that at any other time. She never came to the Midnight Eucharist again. Not in all the years she lived here.'

He became aware of the intense, rapt attention of the three women in front of him. 'So what have you to do with Alice?'

'She was . . .' Jess had to shout to make him hear. 'A

relative. A long-lost relative.' She looked at Archie May. 'Will you ask him – did Alice marry? Are there any children?'

'Marry? Alice?' For a few seconds his body shook with silent mirth at the idea. 'Alice wasn't the marrying kind. Oh no – you couldn't imagine Alice marrying. I don't know what was in her past – perhaps you do. But she was an island on her own, Alice Brodie was . . .' Again, he shook his head. 'An isolated being. That was Alice. Cut loose, somehow. Strange creature.' He looked directly at them. 'But a good soul. Of that I'm sure.'

A thought struck him and he pulled himself spryly out of the chair.

'Let me see now – d'you know, I do believe . . .'

He fumbled round amidst the utter chaos of the shelves, limping along them stiffly, running a finger along the dusty leather bindings.

'There are a couple of albums from the parish – I must hand them over to you, Archie. Not really mine to keep after all. Ah – here!'

Yellowed pages crackled open under his hands displaying faded sepia photographs. He looked through, murmuring to himself.

'Yes – that's the one! The only time we could persuade her to come along. This was the annual parish picnic – nineteen hundred, look. Now that—' his arthritic finger quivered lightly over a face at the end of the solemnly posing line, 'is Alice Brodie.'

The tiny, indistinct face of a fifty-year-old woman looked out at them from the picture from under a dark hat with a brim. Jess could hear Olive's jerky breathing close to her as they peered forward to look.

'Oh God.'

'Is it?' Polly asked.

'It's so small – I can't be sure . . .' Olive laid her hand over her heart, trying to calm herself, staring rapt at the picture. 'It could be, but then – oh my Lord, yes it could easily be . . .'

They all pored over the picture, unable to move away from their one glimpse of Alice, Alice who, after all, had made some sort of life. Jess couldn't stop staring at the faded sweetness of the face, its closed, unsmiling gaze, the thick hair escaping from under the hat. She could sense that had Louisa lived long enough, she too would have looked like this, and that in turn, one day, she herself . . . But the woman's face told so little. Another face among a throng of faces giving nothing away. No clue on the outside, Jess thought. No scars to show us.

'I say,' Archie took in the acuteness of their need to see. 'Thomas – how about giving them the picture? The parish won't miss one photograph – they'll only moulder quietly away on the shelves in the vicarage.'

'Would you like it?' Thomas Chillingworth asked. 'I don't see why not, after all, if it means so much.'

He took an ivory-handled paper knife from his desk and carefully cut the page from the album. Olive took it from him as if she hardly dared touch it, looking up at him in awe.

'I'm ever so grateful – I don't know what to say,' she said tremulously. 'You see – Alice Brodie was my mother.'

They found her name in the graveyard, 'Alice Brodie', carved on a simple stone, positioned close to a young lilac tree which was pushing out fragrant white blossom.

431

They had left Archie May with their stumbling gratitude, and come to kneel on the spongy grass round the
grave in the afternoon sun.

On the stone it said simply, 'Alice Brodie 1850–1912.
Faithful Child of God.'

Olive sat, transfixed by the sight of it. They were
silent for a long time, staring at the little grave, the high
emotions of the day still coursing through them. All
that remained of Alice, then, they could locate here.
This had been her place where she settled at last, and
this what finally remained, this little stone already green
with lichen.

But we remember you, Alice, Jess said, in her mind.
Your family remembers you and you live on with us.
Now you can rest in peace.

At last, Jess gently nudged Polly. The two of them
got up and walked a short distance away. The graveyard
was ringed, beyond the path, with dark yew trees, but
among the graves were lighter, young blossom trees.
They went and stood near one, a flowering cherry still
wearing the remnants of its blossom.

For a moment the two of them put their arms round
one another and held on tight, not speaking. When they
released each other they stood watching Olive still
kneeling by the grave, her bag and the flowers beside
her. They could tell she had begun to speak, the low
murmur of her voice just reaching them though they
couldn't hear her words. After a time, she picked up the
posy of flowers and laid it carefully beside the humble
headstone. Then she got up and walked towards them,
and there was an enormous tiredness about her.

Forty-Five

Picardy, France – June 1919

The car lifted lazy sworls of dust behind it that hot, still midday, the sound of its engine breaking into the silence of the countryside. They had the windows open, so that the burring sound of the tyres over the pavé road came to them more loudly. The sun was almost at zenith, so that the car moved through an arcade of grey shadow thrown down by the trees with knobbly trunks which grew along the roadside.

They had taken the first morning boat to Boulogne, where the lady from the St Barnabas Fund met them to take them south: past Montreuil, through the old city of Abbeville and along the line of the Somme Valley towards Amiens. Now the war was coming very close to them. The names of towns were taking on a terrible familiarity, and as they motored away from the comparative tranquillity of the coast towards the battlefields of North Eastern France, they began to see clusters of graves marked with wooden crosses.

Jess, who was seated next to the rear left window, shifted her position a little, her cotton frock damp with sweat under her. Polly was asleep, leaning heavily against her shoulder, and Jess could feel the moist warmth between their bodies. She felt protective towards Polly, travelling here to face her grief head on. John was also asleep with his head back next to the other window. In front, Peter Stevenson made desultory conversation with Miss Baxter, the St Barnabas lady who was driving the car. She had rich brown hair taken up into a pleat and held tenuously by tortoiseshell combs. They looked so insecure that Jess, sitting behind her, had been waiting all day for them to fall out and her hair collapse, but so far they had held on, letting more and more strands of hair escape from them and blow round her head in the breeze from the window. Jess felt almost a sense of worship for Miss Baxter. She had thought of everything: the route and accommodation and the need to strap John's wheelchair to the roof of the chesty old car. She anticipated their needs, even their feelings. To Jess she seemed one of the most wonderful people she had ever met.

'Not too far now,' she called over her shoulder. Jess loved the sound of her Scottish accent. 'It's a pity we have to make these visits so brief,' Jess heard her say. 'But of course it's a question of the expense, and the sheer numbers of folk wanting so desperately to come. We hope to charge less as things get established.'

Peter nodded. Jess watched him out of the corner of her eye. She had an oblique view of his profile, the slant of his cheek, and she could just see the tip of his nose. She looked out of the window, but kept feeling her gaze drawn back to look at him, at the line of his dark hair at the nape of his neck.

'Were you on the Somme yourself?' Miss Baxter asked.

'No.' Jess heard a stiffness in his tone, his shame at not having done his bit. Peter raised one hand to ease some irritation on his cheek and she saw his long fingers rub the skin back and forth for a moment. 'I was reserved to oversee a munitions factory.'

'Aha. Well – the body is composed of many organs,' Miss Baxter said enigmatically.

Jess sensed, rather than saw, Peter smile faintly. She felt a huge surge of gratitude to him as well. It was because of him they were here. He who had sought out all the possibilities of getting them to France, who had made the arrangements. What had clinched things was that John Bullivant, hearing them discussing the possibility of going to the battlefields, had begged to be allowed to go.

'What on earth d'yer want to do that for, John?' Marion Bullivant had seemed quite alarmed.

'I can't explain it, Mom. I just do. I left me legs over there and I weren't with it when they brought me back. I don't remember 'ardly a thing about it.'

'But John,' Polly said gently. 'Ernie died on the Somme. We won't be going to Belgium.'

'I know that, Poll. But it's still over there, ain't it? The state the place'll be in I should think Ypres and the Somme'd look pretty much alike. I just feel I'd like to come and see it. It took years of my life as well as my legs.'

Polly had glanced across his head at Jess. We can't refuse him, her expression said. But how on earth are we going to manage?

It was Peter who had found out about the recently founded St Barnabas fund. Peter who had then said that he would come at his own expense to help John. Ernie's family had been all for Polly going and they chipped in to help. All of them had savings from the war and in the end they put together enough for the four of them.

Those weeks, as the spring had passed and turned into early summer, were a time of churned up feelings for all of them. Mixed in with the preparations for the journey to France was all the emotion over Alice, the rewriting of her past in their minds. Slowly they grew more used to the idea. It was hardest of all for Olive: to have to accept that her mother had been alive and had not come back to them, and grow to understand and forgive her. Jess saw her quite often just sitting in silence, staring, and knew she was thinking of it. When she did talk about it it was with enormous sadness and regret, not with bitterness. She put the photograph from Whitall parish in an old frame and it stood on the mantelpiece. Having that seemed to reclaim Alice as part of the family.

And there was other turmoil. Bert, after coming home and gleefully returning to civilian life, was now restless and discontented. His face wore a frown almost all the time.

'I'm back 'ere,' he complained. 'Back where I started in a bloody 'ard, filthy job. Four year of my life I fought and for what? What did I get out of it?' Though he had left the army cursing it high and low, he was now talking about joining up as a regular.

'You get used to the life, sort of thing. Moving about. Seeing a bit more of the world. And there're some good lads . . .'

By May he had re-enlisted and said his farewells to them.

'I don't blame 'im in a way,' Perce said when he heard.

Sis looked indignantly at him. 'Well I 'ope you ain't getting any ideas of going off!'

'Not on your life!' He gave her a saucy, affectionate pinch so she squealed. 'I know when I'm well off!'

Jess turned to the car window again, seeing now that

the scenery was changing. They had reached the edge of the town

'Now you can see,' Miss Baxter said. 'We're getting close.'

Jess nudged Polly who stretched, yawning loudly, and woke John. They sat in absolute silence as Miss Baxter steered the motor car slowly, almost reverently along the ruined main street of Amiens, still following the river.

'They make beautiful wool and velvet here – or did,' Miss Baxter said. 'Before it was shelled to blazes. And Albert's even worse. Almost completely flattened.'

It was hard to imagine that anything would ever be made in Amiens again. So many wrecked and ragged buildings, the rubble of stone, the smashed remains of life as it had been before.

'They didn't get the cathedral though – look, quickly, to your right. We're turning off here in a minute.'

Before them, the lead covered spire of the cathedral soared up out of the rubble against the blue sky with a kind of majestic defiance and in it they caught a glimpse of the city's real face, its splendour before the war.

Jess felt a moment of empathy with the huge building as if it were a big strong lady, squatting there, flanked by its flying buttresses like petticoats. She survived! Wouldn't let them crush her. It gave her strength, this thought, as they drove along the sleepy country road towards the ruined town from where Ned had sent her postcards of the basilica, when she had believed love was a sure, unchanging thing.

*

They stopped outside Albert in a tiny roadside café, ate bread and drank black coffee brought to them by a wordless girl who then stood with her back against the wall, watching them. Jess winced at the bitterness of the coffee but it refreshed her. They were seated at a rickety table in a little stone floored room where flies moved above their heads. Peter was beside her. Miss Baxter opposite.

'How did you come to be doing this work?' Peter asked her.

'Well . . .' She spoke slowly, as if reluctant. 'My fiancé was killed not far from here – at Grandcourt.' It came as a revelation to Jess that Miss Baxter was a great deal younger than her old-fashioned manner and style of dress made her appear. 'My family are not without money – I was able to come almost as soon as the war finished. It meant everything to me to know where Duncan met his end. There was no grave for me either—' She looked at Polly. Neither the Red Cross nor the Graves Registration Committee had been able to locate exactly where Ernie was buried. 'But to see the place – be close to him somehow . . .' She spoke with great sadness, but with a kind of resignation, and looked calmly round at them. 'I had to find a worthwhile way to fill my life. You see, Duncan and I were going to go abroad. He'd planned to train for the ministry and I was to teach – in India. I didn't want to go alone: it was our project, our dream to carry out together. So when I heard about St Barnabas I volunteered straight away, to help other people find some sort of peace of mind.'

Polly's eyes filled with tears. John put his hand on her shoulder. Before they left she had gone to a seance at the Blacks' house for what she said would be the last time. John didn't like her going. She had asked Ernie

438

what he thought of her going to France and he had given her his blessing. Miss Baxter's round face looked with great kindness at her.

'It's a sight you'll never forget – out where they were fighting. Beyond belief. But it does help, in a strange way.'

'I just need to know – to see,' Polly said. 'To lay him to rest in my mind.'

Miss Baxter leaned across and laid her hand over hers. 'I know, dear. I know.'

They left behind the ruins of Albert, straddling the River Ancre, and drove the few miles to La Boiselle through a landscape which looked ghostly even on this sunlit afternoon. The fields lay uncultivated along the Front, for the land had to be combed further for the dead. For miles on end stretched the churned up earth, pocked with shellholes. Shoots of grass, wheat and weeds had sprouted across them in uneven patches and here and there, tiny, fragile poppies blew in the breeze. They passed thin clumps of tree stumps, pathetic sticks poking up, barely a leaf in sight, and along the road still, lay the rubble and the human debris of the front line: sandbags, twisted chunks of rusting metal, wrecked wagons, sprawls of barbed wire and discarded belongings – a bleached scrap of khaki cloth here, an old water bottle or rusting mess tin there.

'My God,' Polly breathed. 'What a mess.' She had taken Jess's hand. They were almost afraid to see, much as they wanted to.

'We thought we had it bad,' Jess said soberly. 'But my God, the poor French!'

'There is a little money to be made out of the debris,'

439

Miss Baxter told them. 'I gather copper wire fetches a good price. And uniform buttons, guns – you'd be surprised.'

'Can't say I blame 'em though,' Polly said.

The road climbed gradually upwards and on each side of the road were gentle hills. Miss Baxter pulled the car into the side of the road and swivelled round to face them. She looked at Polly.

'We're very close. Up here the road will cross the line of trenches the Germans were holding in July 1916 when the Big Push began. You can see one of the craters where our boys mined underneath it prior to the attack. It's a massive hole – still full of what they left behind, helmets and so on. And just over the way are our trenches – they were very close together here. Just in the village there's a spot they call the Glory Hole where they were only yards apart.'

Polly gripped Jess's hand. Jess could see Peter watching her cousin, a gentle expression on his face. He sensed her looking at him and his eyes moved to meet hers for a second.

'Can we get out 'ere a minute?' John asked.

Miss Baxter hesitated.

'I'll help him,' Peter said. 'You stiff, John?'

'Ar – bloody stiff.' His voice sounded harsh after Miss Baxter's soft tones. 'And I want a look round.'

Polly and Peter levered John out of the car again and eased him down to sit on the ground. Polly got back into the car, leaving the two men to talk.

'I was going to say to you, Mrs Carter—'

'Please – my name's Polly – this is Jess. You don't need to call me Mrs Carter all the time. 'Specially the way things are and you being so kind to us. You feel almost like family.'

Miss Baxter smiled. 'All right. Thank you. And I'm Isobel. I'd be just as happy if you called me that too. I was saying – as there is no grave as such for your husband, and you can't be certain of the exact spot where he died . . .' She brought the words out painfully. 'There will be memorials of course, eventually. None of them will be forgotten. But for now, I'd suggest you choose a place, when you find somewhere appropriate, to make your peace with him. People find that helps.'

This time Jess squeezed Polly's hand to give comfort.

'Awright, I'll do that,' Polly said huskily. She turned to look out at the fields. 'Oh my God – what're they *doing*?'

Already yards away, on the rough terrain beyond the road, were Peter and John, beginning to climb slowly up the side of the nearest low incline. Peter was bent forward, taking short, determined strides, as John clung to his shoulders. He looked a pathetic sight, flung across Peter's back, the remains of his legs dangling helplessly, Peter's elbows sticking out as he held on to him.

Isobel Baxter was out of the car in a second and Jess and Polly followed.

'Stop – for heaven's sake don't go any further! STOP!' The young woman jumped up and down waving her arms frantically above her head. They saw Peter stop and swivel round. For a moment he loosed John with one hand and waved at them.

'Shan't be long!' they heard him shout. 'It's not far!'

'But there're BOMBS!' Isobel shrieked. She seemed almost beside herself. 'Please stop, you could be killed!' But Peter had turned away and continued to clamber up the slope, a rough rubble of stones, exposed roots, tree-stumps and debris, so that he had to watch every step and it took all his attention.

441

Isobel wrung her hands. 'It's quite, quite wrong to leave the roads and the designated paths. There are unexploded bombs everywhere ... bodies ... Oh dear. Perhaps I ought to go after him.'

'I'll go,' Polly said.

'No.' Jess laid a hand on her arm to stop her. 'Don't. Leave them.'

'You're right,' Isobel said, her eyes never leaving the two men. 'If we all start going it increases the risk. But oh heavens ...' She pressed her clenched fist to her lips.

There was a kind of indistinct path which Peter was following through the rubble. Slowly, ploddingly he climbed. Jess watched, her body so tense she felt she might snap, every fibre of her willing him to reach the top safely, to turn, to come back. She found herself overwhelmed with feeling that she had only dimly known was in her.

Be safe, be safe, Peter, oh Peter, her mind hammered, beyond her willing it. Come back to me ... She laid a hand over her fast-beating heart. She didn't really know how big the risk was that Peter was taking with his own life and John's, but she found herself chill with fright. It was as if all the same kind of longing, the hopes and prayers she had sent out to Ned during the war distilled together in her mind, the intensity of it startling her. Come back to me, Peter my love – please ... This time the words, the longing, was for someone else, and she was shocked by the extent of feeling towards him that had been growing, deep in her.

The three of them watched every move of the two men as they reached the highest point. Peter turned this way and that, so that they could look back towards Albert, then over to La Boiselle. Jess saw him pointing across the landscape with its scarred fields and clumps of razed woodland, its pimples of hills. For a few moments he put John down and they rested, apparently without talking. Jess watched them, saw the curious camaraderie that had formed between the two men. Soon, Peter hoisted John back on to his shoulders and they began the descent. For a moment, halfway down he slipped and almost fell and they all gasped, but he managed to right himself.

'Oh Lord!' Isobel murmured. But soon they were down the hill, safe, and Peter was walking across to the car. Both men were smiling.

'I ought to give you a thorough ticking off!' Isobel ran to them, laughing with relief. 'Please don't ever, *ever* do anything like that again, will you promise me?'

'I'm sorry, Miss Baxter,' Peter backed in through the car door, depositing John on the seat. Jess heard the jubilation in his voice. 'Didn't mean to get you so worried. Got a bit of a better picture up there.'

'You can see our lads' trenches,' John said through the open car door.

Jess looked into Peter's face and he smiled at her.

'Don't suppose you were worried?'

Jess felt her cheeks burn. She had known, in those moments, how much she felt for Peter Stevenson, and now she was vulnerable in front of him.

'I was. Course I was,' she said testily.

'I just wanted John to be able to see . . .'

She could see in his face that it was not just John. Carrying him up there had been a test for him: the duty of a man who had not endured the trenches to perform a service for one who had. A different pilgrimage from the one the rest of them were making, but a pilgrimage none the less. There was a relief, a satisfaction about Peter as they got back into the car.

'Now,' Isobel said. 'Time is marching fast onwards. We have to return to Abbeville this evening, so no more delays – please.'

Polly chose a spot just outside the village of La Boiselle to consecrate a little piece of ground, in her own way, for Ernie. La Boiselle had been fought over so heavily that most of it was a ruin. Looking along what must have been the main street was a poignant sight. So little remained of the buildings of the flattened village and what did was mostly rubble.

'These poor people,' Polly said, even more moved by the sight than she had been in the towns. 'All their homes gone. I think I'll do it somewhere 'ere.'

They walked until she found a little spot at the edge of the field nearest the southern end of the village.

'I shan't be able to keep coming back 'ere,' she said. 'So it don't matter to me if it's only me knows where it is. Look – by that little tree. That's where I want it.'

Close to what looked like the remains of a barn, a young sapling had been smashed, leaving its trunk a sharp stump not much more than a yard high.

'Cut off in it's youth – like Ernie. Like all of 'em.'

Peter helped her, digging a little hole in the ground near the tree with a trowel, which Isobel had had the foresight to carry in the car. John sat in his chair and Isobel and Jess stood nearby watching. Polly had a little wooden box with '*Pte Ernest Frederick Carter – Royal Warwickshire Regt*' carved on the top. Inside, she had told Jess, she'd written a letter to Ernie saying how much she loved him, would always love him, and wishing him goodbye. With it she'd put her wedding ring with a picture of Grace and a lock of the little girl's hair. She broke down as she laid the box in the ground, and knelt by it sobbing.

'Oh Ernie,' they heard her murmur. 'Oh Ernie . . .'

Jess went forward and knelt beside her, her arms round Polly's shoulders, while Peter retreated to stand next to John. Peter knew as well as any of them the need to relinquish the dead in order to love the living, but he also understood how hard it must be for John to watch Polly's grief over another man.

Polly accepted Jess's embrace for a moment, then turned back to cover over the box with earth.

'Goodbye, my dear Ernie,' she whispered. 'I can't do no more for yer now. I wish you'd lived and come home, I do with all my heart, but I know you're gone. Rest in peace, my love. I'll bring up our Gracie right, and I'll never forget yer.'

She patted the surface of the little grave and got up to gather some stones, which she laid in the pattern of a cross over the top of it. Peter came close and took some photographs.

'Grace might want to see when she's older,' he said. Jess saw Polly give a smile.

'Well done,' Isobel said softly. Jess saw that she too had tears in her eyes. 'Shall we all just take a bit of time to walk with our own thoughts before we go?'

They all spread out, each of them leaving the others with their private griefs. Peter pushed John's chair to a place next to the road where he could sit and look. Jess walked back a short distance, and stood with her arms folded looking out across the sombre French fields. The light was fading: it was almost dusk and very quiet, the only sound the gentle breeze which played with the light skirt of her dress. The end of a warm summer's day. They were days like this in 1916, she thought. And only last year guns were firing across these fields. She felt full to the back of her throat with emotion: grief and anguish for Polly and John, and an immense sorrow for all the dead who still lay round. But mixed with the sadness came also a sense of wonder, a restless longing.

Inevitably she found herself thinking of Ned. He fought near here somewhere, she thought. He had mentioned High Wood, and she wasn't sure where that was, how far away, but he had undoubtedly been through Albert. Here, so many miles away from her, when in feeling they had seemed so close. And now she had come to this place herself, he was lost to her forever. How long, how faithfully she had devoted herself to him! She had lived for him and for his love, for their future together, and what had happened to all her high ideas of passion and devotion? She saw Polly, in the corner of her eye, walking along the edge of the field with her head down. Polly with her clear grief. For a moment Jess even envied her. If Ned had died on the Somme, how sweetly she could have remembered him! His life cut short, a decorated hero of the war, preserved for her like a tinted photograph, enshrined in all his perfection. If he were gone, she could still remember him as loving her. As it was he had had to go on, carry his wounds, his confusion into the imperfect future. He had left her a more bitter remembrance than Ernie, who had given everything to the French earth and who by not returning, had lit his own life with a glow of glory.

But Ned *is* gone, Jess told herself. Just as much as Ernie is. She too, had to bury him here and look to the future.

She turned to go and join the others, and as she did so, heard her foot tap against something wooden. Look-

446

ing down she saw a short plank, painted as a rough sign board. Curious, she squatted down and turned it round, rubbing off some of the dried mud. In black paint, above an arrow, it read, 'Sausage Valley'.

Peter came and stood over her. 'What's that you've found?'

'An old sign – look.' She stood up.

Peter read it and chuckled. 'Did you know there's a "Mash Valley" somewhere near it as well?'

'No!' she laughed.

There was silence for a moment as they looked out together across the haunted landscape.

'They're still here,' she said. 'All of 'em. I can feel it. As if they're begging us not to forget them.'

Forty-Six

By the time they arrived in Abbeville the sun had long set. Jess and the others all slept on the journey, while Isobel Baxter drove on steadily, car headlamps pushing on into the darkness. When Jess woke, the engine was switched off and they had pulled up in a dark street. She could make out almost nothing outside except that there were buildings on either side of them.

'Here we are.' Isobel opened her door and Jess stepped out feeling muzzy and confused. The air was warmer than she expected. 'This is our stop for the night. We're rather late, but Madame Fournier should be waiting for us.'

Peter Stevenson and Polly attended to John, and Jess and Isobel carried the luggage into the dim little vestibule, where Isobel, with obvious affection, greeted an elderly woman with hunched shoulders and steel-grey hair. Even in her only just awake state Jess marvelled at Isobel. She seemed to manage everything: even spoke fluent French!

Madame Fournier showed them to their rooms up a staircase with an intricate wrought-iron bannister, shadows leaping around them in the candlelight. It was a sizeable old house and their footsteps sounded loudly along the wooden floors. There were engravings in heavy dark frames along the upper corridor, which smelt strongly of beeswax polish.

Polly carried a candle into the room she and Jess were to share. There was one, grand-looking bed, the bedstead high at each end, made of carved wooden panels, and a crucifix was nailed to the wall above the head of it.

'Look at this!' Jess lay down on the bed. 'Be a bit like sleeping in a ... box.' She'd been about to say 'coffin' but in the circumstances, thought the better of it. A hard, well-stuffed bolster lay along the top of the mattress.

'Ain't it *nice*?' Polly said, looking round. There was a marble topped washstand, a wooden chair with curved arms and a tarnished mirror on a chest of drawers near the foot of the bed. She rested the candle on the washstand and sank down beside Jess. 'This feels like the longest day I've ever had in my life. I'm all in.'

Jess rolled over on to her side, closer to her. 'How d'yer feel, Poll?'

Polly was rubbing her hands over her face. She paused a moment as if trying to assess her feelings. 'Better. I'm ever so glad we came 'ere. I mean, Ernie's been dead a good long while, but it's only now I think I can really put it behind me, now I've said goodbye to 'im properly.'

Jess smiled. 'Good for you. That's why we came. John'll be glad too.'

Polly nodded. 'I'm flaming lucky really, ain't I? And eh – what would we've done without Mr Stevenson?' Polly could never get used to calling him Peter, however many times he asked her to. 'I think the man must be an angel.' She looked closely at Jess. 'You know 'e's done all this for you, don't yer?'

'Don't talk daft – it's for John – and you.'

Polly laughed, head on one side. 'Oh Jess – how

449

much longer are yer going to keep the poor bloke hanging on?'

'Has he said anything to yer?'

'No,' Polly stood up, stretching. Through a yawn she said, ''E don't need to.'

They ate downstairs at a long table of dark, polished wood lit by candles. As it was late, Madame Fournier did not join them to eat. She greeted them with many nods and '*bonsoir*'s, and fed them with omelettes, bread and crisp lettuce leaves on thick white plates, and with it they drank red wine. The meal was served by a solemn-faced girl who looked, Jess thought, about thirteen years old. Since she had been in France she seemed to have seen only the old and the very young.

They were all very hungry and the food was delicious.

'How does she make an omelette as tasty as this?' Peter said, wiping his plate with a chunk of the bread. 'Even the lettuce tastes nicer than anything at home.'

'Well – it's straight from the garden,' Isobel said. 'At the back of here she has quite a little smallholding – vegetables, fruit trees, chickens. The French do like their food very fresh.'

Jess sipped the wine, feeling the alcohol going almost instantly to her head. 'You speak French ever so well,' she said. Isobel was sitting next to her.

'I was lucky enough to spend a year here, before the war. In fact Madame Fournier is an old friend of mine. One of her daughters is my age – she lives in Paris now and has a family of her own. When I started this work we had to find accommodation for people on these pilgrimages, and I thought of Madame Fournier here in

450

this big house. She did take in other lodgers sometimes, and she said that if I thought the folk I was bringing were suitable, she'd provide a bed and food for them. She lost a son at Verdun. She is very *sympathique*, as the French say.'

'Very good of 'er,' John said through a mouthful of bread.

'And are you glad you came?' Isobel asked him.

John nodded, wiping the back of his hand over his moustache. 'Oh ar – very glad. Yes. Thanks very much.'

'And you, Polly?'

Polly smiled. 'Yes thank you, Miss Baxter—'

'Isobel – please.'

'Isobel. I'm all in now though.'

'You must be tired yerself,' Jess said to Isobel. 'Driving all that way while we slept.'

'Ah well – that's all right. I shall sleep tonight.'

Jess understood by the way she said it that sleep did not come easily to her. She was reminded for a moment of Iris: something in Isobel's stoic acceptance of the suffering and loss in her life. I'll go and see Iris when I get home, she thought. I've been selfish, neglecting her while I was all wrapped up in my own feelings. I must look after her better.

While Isobel was advising them all to get a decent night's sleep as they needed a good early start to reach Boulogne in time, Jess looked cautiously across at Peter. She had spent so long avoiding his gaze, that she felt very self-conscious and vulnerable doing so. But tonight was special. This would be their one night in France, and it was thanks to him that they were here. Today she had allowed herself to admit how deeply she cared for him, and if she did not find courage to risk showing him, she might never know if he still felt anything for

451

her. After tomorrow they would be home, with every-thing back to normal, and she might hardly ever see him. The wine made her feel mellow and more relaxed, and she dared herself to look unwaveringly at him. He was listening to Isobel, but after a moment he seemed to sense her watching him and looked back at her. The expression in his eyes was so full of affection and tenderness towards her that she felt her limbs turn weak and had to look away. After a second though, she looked back and smiled.

He came over to her as they left the table, all still talking sleepily, making arrangements for the morning. Sensing him beside her, Jess looked round.

'I'll need to help John get to bed.'

Jess clasped her hands tightly together to try and stop them shaking. 'Yes. Course you will.' This time she didn't look away, knowing he wanted to say more.

'Jess, I was wondering . . .' He hesitated, watching her face, ready at any second to draw back if she showed signs of rejecting him. 'Afterwards – I know it's been a long day, but would you like to come outside – for a walk round? There's the garden . . .'

'Are yer coming, Peter?' John was waiting in the wheelchair near the stairs. 'Sorry, pal – only my blad-der's fit to bust, I can tell yer!'

'John!' Polly ticked him off. 'The whole world don't need to know!'

'Yes,' Jess said softly. All sleepiness left her in an instant. 'I'll meet yer down here.'

'What're you two whispering about?' John de-manded.

Peter gave a bashful grin. 'Give me half an hour,' he said to her quietly.

Upstairs, while Polly was pulling her clothes off and

yawning in great gusts, Jess unlatched the shutters and pulled one of them back. There was a half moon in the sky, silvering the tops of the fruit trees, though she could not see far down the garden. Standing still by the window, she could feel the blood pumping round her body. The muzziness she had felt from drinking wine had left her, and she was wide awake, with a strange, enhanced alertness. She felt as if she could go on without sleep forever.

'What yer doing?' Polly had stripped to the waist and was splashing water from the pitcher over her face and shoulders.

'Looking at the garden.' She turned round. ''E's asked me to meet him – tonight.'

Polly stared, water dripping from her chin. 'Who – Peter?'

'No, Kaiser Bill – who d'yer think?' Jess retorted.

'Ooh–' Polly beamed at her. 'Well about time.'

Peter helped John Bullivant out of his clothes and into bed. He tried to pay attention to the things John was saying to him, when he was trembling with anticipation and all he could think of was Jess . . . Jess. He had waited long and patiently for her, knowing that she was grieving over Ned as he had also to do over Sylvia. He was not an arrogant man, did not assume himself to be irresistible in her eyes. But he knew that he loved and desired her with great, protective tenderness. Tonight, when she looked at him, fear and love in equal measure in her face, he knew that at last his quiet waiting might be rewarded. His body was so taut with urgency to get outside and see her and talk to her in case she changed her mind, that he thought John must feel it. But John was exhausted. He lay back on the wide bed and closed his eyes immediately.

'Thanks, pal,' he murmured.

'Sleep tight.'

Peter blew out the candle. He stood in the darkness for a few moments trying to compose himself.

Jess closed the heavy door behind her and stepped out into the garden, breathing in the warm, sweet-smelling night air. A tinny church bell was striking somewhere nearby, and as she stood still, letting her eyes get used to the darkness, she heard crickets in the grass and the muffled clucking of chickens from some distance down the garden. Jess knew that chickens were usually quiet once they had been cooped up for the night, but these sounded terrified, as if alarmed by something. Stepping carefully, she followed a rough path of stone slabs along the side of the grass and fruit trees. The garden was a good width, and extended over a hundred feet. The bottom third was screened off from the rest by a row of tall conifers and behind them, Jess found the whole area given over to a cottage garden. She smiled with pleasure, making out in the moonlight the rows of healthy look-ing plants. Madame Fournier obviously knew a great deal about growing vegetables. The chickens were squawking just as hysterically, and she was afraid the noise would bring someone out of the house to investi-gate. She could make out the wooden coop up against the end wall, and as she moved closer she saw a moving streak of shadow slink off and melt into the deeper darkness of the bushes at the edge of the garden.

I've just saved your bacon, you chickens, she

thought, waiting to see if there was any more sign of movement. But there was none. The predator had been scared off. She listened to hear if anyone had been disturbed, but there was no sound of anyone coming.

Able to see much better now, she went back nearer the house and stood under one of the trees, looking up into the branches. The sight of the leaves above her, burnished with moonlight, the fragrance of garden flowers and the fact that she was waiting for him to come to her, brought her emotions fully to the surface. I love him, she said to herself over and over. All that time I had eyes for no one but Ned, and this was here waiting for me. This love, beside me all the time. She knew this with burning certainty now. Knew she felt truly sure with Peter in a way she never had in those years with Ned, always hanging on for him, putting her life off until he came back, forever insecure and worried. She longed for Peter to come, to be able to tell him how much she felt for him. Looking up at the windows she wondered if she might see his shadow moving about in one of the rooms, helping John, but there was no sign of anyone. Their window must face out from the front, overlooking the street.

Eventually she heard the door open, then close again quietly and saw him standing outside, a long, lean shape, letting his eyes adjust in the darkness. She enjoyed watching him, knowing he couldn't yet see her. He took a few paces back and forth and she heard him quietly clear his throat.

After a moment she walked out from under the cherry tree and he came towards her.

'Jess?'

She loved the sound of his voice saying her name.

'Yes – it's beautiful out 'ere.' She was very nervous suddenly, looking for something to get them over the awkwardness of meeting. 'Come and see.'

He followed her as she walked down to the dark screen of trees, and they stood looking back at the house. One of the casement windows was slightly open, but there was no light behind it.

'I think that's our window,' Jess whispered. 'I must've left it like that. I'm surprised Polly ain't having a good nose out at us!'

'She wouldn't be able to see much,' Peter said.

'There're chickens down 'ere – no wonder her eggs tasted so nice.' She led him to the far end of the garden. They stood listening, but the chickens had calmed down and were quiet now. Jess felt she could sense, rather than hear their breathing and the close cluster of warm feathers.

'I scared a fox away when I came down before. The hens were making a hell of a racket, poor things. They must've been frightened half to death.'

'How d'you know it was a fox?'

'Well I saw it, sort of. I just know it was a fox!'

'And they could tell it was out here?'

'Oh yes. Smell it a mile off – and it was trying to get in, I s'pect.'

Jess thought, I want to say I love you, and I'm going on about chickens. She knew she was chattering out of nervousness, and told herself to shut up. In the silence that followed, she gradually turned and looked up at Peter, standing like a tall shadow beside her, waiting quietly, she thought, the way he does. She was intensely aware of his body close to her, and of her own, the feel of her dress against her bare skin. Peter leaned down, closer to her. Seeing the way she looked back at him, he held his arms out and drew her into them with a cry of joy that was close to a sob. She pulled him to her and they kissed, holding, caressing each other. She felt his hand in her hair, on her back, pressing her close in his desire for her. Her body responded to his excitement with strong, fiery movements until Peter abruptly pulled away.

'We must stop. I'm sorry, Jess ... I shouldn't've behaved like that. I don't even know if you ...'

'Peter?' She touched him, making him turn to her again, and wrapped her arms round him. 'Don't say you're sorry. You're the best, kindest man I've ever met. I love yer – I loved yer touching me.'

'Do you? Love me?' He stood stiffly in her arms.

She nodded. 'Sorry it's taken me such a long time to know it. Please – put your arms round me again.'

He did, laughing with happiness. 'I can't believe this is true. Oh my lovely Jess. Can you really love a funny old stick like me?'

'That's why I love yer. Because you're a funny old stick with a great big heart inside him and I'd trust my life to yer. Oh – and you're quite handsome really an' all!'

He tickled her so that she shrieked with laughter and they both stopped, looking back nervously at the house.

'That was your fault,' she whispered. Serious again she stroked his face with her fingertips. 'I feel so much for you. As if it was all buried somewhere in me and I've found it suddenly. I've so much love in me I want to give yer.'

'Oh Jess.' Moved, he kissed the top of her head, then stroked his hands lightly down the front of her dress, resting them for a moment on her breasts, free and warm under the light cotton. 'I could do with some love

457

I can tell you. These've been terrible, lonely years. And I've plenty to give you in return. More than you might realize.'

Jess laid her hands over his. 'Oh, I think I do,' she said.

The next afternoon, when they sailed back to England, was one of cloudless sky, the sea a deep, glassy blue. They said their farewells to Isobel, Jess hugging her, to Isobel's evident surprise and pleasure.

'You've been marvellous to us,' Jess said, truly sorry to be parting with her. 'You take care of yourself, won't yer?'

'Oh I will – don't you worry.' She turned back to them with a fond expression as she left and waved a last time. 'God bless you – all of you.'

John and Polly spent the journey up on deck, where Jess and Peter left them sitting together contentedly in the fresh breeze, John well wrapped in a blanket, Polly with a scarf over her hair. Jess and Peter strolled back and forth, stopping to lean over the side for long spells, at all times holding on to one another, arm in arm.

'I should feel tired,' Jess said as they strolled the deck. 'But I don't.' They had stayed up all night, sitting wrapped in each other's arms in Mme Fournier's garden, oblivious of the dew, the time, or anything but each other. They talked, caressed, kissed, until the sun tinged the roof and the leaves of the cherry trees with pink and they looked up, overjoyed by the sight.

'We can soon catch up on a bit of sleep,' Peter said. He looked at her, couldn't stop looking at her, full of wonder. 'You're so lovely. I just hope I'm not asleep now.'

'You're not.' She kissed his cheek, then leaned her head on his shoulder. 'There, you can feel I'm really 'ere.'

When Dover with its chalky cliffs was still just a haze in the distance, they were still standing, gazing out over the sea, Peter with his arm round Jess's shoulders, each too happy for words. But as the land drew nearer and nearer, Peter spoke at last. He removed his arm from her shoulder and turned to her, taking her hands in his.

'I've got to say this now – I just don't want it to wait any longer. I never want to be with anyone except you, Jess. Would you agree to be my wife?'

There was no hesitation. 'Yes!' Jess cried into the wind. 'Oh yes, yes!'

Laughing, he held her close. 'Aren't you s'posed to be a bit more reluctant when someone asks you? You know – think it over a bit?'

Jess grinned up at him. 'Why waste time?'

They found Polly and John on the sunny, port side of the ship, cups of tea on the table beside them, steam whisking away in the wind. Both of them were smiling, their hands clasped in each other's.

'Come on over 'ere, we've got summat to tell yer!' Polly waved at them as soon as they appeared.

Jess tightened her hold on Peter's arm, her joyful eyes meeting first his, then Polly's. 'Yes – so've we.'

Forty-Seven

11 November 1921

'Come on, Mom – we'll be late else!'

Jess looked up smiling as Davey's face, pink with exertion, appeared round the bedroom door.

'Nearly done, pet. Just getting 'er into a nice clean napkin.'

'Will it last long enough while we're out?'

Jess laughed. David, now seven years old, was growing up into a quaint little fellow. He had little memory of his own mother, and Jess was flattered and relieved by the way he had taken her so affectionately to his heart. She had grown very fond of him.

'Oh yes. Don't you worry.'

'Our dad's waiting . . .'

'Awright. You go and tell him I'm coming. I'll be down in a minute or two.'

His scurrying footsteps receded along the landing and downstairs.

Jess turned back to her baby daughter whose arms and legs were waving about with the sheer pleasure of movement. She stuffed a fist into her mouth, clamping her gums over it.

'You're cutting some teeth, madam,' Jess said. She bent and kissed the child's soft tummy. 'Come on, Alice. Yer Dad's waiting for us. Time we was going.'

*

'It's a pretty name,' she told Olive, who had come to see her, dewy-eyed with happiness, after the little girl was born. She kissed her aunt as Olive held the baby in her plump arms, her face softened by the sight of an infant. 'And between us we'll make Alice into a lucky name.'

Olive smiled, eyes still on the child. 'I s'pect you will, bab. Knowing you.'

She had been overjoyed when the four of them came back from the Somme, first of all to see Polly looking so relaxed and cheerful, and then to hear from them all that there was to be a double wedding. Jess could tell how highly she thought of Peter. He seemed to be the one to replace Ned in her affections.

'Louisa would've been so proud of yer,' she said to Jess.

'Well you're the one that's done me proud, Auntie. Taking me in and looking after me the way yer have. You've been a mom to me. You always will be.'

Before the wedding, which they fixed for the September, Jess said to Peter that there was one thing she felt she must do.

'I left my dad swearing I'd never go back there again,' she told him sadly. 'I regret it now, even though he daint seem pleased to see me. He is my father though. I ought to tell him I'm getting married, let him meet my intended and that.'

The day she and Peter sat on the train out to Leamington reminded her acutely of the same journey with Ned. The same smoky, grimy smell of the compartment, the city folding away, fields spreading golden around them. This time it was August, blue sky with piles of puffy clouds. She sat close to Peter, drowsy in the heat. Every so often she turned, found him watching her tenderly and reached up to kiss him.

461

She delighted in showing him some of the village, but when they reached Forge Cottage it looked very run down. The windows were filthy and the front garden had been allowed to run riot. Jess was filled with misgiving as she approached it.

'Oh dear,' she said to Peter. 'Oh look – this is where I grew up, but what a mess! My mom kept it lovely, and my stepmother. There must be summat wrong. Sarah must be ill – she'd never let the place get in such a state. She was a worker, whatever else you might say about her.'

'It's very nice,' Peter said looking down the farm track, clumps of nettles blowing about on the verge. 'I bet you ran wild here.' For a second she expected him to add 'my country wench'. But it was Ned who would have said that.

She smiled, though still looking anxious. 'I did a bit.'

The door was opened by a woman in her mid-thirties with a wide mouth and wide hips encased in blue and white gingham.

'Is—' Jess hesitated. 'Is Sarah Hart in please?' She felt as she spoke that they were not there, that everything had changed beyond her imagining.

'Ooh no. Sarah's been gone from 'ere a while now. Living back over the shop, 'er is, if yer want 'er. Who're you then?'

Jess's thoughts began to race. Had Sarah given up waiting for William to learn to love her and left him? What other reason could there be – what had happened?

'I'm Jess – Hart. Is my father still 'ere then?'

'Your father? William Hart?' The woman looked deeply shocked. 'Don't you know?' She looked back over her shoulder as if hoping there was someone else there who could impart the news. ''E was killed in

Flanders, duck. Back in the war. 'Ow is it you daint know that then? Your own father?'

'In *Flanders*? But 'e was . . .' She was going to say 'too old'. But she knew suddenly that he was not, though he had always seemed so to her. He would have been in his fifties, a fine strong man. Probably told them he was ten years younger and got away with it. The very young, the older men, they had needed them all by the end. But she could scarcely take it in.

'Sorry to give yer such bad news,' the woman said importantly. 'Only I'd've expected 'is daughter to know. Listen – my 'usband knew 'im well. Worked together for years, they did. I'll call 'im for yer, shall I? Philip! Phi—'

'NO!' Jess interrupted abruptly, starting to back away. 'No – thank you. There's no need for that. You've been very kind. Thank you for telling me. We'll be going now.'

Mrs Gill shrugged as if to say 'please yourself' and stood in her doorway as they disappeared down the road.

'Well,' Jess said numbly. 'That settles that. I've no one 'ere now.'

He took her hand as they walked. 'Aren't you going to see your stepmother?'

'Oh no. She won't want me turning up. We never got on. I'd like to see my mom's grave again, make sure it's tidy. And then we'll go. I know the place where I really belong now, and that's with you.'

That November morning the four of them hurried from their little house, Alice cuddled up in Jess's arms, and took a tram through the misty streets into town to join all the others gathering round the Town Hall. Polly had said she and John and Grace would try and meet them at the top of New Street, and as they drew closer, Jess saw them waiting in the spot where they said they'd be. Polly was heavily pregnant, and needed help with John's chair, so John's brother Lol had come along and taken over pushing it. Olive was there in a black hat, holding Grace's hand. She raised her arm straight up, swirling it around, the way she always waved.

'You look nice, Auntie,' Jess greeted her. 'Ever so smart. Awright, Poll? 'Ow yer feeling?'

'Oh, I'm awright,' Polly smiled. 'Considering.'

Dotted about the square, a number of collectors stood with trays on strings round their necks, a little sign on the front saying, 'Field Marshal Haig's Appeal'. The trays contained poppies made out of delicate red cloth and wired paper stalks.

'Poppies in the corn,' John said, when he saw them.

'They make these ones in France apparently,' Polly said. 'To keep the memory of the lads who died and 'elp the ones who make 'em to 'ave a living – injured blokes they are. P'raps they'll do it next year an' all.'

They bought a poppy each, helping each other to pin them on their lapels.

It was almost eleven o'clock, three years to the hour since the war was declared finished, and a large crowd was gathering in Victoria Square under the thick clouds. Along the imposing grey flank of the Town Hall was a platform draped with tapestries of red, gold and purple on which people had begun to lay their tributes of flowers and wreaths, and over to one side of the square, the Police Band were assembled, waiting.

A few minutes before eleven, as they all stood in the now tightly packed crowd, there came a loud, booming

464

explosion as a maroon was fired off, then another and another, and the crowd fell absolutely silent. People began removing their hats and others followed until every head was bare and bowed, waiting. Jess handed her hat to Peter. It was so quiet that she became aware of the faint sound of pigeons scuffling and murmuring high on ledges of the buildings and they heard a train let off a head of steam. Alice moved restlessly in Jess's arms and she rocked gently from side to side to pacify her, not wanting her to disturb the tense, emotional silence. None of them looked at each other, each standing lost in their own thoughts.

After two minutes the Last Post sounded mournfully across the square, and then the Police Band began to play 'Oh God our Help in Ages Past' and gradually people began to sing, the sound of voices swelling around them. Many were in tears, women sobbing uncontrollably. Polly wept quietly, a handkerchief pressed to her face, and as the slow, emotional hymn went on, the raw feelings, still so recent, the overwhelming, immense sadness of it all welled up in Jess. She held Alice clasped tight to her, kissing her cheek, wetting the child's face with her tears as they sang the final verse. There was Alice's new, innocent existence, set against the memory of slaughter of so many young lives, and even greater than that, an overwhelming sense of the nature of humankind, of the way we are, good and bad, so closely woven together. She felt Peter's hand rest for a moment on her back, and looking up at him, saw that he was also wiping his eyes.

The crowd slowly began to disperse, and they were moving towards the platform to look at the tributes when Jess caught sight of him. She saw Mary first, a little ahead of them in the stream of people, holding a baby in her arms and guiding little Ruth in front of her. Jess found herself seeking desperately to see Ned, like a bad habit she still couldn't break. She stood on tip-toe and found him moving along just in front of Mary. When he reached the platform he leaned over and laid something on it, then turned and spoke into Mary's ear, his head close to hers. Seeing him with Mary touched an old nerve, just for an instant. He looked pale, less tall than she remembered, still much the same, yet somehow he had faded into ordinariness. The sight of him affected her, made her stomach flutter with nerves, just for those few seconds. But then she felt within herself a deep calm. They had not spoken to each other in three years and she had not missed him. He was nothing to her now, except a memory which could be folded away. Her heart had moved on. In a moment it was their turn to look at the floral tributes. The British Legion had contributed a plain wooden cross surrounded by poppies and framed with laurel leaves. On it were the words,

'To those who fought and fell, from those who are fighting on.'

There were offerings from public departments and societies, and from individuals. Moved, Jess's eyes swept over them. She found herself looking at the spot where she was sure Ned had laid his tribute. It was his handwriting that made it stand out for her. Instead of a bunch of flowers she saw a single sprig of heather, and a little note attached to it, 'Jem – Rest in Peace'.

She stood looking for a few moments, then turned, and Peter said, 'Ready to go?'

Jess nodded. She knew Ned would be moving away through the crowd, that she might not see him again, might never, but she did not look back. She was filled with a great surge of joy in the present. What she had now was truly built upon rock. She smiled up at Peter over Alice's head and he was moved at the sudden radiance of her face. You are my love, her eyes said. Love is what I always wanted, and it is you I have given my heart to. She knew that he, in turn, had given his.

He put his arm round her shoulders, holding David's hand the other side, and they edged through the remaining crowd who were all decked out in the poppies, a flowering of remembrance pinned close to the hearts of the living.

In the middle of the throng of people, David pulled on Peter's hand to get his attention. Peter stopped and bent down close to him.

'Will I have to fight in a war, Daddy?' He looked up, steadily, into Peter's eyes.

'I hope not, son.' Peter smiled and ruffled his hair. 'I hope not.'

47

extracts reading groups new events
competitions books new
discounts extracts
competitions extracts discounts
books new
events books
extracts
new reading groups
interviews
events extracts
discounts
new books events
events new
discounts extracts discounts
www.panmacmillan.com
extracts events reading groups
competitions books extracts new